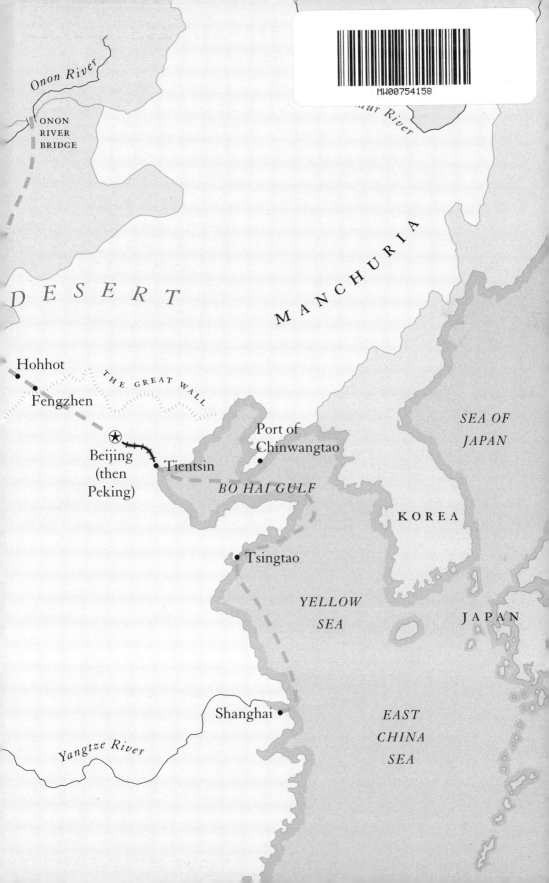

Onon River

ONON
RIVER
BRIDGE

...ur River

D E S E R T

M A N C H U R I A

Hohhot

Fengzhen

THE GREAT WALL

★

Beijing
(then
Peking)

Tientsin

Port of
Chinwangtao

BO HAI GULF

Tsingtao

SEA OF
JAPAN

K O R E A

YELLOW
SEA

J A P A N

Shanghai

EAST
CHINA
SEA

Yangtze River

WARNING OF WAR

WARNING OF WAR

—

A NOVEL OF THE NORTH CHINA MARINES

JAMES BRADY

THOMAS DUNNE BOOKS
ST. MARTIN'S PRESS ✹ NEW YORK

This book is for my daughters, Fiona and Susan.
And for Sarah, Joe, and Nick Konig, my grandchildren.

It is dedicated to every United States Marine who ever fought.

THOMAS DUNNE BOOKS.
An imprint of St. Martin's Press.

www.stmartins.com

Library of Congress Cataloging-in-Publication Data

Brady, James.
    Warning of war : a novel of the North China Marines / James Brady.—1st ed.
        p. cm.
    ISBN 0-312-28018-1
    1. United States. Marine Corps—Fiction. 2. China —History—1937–1945—
Fiction. 3. World War, 1939–1945—China—Fiction. 4. Americans—China—
Fiction. I. Title.

PS3552.R243 W37 2002
813'.54—dc21

                                                                    2001054806

10 9 8 7 6 5 4 3 2

AUTHOR'S NOTE

I am indebted to retired Marine Captain George Howe, who served in North China and a decade later was still fighting in North Korea, for his generous and wonderful letters about pre-war Shanghai and Chinaside duty. And to Colonel Richard Camp, USMC (Retired), whose gripping articles about the North China Marines of 1941 in *Leatherneck* magazine provided so much richly descriptive narrative material, from which I have shamelessly cribbed, in Chapters 12 and 14 especially.

Much of what I've written about Marine legend Lewis B. Puller derives from my reading of Burke Davis's biography, *Marine! The Life of Chesty Puller*.

My thanks to two successive editors of *Leatherneck* magazine, Colonel Bill White and Colonel Walter G. Ford, and to associate editor Master Gunnery Sergeant R. R. Keene.

And to Lieutenant Colonel Ward E. Scott II, USMC, of the Marine Corps Historical Center at the Washington Navy Yard.

I am most grateful to Marine Commandant General James L. Jones for his generous comments on my earlier books about the great Corps that he leads. And in which it was my honor to serve.

If the Army and the Navy
Ever look on Heaven's scenes;
They will find the streets are guarded by
United States Marines.
                    — "THE MARINES' HYMN"

PROLOGUE

IN November of 1941, with half the world at war and the other half about to join in, a thousand United States Marines in their forest-green uniforms, their canvas leggings, with their Springfield rifles and tin hats, stood sentinel over the last days of an uneasy truce in chaotic North China.

Which is where this story begins, what in tradition, a regimental toast, among retired Chinaside Marines, and old grads of his class at the Naval Academy in Annapolis, came to be known as "Billy Port's Ride."

Marine flag officers of the time were too occupied with fighting and defeating Japan to confirm details of the story. Nor would latter-day officials, lacking personal knowledge or reluctant to roil Cold War tensions, speak authoritatively on the matter.

Perhaps it would be better simply to forget the whole business.

Chesty Puller believed in Billy's "ride." But then, Chesty was himself a bit of a maverick, and had been Captain Port's commanding officer and friend, and therefore suspect.

What is not in question is that on November 27, 1941, a matter of ten days before the attack on Pearl Harbor, Washington knew that the Empire of Japan was about to go to war. Neither the president nor Cordell Hull, his secretary of state, War Secretary Stimson, nor Navy Secretary Knox knew just where or precisely when the attack would take place. But they were sufficiently alarmed as to authorize an immediate "warning of war" to be sent to American military bases and forces in harm's way, including the North China Marines.

Neither today's Pentagon nor the Department of the Navy or anyone else in Washington will go beyond that, nor understandably will the government of Japan, or the Mongol authorities at Ulan Bator, and Moscow, enjoying its newly cordial relationship with us and unwilling to muddy waters, is certainly not likely to speak out. No government is going to say on the record that what Captain Port is gloriously remembered for having done actually occurred.

Nor does anyone claim these things didn't happen. Or that Billy Port never made his ride.

1

If you were a Marine, Shanghai was the place you wanted to serve.

THE Great Wall of China that tourists know today was constructed during the Ming Dynasty (1368–1644) on the footprints of earlier walls dating back to the millennia before Christ. It was intended to shield the country's rich and ripe "northern crescent," those provinces open to the raids of the barbarians of the time, and later to the Mongols and Manchus, Muslims and Japanese, the Koreans and the Muscovites.

Despite battle, vandalism, and erosion, the Wall remains, immutable and largely intact, meandering for four thousand miles along the steep ridgelines of North China, silent and forbidding, a broadly paved road atop its walls facilitating the swift deployment of Chinese defenders. The Wall is no longer a military factor; if you wish to get through the Great Wall of China, you don't need an army. You simply bribe the fellow who watches over one of the many fortified gates and "passes" tunneling through the ponderous Wall at its base, which render it if not entirely vulnerable, then certainly . . . susceptible. The bribe, at Depression exchange rates, might cost you several dollars. Imagine! A lousy couple of bucks to invade a country. By the time of this story, midway through the twentieth century, the price had gone up slightly, but the Great Wall wasn't truly an obstacle to enemies; merely an interruption.

Yet it remains standing, seemingly untouched, like China itself. You beat on it and beat on it for a hundred years, and in the end it is still there and you are gone, exhausted or dead, your pick and maul and sledgehammer broken. Europeans and Asians, Turk and Hun, and occasionally the Americans, we all took our shot and when we had finished, the Wall was still there, contemptuous of our efforts; China was still China.

As the individual Chinese in the street mutters even today under his breath as we pass, "Foreign devils!"

———

Hundreds of miles south and east of the ancient Wall, it was in the city of those "foreign devils," the great international port of Shanghai, that late in 1941 the adventure began.

Shanghai—arrogantly self-absorbed, unshaken, bustling, and disdainful—was riding out the war with Japan in fair shape. Then, on a November evening, the White Russian General Rostov, out of sorts, depressed by something or other, shot himself to death over cocktails at the bar of the Imperial Club.

This small but shocking act of violence in the midst of a major war was shrugged off by most Chinese (what did one fewer foreign devil matter?), but it made the front pages and certainly got the international community's attention. Was even blasé Shanghai succumbing to war nerves, these persistent rumors of a wider war? Was there a dimension to Rostov's death that went beyond one man's tragedy? Or was the Foreign Quarter reading too much into just another neurotic émigré suicide?

Rostov was an aristocrat who'd fought gallantly under the tsar against the Germans, the Austrians, and briefly the Turks, before commanding a cavalry division against Stalin during the Civil War of 1920. His death was especially shattering for the small, influential, foreign set in Shanghai, the diplomats and soldiers and wealthy men who circulated about the hub of the Imperial Club. It was upsetting to have a decent fellow like Rostov shooting himself anywhere, but to do so in an establishment so admired for its elegance and class? Symbolically at least, the suicide signaled a bleak watershed for the city's better sort. Until then, people said, wartime Shanghai, especially the International Settlement and the French Concession, both dating back to the Boxer Rebellion, had been enjoying a splendid season.

Despite the war.

In the vast interior of the country far from the sea and the big port cities like Shanghai, the war threatened to go on forever, the Japanese winning most of the set-piece battles but the Chinese giving ground grudgingly, and with their inexhaustible manpower, chewing up Japanese troops by the score in every skirmish, sometimes by the hundreds, even thousands. A contemporary war correspondent with a poetic streak and a tolerant rewrite desk compared the combat to "full-grown tigers fighting," the bloody metaphor apt.

The Sino-Japanese War began July 7, 1937, with a night exercise during which Japanese troops fired blank cartridges into the air to simulate combat conditions. Startled Chinese troops, believing they were under attack, replied with artillery fire. The misunderstanding occurred at the Marco Polo Bridge outside Peking, a vista so famed for its beauty, we are told by China historian Jonathan D. Spence, that "the Emperor Qianlong wrote a poem on the loveliness of the setting moon when viewed there in the first light of dawn."

The skirmish at the Marco Polo Bridge was nothing, but not the rhetoric that followed. In Tokyo, Prince Konoye mobilized five divisions and demanded a Chinese apology. Chiang Kai-shek, always to be counted on for xenophobic histrionics, declared, "If we allow one more inch of our territory to be lost, we shall be guilty of an unpardonable crime against our race." Both irate statesmen would soon get their war. Even though Tokyo would, for its own reasons and with considerable understatement, continue to refer to it as "the China Incident."

By the autumn of 1941 two great and cultivated Asian nations had been grappling for more than four years in total, brutal combat, and millions were dead (including 160,000 Japanese soldiers), if not of wounds, then of famine, disease, and exposure. General Hata, commander in chief of all Imperial forces in China, knew his was the superior army, yet he feared "bogging down" in the morass of sheer bodies the Chinese could put into the field. Yet here in Shanghai and in four other "treaty" ports (set up and guaranteed after the Boxers were disarmed forty years earlier), international trade and something approaching normal commerce, industry, even the stock exchange continued to function. Smuggling, a Shanghai art form, was enjoying a wartime boom, the familiar harbor sampans laden deep with goods, much of it contraband. If you but had the money, you could buy just about anything: Singer sewing machines, opium, cartridges, pickled snake, White Russian girls, industrial diamonds, a slightly used trench mortar, rhino horn aphrodisiac, beautifully forged documents, single malt Scotch whisky by the case. Oddly, the national telephone system worked about as well during the war as it did in peacetime, permitting callers to reach a party on either side of the "enemy" line. At the worst of the fighting, the city's "Wall Street" in downtown Shanghai, with its art deco, Tudor, and neoclassical facades, numbered 113 fully operational financial institutions.

Although the Japanese first occupied Shanghai in 1932 during a pre-war skirmish, and then five years later fought fiercely to retain it, these International Settlements of the big cities were left sacrosanct and virtually untouched, islands above the storm, each with its own bureaucrats and small detachments of foreign troops to keep order. As late as 1941, the inspector general of the port of Shanghai, the official who collected customs, was neither a collaborationist Chinese nor an occupying Japanese, but an Englishman.

"The English are bloody," so said sophisticated Shanghai merchants, "but they don't cheat us." The French, they held, weren't "bloody," but they cheated. As for the Germans, well, they cheated *and* were bloody.

Here in Shanghai, and in Canton and Peking, Tsingtao and other places, Chinese government buildings and many of the hotels (the so-called "Grands" were immune) had been requisitioned by the Japanese. Yet the economies flourished with the comings and goings of all manner of moneyed people, whatever the shady source of their wealth (opium, sewing machines, pickled snake?) or the purity of their souls. And many of the foreign inhabitants, including the Brits and Yanks among them, lived very well, sometimes better than well. In the very heart of the city, the Shanghai Race Club operated a fully equipped thoroughbred racetrack (they'd recently introduced parimutual betting), where the season's race meeting became the city's primary social event. On Nanking Road was Jimmy's Place, the most popular nightclub in town, owned and managed by Jimmy Jones, featuring a swing band composed mainly of Black American musicians from Chicago, most of whom had settled in as residents, marrying or carrying on a semipermanent relationship with White Russian girls or the local Chinese and Eurasian beauties.

If you were Chinese, of course, Shanghai life was harder. Wartime shortages, inflation, and the Japanese saw to that. All these additional burdens piled atop the accepted colonial racism and snobbery. A lovely English park on the Bund had a sign: NO DOGS OR CHINESE ALLOWED.

Captain Billy Port lived well. Captain Port—full name William Hamilton Thomas Port, of Pinckney Street, Boston, and the United States Marine Corps—was a member of the 4th Marine Regiment which, with its understrength 1941 complement of 1,008 officers and enlisted men, had for a decade looked out in China for American interests: commercial, cultural, financial, even religious. There were hundreds of Catholic and Protestant missions, thousands of priests and nuns, ministers and their wives, doctors and nurses, teachers, schools and hospitals, all doing God's work in their own busy way. The Marines also made up the guard detachments at the Peking (some were starting to call the capital "Peiping") embassy, and the consulates and legations in Shanghai and elsewhere in the war-battered country, where they sought to maintain a nice balance between two warring armies, and carry out their regimental duties, without being caught up in the fighting.

In many ways, if you were a pre-war Marine, Shanghai was the place you wanted to serve. It was exotic, cheap, glamorous, and exciting.

The Marines were in China as a political, rather than military, counterweight to the Japanese, showing the flag above American properties and enterprises in a violent land. In the international quarters of Shanghai, Peking, or Canton, the Americans and the Japanese troops, who had actually stormed and captured and now occupied these cities, eyed each other uneasily but with a certain professional respect and even formal courtesies. Naturally, in such fluid, chaotic conditions, there were times when the Marines had to fight. And fighting was an occupation at which Billy Port was something of a virtuoso.

Although when he left Boston in his wake a dozen years before and tried to explain to family and friends just why he'd applied to Annapolis and later become a Marine, Billy wrote home with the self-consciousness of young men:

"Try not to be overly upset by my present mission (as a lieutenant seconded to the Guardia, the Nicaragua militia trying to put down the Sandinista rebellion). I have long felt that I might have been cut out for things away from the beach and the country club . . . this might be a good foundation. Since I have no calling to the cloth nor talent for teaching or medicine, this proud and disciplined Corps may be my route to the principles of a constructive life."

Like most decent if unformed young men, Billy didn't quite match or live up to his own aspirations. Which doesn't mean he wasn't successful in his career. His commanding officer in China, and earlier his superior in the Nicaragua insurgency of 1932, Major Lewis B. "Chesty" Puller, once said of Port, "I'd as soon go to war with Billy Port as any man I know. Marines will follow him anywhere. An officer either has command or he doesn't. Billy has it. And besides that," Major Puller remarked, there was one small but important matter, "he knows how to kill a fellow and has the stomach to do so."

When a disapproving colonel remarked that for all Port's warrior virtues, his men didn't march all that smartly, Puller responded: "I have several times on seagoing duty been sent by the Asiatic Squadron to show the flag in ceremonial roles. Once in command of the American honor guard dispatched to pay respects at Admiral Togo's funeral (Togo being the Japanese seaman that 'crossed the T' with his battleships at Tsushima and sank the Russian fleet). On the solemn occasion of that great man's funeral, I handpicked Marines who were crackerjack in drill and precisely trained on the parade ground, but I was most particular that they were all of them taller than me. And consequently, taller than any of the surrounding Japanese, above whom they towered. And I would think, impressed."

"So?" the colonel said, not really getting the point. Which Puller proceeded to supply.

"And if he had been serving with the Asiatic Squadron here at the time, I would have chosen Billy Port for that honor guard."

This was too much for the colonel. "Neither Port nor his men even pretend to work at their close order drill. But kind of saunter along."

"Yes, sir. But the colonel will agree Billy is an impressive young officer..."

Major Puller paused.

"...and tall."

2

"Harry Luce doesn't think there's going to be a war,"
said Joe Haynes of Time.

THIS deep into November, nearly Thanksgiving, you could still get in a decent game of doubles on the clay courts of the International Settlement near Embassy Row. But when a chilling wind came in off the swift, brown Whangpoo River, one of several tributary streams that flowed through the delta of the great Yangtse, the ball tended to float on the breeze, and most men wore smart wool sweaters, of the sort Fred Perry or Tilden favored, over their tennis whites.

Now, on a Tuesday morning at eleven, the foursome in play was a familiar one. The talk, much of it, was of the unfortunate Rostov whom they all knew. Port the Marine; Lonsdale of the British embassy staff who was spoken of as a future foreign secretary; Joe Haynes of *Time* magazine, a favorite of Henry Luce; and nimble, bouncing Jesse Irabu, a youngish Japanese Special Naval Landing Force colonel born in Modesto, California, to first-generation, and rather wealthy, Japanese-Americans who owned and cultivated substantial agricultural acreage. Irabu had graduated from UCLA, and for some reason later returned to Japan, dropped his U.S. citizenship, and entered government service. That was a dozen years ago and Colonel Irabu didn't bother to explain his motivation; nor did his tennis partners feel it was their business to ask. Not of Irabu, one of the few Japanese that people in the Quarter could stand, and whom some Westerners, though not all, agreed was actually "okay."

The American, Billy Port, had the sleek, combed-back hair and dark good looks of the day, redeemed from conventional motion picture handsomeness by a broken nose that had been set badly following the Navy-Penn football game his senior year at the Academy, giving him the look of a club fighter. Port was very fit and had just turned thirty-two, so he thought about age a bit, though not brooding on it precisely. In another eight years he'd be forty. Now that would be a birthday to get a man's attention, especially if he hadn't yet made major. As seemed likely, given the recent little heart-to-heart with his regimental C.O. Not that Port blamed Colonel Howard; he'd had it coming. Nobody, not even the colonel, liked the boorish Sebastian, but why did it have to be Port who confronted the man at the officers' club? Ten years a Marine, and the son of more or less "proper" Bostonians, you'd think Billy would have more sense than to kayo a drunken fellow officer in front of "the ladies." Or so he told himself.

Now there was this Rostov mess.

Rostov, and of course the war, made the between-sets conversation as the four players toweled off and got their wind while a couple of elderly Chinese women swept the court and the white tapes clean of red clay dust. The first two sets went to Port/Irabu 6–4, Irabu's savage, slashing net play the impressive difference. The third wasn't even close as Billy and the Japanese colonel closed out the match easily.

"Brutal and licentious soldiery," Lonsdale grumbled in his Oxbridge drawl. Billy played to him with an exaggeratedly wolfish look and encouraging if crooked smile. He liked Lonsdale, liked the English, admired their cars, their clothes, and especially their women, and may have been the only officer of American Marines who had his uniforms tailored in Savile Row by Henry Poole of Cork Street.

After they showered, the four men took coffee. Irabu, with his divided loyalties (Japan and UCLA, whose tennis varsity sweater he still sported), was as usual being teased by the English diplomat. This time about a very odd occurrence at last week's Chamber of Commerce lunch. A visiting Japanese bureaucrat, Kawai Tatsui of the Foreign Office Information Bureau in Tokyo, told his mainly Chinese audience of businessmen that in order for China and Japan to effect sincere friendship, "The two nations must be naked in their minds." At which, the bureaucrat rather dramatically shed his clothes "and danced in the nude for his hosts." Mr. Tatsui's performance, said the local newspapers, was "heartily applauded" by the Chinese, who were of course at war with Japan.

"Ah, yes, the mysterious East," said Lonsdale. "What was all that about, Colonel?"

Irabu, brow wrinkled, was swift to respond. The casual Californian in him gave way to the proud (and slightly touchy?) Japanese: "Have none of your countrymen in their enthusiasm also gone too far?"

"Don't often take off their trousers in public. But give the fellow marks for trying," Lonsdale offered archly.

Port gave Haynes a lift back downtown in the open Bentley.

"Harry Luce doesn't think there's going to be a war," Joe said. Both men understood there already was a considerable war in Europe as well as the one going on here in China, and that Henry Luce was talking about a war that would have Americans in it.

"Yeah," said Port, "but he also considers Chiang Kai-shek to be approximately God."

Luce's curious hero worship of the photogenic but corrupt Chinese "generalissimo" was hardly a secret. How many times had Chiang or his smart and beautiful "Missimo" been on the cover of Luce's *Time*? Or his enormously popular new weekly "picture" magazine, *Life*? Henry Luce, son of an American missionary and reared in China, loved the place and cheerfully admitted having a rooting interest in the home team.

"Don't get me started," Haynes said. Then, "Lot of hostility in your pal Irabu, Billy. I thought he was going to kill me with that overhead smash, drive me into the damned clay."

"He just likes to win, Joe. He's like Tilden."

Haynes shook his head.

"He's wound so tight he's scary. As if it's Jesse against the world. That's dangerous."

"Oh, hell," Billy said. "He's okay. You ever consider what it might have been like to grow up Japanese in southern California? Might leave a youngster as proud as Jesse rubbed a little raw."

Haynes shrugged. Then he dropped Colonel Irabu as a topic, and the journalist in him emerged, pressing his pal Port.

"What do the Marines think, about our getting into a war, I mean?"

Billy had come to trust Haynes's discretion about quoting an officer by name so he spoke honestly.

"I think it's coming, Joe. And it's time. Twenty years since the World War. The Japs throwing their weight around out here. And brutally, too. Arrogant as Irabu can be, he's a sportsman, and not many of his pals are. We've got Germans sipping aperitifs on the Faubourg-Saint Honoré, bombing hell out of London, and battering at the gates of Moscow. With Mussolini, God help us, threatening Egypt and the Suez Canal. Maybe time we got into it."

The Japanese had been rattling sabers for so long not everyone took them as seriously as Billy did. Some Tokyo-watchers thought all their talk of a Greater East Asia Co-prosperity Sphere opposed to the U.S.

and Britain was nonsense. Captain Port didn't. He'd seen the Japs fight on the Amur River against the Russians eighteen months ago in a brisk and bloody, if "undeclared" war, over where the borders of Soviet Siberia ended and those of Japanese-occupied Manchuria began. He and Chesty Puller had been among the small group of Western officers sent up there in the summer of '39 to Nomonhan as neutral military observers. General staffs like to take the measure of the other fellow's troops, the way major league teams send old ballplayers ahead to scout their next opponent. It was at the Amur where Billy first met Irabu whose battalion had performed gallantly against the Russians, charging with bayonets against the machine guns, breaking through the outposts and into the main Soviet line, forcing Georgi Zhukov to throw in his heavy armor and call down Russian artillery. Irabu's courage and dash earned him a cushy attaché's post here in Shanghai and a place in the weekly doubles match.

While General Zhukov's powerful riposte got him invited to the Kremlin and ticketed for higher Red Army command.

Port dropped off Haynes who turned down lunch. "I've got to get a line off to New York about this new 'peace mission' they're all talking about. For what it's worth, Prince Konoye's given his blessing." Two envoys, Kurusu and Ambassador Nomura, had boarded a China Clipper to the States to meet Roosevelt and confer with Cordell Hull at State.

"Sure." Port was only a company grade officer and enjoyed listening to reporters airing the world view, the larger picture.

Konoye, who also liked the English (aping them by affecting striped trousers and morning coat), had but recently been ousted as Japanese prime minister, and succeeded by the bullet-headed little army general Tojo, who was never seen out of uniform. Diplomats found such fashion notes significant and read much into them. Critics carped that Tojo resembled a monkey and was mentally deficient (and those were Japanese critics!). And the cynical suggested the trip to meet the American secretary of state had been cobbled up as a face-saving device for the now-deposed Prince Konoye. More weighty men spoke in despairing clichés of "one last chance for peace."

Captain Port, commanding Dog Company of the Fourth Marines, one of the nine understrength rifle companies that made up the regiment's cutting edge, spent the afternoon meeting with his platoon leaders and senior NCOs, planning a field problem to be run next week. The paperwork, a drowsy chore he disliked, he pushed through reluctantly. If there was a crisis, if war were about to break out, it hadn't yet ruffled Dog Company. That night, as if Rostov hadn't happened, Billy was at his usual stand at the bar of the Imperial, nursing the club's very good vodka over ice with pimento-stuffed olives.

When Mannerheim, a cousin of the Finnish field marshal and a charter member of the club, mentioned Rostov, Billy responded crisply.

"I should have seen it coming," he said of Rostov's death.

"Oh?"

"We dined last week at Madame Pearl's. He was being very hard on himself for not having gone back to Russia this summer when the Germans came. Defend the old homeland. That sort of thing."

"One of Deniken's cavalry commanders? The Reds would have shot him on sight. Rostov fought against Stalin, y'know, in the Caucasuses during the Civil War. Whipped him, too, he claimed. Rubbed it in, sneering that Stalin was nothing but a second-rate bank robber. Stalin has an inferiority complex and hates men like Rostov."

Billy shrugged, not buying the line. "Rostov disagreed. He thought it might be pulled off. Said he saw a brief window of opportunity in those first weeks of the blitzkrieg when the Kremlin just might have issued an amnesty to some of the old Whites. Unify the nation, we're all Russians now, Reds and Whites both, standing firm against the invader. Stop the Hun. Rather like Alexander Nevsky's call to arms against the Teutonic Knights. It's an appeal that might have worked. Even Stalin might have seen it . . ."

"He's a brute. And a Georgian," someone snarled amiably. Port wasn't quite sure which was meant to be worse.

Out of the corner of an eye he could see Prince Yusopov occupying an armchair, sitting under a portrait of the tsar and Alexandra, listening, nursing a drink, paging through a copy of *The Field,* not saying anything. Nicky Yusopov was only in his early forties yet had the respect of older men. His father, after all, had been one of the aristocrats who assassinated Rasputin. Once, in a pensive mood over a glass, assessing his own countrymen, Yusopov confided to Billy, "Everyone in Russia is a little mad."

Count Vasily, who did more talking than listening, piped up.

"But why would a man like Rostov . . ." Vasily began.

That was the point, wasn't it? Port told himself. No matter how bad things got, why would a man pull out a revolver at the bar and shoot himself? Over politics. Or anything else. A man like General Rostov. The American knew how depressed he was. But just why?

"Bad manners, at the very least, to do it in the club," Mishka said. But then Mishka, a rational man in an irrational time ...

"Rubbish!" someone else put in. "That wasn't politics. It was an obsession. He was fixated on a return to Russia. It's what we all, endlessly, dream about. You, Port!"

"Yes?"

"You ever lose a country? Your whole damned country? And you're never again let back in? *Never?*"

"Not yet I haven't."

"Ha!" offered Vasily. "Talk to your American Indians, your red-skins, Port. The Sioux and Comanches might enlighten you as to what it's like, losing a country. Which is *our* situation, precisely!"

Jesus, Billy thought, why pick on me? You'd think I was George Armstrong Custer. Now Yusopov, from his chair, spoke for the first time, his voice low, making it even more impressive.

"Don't make a bigger ass of yourself than usual, Count."

The advocate of American Indians half bowed. But did shut up. And instantly. "My prince," he responded, suitably cowed.

Billy Port thought it time to defuse passion. He was only an honorary member of this club of tsarist officers, the only American except Puller they ever accepted, and it wouldn't be seemly of an outsider to generate a brawl. He was quite capable of doing that at his own officers' club.

"I never heard the count's remark," he said mildly, earning a grateful nod in his direction from the Russian. Then Billy said, "With Rostov, of course, there were other concerns, as well."

All about the room men nodded. My God, of course there were! Women, for one. Heavy gambling debts for another. And what of Rostov's health, carrying all that weight at his age, and he a cavalryman?

"There was a girl, I believe," someone said.

Men nodded. This was more the Rostov they all knew. A girl.

"A Russian? A Eurasian? A young blonde? Chinese? Wager she was a beauty," Vasily put in. "She must have been, Port, wasn't she?"

"Is there any other kind?" Prince Yusopov asked rhetorically, a laugh behind his words, but getting his answer, regardless.

"Not for Rostov."

Captain Port snapped his fingers and the barman served up another round for all there.

"To General Rostov," Billy said, lifting his vodka, relieved to be off the subject of Rostov's love life, which was cutting uncomfortably close to home.

"To Rostov! And the tsar!" he was echoed by a dozen White Russian officers as they flung emptied Waterford glasses smashing into the stone fireplace, all of them former officers of the late tsar, most of whom by now considered Billy Port of Boston and the Marine Corps an honorary Russian, marooned like them in a foreign clime.

3

London and Washington didn't want war over a few cops on Shanghai streets.

WHEN Port left the club his car was there waiting, motor idling, the top up against the November damp, the Chinese chauffeur alerted by the doorman, and smartly at attention with the curbside rear door already opened, so that the captain, with a nod to his driver, climbed easily into the backseat and was soon rolling smoothly in the big Bentley up Bubbling Well Road, turning at the intersection of Gordon, toward the Bund, Shanghai's waterfront esplanade on the Whangpoo River, where old mansions graced the hillsides sloping to the breakwaters and the quays, with their views of Shanghai's harbor. In decent weather, what a gorgeous sight it was: tankers and merchantmen and passenger liners and junks, mahogany speedboats and small yachts, pinnaces and tugs towing barges and the familiar bustle of great ports everywhere, and the East China Sea beyond. And the sweet and reeking smell of it. He had his own, less poetic memory but preferred to recall George Howe's eloquent description of the smell that first day in 1936 that Howe landed at Chinwangtao to join the regiment, and jotted an instant appreciation of it, "A blend of spices, coffee, tea, human excrement, the river and the land."

Also in view, the flotilla of destroyers and two cruisers and the hurrying avisos and patrol craft and tugs, all of them quite trim, fore and aft, and properly nautical, bravely flying the flag of the Rising Sun, let's not forget those. You didn't have to occupy a port city to rule it.

As his car rolled through darkened Shanghai, Captain Port couldn't help but notice the Japanese patrols, a dozen men, no more, rifles slung, but helmeted, armed, and alert.

This was new in the International Settlement. But several Japanese officials had recently been assassinated. As had several senior Chinese working with the hated invaders in collaboration. The Japanese, understandably irritated, demanded the right of patrol from the concession powers, and got it. London and Washington and the other powers didn't want war over keeping the peace in Shanghai streets, over putting a few cops on the beat. That, after all, wasn't politics, just good sense.

"Turn here," Port ordered.

"Yes, master," the driver said. He was a new man and Billy wasn't yet sure of him.

"Sir. Or captain," Port corrected. He didn't like this "master" business; it had about it the whiff of rickshaws and pith-helmeted colonials. Leave that sort of thing to the Brits, who did it much better than we did. Besides, "captain" was an honorable title and carried sufficient weight for anyone.

"Yes, sir."

Like many of the 4th Regiment's officers, Port lived off-base. The married officers, of course, had private homes, apartments, or houses in the International Settlement, despite exorbitant war-inflated rents (a six-bedroom house with five servants might set a man back eighty dollars a month). There were the usual Bachelor Officers Quarters with private rooms but a communal shower, so Port kept a room at the BOQ and slept there when he drew officer of the day or if they ran a night problem or had some sort of alert. But if one could afford it, and he could, a single officer had his own digs. More privacy, no protocol, and it distanced you comfortably from the routine of barracks life. And the odd bird down the corridor.

First Lieutenant Diggs, for example, was given to nightmares and would wake a barracks with his midnight shouts. Major Holland drank. And when in the mood threw open windows to fire his .45 into the night sky. Joe Owen kept snakes and from time to time you found one in the big shower room, a cobra or a small python slithering across the tiles.

He liked Joe but who needed that?

"Your house, sir," the driver announced as he pulled into the driveway that led up to the big, squat, gloomy, red-brick rented mansion with a cobbled courtyard that once belonged to a now-exiled textile magnate.

"Yes," said Captain Port, looking up to see lights turning on and the front door flung open, as a young girl in her white schoolgirl's dress ran barefoot toward him down the steps and across the damp November cobbles, blonde braids bouncing.

He waited for her to get to him and then folded her into his arms, where they kissed as she leaned close against him feeling the buttons of his uniform and its campaign ribbons. And suddenly the big house was no longer gloomy but full of light, with the majordomo, Leung, holding the door for them, for Captain Port and for the beautiful young woman curled against him with her slender arm through his.

"Your feet will be frozen," Billy said.

"Oh, poof!" She laughed. "You know nothing of girls. Absolutely nothing."

This was "the Schoolgirl," a nineteen-year-old, stateless White Russian named Natasha. Who for a time had belonged to General Rostov.

4

Let the Kennedy boys squire debutantes and get in the columns.

BILLY Port was one of the wealthier serving officers in the Marine Corps, or in any of the American services in the years between the wars, on a short list Dun & Bradstreet might have compiled, headed by George S. Patton (he kept a yacht and had strings of polo ponies), the army's dashing, early exponent of tank warfare.

In school Billy'd been teased about the source of his family's money by Boston's "better sort," Saltonstalls, Lodges, Peabodys, Cabots, Endicotts, and the like. And though it was no longer held against him personally, Port had always been aware of where the money came from. Illegal liquor. Sold, noisily in blue-collar speakeasies, and quietly, quite discreetly, to those same Saltonstalls and Peabodys who snooted Billy over his family's business.

Prohibition had its Capones, its Dion O'Bannions, and Mad Dog Colls. It also had "proper" Back Bay Bostonians like his father, a Harvard man and the son and grandson of Harvard men for a century back. Mr. Port had trebled the family's already substantial fortune by bootlegging liquor during Prohibition, earning the admiring nickname "Vintage" Port for the unwatered quality of his booze. Also picking up along the way something of a rap sheet. To cope with which, Port Senior retained one of the finest old whiteshoe law firms in Boston, which succeeded in getting most charges plea-bargained down to a slap on the wrist or "time already served."

Following Repeal on December 5, 1933, the elder Port, regretting his transgressions, and seeing in which direction the world was headed, set up in the legitimate and profitable high end of the distillery business, filing papers with the state, the county, and the city, all legal and aboveboard and in triplicate. If you could make money by breaking laws, how much more might you make when the law was on your side? Overnight, the bootlegger Port became a big businessman, and in so doing, the Back Bay, Boston WASP rival, and a very bitter one, to Irish Catholic Joe Kennedy of South Boston, another who had made his stake selling moonshine. And also had gone straight.

By now both men, the Catholic Kennedy and the Protestant Port, were considered at least marginally respectable. Marginally. And between the two of them in the 1930s, Kennedy and Port had come to dominate (with Bronfman and a few other Jewish Canadian firms) the North American trade in quality imported Scotch, Irish whisky, old brandies, London gin, and first growth Bordeaux and Burgundies. Young Billy Port and his kid brother Ned studied at Boston Latin and, while still in school, were entered at Harvard, following the family line. While the "arriviste" Kennedy, unwilling to take second best to "Vintage" Port, and having the cash, spent freely to get his Catholic boys into WASP Harvard as well, and spent even more freely to reelect Roosevelt and earn himself first the SEC chairmanship and later an ambassadorship. To London, to the snob Court of St. James, no less, where Kennedy made himself less than popular by showing off his Hollywood connections, throwing his money around, flaunting his Catholicism, and predicting the inevitability of Hitler.

Though Port's father found Joe Kennedy's strivings cheaply amusing, he had to admit to a certain envy when first Joe Kennedy Jr. and then brother Jack matriculated at Cambridge. While his own firstborn son, Billy, stunned the family and defied his father by snubbing Harvard and wangling a congressional appointment to Annapolis. And then, confounding Port pére yet again, by choosing a military career as a Marine officer rather than going into the family business after graduation, as New England elder sons were supposed to do.

But why Annapolis? Why the Marine Corps?

This was the root of an estrangement between father and son that lasted several years, ending only when it became obvious young Port had an absolute gift for war. But where did that come from? Why was Billy so good at it? The elder Port had never even been a Boy Scout. A Port granddad had bought his way out of the Union Army by paying off a substitute. And then, astonishingly, Billy was awarded a medal for gallantry. At which point his father grudgingly accepted the situation, and taking belated pleasure in his boy's achievements, settled a little money and a block of stock on him. Let the Kennedys squire debutantes and make the gossip columns, his son was pacifying Latin America and shooting bandidos.

Billy Port was different, something his own flesh and blood couldn't quite fathom. It impressed them; it scared them, what Billy did and was capable of doing. The young man's epiphany, the event that would shape his life, took place two thousand miles south of Pinckney Street.

In a homicidal firefight raging through the tropical jungle night and into the next day, Port was written up for a Medal of Honor, later negotiated down to the Navy Cross, for his leadership against superior rebel Nicaraguan forces that had earlier ambushed, captured, and then gruesomely tortured to death several other Marine officers and NCOs, a few of them Billy's close friends. Port didn't have any apologies for his murderous rage.

"Shooting soldiers is one thing, but nailing them to the ground atop an anthill, driving knives through their hands and feet, slow-roasting them over low fires, tugging out their intestines with a hooked stick, and taking a damned long time to do it, that's something else. You can kill brave men; you don't reduce them to howling animals."

That was part of Billy Port's philosophy. Kill, but kill clean. As he had done, though twice wounded, killing every Sandinista he and his men caught up to. Even his great pal, role model, and (slightly) superior young officer, Chesty Puller, who had himself won the Navy Cross (several of them) in combat, and who considered Billy a friend, was somewhat in awe of him.

Years later, in China, Puller said, "Sometimes it's necessary to kill. But to enjoy it so much? I love Billy; but he makes me nervous."

So spake Major Puller, who was *never* nervous. At Shanghai he was Captain Port's battalion executive officer, and tended to keep what seamen call "a weather eye" on him. "He's known success early in his career. That can turn a fellow's head. Judgment and maturity; they come later with most of us. Or so it is to be wished."

And as much as Puller, the defender of wild young men who happened to be good Marines, admired Billy, he did permit himself to wonder how the young man served two years at the embassy in Paris without having been challenged to a single duel.

5

Chesty Puller said, "I'll fight my way the hell back to Frisco."

As early as 1938 things in China got so tense the U.S. Army pulled out its 15th Infantry Regiment billeted at Tientsin in the old German barracks there. Shortly after, also at Tientsin, the British refused to turn over several Chinese "terrorists" to Japanese authorities and the Japs responded clumsily, enraging Britain by strip-searching at bayonet point foreigners attempting to enter the British compound, even the women. The very thought of Asian troops pawing naked English-women in public nearly brought the two powers to war, though Chamberlain backed down. A hint of Munich to come? Some thought Tientsin and the embarkation of the 15th Infantry should have been a signal for the 4th Marines to get out as well. It wasn't, though in November of 1940 in Shanghai, officers were asked if they wished to evacuate their families. Puller was among those who did, and his wife and daughter Virginia sailed aboard the *President Coolidge*. Now, as 1941 waned, Major Puller himself was being shipped home, no longer to serve Chinaside, but returning to the States to a new command, the 1st Battalion, 7th Marines, at a just-activated base in North Carolina called New River, the beginnings of what would be a 2nd Marine Division. Puller and Captain Port dined one last time before he sailed.

The two men, friends and literally comrades in arms for ten years, easily fell into alumni reunion nostalgia:

"Remember that night in Managua at the officers' mess, Billy, when all hell broke loose and we fought a battle in our dress whites?"

"I surely do, Major."

That was the time Puller commandeered a passenger train and chased Umanzor and Benavides and their outlaws, as splendid a band of cutthroats as a man could ask, all night and into the next dawn, and then fought it out with them along the railroad right-of-way between Leon and El Sauce. Until, in the end, everyone was so shot up, the Marines couldn't prove whom the bodies belonged to, Umanzor or some poor peon, or that they'd actually gotten Benavides himself.

"I doubt we did, Billy," Puller admitted, "but the general slaughter so delighted His Excellency el Presidente, he promoted everyone right there on the spot, and passed out medals with his own face on them."

"Those were the days, Major. M Company of the old Guardia Nacional."

"Even if it wasn't the Marine Corps, Billy," Chesty said.

"Well, sure. But in between firefights in the Guardia, it was nice and relaxed. *Muy bonita, sabe?*"

Billy Port wasn't much for going around explaining himself to people. But Chesty was different, and now, over a farewell meal and a glass, he said, "I went to Annapolis because I needed discipline, some sort of structure. And I had to get out from under my dad. With him it was always Us versus Them. I didn't want to live my life hating old Joe Kennedy and his kids. When I was still in high school, I went to a dance with one of the Kennedy girls. Only a cousin, not one of the sisters. I heard about it for weeks. It was the Montagues and the Capulets all over. I decided, to hell with it! That was my dad's life, not mine. When it comes to blood feuds, Major, there isn't that much difference between Boston and fifteenth-century Italy.

"And after Annapolis, I thought the Corps might supply the rest of the tightening up I needed. And here I am yearning for the good old days in the Guardia, wine, women, and song."

Chesty listened, nodded.

"Yes, and shooting bandits, don't forget. And not getting killed yourself. Billy Boy, you tightened up all right; you were a natural at it."

Then Port said, very serious, "Major, I never told you this. But in all those fights, all the killing, I was always, you know, enjoying myself. And then I realized I was really scared as hell. But didn't know it until the shooting stopped."

The two men talked some more. And since it would be their last talk until only God and the Marine Corps knew when, Puller parceled out a little advice.

"When we get in the war [most of them were no longer saying "if"] there'll be a quick buildup of the Corps to two, maybe four divisions. There are seventy-five thousand of us now; pretty soon, maybe a quarter million. And with casualties, men are going to be promoted fast. It'll be a fraternity rush. A year or two and you'll maybe be a light colonel, commanding a battalion. I might myself make colonel. Brigadier, even."

Port shook his head. "I don't think I'm ready for a battalion, Major. Unless it was in the old Guardia."

"In the Guardia we'd both be field marshals. But at a high cost."

"Which is?"

Puller's voice grew serious.

"We missed the last World War, you and I, Billy. Don't want to miss out on this one. This time Marines will have the opportunity to confront with force of arms the Samurai warriors of the Empire of Japan. That is going to be one dandy of a war. Men dream of such blessings, Billy, but to only a few of us are they granted."

Port nodded and Puller went on. "So what I'm saying is, throttle down a bit. We all make damn fools of ourselves, Billy. You're hardly the only one. Though you are nationally ranked."

"Thanks, Major. My old man would hate to think I wasn't. As Red Sox fans do, he keeps a scorecard on me."

Puller laughed.

"I remember a few years back I was asked to dinner by a U.S. Navy captain who was entertaining two Japanese officers. One of the Japs was the damned politest fellow you'd ever want to meet. Bowing and smiling and agreeable. Then he got drunk. Which was when his good manners disappeared and he snarled and told my pal the captain we would soon be at war, the Japanese in his destroyer, the American in his cruiser, and the Jap said, 'We will sink you and as we steam by, you will shout from the water, 'Help me, friend!' Then I will stop my ship and kick you down with my boot in your face and say, 'Die, you American son of a bitch.'

"Until then," Chesty said, "Emily Post could have taken lessons from this boy. But underneath it all, there was hostility. The booze just brought it out."

Port nodded. "Well, I drink too much, too, I guess."

"Sure, Billy, but mostly I think you're just ornerier than most people."

Major Puller talked more than he usually did, the Virginia voice soft in the night over dinner against the pleasant ambient sounds of Madame Pearl's, the music, the laughter, the tinkling glasses, the scurry of waiters, the relaxed chitchat of people in the right place at the right hour.

Chesty'd arrived Chinaside in 1933 but even back then, there was talk about just how, if a full war erupted, the Marines could get out. That's how fragile the peace was, how turbulent the country, under an uneasy truce between the Chinese and the Japanese, who occupied Manchuria and the coastal cities. Puller was astonished to learn that the regimental plan was to evacuate by horseback.

"But we have plenty of big trucks," Chesty protested. Well, yes, but weren't horses more reliable than machines?

Major Puller had only a slim patience with such stupidity. Yet, to cover all the bases, he kept a Mongol pony stabled on the city outskirts in the hands of a friendly (and well-compensated) Chinese hostler. Chesty's plan was to don Chinese clothing (he spoke pretty good Chinese by then), make his way to the stables, and then ride through bandit territory until he could join the Chinese army.

But like all good soldiers, Chesty retained his options. One night a sergeant emboldened by drink asked what the major planned to do if the shooting started.

"I don't know what the government will do. Or Headquarters, either. But with no orders to the contrary, I'll take the battalion and fight my way the hell back to Frisco."

Chesty had a gift for the memorable line.

Billy loved Puller and would have served under him anytime, anywhere. But what Puller could do, so too could he. Nicaragua proved that. Which is why he occasionally asked himself what he was trying to prove, navigating edgily between self-confidence and arrogance, in trying to keep up with legends, his father and Puller.

Or was this restlessness just the perfectly healthy and understandable yearning of a career officer for another good war?

6

A thousand Japanese soldiers shouting, "Japanese soldier is frightful."

THE temptation, of course, is to say that war between the United States and Japan was inevitable from the first uninvited visit of Commodore Perry. Which country would end up dominating the six thousand miles of ocean that separated them? Maybe only a war could settle that. Hull, the Tennessean who was Roosevelt's secretary of state, did not share the inevitability theory. War, he thought, was likely but not entirely unavoidable. Hull was a country lawyer who had been Alvin York's congressman, the same wild, hillbilly Alvin who pleaded conscientious objection to going into the army in 1917, and ended up the country's greatest hero as Sergeant York.

Hull was not a sophisticated man. But he was smart, honest, shrewd, and worked at all three. Much as he knew local precincts and how they tended to vote in Memphis and Nashville, he understood that in Japan there was a "war" party and a "peace" party. Several recent Japanese prime ministers had been assassinated for opposing a broader war in China or a totally new one with the Western powers in Asia, the East Indies, and the Philippines. The home minister, Admiral Suetsugu, speechified grandly of a Japanese eminent domain beyond the seas, of a "moral purification drive" in the home islands. A finance minister was bumped off for sneering at Suetsugu and the Hawks. So, too, several corporate chairmen and influential journalists. The emperor seemed to vacillate, tugged at by the war and the peace parties. The new premier, Tojo, was the role model and idol of the militaristic young officers who demanded a showdown with the West.

Secretary Hull read the cables, knew the war party's message: How dare America, France, the Netherlands, and Britain declare a boycott on shipments of petroleum? The Dutch and the French had been defeated by the Nazis and occupied; the British were already fighting on several fronts and not doing all that well. London and their other great cities were being flattened and burned by the Luftwaffe. The Americans, well, who knew where their self-interest lay?

Now came Ambassador Nomura and Mr. Kurusu to talk peace.

And whatever they were selling, Hull wasn't buying. Not yet. Nor was his boss, the president, who appreciated that for diplomatic reasons and the American image, the Japanese envoys had to be received politely and even cordially. But he issued a final instruction on the eve of the talks.

"Cordell, with all due respects to our visitors, and to your handling of their mission, the time may be approaching when diplomacy may no longer be sufficient."

Hull understood the president was telling him the country could soon be at war. And telling Hull to be firm.

Lacking subtlety, Secretary Hull overstepped himself, getting off to the Japanese what could only be termed an ultimatum. A clumsy one at that. On November 26 the note went off to our man in Tokyo, Ambassador Joseph Grew, to be hand-delivered to the appropriate Japanese officials early in the morning of the twenty-seventh.

Japanese diplomats were "dumbfounded and despairing" when they read Hull's letter.

The Army, of course, was delighted. "This means war." And the Imperial Army wanted war.

To the Japanese Navy, which thought it was outgunned and not yet ready to challenge America, Hull's letter was "a jarring blow."

The secretary, not a career diplomat, had blundered. No true diplomatist ever drives his opponent into a corner with no options, no chance to save face. The Hull note demanded that the Japanese immediately pull out of not only Indochina, where they were but recently arrived, but also from China, which they had been fighting for years. And the Japanese knew not only that they were being bossed around, but were considered something of a joke.

In Japan, people were ready to believe the worst rubbish. "Americans think of us as bespectacled bunglers." There was a popular fairy tale that the British, who contracted to build a number of modern Japanese warships, had purposely constructed the ships so top-heavy that at the very first broadside, they would immediately capsize.

The Japanese reaction was such that Cordell Hull on November 27 said to War Secretary Henry Stimson, "I have washed my hands of it and it is now in the hands of you and Knox—the Army and the Navy."

It was on this day, November 27, that a "warning of war," went out to American forces. All the great powers had over the years issued such alerts. In 1914 Germany sent out its *"kriegsgefarh,"* its "danger of war," before Bethmann-Hollweg declared war on tsarist Russia, while piously pleading, "The sword has been forced into our hand." The Russians announced a "period preparatory to war," the French had their *"la couverture,"* which summoned reservists to the colors.

Stimson's version of the alert went to MacArthur in Manila, to General Short in Hawaii, and to other Army and Air Corps brass. Knox's warning went through Admiral Harold "Betty" Stark to Admiral Kimmel of the powerful Pacific Fleet at Pearl Harbor, to Admiral Hart commanding the understrength Asiatic Fleet in Manila, and at Headquarters Marine Corps in northern Virginia to its commandant, General Thomas Holcomb.

The general, who'd fought at Belleau Wood and Soissons against the Germans, was an actual chum of FDR's, both men being amateur sporting marksmen and Holcomb a member of the Marine rifle team. Among the senior USMC officers to whom General Holcomb now passed on a warning was Colonel Samuel L. "Sam" Howard, commanding the 4th Regiment of Marines in China.

One of the several teletyped, classified versions, the one that went out to the admirals, and to HQ USMC, read like this:

"This dispatch is to be considered a war warning. Negotiations with Japan looking toward stabilization of conditions in the Pacific have ceased and an aggressive move by Japan is expected in the next few days. The number and equipment of Japanese troops and the organization of Japanese task forces indicates an amphibious expedition against either the Philippines, Thai or Kra Peninsula, or possibly Borneo. Execute an appropriate defensive deployment preparatory to carrying out the tasks assigned in War Plan 46 . . ."

The warning mentioned just about every place but Honolulu.

Yet the diplomatic minuet went on. That same day, Kurusu and Nomura called on FDR in his office at the White House. It was a pleasant visit that accomplished nothing. Except to convince Roosevelt that he had one more chance to avoid war; by communicating directly to Emperor Hirohito with a carefully crafted and genuine appeal.

Accustomed to wielding power, Roosevelt overestimated the emperor's actual authority, which was mostly symbolic. FDR thought it was possible to make an end run around Tojo and the Japanese government. To reach, and influence, the emperor.

The president was mistaken.

But then, on the other side, the Japanese were also indulging their imaginations. A thousand Japanese infantrymen who were scheduled on December 8 to land in Thailand, preparatory to invading British-controlled and neighboring Malaya, were undergoing a crash course in English. When they came ashore, they would be wearing Thai uniforms, and then, commandeering twenty or thirty buses and rounding up some café and bar girls to accompany them as camouflage, their orders had them driving "merrily" to the Malay border, waving Thai and English flags, and under instruction to sow confusion by yelling: "Japanese soldier is frightful." And "Hurrah for the English!" while showing the Union Jack.

Meanwhile, the Japanese aircraft carriers steamed, undetected and keeping radio silence, through the northern Pacific toward Hawaii.

7

The jaunty MacArthur's divisions were unarmed, still learning how to salute.

THE regiment would be leaving China after ten years and doing it in a matter of hours. Colonel Howard knew this the moment he'd read his copy of the war warning. Which was followed almost immediately by a message that two passenger liners had been ordered into Shanghai to pick up his command and transport the 4th Marines to Manila.

But first, Sam Howard got off a calculated protest to his superior officer in the Far East, Admiral Thomas C. "Tommy" Hart, commanding the Asiatic Fleet. Colonel Howard reminded Hart that some two hundred of his men weren't even here in Shanghai to be evacuated. They were spread out across hundreds of miles of North China from Tsingtao to Peking and points north and west. And he, Sam Howard, wasn't sailing out of Shanghai without them. The colonel, having issued his cry of rage, was not very politely handled.

"Sam," said "Tommy" Hart, who placed the phone call himself, "don't hand me any sob stories about your North China Marines at Peking or anywhere else. I want you and your regiment to hell out of Shanghai by tomorrow, day after. When you land safe and sound at Manila, we'll go back for the others. One of the two liners, the *Harrison,* will pick up the North China detachments at the port of Chinwangtao no later than ten December. You got me now, Colonel?"

"Aye aye, sir," said a chastened commander of the 4th Marines. In all fairness, he should have known that "Tommy" Hart wasn't the kind of man, or officer, who would abandon a couple of hundred Marines without making some effort.

Nor could the Marine commander know of even larger problems weighing on Admiral Hart. The appalling military unpreparedness of the Philippines, for one. Hart had just days earlier asked Douglas MacArthur for a readiness report. MacArthur, for whom a "field marshal's" title had been cobbled up to satisfy his amour propre, airily told Hart that by next April he would have some five hundred warplanes and two hundred thousand trained men. That would be "dandy," said Hart dryly, but what about today? It turned out the jaunty MacArthur had fewer than 150 aircraft and his newly formed Philippine Army divisions, little more than Boy Scouts, were unarmed and still learning how to salute.

In Shanghai Sam Howard spoke to his men. The 4th Marines fell in, platoon by platoon, skeleton company by company, onto the great square that functioned as a parade ground of Marine barracks, Shanghai, one of the most exotic and storied Marine bases in the world. At one time the Marine Expeditionary Force in China had comprised more than four thousand men (and at one point, two regiments, the 6th briefly here beside the 4th) but at the strident urging of the very same Admiral "Tommy" Hart, who saw war coming, Headquarters Marine Corps had permitted the strength to run down to just over a thousand. After all, if war came, the Marines would have to get out quickly if they got out at all.

The only jarring note as the colonel spoke, a wisp of smoke rising from the chimney of headquarters where the regimental sergeant-major was already supervising a shift of clerk-typists burning papers. Not that an infantry regiment kept on file many state secrets. But why give the enemy the gift of anything?

Colonel Sam kept it brief. He told his officers about the ships coming to take them to Manila and to get ready. "At officers' call later, I'll fill in the details. Dismiss the men."

Heels clicked and Springfield rifles slammed.

The 2nd Battalion, including Captain Port's Dog Company, was scheduled to depart the barracks last, in line behind the 1st Battalion and Headquarters Company, tidying up and functioning as rear guard. Port was going over rosters and lists with the executive officer and the platoon leaders, the paperwork he hated, when his top sergeant squeezed into the cramped company office.

"Colonel wants you, Captain."

Rafter was never one for wasting words. Not with an upper plate that occasionally slipped when he spoke.

"Where is he?"

"Just outside, Skipper. Came over his own self asking for you."

What the hell had he done now? Billy wondered. Captains went to colonels, not the other way 'round. Outside the company office idled the colonel's car, a corporal at the wheel, the colonel pacing alongside.

Port saluted. "Morning, Colonel."

"Morning, Port. Come walk with me to HQ."

"Yessir." Billy fell in alongside his commanding officer, making a conscious little skip to get in step, adjusting his stride to that of the shorter man. He knew the colonel's opinion of his marching and wanted to make a decent effort.

Marines saluted as they passed but Colonel Howard spoke only to Port, and that in a low, conversational tone.

"They'll miss Shanghai."

"They will, Colonel. Chinaside Marines put down roots after a few years."

"I'll miss it myself."

"Yessir. As will I." And he meant it. Though he was thinking not just of the country or its people, but also of this Natasha he'd been saddled with. And with the regiment leaving, what *was* he going to do with her?

"That's what I want to talk to you about, Port."

Billy thought then he was going to be questioned about the young woman living with him.

Instead, the colonel said, "I want you to stay behind in China for a bit, Captain."

8

"Favorite? Port, you're a freebooter and a pain in the ass."

THE two officers were now at regimental headquarters and as men passed in and out, hurrying, they saluted and made way.

"My office, Port."

"Yessir."

When the door closed behind them, a clearly puzzled Billy Port asked, "You want Dog Company to watch the regiment's back, sir?"

Rear guard? Traditionally the position of honor. Well, well . . .

"Not your company, Port," Sam Howard said, "you and a few good men. To tackle a tough job, maybe an impossible one.

"I've shared this war warning with the officers and staff NCOs so you know what I'm talking about. Something big's coming. Quite probably war with the Japanese. So we're getting out of China. No single understrength regiment of Marine infantry is going to take on the million men of a very good Imperial Army.

"If all goes well, and depending on the tides, the regiment will be at sea tomorrow night. Maybe sooner. But this message from Headquarters Marine Corps caught us by surprise. I've got another two hundred Marines out there that won't be aboard the *President Harrison* or that other tub tomorrow. Fourth Regiment Marines, at the embassy or on detached duty guarding legations or missionaries or pulling duty as circuit riders, to hell and gone across North China. No way I can get them all back here to Shanghai by tomorrow. The Asiatic Fleet swears they won't be forgotten, that they'll send another ship up there to Chinwangtao on Bo Hai Gulf, to pick up as many of the two hundred as can get there. But they can't promise to have a ship at Chinwangtao until December tenth. By then, we could be at war.

"I don't mean to leave those men behind. The Fourth Regiment doesn't abandon its wounded or its dead. Or, by God, its living. I want to give those boys an option, a second way out so to speak."

He got up and went to a large map table.

"Look here, Port." There was steel in his voice. Port felt it, felt the steel.

The colonel traced a finger south across the map. "Half-dozen men down south at Canton guarding the consulate. I told them to make their own arrangements. There are a dozen neutral merchant ships in Canton harbor. They ought to be able to bribe or bully their way aboard one of them. We have a detachment at Chungking, with the U.S. Mission to Chiang Kai-shek's headquarters. No problem. The Japanese have been trying for two years to take Chungking and haven't come close."

His finger moved north, along the coast. "It's our North China Marines that are at risk. Tsingtao and Tientsin"—he poked a finger at the two northern ports—"a platoon under Major Luther Brown at Tientsin. At Tsingtao, a corporal's guard drops in every week or so to check things out. I tried to tell them what I told Canton. You've got waterfront property. There are plenty of ships. Get yourself out any way you can. Hijack a junk if you have to. Tientsin seems to be waiting for Peking's lead. There's twenty-two men at Chinwangtao under a Lieutenant Huizenga. They'll get out if the SS *President Harrison* ever gets there.

"Peking. That's the hard one. A hundred plus Marines at Peking and they're eighty miles from the sea. They're going to try to reach the coast by rail. But Colonel Ashurst tells me the Japs are discouraging travel. The express trains are all running local. Or having breakdowns. As if something was about to happen. Anyway, Ashurst favors getting to Chinwangtao somehow, and then out by ship." His finger then moved north and slightly east. A long way this time. "You know a Mongol town called Hohhot?"

"Nossir." Port had never heard of it. The colonel poked at it on the map.

"West northwest of Peking, couple hundred miles. On the fringes of the Gobi, what's known as 'Inner' Mongolia. 'Outer' Mongolia's independent but under Soviet influence. 'Inner' is still Chinese. Except where it's occupied by the Japs. We've got Marines up there at Hohhot or nearby. No way they can reach Chinwangtao and sail for Manila."

"Oh?" What Port really wanted to say was, "What in hell are they up there for?"

"It's pretty wild. A sort of no-man's-land. No Japs to speak of. A few self-elected warlords. Plenty of bandits. Killed a couple of American missionaries at someplace called the Celestial Joy Mission in September, and Washington sent a squawk. One of the dead preachers was the niece of a congressman. Before they killed her, they raped her. Congress will put up with a few Americans being killed here and there. But they won't have American women raped, by God. I ordered out a detachment from Harbin, a savvy sergeant and a dozen men, and now they're marooned at Hohhot (or that's where we think they are), nursemaiding what's left of the holy joes. Harbin then sent another patrol to relieve the first bunch but they seem to have gone missing. Never reached Hohhot. Our people at Harbin are headed for Chinwangtao. Don't know if they'll get through but they're not your concern. Nor are the big detachments at Peking and Tientsin. It's the two small patrols near the Gobi. Maybe two dozen Marines.

"I want you to go up there, find them, and get them out.

"You'll lead a light column north, moving fast, by whatever route you think best, and pick up any Marines you come across. Pick your men, pick your route, and get 'em out. By land or by sea. Buy a ship or steal one. Link up with the Nationalists. Slip across borders into Siberia. Find a weak link in Korea. Up to you. I don't want to be enjoying a cold one in Manila thinking about Fourth Regiment Marines sitting in Jap prison camps. Or lying dead in the streets of Peking. Or the Gobi. Or any other damned Chinese slaughterhouse."

Port looked at Colonel Howard, questioning, actually respectful. This seemed to unsettle his commanding officer, more comfortable with the edgy Port he'd come to know. The colonel let the silence between them hang for a moment. Then he said, "Let's hope Ashurst at Peking and his men get on that damned ship and sail home. But if they don't, trekking overland through bandit country may be their only bet. Even if it means joining up with your bunch and fighting your way out. Ashurst is a by-the-numbers officer who'll probably tell you to go to the devil. But if they can't get away by sea, I want them to have some option, no matter how desperate. I'll give you a written order to that effect. Ashurst can ignore it, probably will. But you can't."

Port nodded. He understood the assignment and the job made sense. Did Colonel Howard credit, in fact. Yet he had one question.

"Why me, Colonel? I'm hardly your favorite Marine."

Sam Howard gave him a withering look, one bred of twenty-five years in the Corps and eagles on his shoulders.

"Favorite? You're a freebooter and a pain in the ass and I can't say I like you very much, Port. You're impudent and a rebel and very close to insubordinate."

Billy listened that far and then he said with a grin, "With all due respect to both of you, Colonel, you sound like my father."

The colonel blinked. That stopped him. "I sound like 'Vintage' Port? Your father is a very"—he seemed to be searching for the adjective, ending lamely—"famous man."

"Yessir, he is. As he informs me from time to time. He is also, and I love him, the most manipulative, vindictive, opinionated man I know."

Colonel Howard gave him a cold look. Really cold. Sam Howard didn't much like a man who spoke ill of his own father.

"Then, why did I pick you for a dirty job? Because I hate your guts? Is that what you think, Captain?"

"It had occurred to me, sir."

"Give me a little more credit than that," the colonel said, his anger palpable. Port knew he'd been unfair.

"Permit me to withdraw that remark as unworthy, Colonel."

"It's withdrawn," the colonel said, accepting the apology but not going out of his way to smooth things over with a smile. He still didn't like Port.

"I have three reasons for sending you, Captain. First, I know about your Navy Cross and what you did in Nicaragua, in the jungles. I know that you're a good man in a tight place. And this may turn out to be a very tight place.

"Second, because Chesty Puller vouched for you."

There was a pause. And Captain Port, curious, said softly, "That's two reasons, sir."

Colonel Howard nodded, very brisk, cool, and unemotional.

"The third reason? If it's possible, you'll *get* them out. You'll bring those Marines back to the regiment. You served in Paris and probably know the French have a word for it. I recall it from Soissons during the Great War. '*Débrouillard,*' muddling through somehow, finding your way in the fog. You may be the only officer in the regiment who can."

"Yessir."

Sam Howard looked Port up and down, thawing just slightly.

"Find our wayward Marines up there in the Gobi Desert, Captain. Find 'em, get 'em out, bring 'em home. I'll brief you as best I can, but beyond the Gobi, it's up to you. Reach the Gobi and you're on your own."

He and Port then went over maps and names and numbers in detail, two professional soldiers working together, sizing up the problem and conjuring up solutions, as their regiment went to war.

9

They danced then, to Glenn Miller. And very close.

"GET me the first sergeant," Port told the company clerk, "and quick about it."

The clerk trotted off, sulkily aware that Billy had just come from seeing the colonel, and assuming he'd been chewed out. That's how officers were: taking it out on the first enlisted man they came across.

Master Sergeant Rafter was a Virginian, very neat and trim, with close-cropped hair and jug ears, a country boy who'd been a Marine since 1917, had fought the Germans as a rifleman in the 6th Marines at Belleau Wood, advancing "through the wheat" as they called it, men who never forgot that slaughter. And he'd served both in Haiti and Nicaragua. He was forty-two years old and didn't look it, a middleweight in size, and quiet, and the best top soldier Port had since Billy made captain and was given a company to command. Port waved Rafter into his tiny office and gestured him to close the door.

"Sit down, Top. The company ready to ship out?"

"Nossir, but they will be. Lot to do in twenty-four hours."

"All present or accounted for?"

"Yessir. Corporal Schultz went missing last night but we know the bars where he hangs out. I've sent a platoon guide down to Nagasaki Joe's. We'll have him by the time we board ship. He may not be sobered up but he'll be aboard."

As a good company commander should, Port knew, or knew of, Nagasaki Joe's, a tough joint where the bar girls sat on Marine laps and opened the beer bottles with their teeth.

"Good. Except that I'm not boarding ship with the company. The colonel's got me going upcountry to pick up stragglers and try to get them out. Small detachments at a couple of way stations. The exec doesn't know it yet but he'll be taking the company to Manila."

The Dog Company executive officer was a relatively new first lieutenant they were both still measuring. Rafter pursed thin lips, wondering where all this left him.

"I'll be traveling fast, traveling light. First leg by ship up the coast to Tsingtao, probably. I don't want to take too many men. Maybe a reinforced squad. Three or four empty trucks with drivers for the men we pick up. Cold-weather gear for us and any stragglers who join along the road. Couple of petrol tank trailers hooked up. No Esso stations out there."

"Yessir. I'll pick the men."

"Good. And I'd like you to go with me as second in command."

Rafter had half seen it coming.

"Begging the captain's pardon, but I'd rather sail with the regiment, sir." The first sergeant was hard and fit, but no longer young. Though only graying temples and his false teeth spoke truly to the aging process. Manila wouldn't be a bad duty station for a career Marine with a few years on his sleeve. Warm sun, beaches, nut-brown girls, a good Staff NCO Club. Rafter liked this company, liked being its top soldier. And didn't at all like the idea of being scooped up by the Japs as a prisoner of war.

Billy Port didn't sweet-talk the first sergeant. "I need a good man who's been around. This is going to be hard duty. You decide."

"I don't suppose I could think it over, Skipper."

"No." Port spit out the word. "I don't have the luxury of time. Nor do you. Make up your mind now. I want you. But you decide."

Rafter didn't like it. But what he said was, "I'm your man, then. I'll tell the gunny to take over the company from me and I'll start picking our squad."

Rafter didn't say anything more but he was going. It would be nice, Port thought, if all life's knotty little problems could be as swiftly solved as those between a good first sergeant and the officer for whom he worked.

Billy was thinking, among other things, of Natasha. With a young girl, you wanted to do the right thing. And what was that?

He and Rafter and a staff sergeant and a couple of corporals put in the rest of the morning and all afternoon assembling their little task force.

"One eight-man squad enough?"

"I don't need a lot of men. But I want firepower. Instead of one BAR per squad every other man should have one." A BAR was a Browning Automatic Rifle, the best infantry weapon the Marines had.

They were still arguing supplies and logistics when Port broke away. This was the aspect of *la vie militaire* Billy hated and on which men like Rafter thrived, the picayune details of peacetime service where every Marine prudently carried a little packet called a "housewife," containing scissors, needles and thread, spare buttons, and the like. About eight o'clock when he left them, the top was deep in a discussion of where in Shanghai they stocked goosedown sleeping bags, the sort of light, warm bags alpinists or climbers on Everest might need, and ordering a corporal to round up axes, saws, shovels, planes, and other tools that might come in handy for building shelters against winter. If someone told Rafter it was treeless where they were going, Billy suspected the first sergeant would lay in seeds, saplings, and fertilizer, begin reading up on the cultivation of forests.

Port was taking the girl to a final dinner at the Imperial Club. He wasn't likely to see the Russians again. Maybe they'd go on later for a nightcap at Jimmy's Place, listen to the music. Marines were practiced at farewells. Whether at Nagasaki Joe's or Jimmy's Place. Or a private club where generals and princes drank and toasted the tsar.

The Corps moved you around and by now Billy Port was an expert at saying good-bye. He had even been married. Once. It didn't work out. He was very young, a year out of the Academy, and she was a Nicaraguan aristo whose grandfather had been president of the country. She was a great beauty as well, and astute.

"From our very wedding day," the bride complained, "he had a mistress, the Marine Corps. Billy's father came down from Boston for our wedding. At the reception, he told me, 'It won't last, you know. If he defied me over the Marines, he'll do the same to a wife.' "

And Billy had.

Dinner at the Imperial went well. He and Natasha made an attractive couple, the captain in his dress blues, she with her blonde hair down, set off against the black velvet of her evening dress. She had a few nice jewels, understated, which made them richer. He assumed they were gifts from men. You didn't buy jewels like these on a nightclub dancer's wages. There was laughter, caviar, dancing, the gypsies played, there was plenty of champagne, the tsarist officers, who recalled Natasha from her time with the late Rostov, were all very gallant. Only Prince Yusopov sensed Billy's dilemma. Though the American had said nothing.

"So the regiment will sail."

Port nodded. Hard to have a thousand Marines kissing the girls good-bye and buying last drinks without the word getting out. He hoped none of the men Rafter conscripted were big talkers. Not that he'd told them much. Simply that they'd been assigned a mission upcountry, where fellow Marines, members of the regiment, were counting on them.

Yusopov knew quite a bit, it turned out.

"But without you, Billy?"

"Looks that way, Prince." He hadn't told Natasha a thing, not yet, and he shot Yusopov a cautionary glance. There were few men Port trusted in Shanghai and the prince was one of them. If he couldn't get out of China by sea, the nearest friendly border was Siberia's. Which meant Russia. Which meant Billy had already half decided to pick Yusopov's brains. The prince was a White, deadly enemy of the Soviets, but might have sources within the Red Army officer corps. After Yusopov danced, quite sedately, with Natasha, he and Captain Port agreed to keep in touch. Nothing more than that, with Billy careful not to tell even the trusted prince too much.

Now Port could no longer put off telling the girl something. Not everything. But he had to say something.

They skipped Jimmy's and in the Bentley she was more than or-dinarily silent, huddled close to him, but Billy didn't trust this new chauffeur, and when he started to say something, he bit off his own words. When Leung had let them in, they went into Port's study for a brandy. A servant brought a tray and ice but Natasha shoved Port gently back from the wet bar. "Pretend we're at Nagasaki Joe's and I'll play bar girl."

He looked at her.

"Only if you uncap the beers with your teeth."

"If I had to, Beelee, I could learn that as well."

He bet she would.

When she'd poured the cognac into the snifters, Natasha switched on Billy's new Victor gramaphone. It was big band music, unmistak-ably American.

"Glenn Mee-lair," she said. "I love Glenn Mee-lair."

Also, she loved "Artur Shaw" and Krupa on the drums. With that name, "Krupa" might actually *be* Russian. And Cole Port-air. 'Arry Shames. Natasha had good taste in American swing. They danced again. To Glenn Miller, this time with no Russians gallantly cutting in. She looked up at him as they danced, and then pulled down his head to kiss him on the mouth, her eyes open, her eyes locked on his.

"Beelee, so you will be leaving me?" she asked.

10

"Oh," she said, "you got shot."
"Yes," Port said, "but years ago."

NATASHA had come to him as an afterthought. Months ago, increasingly moody, General Rostov had done what he considered "the decent thing," telling his young lover, "You deserve better than me, Nataly [the form of her name he favored]. A man with a future and not, like me, all past. There are plenty in Shanghai would die to have you, my dear..."

The girl doubted him, but gently, with a smile, stroking his steel-gray hair with a strong, tanned young hand.

"Poof, they only want to sleep with me. I understand that."

"Believe me, Nataly, I see how they look at you when you pass. Even the serious fellows."

"Hush, my general, and don't be so noble. Come to bed."

But he knew better than she. Perhaps he was already thinking about death. And when Natasha did nothing constructive about moving on to someone with a future, or to that most famous of phrases, a more "suitable arrangement," Rostov took the initiative. As a dashing cavalryman who'd served with Deniken, he cut immediately to the point: "That American Marine, Port..."

"The tall one?"

"Yes, he's a decent young chap and quite wealthy, I'm told. Has a large place on Embassy Row. No wife. Men at the Imperial Club agree he's a gentleman. Major Puller testifies to his worth as a soldier. I could speak to Captain Port for you and..."

"Whatever you wish," she said. Passivity came naturally to a girl of her... training. Even one of such resilience. It was one of the techniques of survival in a hostile clime.

Natasha had been born in Shanghai to a Russian girl in the corps de ballet (that sounded so much better, didn't it, than "chorus line"?) of one of the big international nightclubs of the twenties and thirties. No one was quite sure about the father. And Natasha'd been on her own since she was fifteen, tall, healthy, energetic, blonde. Smoking cigarettes and passing for seventeen or eighteen, she hit the same club circuit as her mother. By 1941 the Shanghai nightclubs were even larger, grander, glossy as an MGM musical. The Chinese proprietors of such places favored Western girls and there was always a market for blondes. Natasha didn't tap-dance terribly well but the long legs made up for that. And she was still so young the other dancers christened her "the Schoolgirl." Rostov was hardly the first man she'd moved in with. There'd been another Russian, one Brit, a wealthy Chinese to whom money was of little concern when it came to "face," to making an impression, with a mistress who looked like this one.

If General Rostov wanted her out and Port didn't object, well, she had no prior commitments. And with the Japanese becoming ever more pushy, territorial, the idea of an American protector made sense. And a rich one at that. Along with her other virtues, Natasha had a nice, practical bent.

What she didn't count on was falling for Billy.

At first, and grousing about it as habitual bachelors do, he'd agreed to put her up in a spare bedroom, a favor to his pal Rostov. At this stage of the affair, he was offering little more than a bed and breakfast. "Until she finds a suitable arrangement," he assured himself, echoing Rostov. That season Billy was full of assurances and, so far, the best of good intentions. Then, one night in the late September, and entirely on her own, she made her way down corridors and up flights of stairs and into his bed.

"You're my first American, you know."

"And?"

"I find I like Americans all right, yes."

"Why, thank you."

"Am I your first Russian girl?"

"Oh, yes, the very first," he lied. But then, perhaps she was lying as well?

She ran a hand over his body.

"Oh, you got shot."

"Yes, but years ago."

"Rostov also got wounds. Saber wounds for him."

"Well," Billy said vaguely. There was also a machete cut on one shoulder that he could have passed off as "saber wounds," but he didn't really intend entering a competition for "best wounds," or going into clinical details.

"The good men usually have scars," Natasha said thoughtfully, clearly a student of the matter, "very seldom the bastards."

"I guess so." The conversation smacked of a coroner's inquest and he hoped she was going to drop it.

"Do you mind that I smoke?"

"No, not at all."

"I drink, too."

"And what else do you do, Natasha?"

"Oh, various things," she said cheerfully, and then proceeded to do a variety of them. The subject of wounds, blessedly, did not again come up.

From that night on she shared Captain Port's bed. And now a bigger war was coming, from which not even the proud, disdainful treaty port of Shanghai with its international quarter would be immune. Just as this gorgeous kid—generous, sensible, funny—had insinuated herself into his life, along came an inconvenient war.

One of those first weekends, with the leaves turning but the delta still green, they drove out into the countryside in the Bentley with the top down, past Japanese infantrymen marching under heavy packs, and swinging wide around Chinese oxcarts, and the occasional Jap Army truck or motorcyclist. Leung had had the kitchen girls pack a picnic hamper, cold pheasant, Carr's English biscuits, a wheel of brie, salad, fresh bread from his own kitchen, two bottles of chilled Côte de Beaune, and they parked about a dozen miles out on the grassy, flowering banks of the Whangpoo under an autumn sun, picnicking as sampans floated by and freighter smoke smudged the high blue Asian sky.

"Your automobile is so beautiful, Beelee."

"Do you want to drive it going back?"

"I can't."

"You don't drive?"

"Of course not. There are taxis. And men send their cars for me."

"I'll teach you. It's fun driving a good car fast."

"Ha! You've seen me dance. I fall over my feet. And you think I could drive a car?"

She and the Bentley, of course, were made for each other, sleek, beautiful, and fast. And that September and October and into early November Natasha and Captain Port drove out into the golden coun-

tryside of a China at war to peaceful places: to tea ceremonies and historic pagodas and old shrines where they dropped a few coins of tribute
into the bowls of all variety of monk. Or they cruised slowly through the
teeming city (concerned about his fenders, Billy was at the wheel in traffic!) to little waterfront restaurants or to Jimmy's or the Imperial Club
or the French theater, and enjoyed all these fine places, and he wondered, Is this what love is?

Natasha didn't wonder; she was quite sure of it.

"Where else will we go?" she asked, very much still "the Schoolgirl." "Is San Francisco near your Boston? I would also love to see
Hollywood and meet movie stars."

Hedda Hopper's Hollywood gossip column ran in the English-
language Shanghai paper and Natasha followed the scandals closely.

"And Miami Beach," which she called "MEE-am-ee," "and sail in
glass-bottom boats."

"Why not all of them?" he replied. "And wait 'til you see snow
falling over Boston Commons and attend parties at the Ritz Carlton.
And Fenway Park in the spring when . . ."

"Is that your botanical gardens, Fenway Park?"

"No, but it has nice grass and Joe Cronin."

"He is a friend of yours?"

"A good-hitting shortstop; we're inseparable."

"And would you really take your mistress to Boston? *Quel choc* for
the family."

Her tone was flirtatious, his serious.

"You're nobody's mistress anymore, Natasha."

She kissed him then on the mouth, but chastely.

"I do love you, Beelee."

He'd left behind other women. Funny, wasn't it, how things happened when you had absolutely no intention of getting involved?
Damn that Rostov!

No, that was unfair, wasn't even honest. Instead, all hail, Rostov!
For sending him Natasha. He recalled the dictum: to the victors belong the spoils.

Except that when this new war began, at least here in Shanghai,
the Japanese would be the victors. And their spoils, undoubtedly,
would include stateless Russian girls left behind by their American
boyfriends. That was bitter tea to swallow, Natasha belonging to the

Japs. Few of whom would ever be confused with Jesse Irabu. He knew what they'd done in the so-called but apparently quite literal "Rape of Nanking."

How could he leave her alone here in China? He didn't have the answer and nagged at himself, "Come on, Billy, boy, you've got dough, connections, you'll come up with something. You can't just dump a girl like this." Especially since there were no girls "like" Natasha.

There was only Natasha.

In the morning Billy drove to the barracks to focus on concerns for which he *did* have answers, spent a useful hour with Rafter going over guns, ammo, radios, weapons, canvas tents, vehicles, drawing cold-weather gear, maps, and still more money. Plus four little tanker trailers filled with truck fuel.

"Food. God knows what we'll find up north, if we can live off the country. Probably not in winter. Canned goods, hams, corned beef, peas, and apple sauce and canned peaches and pears, pork and beans, dried sausage and liverwursts, sardines, tuna fish, Campbell's soup, cereal, whatever else you can think of that we can eat and won't spoil. See to it, Rafter, you know what to take. See to it."

And he did. And the chow materialized. The Marine Corps was very simple for an officer with a good top soldier. You just said, "See to it, Rafter." And it was done. Usually by someone else told to "See to it, Corporal."

"And one foot locker per man plus one duffel bag," Port resumed. "And have the men pack their dress blues; useful if we have to put on a show."

The uniform of the day would definitely include overcoats, bulky, below knee length, weighty as they were. It would, after all, be December in a day or two. And they were traveling north.

"And get the men's hair cut. I don't want people thinking we're running a loose ship."

Colonel Howard was hell on haircuts and Port saw no reason to unnecessarily annoy his commanding officer in these final hours.

11

Warlords at the Gobi who'd trade a favorite concubine for a heavy machine gun.

THE colonel and his staff were standing at a map table when Port and First Sergeant Rafter entered Sam Howard's office, doing business as the regimental command center.

There was some chat and then the executive officer, Lieutenant Colonel Curtis, said, "We have a ship for you, Port. A Portuguese coaster registered out of Macao. An old tub but it ought to get you to Tsingtao. Or to Tientsin, if that's your play. Ridgely has all the dope. Called the *Vestal Virgin,* something poetic like that."

"Yessir," Billy said, turning to Major Ridgely with a nod and a grin. He was going to owe Ridgely, the quartermaster, who'd agreed, well, sort of, to get Captain Port's wine, civilian clothes, books, a favorite French painting, and other creature comforts aboard one of the liners carrying the regiment to Manila. Never too early to be genial to a man doing you favors. Billy had already presented Ridgely with a case of Latour '37. The wine wasn't yet quite drinkable but Ridge could wait, while he, Billy, mightn't be able to. He'd even wondered aloud if the ingenious Ridgely thought he could get Port's Bentley aboard ship.

"Useful to have in Manila if I ever get there, Ridge."

Ridgely just gave him a look.

"Sam Howard would have my ass, Billy."

"Sure, sure. Just an idea."

"You'd better see me about money," Curtis told Port. "You'll probably be overcharged by the Portuguese and who knows how many bribes you'll have to pay even to clear the harbor. And in North China you'll be negotiating with the friendly local warlords."

It was one occasion when the Marine Corps, usually parsimonious and proud of it, was freely tossing about the cash.

"How many men you taking, Port? You're keeping it small, I hope."

"I am, Colonel," he told Sam Howard. "My first sergeant's picked a squad from a good rifle platoon. Job like this, you want Marines who've worked together as a unit. We're adding a corpsman, a radio-man, and someone savvy from motor transport to keep the trucks running. There may be a couple others, a driver or two," he said, purposely keeping it vague.

Colonel Howard nodded. You gave a man like Port a job to do and didn't inquire too closely as to method. Better off not knowing in case something went wrong. Which on this mission was virtually guaranteed. Curtis took up the thread.

"Give yourself free rein at the armory. I don't want to leave much for the Japs. You've got how many trucks?"

"Four. I figure starting off with four empty six-bys, in a best-case scenario, with no breakdowns, we could carry a hundred, a hundred twenty men packing them in."

Billy didn't mention the Bentley. Or several people he might add to his task force. At least one of them, Leung, not even an American. Why court trouble?

Curtis, as regimental exec, went on: "I'd shove a 60mm mortar and a couple of heavy machine guns into one of those trucks. Come in handy in a firefight. Plus you might want to do some trading up north, a little barter with the warlords."

The regimental sergeant major, who'd been Chinaside since 1927, permitted himself a laugh.

"Yessir, I've met warlords other side of the Great Wall that'd swap their favorite concubine for a good watercooled .30-caliber Browning heavy."

Even the senior officers enjoyed that one. Billy laughed along, taking care to shoot yet another very sincere smile in Major Ridgely's direction.

The air officer was there, Ramon Gibson, which was a matter of considerable local amusement, since the regiment had no planes. Port turned to him. "Ray, can we expect any air cover? Those Flying Tigers of Chennault's?"

The colonel answered instead of Gibson. "I asked already. Chennault's Tigers are wild men but pretty good. But they're five hundred miles from here, a thousand from North China."

Gibson fleshed it out: "That's right, Colonel. P-40s don't have the range. And for all the headlines, they have only about eighty pilots and sixty pursuit planes. The Japs have hundreds of Zeroes and maybe five hundred bombers in China alone. The Flying Tigers are up to their ass handling them."

"So don't delude yourself, Captain," Sam Howard concluded, "once war breaks out, you and your dozen men and four trucks are on your own."

There was some more chat, Port was given a bank letter of credit on the Marine Corps account, keys to the armory and other buildings, and a full set of rolled maps, large scale and small. Three men from logistics and supply, the exec said, were also being left behind in Shanghai. But on purpose, directed to tidy up affairs, pay bills, hire civilian security people to watch over Marine Corps property, and so on. And if need be, turn themselves in to the Japs, plead diplomatic immunity, and ask to be repatriated home. Rafter raised an eyebrow over that one; there was an assignment he didn't envy. Fighting their way out was bad enough. Then Colonel Howard picked up the phone.

"Send in that sailor."

A young Navy lieutenant, junior grade, in very proper blues, entered the room and stood at attention. He was a sizable, rangy kid, but baby-faced, and to Port he looked about nineteen.

"This is Lieutenant Edmund Cantillon, Port. Of Yale University and the United States Naval Reserve. I'm assigning him to you. He can navigate if you get away by sea. Also function as second in command. So if you get killed, Mr. Cantillon can take over."

The colonel, enjoying his own stab at gallows humor, fixed Billy with his gaze as if expecting argument.

Billy didn't intend getting killed in the foreseeable future but wisely didn't say so. For this once he kept his mouth shut. In another day or two the colonel would be at sea, en route to the Philippines, and Captain Port would decide who was his number two and who wasn't. Until then, the matter was theoretical. Cantillon, who looked uneasy, sensing Port's unspoken protest, realized he was the proximate cause of it.

Then, cutting off a debate that hadn't yet happened, Colonel Howard called on the adjutant.

"Sir, the regiment's official duty roster lists two hundred four officers and men in the North China garrisons."

"Well, as of the moment the regiment sails down the Whangpoo

River to the East China Sea, any of those two hundred four Marines of the Fourth Regiment could be Captain Port's concern. The adjutant at my request prepared a one-sentence order to Captain Port." The colonel now read his order aloud so there'd be no confusion.

"You will as of the date and hour of this letter assume control of all detached Marine personnel of the Fourth Marine Regiment, commissioned, noncommissioned, and enlisted, not otherwise commanded by senior officers serving on active duty anywhere in China north of the Yangtse and south of the Amur Rivers, including the Gobi Desert to the west and east to the Yellow Sea and the East China Sea."

Sam Howard was again looking at Billy. This time, almost affectionately.

"That means Colonel Ashurst, being in command on the ground, makes his own decisions. If he wants to send some of his men with you, fine. If not, that's his call and you're on your own. That all satisfactory, Captain?" he asked quietly, appreciating the job he was assigning this officer, and very close to fatherly.

Port, who had his own sensitive moments, though not often, just as quietly replied, "Yessir, quite satisfactory."

An armistice between the two, perhaps only pro tem, had been initialed.

"Good. I will date and sign that order tomorrow, or after tomorrow, prior to embarking with the regiment and departing China."

"Thank you, sir," Billy said, quite deferential. After all, Colonel Sam hadn't sailed yet.

When Howard closed the meeting, Billy shook hands all 'round the room, earning a knowing wink from Major Ridgely, a slap on the arm from Curtis, a brisk nod from the colonel. Out in the hallway he said to the naval officer, "Where are you billeted, Mr. Cantillon?"

"The Park Hotel, sir."

"Please check out at six tomorrow morning and report to me at the Marine barracks. With all your gear. There'll be plenty of room to put you up at the BOQ. We may be leaving on short notice and I don't want you having to go back and retrieve your sidearms or anything."

"I don't have sidearms, sir."

Port looked at Rafter. "Top, see that our guest is issued a weapon, helmet, and web gear in the morning. And anything else he needs."

Cantillon, perhaps surprising himself, said, "Begging the captain's pardon, but I'm not his guest. I've been ordered to report to the captain and I have."

Billy sized him up. He could have chopped the kid off at the knees. Instead, he said, "Well stated, Mister."

Maybe they could make a Marine of this boy.

12

A kilted Scot, tears streaming down his face, played Highland tunes.

A crackling tension gripped Shanghai that Thursday, November 27, 1941, as the regiment, after ten years of duty Chinaside, prepared to sail. The mood, both among the Marines and the city they were leaving behind, was a strange mix of fear, sweat, and an excitement rippling with blended anticipation and dread.

Admiral Hart, commanding the Asiatic Fleet, had been lobbying Washington for months to withdraw the 4th Marines from what he considered nothing more or less than a trap, and had withheld replacements, shrinking its strength. Now, with the warning of war, half the regiment, the 2nd Rifle Battalion and some of Headquarters Company, would board the *President Madison* on Thursday, the First Battalion and the remainder of Regimental HQ to take ship aboard the *President Harrison* the next day. If all went well, the Marines should be landing at Manila early the following week.

Billy Port couldn't stay away from the waterfront. He wanted to be there when they left. In an issue raincoat, the captain had found a half-sheltered vantage spot on a small balcony of the headquarters building, from which to watch the regiment cut its ties with China.

Colonel R. D. "Dick" Camp Jr., USMC (Ret.), memorably set the scene of that cold, rainy November Thursday at the Marine barracks, ending an era that began before the Boxer Rebellion.

Groups of men huddled here and there, trying to get out of the rain and avoid the noncommissioned officers and their insatiable demand for working parties. Cupping cigarettes in an illusion of warmth, they engaged in desultory conversation trying to make sense of the day's events. A few stood by the yard's chain-link fence, quietly talking with their White Russian girlfriends who had come to say farewell. One girl, not older than fifteen or sixteen, seven or eight months pregnant, and wearing a babushka, stood at the fence weeping quietly and steadily. There did not appear to be any conversation taking place between her and her boyfriend, an uneasy private first class who looked as if he could hardly wait to be given the order to fall in, might even welcome a summons to one of the working parties.

Port couldn't help empathizing.

A half-dozen or so Chinese "ladies of the night" also had come to say good-bye. They stood in a neat little rank at the curb and waved gracefully while calling out, "Bye, Johnny," "Bye, Charlie," "Bye, Jimmy." The men looked sheepish and tried to ignore the women but fellow Marines hollered to them that they were being paged. As the troops formed up, the girls called out the traditional pidgin English farewell: "Long time no come no see."

A small knot of rickshaw drivers waited gloomily by their vehicles in the rain. Marines were among their most generous tippers, especially when drunk, although some of them, the cruelest, forced them to run races in the manner of Roman chariots, the Marines betting heavily on which skinny-legged coolie was fastest or more reckless.

Right on schedule the big double-decker buses pulled up and the men filed aboard for the trip to the Bund, on Shanghai's waterfront. As the buses reached the intersection of Bubbling Well Road and Gordon Road, a fleet of taxicabs was lined up. Each had a huge letter painted on a sign hung over the cab. Together they formed the words "Good Luck." A sad day for the cab company, losing its best customers.

Port had now slipped away alone and took a cab to the waterfront to see what happened next. There were crowds, despite the rain. A Chinese man wearing a little gray felt hat and a traditional long black robe materialized out of the crowd and seemed to be focused on the officers, causing the Marines to show concern. He suddenly raised his hands, many thinking that he had a gun. Instead, he shouted in English: "Three cheers for Chiang Kai-shek, three cheers for President Roosevelt," and then off he went, disappearing back into the crowd.

"Hell of a thing!" marveled Curtis, executive officer of the regiment.

At a command, the Marines boarded a lighter for transport to SS *President Madison,* swinging at anchor out in the stream. A Chinese Boy Scout band tooted and banged away on "Aloha," "Roll Out the Barrel," and finally its version of "The Marines' Hymn."

That night, back at the barracks, Port, accompanied by Rafter, met again with Colonel Howard and other officers who were still ashore, including by now young Cantillon, nicely togged out with a cartridge belt and holstered .45 over his proper blues.

The colonel said Port's Portuguese coaster out of Macao should make Shanghai within thirty-six hours and that the charter arrangements were set. Then one of Howard's staff said, "The embarkation this morning was smooth. But we may have trouble tomorrow. The Japs made loading the *Harrison* bloody hard work this afternoon. We're working through the night with about two hundred of five hundred total tons yet to load."

This was Major Ridgely, Port's quartermaster buddy.

Ridgely said the Japanese shut down a key bridge leading to the waterfront, ordered Chinese customs officials to inspect all Marine supplies and cargo, and instigated three strikes among laborers loading the lighters. "It took Colonel Howard to get their senior officer to have the bridge opened."

"It did that," said Sam Howard, "which brings me to you, Captain Port. My hunch is each day the Japs will get ornerier. So the sooner you can get the hell out of Shanghai the better. They made Ridgely's life miserable today and may do likewise tomorrow. When it's your turn to be hazed and harassed, you won't have eight hundred armed Marines backing you up as we did today."

"Yessir." That was Port's assessment as well.

Howard had one more thing to say and he tugged Billy aside.

"The more I think on it, the better I like your chances up there in North China the other side of the Wall. That's the badlands, the worst place in Asia. Even the Japs steer clear if they can, pretty much stay out of Inner Mongolia and the Gobi. So you ought to be able to slip through the net. It's sheer chaos from what I can learn, bandits and warlords, Mongol separatists, food riots and fuel shortages, Chiang and the Reds fighting each other, the Japs fighting both and pared to the bone on manpower, all those troops being shipped elsewhere. I don't envy General Hata his task.

"But my concern is the Fourth Marines. If you're still on that tramp steamer when war breaks out, you're screwed. Just hope to hell their destroyers are doping off, and run for it or scuttle. But if you get into North China, and can work your way past Peking and clear the Great Wall without being rounded up, you've got a chance, Port. I don't put your odds at any worse than three to one against."

Billy couldn't resist a grin.

"Much appreciated, Colonel."

Friday morning November 28 was again cloudy. Colonel Howard had decided to march the rest of his command through town rather than use buses. If the regiment was bidding a final farewell to China they were going to do it in style. Colonel Dick Camp supplied details.

There was reveille but no breakfast as the troops were scheduled to eat aboard *Harrison.* The uniform of the day prescribed winter greens, campaign hats, heavy marching order—packs with clothing and field equipment—and personal weapons, rifles or pistols. The order of march stipulated: regimental staff, color guard, 1st Battalion HQ, hospital staff, band, A, B, and D Companies. D, or Dog, was Port's, though he wouldn't be with them. The route went from Gordon Road, west on Avenue Road, left on Ferry, left on Bubbling Well to Nanking Road and onto the Bund.

The heavy machine guns on their rubber-wheeled racks would be trundled along by the gun crews. Heavier ordnance moved by truck.

The men formed in column along Ferry Road in front of its compound, now deserted but for Port's command. Colonel Howard and his small staff were positioned in front, and the color guard, bearing the regimental colors and the national ensign, was behind the lead company. In all there were 350 officers and men in formation.

As the units were called to attention, a deep silence fell over the column, despite a cold excitement stirring. Yesterday had been overture; this was the final curtain. As the column stepped out, the drum major brought his baton down, and the drums boomed out the first beat, joined by the snare drums rolling out their complicated rhythm to the set of the cadence. The last China band was composed of both men from the 4th Marines, those bandsmen earlier withdrawn from the Embassy Guard at Peking, and the field musics—buglers and drummers—from the infantry battalions, almost fifty men strong. Some of these NCOs were veteran China hands and had formed permanent relationships with local women, always returning to them after separations. This time would be different.

Some spectators occasionally broke out of the crowd and ran up to the drum major to shove a gift under his arm, the gifts shaped like bottles. Others passed packets of fruit, cakes, and other gifts to the men in ranks. Occasionally, one of the crowd, a barkeep or landlord, would wave something other than a gift—an unpaid bill.

As they passed the Park Hotel a middle-aged Scot, in proper regimental kilt, lustily played Highland tunes on the bagpipes, tears streaming down his face. He had set the rhythm of his music to the cadence of the drums and piped the entire column by, honoring the Marines in the only way he knew, sounding out the haunting strains of his own land. After passing the hotel, the band opened up into "Semper Fidelis."

Then, as the column entered Nanking Road, they struck up "The Marines' Hymn." The onlookers seemed to recognize the tune and with the greatest goodwill and warmth of feeling shouted good-bye to their "Molines." Over the years the Chinese had grudgingly gained a respect for at least these green-clothed "foreign devils."

Farther down Nanking Road they marched past Jimmy's Place where Jimmy Jones (or was it Jimmy James? even Jimmy changed his story from time to time) had assembled his cabaret orchestra, playing American swing music. As they passed, Jimmy swung his band behind the line of march to the tune of "Battle Hymn of the Republic."

Unnoticed at the time, Japanese Army photographers were taking movies of the scene, which would come back to haunt Jimmy in his days in the internment camps.

At the Bund the men began boarding lighters while Colonel Howard and his staff lingered, paying their respects to local and foreign officials who jammed the Customs Jetty. In the midst of this crowd, standing rather conspicuously, the commander of the Japanese Special Naval Landing Force and his aides, who now approached Sam Howard and, smiling insincerely, it was thought, shook his hand and then departed the area.

It was then that Captain Port, having spoken to and wished godspeed to the men of his rifle company, came up to Colonel Howard and saluted.

"Good luck, sir."

"And you, too, Port."

That was all. There was still a chill. Then Sam Howard broke it.

"God bless you, Port. Get my men back to the regiment."

"Yessir."

They shook hands then, two professionals doing the same job but heading off in different directions.

The last lighter filled now, with Howard and his staff and the band, and as it pushed away from the quay, and to a great cheer, they once more played "The Hymn." And then a chorus of "God Bless America," as the few Americans on the docks and piers, mostly civilians now, wept openly.

This would prove to be the last piece of music the band of the 4th Regiment would ever play.

Just then, the morning's first sun broke through low cloud and illuminated the scene: Shanghai, the Bund, the disappearing lighters, the big liner at anchor beyond. Port turned to Rafter.

"Work to do, Top. It's time."

"Yessir, it is," said the first sergeant, who had no patience for either tears or emotional farewells.

13

You see Malraux's twitching eye and then he jumps up and shoots a fellow.

FOLLOWING the Nicaragua fighting in 1932, and his Navy Cross, Second Lieutenant Billy Port was assigned to teach small-unit tactics at the Marine Corps Schools, then located at the Philadelphia Navy Yard. Guerrilla warfare wasn't yet on the formal curriculum, but senior officers thought they might as well put Port's talents to constructive use. "A promising young officer," people said. To which some added, "If a bit wild." He was asked to write a manual for the class but begged off. Billy knew what to do in a fight but couldn't get it down on paper. He commanded a rifle platoon at Guantanamo Bay in Cuba and in 1936 was transferred to Paris and the embassy. Supposedly this was duty of a ceremonial sort. What it actually was, was intelligence-gathering, amiable spying, which is what military attachés of all nations really do when not attending parades and looking smart at cocktail parties. Paris was very clearly one of the places there really was intelligence floating about.

The Germans had just marched into the Rhineland and gotten away with it. Hitler was making ugly noises about Austria. Mussolini strutted about, calling the Mediterranean, "Mare nostrum . . . our sea." The French were touting their Maginot Line (*Life* magazine put its turrets on the cover; called the thing "impregnable"). The Civil War in Spain was a year away but Madrid was shaky and the situation bore watching. In Soviet Russia Stalin was suspicious of his own officer corps and contemplating purges. French governments fell every three months and in the streets Communist labor union members clashed with Royalist bully boys. While Paris itself overflowed with refugees and émigrés cooking up plots, and with promising young men from colonial Africa and Asia, in France to get an education, make trouble, and sleep with French girls drawn to the exotic. The Vietnamese Ho Chi Minh was an early professional student-cum revolutionary in the twenties, then returning home to organize Communist cadres and rhapsodize about la vie Boheme. One of Lieutenant Port's assignments was the attending of low-level diplomatic functions and cocktails at which he was supposed to chat up other young officers and pick their brains. Mostly he spent time with attractive young women. But it was during one of these minor intelligence-gathering events that Billy struck gold, meeting a Chinese intellectual called Chou En-lai.

Now, five years later, Chou was one of the leading men in the Chinese Communist movement, whose Red Army, commanded by Mao Tse-tung, was fighting wars against both the Japanese and Chiang Kai-shek's Nationalists. And Port was one of the few Yanks to whom Chou occasionally talked. Unlike the less-educated Mao, Chou was open to ideas, to alien cultures, to philosophical and political debate—which didn't make him any less a Communist, just a more interesting one.

For one thing, both Chou and Port read Malraux. The French soldier of fortune/intellectual André Malraux had been in Shanghai in 1927 when Chiang put down the Reds and their union allies, smashing their ranks and eliminating their leaders with a terrible ferocity. Malraux had written of the events in his fictionalized *Man's Fate*. More than simply an observer of the scene and an artist, the Frenchman had been a bloody part of it. Port had seen Malraux around Paris, once met him at a literary cocktail, but Chou actually knew the writer. "What a fellow he is," said Chou with very genuine enthusiasm, "the twitching eye, the chain-smoking, the women, and the words, always the words, gloriously infused with fire. A poet and a revolutionary both. And a fighter. Not nearly the tactician he thinks he is, but not bad. And bold, with courage. You see Malraux's eye twitching and you think he's terrified and then he jumps through a window and shoots a fellow."

Chou shook his head in admiration of the Frenchman. Port suspected that in praising Malraux, Chou was also describing himself, the poet-rebel, the fighter-artist, the thinking man of action.

Chou's acquaintanceship (the two were hardly pals) with Port had its pragmatic side. Why not know what the enemy, or future enemy, is thinking, doing, what he fears? The American's motivation was equally self-interested. There were half a billion Chinese. If the country did go Red, they would be a mighty force to be confronted. Now, in Shanghai in the late November of 1941, Billy had a specific need for information from Chou En-lai.

After calling and being told he had the wrong number he called back precisely four minutes later and was given a different number. Chou slipped in and out of Shanghai through Japanese lines with such apparent ease (after all, he and the Japs were at war, weren't they?), Port assumed a deal had been cut. The Reds might discomfort the Japanese; they played bloody hob with Chiang. And wasn't it said, "The enemy of my enemy is my friend."

By good fortune Chou was in town and the two men met in a tea house both knew. As if to establish his bona fides, Chou En-lai was already seated, paging through an impressively current issue of *Time* when Billy entered.

"So, America too is going to war?" the Chinese Communist asked with a half smile. "You and Generalissimo Chiang and we poor Communists, all on the same side. What a gathering of eagles." You couldn't miss the sarcasm.

"Looks that way. No one knows the date. At least we don't."

"It's so very typical for you to assume that we all understand you Americans would never start a war. That surely it will be the Japanese who strike first."

"Touché!" Port agreed with a smile. "It wouldn't occur to me that we'd fire the first shot. Parochial point of view, I'll concede."

Chou sipped his tea and smiled.

"But in this instance, I'm with you. Everything we hear up in Shensi is that the Japanese are about to move."

"That's something else we don't know," Port put in, eager for information, for any edge he could get. "Just where? The Dutch East Indies? The Philippines? And when? Any hint on the timing?"

Chou shrugged ignorance. Valid? The two men haggled for a time and then, without going into detail, the Marine told Chou about his mission, hoping to get more from him.

"So there are some North China Marines left up there and I'm trying to get them out. If I get as far as Peking before war breaks out, which direction would *you* take, Chou? A ship to Vladivostok?" His question, ignoring the impressive presence of the Japanese Navy, was a phony; he was just drawing Chou out.

The Chinese drew an invisible map on the table with a finger.

"Forget the Yellow Sea. Their destroyers are very good; you wouldn't get fifty miles. I'd go inland from Peking. Once you get into Inner Mongolia, you'll find plenty of bandits, some Nationalists, but not all that many Japanese. Then the territory of the warlords. Outer Mongolia is a client state of the Soviets but it's so big, so empty, and the Russians are so busy with Hitler, they've rather left Outer Mongolia to the Mongolians. They're not a very reliable people; you can expect treachery at every turn. Farther west you'll encounter our Fourth Chinese Route Army. In those provinces, we rule; there is stability. You have no objections to being among Communists, do you, Port?" He was teasing, and Billy knew it.

"I'm a registered Republican, but no."

They shared a smile over the feeble joke. Billy wasn't giving that much.

The Communist understood. Nor did he take offense. He picked up his copy of *Time* now and slapped it furled on the table for effect.

"Your friend Haynes is a good reporter. He's interviewed me. Once even talked to Mao. But what Joe Haynes writes for *Time* gets changed in New York. Never appears in the magazine. Mr. Luce is the boss and Mr. Luce has his biases. That's the way of the world. But it would perhaps be helpful for future relations if a few Americans, men like yourself, told the U.S. about *our* fight, the Chinese Communist battle against both the Japs and Chiang Kai-shek. No?"

Billy grinned, recognizing he was being suborned.

"Chou, you're persuasive, but you're talking to the wrong guy. I'm neither diplomat nor journalist, just a Chinaside Marine trying to make a living."

Nor did Chou hold his refusal against him. Or didn't seem to. With the Chinese, who knew? But Chou did volunteer a final morsel of advice: "Don't underestimate General Hata." This was the Japanese commander in chief. "He administers a vast territory efficiently, usually shoots the right people, and runs an army rather well. If you annoy Hata and he takes a dislike to you, Port, you'll have trouble. Even Mao tiptoes around him, fighting Hata but never causing him to lose face. Slip quietly out of China and don't spit in the soup as you go, eh?"

Billy valued the advice and enjoyed the old French wisecrack. "I appreciate your counsel, Chou. Thank you."

The men concluded by shaking hands in the Western manner and then, recalling their Paris days, the Communist leader departed with a jaunty, *"Au revoir, mon vieux,"* his French pretty well accented. It had been said in Paris that Frenchwomen found Chou an attractive quantity.

Billy and Top Sergeant Rafter had huddled with their rifle squad leader that morning. "I know he's a great Marine, Top, and runs a tight ship. But Federales is old as hell. He's got to be fifty. I don't want my squad leader keeling over halfway to Peking."

"He's forty-three, Captain. I looked him up. Year older than me. And he can outmarch and outshoot any twenty-year-old we got short of maybe Buffalo." Buffalo was Port's company runner, his bodyguard, really, and for endurance and strength already a legend. A big blond kid with muscles. But this discussion was about Sergeant Federales on whom both Port and his first soldier would have to rely.

Federales's real name was Limon and he was a Mexican Indian from the borders, from just south of Nogales, and had fought in France at Château-Thierry with the 5th Marines in 1918 as a twenty-year-old scout-sniper. He'd been a Marine nearly twenty-four years now. His nickname derived from the Pancho Villa campaign in southern Arizona and northern Chihuahua, when he scouted for General "Black Jack" Pershing's American Expeditionary Force across the Rio Grande, cooperating with Mexican soldiers and Federal Police, the "Federales," in hunting Villa. Young Limon was a federal scout who caught Pershing's eye. Except that, after the campaign, when the young man crossed into the States and tried to enlist in the U.S. Army, bearing a personal reference from "Black Jack," he was turned away as "a Mex."

A Marine recruiting sergeant in Tucson, less particular, less biased, or maybe just needing to fill a quota, welcomed Federales to the fold, and the Mexican had been in the Corps ever since.

"That's the other thing besides his age that bothers me, Top. I've heard every one of his war stories. And I'll be damned if I'm going to spend a month listening to Federales. You know, 'Me and General Pershing during the Great War . . .'"

"I know, Skipper. I'll speak to Federales about that."

Port continued to grouse. "I never saw an American Indian talk so much. What the hell ever happened to the silent, noble redman?"

"Yessir, Captain," Rafter agreed, not wishing to annoy Captain Port by reminding him Federales was a Mexican and not an American Indian.

Billy had one more shot to take.

"Does he really want to go with us? Or would Federales rather be with the regiment?"

Rafter looked at Port, knowing he was still on his shit list for not leaping at the chance for glory in North China instead of sunning himself in Manila.

"I don't have discussions with Federales, Skipper. Told him the captain needed the best rifle squad in the company for a patrol. He volunteered for all of them."

"Good," said Port, caving in on Federales. "Now we need a couple of fellows you may have to pressure."

"I got 'em, Skipper. Most of them."

The radioman, "Sparks" (in keeping with shipboard practice, all radiomen were "Sparks"), hadn't had to volunteer. "Sparks" was in the brig and delighted to get out.

"What was he in for?"

"Madness. Running around the parade ground stark naked one night, singing 'The Marines' Hymn.' Slugged the corporal of the guard that came for him."

Rafter vouched for Sparks. "The warders told me he was like a child, mostly. Easy to handle. Except during a full moon."

Billy thought about that for a bit. "When's the next full moon, Top?"

"We got a couple weeks, sir."

The motor transport expert who would keep the trucks running across China for a thousand miles, if need be, was more complicated. He was a big Pole who'd been a master mechanic for Ford, he claimed, and he wanted a sit-down with Captain Port before he committed.

"I'm entitled," Jurkovich told Rafter. "There ain't a better mechanic this side of Detroit."

"Then why'd you leave a big money job at Ford for this?"

The man was stubborn. "I'll tell the captain."

It turned out that Jurkovich had been the first master mechanic to sign up with the new United Auto Workers, Walter Reuther and his brother, against management. And was beaten up by Ford thugs. Then he was downgraded to journeyman with a cut in pay. Then his wife cursed him out. "My ma told me not to marry a Polack," she snarled, before departing for more promising territory.

"In the end," said Jurkovich, "I got the hell out. Quit Ford and the union both and divorced my wife. Joined the Marines and ended up running the Motor Transport Battalion whatever duty station I was at."

Port bought the story. But he had questions.

"You game to keep our vehicles running no matter what? I'll want you to drive one truck and pick three more drivers. You pick 'em and make sure about 'em."

"Aye aye, sir."

"And do a little fighting along the way if need be?" Billy asked.

"Yessir, Captain."

Port shook his head.

"No wonder you joined the union, Jurkovich. Man who signs on easy as you needs the Reuther brothers to negotiate for him."

That, at least, won a grin from Jurkovich. But Billy Port had one final test question.

"You know passenger cars. What d'you think of the Bentley automobile?"

"First rate, sir. Won all the big road races in Europe years ago. I follow the races and I know. A great motor vehicle, none better."

"Sign him up, Top."

The medical corpsman was simple. "You're it, Doc," the first sergeant informed Dog Company's best and only corpsman, a onetime student of veterinary medicine at Texas A & M, "Doc" Philo.

"Aye aye, Top," said Philo, who was already pondering what medical supplies they might need along the road, unguents and nostrums of all manner and sort beyond the usual. "That's what veterinary studies do for a man," Doc liked to say, "broaden his range of treatment, offer alternative medicines." It was Doc Philo's notion that a vet was less tied to traditional methods and techniques than an M.D., and he had long talks about it with the regimental surgeon, who conceded there might be something to Doc's thesis, since a vet's patients rarely complained.

And absolutely never sued.

14

Thibodeaux, from the bayous, addressed even the colonel as "ma cher."

FEDERALES paraded his squad of riflemen for Captain Port.

"Fall them in, Top."

The little ritual played out on the strangely vacant parade ground in the chill morning. They'd talked with Sergeant Federales; now Billy would tell the men what they had to know about the job and not a sentence more. Federales, small and dark but not a man who moved or acted old, inspected the squad and, when he was satisfied, presented them to the captain.

They looked good. Which might have been important to Colonel Sam. More significant to Port, they were men he'd trained and would now lead through hostile country. Once Billy took a good NCO's word, Rafter's assurances about Federales, the decision became his; he didn't second-guess. He was happy with both the Mexican and his squad.

Looking them over in their green overcoats, Billy was reminded of a novel he'd read last winter on a long train ride to Peking. It was a Kenneth Roberts yarn about the French and Indian Wars, in which Major Rogers, reviewing his crack, green-clad Rangers, remarked with a certain smugness, "With a few men like this, I could take Quebec."

Well, Billy Port thought, "Let's get to Tsingtao and play it from there. We can invade Canada next spring."

The men sounded off. A few, like "Mad Red" Donnelly, he knew to be outstanding Marines. Corporal Kress, known for obvious reasons as "Fat Ass." When they got to "Thibodeaux, James P.," Port stifled a smile. If you were in the regiment, you knew Corporal Thibodeaux, from the bayou country of Louisiana, who habitually addressed everyone, male and female, American and Chinese, officer or enlisted, as *"ma cher."* He'd even tried it on the Colonel. Not scoring well there, however.

After Port told them they'd be trekking north to pick up some North China Marines and get them back to the regiment, Federales dismissed his men. Seeing Port shaking his head, Federales asked Rafter, "Amigo, we got a problem here?"

"No problem with your squad, Sergeant. It's them damned overcoats that bother the captain."

This was a cue Federales could pick up on.

"Back in the Great War, Top, remember how them British officers in the trenches just chopped off the long skirts of their raincoats. That's how they invented the trench coat. Captain Port's right. Even General Pershing used to ask, how the hell do you go over the top in those damned things?"

"Okay, Federales," said an impatient Rafter, "now put a cork in it."

Overcoats were annoying but hardly Port's top priority. They still didn't have a ship. The *Vestal Virgin* was running late.

"That's the damnedest part," Billy Port groused to his sergeants, "we could be halfway to Tsingtao overland by road if we started the day the regiment sailed. The Japs aren't going to postpone this war indefinitely."

Tomorrow would be December first. And in Singapore British authorities pondered a "state of emergency" based on rumors of a coming Japanese attack on the jewel of Britain's crown colonies. Their version of a "war warning"?

The Portuguese coaster out of Macao chartered by the Marines, indeed named *Vestal Virgin* and inarguably a "tub," was helmed by a skipper so money-grasping he had run his vessel aground on a mud bank at the mouth of the Whangpoo rather than pay the $115 the harbor pilot wanted to bring the *Virgin* safely into port. Now, on the first high tide Monday, a tug was attempting to get the Portuguese afloat and either nose it up to the quays along the Bund or to an anchorage in the stream.

"Depends on what she draws, Captain," Cantillon said. "My Portuguese is nonexistent and over the radio telephone the ship's captain was pretty vague."

Cantillon himself, Port admitted though didn't say, was turning out to be okay. Sensible, practical young man who didn't throw his weight around but was almost deferential to the least Marine private. Kept his eyes open, as well. Even Rafter seemed satisfied. Though of course they didn't yet know if the naval officer could actually navigate at sea.

Or if he could fight.

The delayed arrival of the *Vestal Virgin* gave Billy twenty-four hours more to tidy up loose ends. His own, not the task force's, which Rafter and Sergeant Federales were handling deftly.

Wouldn't it be swell if Marine sergeants could take care of Natasha. Saying good-bye had never been tough before, a kiss, a gift, a graceful exit stage right. Not this time, not with her.

He'd done all the logical, doable things: arranged a bank draft, handwrote a detailed letter to his brother Ned in Boston, called in markers from people in Shanghai who owed him, local Chinese officials, American diplomats, his bankers, a couple of Yank businessmen who might be of help because they knew of Boston's "Vintage" Port, and were reluctant to cross his eldest son. On a more personal note, Billy had already given Natasha the tiny, elegant Degas he'd bought in Paris, a very young girl dancing. It was a picture she loved; it was also quite valuable and could, in a pinch, be turned into negotiable coin. Left unanswered, just how would Billy say adieu?

War was coming closer. You could sense the tension rising throughout the city as other men and women, desperate, tried to get out, tried to sell prosperous businesses, expensive cars at distress prices, attempted to unload lush apartments or comfortable houses. Shanghai shuddered: public drunkenness, drug overdoses, the number of suicides, always high here, rose. Most didn't even make the newspapers. One that did, the death of a prominent Dutch diamond merchant, a Jew, depressed over reports his family in Rotterdam had been sent to the camps. Had he known something about a possible crackdown on Jews by Berlin's new friends, the Japanese? Was he himself about to be arrested? There were rumors, disappointments, nervous breakdowns, betrayals, shocks, the unexpected.

One surprise was Laurent.

This was the French race car driver they all called Monsieur, one of the few auto racers who'd won both the twenty-four hours of Le Mans and the Mille Miglia, a man to be mentioned in the same breath with Ascari, Nuvolari, perhaps even Fangio. Why should Monsieur want to join the Marines? And specifically Port, who knew the man, and was painfully aware of his weaknesses and vices?

Billy, in uniform, was headed for the harbormaster's office at the

Bund when Monsieur hailed him, sprinting perilously through traffic to catch up. The Marine watched him come, dapper in his gray hat, pinch-waisted pinstripes, a double-breasted suit and pleated trousers, sporting like Jay Gatsby "a gorgeous rag" of a shirt and tie, polished shoes that whispered Lobb, a Cartier watch on a powerful wrist.

"Hell, this place is washed up, Captain. I know a loser when I see one. Time to join the Free French," Laurent explained his unexpected request. "Help de Gaulle kick the Boche out of France. Get to Dakar and enlist. I figure you might try to get out through French Indochina. Take me along. I could be useful. I drive a good car, you know."

That rare understatement stopped Billy, who was about to deliver a flat refusal.

"This sudden patriotism of yours, Monsieur? The Boche have been in Paris a year and a half."

The Frenchman cast dramatic glances, as if to suggest the Gestapo was on his trail.

"I have sources, Captain. In the Resistance. These are crucial moments for France."

"I'll think about it," Billy said. The Frenchman was a divertissement, as the French put it. But how stable was he? Laurent gambled money he didn't have, treated women badly, had fought a duel. Some men thought Monsieur a cad. Others used stronger terms.

As Joe Haynes once put it, "The man's a shit, Billy."

Despite this fairy tale about joining de Gaulle at Dakar, Port listened out of nostalgic affection for a driver who'd won some splendid races, and was surely down on his luck, for one reason or another. Monsieur, sensing the vulnerability of gentlemen, pushed Captain Port.

"If you're taking that Bentley of yours, you'll need me. Not as a luxury but a necessity. You can't put a car like that in the hands of hacks and sou chefs. I could drive for you, play mechanic as well. You know I know the underside of a car as well as the wheel. And in China, or Laos or Vietnam, wherever you're headed, sir, that's all you'll encounter, butchers. Can you permit them even to touch a car like yours?"

"We have a master mechanic from Ford, Sergeant Jurkovich."

"Did he ever drive at Monza or Le Mans?"

Port shook him off with the uneasy feeling Monsieur didn't believe "no" really meant "non." In whatever language. From women. From the finance officer at the bank. Or from Marine officers of whom he was begging favors.

More complex, Billy's Japanese pal Irabu. Or was Jesse a pal?

He'd seen him fight, admired Irabu as a combat soldier, and they'd become, if not friends, then partners at tennis. But how much did he really know about Irabu, how far could he trust a Japanese officer, with a war with Japan coming on? Should he meet him for a drink, sound him out on what the Japanese planned? Would that put Jesse on the spot with the Jap brass? Or would Billy put himself at risk by speaking candidly to a potential enemy?

These were hardly the only questions pressing in. Just what did Yusopov have on his mind? Where the devil was his ship, the *Vestal Virgin*? Was it damnfoolery to take the Bentley along, with or without Monsieur at the wheel? And, the one problem he kept postponing, there was Natasha.

Fortunately, there were few questions dealing with Leung. Billy asked his Chinese major domo if he would leave Shanghai to accompany his employer on a chancey ride north? The man hadn't hesitated. "Of course, sir." Leung was Chinese-speaking, loyal, the keeper of the money box that Port called "the old exchequer." And Port knew what culinary wonders Leung could achieve in a kitchen when the servants were absent or the captain wished privacy. Could Leung duplicate such marvels over a campfire in the Gobi? Perhaps they were going to find out.

Billy directed Leung to settle the final six months on the lease, pay their bills, furlough the servants with a bonus (and letters of recommendation), shut off the phone, the electric and gas, provide forwarding addresses (Pinckney Street, Boston, and in care of the regiment in Manila) to the post office, and stand by for instructions.

"Yes, sir," said Leung coolly, a man for whom the adjective "inscrutable" may have been invented.

With the clock running down, Port made his courtesy calls of farewell. The Marines trained their officers to do things like that. Joe Haynes was already gone, called back not to Manhattan but to a "safer" post in Honolulu (and just consider the irony of that!) by the foreign editor at *Time*. Lonsdale, the Brit, was busily encoding and decoding at the embassy. The Brits too had good manners. "I also get to burn the state secrets, dear chap. So don't count on me this week for cocktails. See you after the war? Chin-chin."

On the other hand, the Irabu initiative played beautifully.

They met, the captain of American Marines and the Japanese colonel, for the first time since the "warning of war" went out from Washington (and surely had been intercepted by Tokyo), and amid an understandable tension. Gnawing at Billy, just why had Irabu, the UCLA tennis star, the rich young man from Modesto, California, bailed out on the States and reverted to being a Japanese, and a ranking naval officer at that? Was this to be their last meeting? Could he ask?

The previous time they'd met, both men were in tennis clothes. On this occasion, it was civvies. Wearing a gray flannel Poole's suit and repp tie with a snap-brimmed fedora, Port met the colonel, wearing brown worsted and a jaunty English tweed cap, in the late-morning quiet of Jimmy's Place, a big city nightclub, in the morning, being the emptiest place in town. As they waited for the girl to fetch their coffee, Irabu opened the bidding: "Billy, I don't want to know a thing beyond the fact you've chartered a tramp steamer and are leaving Shanghai. But not for Manila. Can I help?"

Port recalled how the Japanese harassed the regiment's departure, blocking a bridge, fomenting a longshore strike. "Can I get a laissez-passer of some sort so we clear the harbor without complications?"

"There's a faction that would like to see you delayed here indefinitely," the colonel said.

Port's face must have gone bleak. Was he going to have to fight his way out? Irabu hurriedly scribbled a note in Japanese characters on an official-looking letterhead.

"Here, this is pure rubbish that won't stand up in court, but it ought to impress a Japanese MP or a Chinese functionary. I don't want you starting a war over the harbormaster's red tape."

Billy tucked the note into his wallet.

"Thanks, old man."

"A word about Tsingtao," Irabu said, his voice conspiratorial.

"Yes?" Billy hadn't mentioned Tsingtao. Irabu's dope so far was pretty keen, alarmingly so.

"They've got the best German brewery on the China coast. If you put in there for supplies, take on a few barrels. I can recommend it highly."

Beyond that, both men consciously fenced. They had tennis in common, they had the Marines, Irabu's Japanese, Billy's the U.S. variety, they got along. But they were serving officers for two countries that any hour might be at war. Given the war situation, the matter of Jesse's citizenship, his allegiance still hung in the air. Irabu wasn't saying anything about it and it was clearly inappropriate for Port to ask. Or was it? Only at the end when Irabu insisted on paying for their coffees, and they shook hands, did either speak with sincerity.

To hell with it, Billy thought, I'll come right out and ask. He can only tell me to stuff it.

"For what it's worth," Port said, "I'm sorry you won't be on our side if the balloon goes up."

"Thanks, Billy. You can't understand this, but at one point some years back, I just felt I'd be more comfortable in my skin, being Japanese than a Californian."

"I've wondered about that. But it wasn't any of my business."

"It wasn't. But the fact you didn't grill me about it does you credit, Billy. One reason we get on. Since we won't be playing doubles again for a while, I'll answer the question you never asked. Just put it down to . . . I dunno, unrequited love. Is that the phrase? I was twenty-five and there was a blue-eyed blonde from UCLA who lived at Newport Beach. My people had a little money, so did hers. We were doing very nicely, she and I. And then her family got in the way. Didn't want any slant-eyed little grandchildren. Subtler than that, but I got the message. I got sore, raised hell, sulked for a while. And then I realized she belonged there and I didn't. That maybe I belonged . . . somewhere else.

"For years, ambitious young Japanese like my parents had been getting out, trading in a rather stuffy, dull, old-fashioned medieval homeland for a contemporary lifestyle in the States. And for some of them, like our family, it worked. And then America got up on its hind legs and kicked me in the teeth. So I came home, to the dear old Land of the Rising Sun, to what I realized *was* home, and haven't looked back."

"Oh, shit. I'm sorry."

"I was sorry, too, at first. The Japanese I ran up against shunned me as a freak. Maybe I was a spy? What could be my motives? Those first few months I was as unhappy in Japan as I'd been in southern California. Then some shrewd and influential people in Tokyo concluded that this might be good business, a successful Japanese-American bailing out on Uncle Sam and coming home. A reverse emigration for a change. Almost overnight, I became a sort of symbol: someone who of his own volition chose Japan over the West."

"Local boy makes good."

"Yeah. Gradually, people opened up to me, encouraged me, made me feel welcome. While back in California I was still a lousy Jap, whose folks hadn't come over on the *Mayflower.*"

Port snorted in derision. "Don't give me that, Irabu! It was prejudice like that which drove the *Mayflower* crowd out of England in the first place and you know it . . ."

Irabu nodded. "Yeah, funny, isn't it?" Then, shifting gears: "Look out for yourself, Billy. This time it isn't going to be bandidos and machetes in Nicaragua . . ."

"I know, Irabu, nor tennis either."

Both men knew that when war came, it would be vast, waged across oceans and continents, even hemispheres. Hardly likely that two soldiers, serving on the opposing sides, would meet again over hostile gun sights. This wasn't the North and the South and boys at college together, but a Boston Yankee and a California Nisei who'd gone home. Though, you never knew, did you? And so they indulged in good-spirited josh and mock threats, a couple of good, tough combat soldiers who used to be tennis partners, walking away from friendship and into a war. Casual as that.

Except that, Billy knew, wars set their own rules, and if it came to it, I'll kill Irabu. Because he knew that if he didn't, Jesse'll kill me.

The drama, such as it was, would come later in the day from quiet, cerebral Prince Yusopov, suddenly brimming with fire and decision.

He'd called, asking Billy to come by without notifying anyone. Port, puzzled, agreed, and had Leung call a cab, the Bentley being so recognizable. And when a servant showed Captain Port into Yusopov's house, the prince, without an apology or remark about the weather, what you expected of a man with his old world manners, declared, "Billy, I want to go along with you and your Marines."

Within moments, they were sitting over coffee, in Yusopov's large, comfortable house in the Pudong district between the delta and the sea, what passed in Shanghai for the suburbs. Nice piece of ground, nice house, nice room. The prince lived quietly but well. And to what end, why give all this up now? Wasn't this rather rash for the calm, deliberate Yusopov? It was the Russian who spoke, his words gushing out.

"Rostov was right. An even bigger war's coming, perhaps in a matter of days, and I want to be part of it. This limbo we émigrés call Shanghai is a half-life. Russia and the U.S. are lining up, both of us against the Germans and Japan, and it's going to be a war worth fighting."

Port sipped his coffee. What could he say to that? Yet he hesitated to encourage Yusopov. He didn't need another Russian aristo on his conscience. Look what Rostov got him into.

The prince went on, solemn as Lent. "Just days ago, the Germans were within thirty-five miles of Moscow. Our forces [Billy noted the "our," odd for a White to so refer to the Soviets] are fighting for every mile. Blizzards have closed down the Luftwaffe and they say fresh Siberian reinforcements are reaching the capital by train from the Far East. My God, man, one of the great battles of history is shaping up at Moscow and here I am, a Russian and a soldier, five thousand miles away, playing bridge, handicapping the horses, toasting the tsar at the club every night. Can one imagine a more vacant life?

"This is a fight I can't sit out, Captain Port."

"But will they take you? Even Rostov thought the odds favored getting shot. Stalin holds grudges, you've said that yourself."

"No argument. I still want to give it a try."

"Then just go back. Through the Middle East and Turkey. Or get to Scandinavia somehow and cross through Finland. Who knows where my detachment is headed once we clear North China. *If* we clear it. You could end up toasting the tsar and playing bridge in Manila."

"North of North China is Siberia." The prince wasn't falling for Billy's wit.

"Yeah, but we might get away by sea. That's an option. Where does that leave you? Or cut west through the Gobi and Mongolia and link up with Chiang. Or even with Mao and his Commies. Hell of a diplomatic fix for both of us then!"

"I'm wagering you'll cross into Russia itself at some point and be embraced gloriously and drunkenly by your brand-new allies, the Red Army. That's why I want to come."

"So you can be shot by the Soviets rather than the Japs?" Port said with a mocking grin.

"Well, I won't have missed the war entirely. And I'll have gone home . . ."

A Chinese maid fetched fresh cups and sweets.

"You ever been back?" Billy asked.

"Yes, twice since the Civil War. Clandestinely both times. Once, some family matters, papers, jewels, a few pictures, books, trinkets I'd hidden before getting out, and that I wanted to reclaim. As the song goes, a sentimental journey. The second time, well, that was also an errand."

"Oh?"

"Yes, that time I had to kill a man."

"A Red?"

"No, one of us. I don't hate the Reds anymore. Maybe Stalin and Molotov and that bunch. But not your everyday Soviet. This fellow was a White, a tsarist general of impeccable credentials. But in the battle for Grozny in the Caucasus his flank was turned and an entire White Army corps was lost. Regrettable, but in war such things happen. The poor fellow felt it the worst of all of us. Or so I believed.

"Subsequently we learned he'd been bought."

"And?"

"Several of us who'd served with him drew straws. I won. Or lost, depending on one's point of view. I was smuggled back into the Soviet Union, took a trolley to his Leningrad flat, removed a music hall disguise so that he'd know who I was, why I was there, and shot him through the head. Didn't take long. I walked downstairs and swung aboard the next trolley car that came by. Someone got me into Finland and a month later I was in Shanghai. I wasn't yet thirty and I've not seen Russia since."

Port nodded, thoughtful and not at all sure what to do. The prince helped him.

"You and your Marines are resourceful people. You'll likely get away from the Japanese. But if you head north, and your route is for Siberia, I can help get you there. There are White Russians scattered all over Siberia, Mongolia, and North China and I know a few of them. And most, I can say, probably know of me. I can talk you into Russia, Port, of that I'm certain. I can get you and your men into Siberia!"

"And then?"

"And then," he said, less impassioned now, quite calm, "I'm sure of absolutely nothing. They'll rehabilitate me or not, shoot me or they won't. But you'll be safe, you and your Marines both. And I will have gone home . . ."

15

After the war, vodka could be the new gin. She might even impress Old Man Port.

HE could no longer stall Natasha.

Until the prince made his startling proposal, Billy was thinking of asking Yusopov to look out for the girl when the Marines left town. That option was no longer in play. So it was up to him to tell her, to attend to a few small matters, to say good-bye, and to do so now.

He braced himself for scenes. Not for the first time, she surprised him, so cool, so in control.

"I don't mean to pester you, Beelee, but just *when* are you leaving? I'll have to make arrangements, of course. Calls must be made, housing found, people seen. You understand."

"Naturally." It was as if they were arranging a hand of bridge later in the week.

With the afternoon fading and the light going he led her out into the back garden behind the mansion. "Here, this is a .32-caliber Colts revolver. Six shots. Small, not too heavy, simpler to work than an automatic. Keep it with you and keep it loaded. See that chipped brick in the wall, about waist high. Good. Where you want to shoot a man, in the middle. Just hold the gun steady in your right hand, aim at the chip, and squeeze the trigger slowly. Don't pull, squeeze."

The shot echoed around the walled garden.

"Good. Now do it again. Set your feet apart, knees relaxed, as if you were going to hit a tennis ball. Now, fire again."

To a civilian, it might have seemed ghoulish to be teaching a young woman how to shoot just before leaving her, but to a soldier who knew what happened in cities when wars broke out, knew what happened specifically to young women, it was just common sense. When he'd reloaded the revolver a third time, she was hitting the chipped brick or close to it with almost every shot.

"I did okay, *mon capitaine?*"

"You did great. The Corps will have you firing for medals in the next Olympics."

There was time for no more lessons. But then, they both knew that.

Marksmanship 101 over, she sat next to him at his big, old-fashioned, rolltop desk to do the paperwork.

"I'm seeing Art Leavis once more at the consulate. He's out of his mind coping with Yanks trying to get out, so stateless Russians are nowhere in his priorities. But Art's a good guy and he's promised to do his best. Meanwhile, there are things I *can* do."

Billy had earlier written to his brother Ned, and now gave her a second version of the letter to hand-deliver, if and when, at Pinckney Street.

"Don't lose this. Ned knows my hand. I've left a blank here," he said, showing her the letter. "Your last name. I never knew it. What do I put down? Natasha 'what'?"

She chewed a lower lip. Then, "Who knows? Could I be 'Nataly Rostov'? He always called me 'Nataly' and he was a good man. Who bore a fine name, 'Rostov.'"

"Okay, but let's leave it 'Natasha' Rostov so I don't have to rewrite the whole thing."

"Okey-dokey." She enjoyed the slang. "I don't think the general would mind."

"He'd be proud."

Then there was the matter of money. "I'm getting you several checks certified by Barings. As good as cash. Anyone in the Orient will honor them. One for short term, the other, larger, long-term expenses. Plus ten thousand in U.S. dollars cash. You'll need it. Bribes and the like. Get a money belt or something."

"I understand." She didn't object or go all modest and protesting. She knew this was serious stuff and she fell into his mood, efficient and practical.

"I want to give you other things but am not sure what. You have the Degas, the young dancer. It's worth something if you have to sell it. If you don't, keep it as a memento. Toss the frame. The canvas itself doesn't weigh anything and you can slide it in between the pages of *l'Officiel* or one of your other fashion magazines and carry it that way."

She was taking notes. Without writing them down.

"Yes, Beelee. That's good sense." Could a well-bred nineteen-year-old in Boston have handled the situation as impressively as "the Schoolgirl" was doing?

When they'd finished their bookkeeping she made vodka cocktails and they drank them, smoking cigarettes, while Leung got the kitchen busy preparing dinner. It might be the last.

Port returned to those letters to Ned.

"We're New Englanders, Natasha. Episcopalians. So it's important that we have a business reason for the things we do, not just being gracious or helping a friend. That's why in writing brother Ned I stress your background in the hospitality industry and exaggerate your expertise with vodka. After the war, when the world gets back to normal, vodka could be the new 'gin,' especially in the States where people love a novelty. So if Ned, or anyone, asks you about vodka, you're the world's greatest expert, okay? You know all the top people in the vodka apparat. Lay it on thick. Ned won't buy it all but he'll understand. It may even impress my old man. The Ports will welcome you because I ask them to, because you're my friend.

"But they'll like you even more if I make you sound like there's an honest buck to be made out of you. That you're the Shanghai 'Billy Rose.' "

He didn't even have to explain who "Billy Rose" was since she'd read all about his entrepreneurial genius in *The South China Morning Post*.

Billy'd flirted with the idea of signing over the lease of this house to Natasha and letting her stay here until she could get out of town.

"But I don't like you being all alone rattling around in a big house with a couple of servants. There's craziness coming and a place like this just demands to be looted. Or requisitioned by the Japs. It's why I want you to have the Colt. And why I'd rather have you downtown in one of the big hotels. The Park okay?"

"The Park is fine, yes."

Port knew the manager and didn't waste time. After a brief phone conversation he said, "They're expecting you in the morning. No suites, unfortunately, but a good room. Leung will have you and your things driven over." He'd earlier bribed the manager. Twenty-five hundred American dollars.

Toward the end of dinner she asked, "I haven't been too much burden, have I?"

"You've been wonderful."

"I never wanted to burden poor Rostov, either. All I ever sought was a suitable arrangement."

"And have I been 'suitable'?"

"Yes, darling. Entirely, and more than entirely." She got up from her side of the table and crossed over to sling her arms around his neck and then kiss him.

"Now, Beelee, can we stop talking beezness? You are going away and I understand more than you think I do. So now, I want to drink some champagne and listen to Glenn Meelair or 'Arry James, and dance together with you. Okay?"

Port got up smiling. Beezness? He thought he was talking about her life, her future.

"Yes, Natasha, let's dance. And not write any more letters to my brother . . ."

He rang for a houseboy to bring the wine.

"Good!" she said firmly, and very pleased, her hips moving as she went to the phonograph. "May we have the Veuve Cliquot? I do like the Veuve."

"It's done, Nataly."

He realized he was calling her by the favorite name of General Rostov. Who also left her.

16

*The bar girls sang: "Goddamn, son of a bitch/
United States Marine Corps."*

DECEMBER 1, 1941, was a Monday, first day of a new week, the fresh start of a new month. Good omen? Billy Port hoped so.

As a boy he'd read Conrad, Robert Louis Stevenson, and Captain Marryat, and now, at dockside with the East China Sea just beyond, and with hostile Japanese all about and perhaps within hours of capturing or killing Port and his Marines, he came up against Captain Henriques, a character the equal of any fictionally created in seafaring literature, even by the great Joseph Conrad.

The commanding officer of the *Vestal Virgin* was large, beefy, whiskered, and stank of gin, fish, and sweat.

"Yes, Capitan Port, your Major Ridgely chartered me for a month. Do not, sir, imagine I am impressed by any of this."

"You are a day and a half late, Henriques. Our trucks have been sitting on the dock since day before yesterday. My men have been delayed. Why didn't you take on a harbor pilot? The Marine Corps included his payment in the charter fee."

"Go to hell, Marine. I don't answer to nobody. And not you bastards. This is my ship. You don't know the tides and I do. I command here, decide when we come, when we go."

Port looked over at Rafter.

"What did Major Ridgely pay this fellow for a month's charter? Do you have the figure there, Top?"

"Yessir. Ten thousand dollars, paid in advance."

Port turned back to Henriques, behind whom his fifteen or eighteen crewmen—lascars, Portuguese, a few Chinese, and a couple you couldn't tell—enjoyed their captain's telling off the latest poor souls to pay actual money to sail on the *Vestal Virgin*. They looked like a tough bunch, several of the men with useful-looking krises shoved in their belts, bare blades gleaming. Those knife blades were impressive: they may have been the only thing aboard *Vestal Virgin* that was clean.

Port also had an audience, his Marines, standing easy, but armed and ready, businesslike in their tin hats, forest-green uniforms, and yellow canvas leggings, rifles slung. Every one of them was now also packing sidearms, the .45 automatic pistols holstered and strapped on. Plus a tall young American naval officer, standing a little less easy. But then, he was new, wasn't he? Though they had gotten him a tin hat and a .45 automatic of his own, and some leggings, which didn't look all that incongruous over the navy blue. Looked pretty good, in fact, or so Cantillon thought to himself.

All around them work went on, the four trucks being winched aboard and dropped easily and slowly into the hold; the Bentley, they were lashing that on deck. On the dock rickshaw coolies and idlers enjoyed watching other men work. Especially the "foreign devils." You could hear the cranes working and winches squealing as Port and Henriques haggled.

"Okay, Captain Henriques. Now, what would you think this ship might be worth?"

"A month's charter, that's what you got. Ten thousand in dollars. Don't try to wiggle out of a deal, *Capitan*. Too late for slim dealing with a fellow like me who knows his stuff. Just because you a Marine don't mean . . ."

"I mean, to buy this tub. How much would that cost me? Cash."

Henriques blinked. He'd cheated greenhorns in his time. But what kind of crazy bastard would buy a floating disaster like the *Virgin*? As he pondered, three large rats scampered past.

"I don't know. I have to talk to owner. In Macao."

"Call him on the radio."

"He's drunk. Eleven o'clock in the morning, he's always drunk by now."

"Make an estimate, Captain Henriques. Take a guess. A price that would please your boss and maybe a nice percentage left over for Captain Henriques. An educated guess. How much?"

Billy enjoyed confrontation. With a slob like this, it was fun. His Marines were enjoying it, too. Henriques's crew, now, as well. They were his men, and a tough bunch, but, well, he wasn't too popular with them. What seemed to be a mate, a slim young Malay, was grinning openly. Henriques was a hard master and the crew enjoyed his discomfiture.

"How about it, Captain Henriques? How much? Cash transaction."

Henriques, no bluster now, went sly. Greed was taking over.

"Forty thousand dollars American. Not a sou less."

"Forty thousand, to buy your ship."

"That's right, *Capitan*. In U.S. You damned Marines got money like that? Cash money?" Clearly the Portuguese doubted it.

Port turned around to where his majordomo waited. Port tugged out a checkbook and his Waterman pen.

"Leung, take this check and go downtown to Baring's Bank. Bring back the cash. Top, in the absence of lawyers and such, can you write up a one-sentence bill of sale, dated properly and witnessed, that Captain Henriques can sign when he's paid."

"Yessir." Rafter had served under Port almost three years but buying a steamship was a first.

While they waited for the exchequer to be replenished, a Shanghai cab skidded to a dramatic halt on the pier and Monsieur Laurent, followed by two honeys with a champagne bucket and glasses, got out. You couldn't say Shanghai was dull.

"Ahoy, Captain Port. It is I, your driver, Laurent."

"Skipper?" the top sergeant asked, not in on the joke.

Laurent was togged out in whipcord jodhpurs, polished boots, a white silk scarf, belted leather aviator's coat, and flying helmet, the von Stroheim effect out of Cecil B. DeMille. All it lacked was the megaphone and his name stenciled on the director's chair. The girls poured the champers for the three of them, while a lackey humped the luggage.

"Captain," Laurent called up again, not having yet been welcomed. The two girls didn't seem to know whether to smile or burst into tears. Apparently they were waiting the Frenchman's cue.

"Yes, Monsieur?" Billy responded at last, his face stone.

Enter Jurkovich, the master mechanic from Detroit. He was on the dock overseeing the winching aboard of the trucks.

"Top," he called. "I'm short one driver. They tell me he's shacked up somewhere. You want me to go down to Nagasaki Joe's, see if I can find him?"

Rafter looked to Port. Billy didn't know quite why, but this Jurkovich was pulling a fast one.

Port shook his head and Rafter shouted down, "No, keep working the winches on them trucks."

Billy'd already decided to take the Frenchman. A good driver/mechanic came in handy when you were moving fast. Clearly, this last-minute defection of a "shacked-up driver" was a phony cobbled up by Jurkovich and the Frenchman. But just why? Had Monsieur bribed his motor transport expert?

Jurkovich, not the most subtle of men, quickly supplied the answer.

"Top, I happen to know this French fellow's reputation, Monsieur Laurent. It would be an honor to have him drive for us. I swear to God, anyone in the automobile business can vouch for the man's abilities. Why, at Le Mans one year he . . ."

So that was it. Hero worship. The grease monkey and the glamorous race car driver. On the quay, Monsieur sensed the balance was swinging his way, and again called up to Port.

"Did I ever tell you about the first Bentley I drove in competition, Captain? It was in Monaco in '34. The Auto Union car and the Ferraris were running one-two, when I, in my so beautiful Bentley . . ."

"Come aboard, Monsieur," Port shouted down, "We sail on the tide. And *without* the ladies . . ."

"But of course," Laurent called back.

When Leung returned to count out the money, and Henriques had stuffed it into various pockets, Billy Port shoved the first sergeant's bill of sale at him and held out the Waterman.

"Right there, Captain. Just sign."

Then Port snapped off an order.

"Which one of you is first mate?"

The Malay stepped forward. "Me, Tuan. First mate since the other fellow drowned. Almost one year. Was second mate four years before that."

"Have you got a master's card?"

"No, sir. Have taken preliminary examinations."

His name, he said, was something that sounded like "Bangalore Johnny."

"Okay, Bangalore Johnny. We'll give you a fair trial at the helm. Mr. Cantillon?"

"Yessir."

"Take the bridge. You and the mate are in charge as long as it works out. If it doesn't [this with an histrionic grin at the newly promoted mate], Buffalo can throw him overboard, too. Signal for a harbor pilot to come aboard, and keep me informed. Rafter!"

"Yessir."

"Finish loading cargo, Top. I want to sail on the tide."

"Hey," Henriques protested, sensing he was missing something, not knowing just who "Buffalo" might be and why he would throw anyone overboard. "You buy the ship, you buy the *capitan* also. Rules of the damned sea. I command here. I get you to Tsingtao. No problem, don't worry about nothing." He was still pretty excited to have all that money in his pockets. Billy briefly indulged him.

"Sure, pal," Port said, smiling. Then, his voice again a whiplash, he told Federales, "Sergeant, have your men unsling rifles and stand at the ready, locked and loaded."

"Aye aye, sir." Henriques and everyone could hear the bolts being slammed home on the Springfield rifles, on the Brownings, cartridges sliding into the chamber.

Then Port called the company runner, the big kid with muscles that everyone called "Buffalo."

"Skipper?" the youngster inquired, standing at attention.

"Don't injure him, Buffalo, but I want you to throw Captain Henriques the hell overboard. On the starboard side so he'll hit water and not the pierside. I assume he can swim. And might welcome a bath."

The Marines liked that one and laughed as if on cue. Buffalo, a literal sort, restricted himself to: "Aye, aye, sir."

Before Henriques could bluster profane protest, he was lifted high above Buffalo's head, rushed toward the starboard rail, and hurled into space.

Even the lascars applauded at the splash. Grins all around.

Port, who liked a happy ship but demanded an effective one, now got everyone's attention with an order to Rafter. "Top, this tub may look like a damned sorry merchantman, but as of right now it's pretty much the last man-of-war left of the American Asiatic Fleet on the China coast. So let's look smart and break out the machine guns."

"Aye, aye, sir."

Almost immediately, the big heavy machine gun materialized atop its cradle and tripod on the *Vestal Virgin*'s bow, and the two light guns on their pintles and lighter tripods were emplaced port and starboard amidships, two Marines manning each of the three guns, and already threading ammunition belts through the action and noisily (and impressively to the ship's motley crew) working the bolts to slide the first cartridges crisply into place.

"All guns locked and loaded, Skipper," Rafter sang out.

"Good, Top. And we might as well set up the 60mm mortar. Just in case."

The ship's crew had edged away as Port's Marines positioned the machine guns and then dashed off for additional metal ammo boxes. Now a mortar crew prepared for firing from between the cargo hatches, just forward of where Billy's Bentley rested, lashed down securely atop a hatch cover. None of this was going to intimidate a light cruiser but in the Marine Corps you were paid to be armed and alert, and Billy had his ways.

With all guns ready for firing, Rafter now called on Sergeant Federales to fall in the men.

"We'll have the flag now, Buffalo."

For all of Captain Port's disdain for marching, he was particular about some things. And when a detachment of Marines went to sea, they flew the American colors, by God.

"Call the company to attention," Port ordered as they stood on the aft deck, the civilian crew watching curiously.

With his men smartly fallen in, Federales barked out commands, and they presented arms, as big Buffalo ran aft to raise the flag. Port, Cantillon, and Rafter saluted, and the others, Yusopov and Leung and even the jaunty Monsieur, fallen silent, stood motionless. It was all something to see and it went off pretty well. Men like the deposed Henriques's crew who sailed the coastal waters from Macao to Tientsin and back had seen plenty of American Marines in their time, drinking and dancing with bar girls in waterfront bars, or during drunken fistfights in the streets.

Probably they also recalled the familiar, if not terribly respectful, North China waterfront ditty all the bar girls sang:

> *Goddamn, son of a bitch/*
> *United States Marine Corps/*
> *Every day/A holiday.*

This newly revealed martial snap, and warlike precision, of Port and his Marines were a surprise, and certainly impressed the crew of the *Vestal Virgin.* Several of whom, they later remarked as they whispered among themselves, had never before seen a sober Marine.

17

"I flunked navigation. At the Academy, they cut football players
a little slack."

THE run to Tsingtao was cake, a piece of cake.

Accompanied at first by that Japanese light cruiser with its menacing six-inch guns, later by two destroyers, the *Vestal Virgin* hugged the coast north from the East China Sea into the Yellow Sea, over the 280 miles that took forty hours to traverse.

Captain Port spent their one overnight at sea on deck, bundled in his overcoat and fur-lined leather gloves against the chill breeze, not up on the bridge with Cantillon and the mate where there was artificial light, but back on the darkened fantail where he could smoke his cigar and enjoy the stars and sliver of moon and phosphorescent wake, and even the quick rain squall that briefly masked the sky. Nor could the running lights of the Jap destroyers spoil the night. It was an ocean cruise without tourists and their Kodak Brownies. Though he could have done without the scurry of rats or the occasional large roach. He went below twice for a head call, again for black coffee. But he returned each time to the deck, to the oceangoing night.

Billy liked the sea, liked the look and smell and feel of boats and ships under way. He might have made a pretty good naval officer if it were all sea duty punctuated by riotous leaves, and none of that buttoned-up, stuffed-shirt naval base white-gloved rigamarole of calling on the admiral and leaving your card, of making conversation at cocktail parties, always aware that the woman you were chatting with might be your commanding officer's wife.

Not that he didn't like cocktail parties.

That got him thinking about home, and about Natasha, this first night at sea out of Shanghai. China cast its spell; so did women. Old China hands sometimes called Shanghai "Sugartown." It was all so sweet.

It had been sweet for Billy and now it was finished.

Right now, with Christmas coming and maybe the first snow falling on Boston, he permitted himself a fantasy: a cocktail party at the Ritz with Natasha, getting out of a cab at the hotel in the cold Massachu-

setts night, and going inside to the warmth and the Christmas lights
of the lobby and the hubbub of greetings and friends calling out and
people kissing and grabbing you by the arm and calling you "Billy,
boy!" and saying, "By God! It's good to see you again!" and all this
in distinctive Bostonian nasal accents so you knew you were home.
And when you introduced your girl around, women wondered, "But
who is she? *Where* did Billy find her?" and men dug an elbow and
growled, "The lucky dog." And Billy hugged all their secrets to himself. After he checked their coats (hers would be sable, he thought,
very "à la russe") they would go into the cocktail lounge off the lobby
on the right and to his favorite waiter, sometimes it was George, sometimes it was Nick, who would greet them and bow slightly and then
bring them the two best dry martinis with olives that either Billy or
Natasha had ever had, and they would touch their tinkling rims just
slightly, and toast each other. But only with their eyes and the glasses
and without words. Who needed words?

On the run north to Tsingtao these were among the things that,
along with the coming war, were on Captain Port's mind.

They snugged up to their berth in fine, chill weather on the morning
of December 3. The disreputable *Vestal Virgin,* well rid of Captain
Henriques, sailed purposefully if without much style, and the combined efforts of the mate and Lieutenant Cantillon turned out to be
more than adequate. When Port issued a brief compliment at daybreak
about their navigation, Cantillon was emboldened to remark that Captain Port, a Naval Academy graduate, could easily have handled the
chore himself without help from a lieutenant junior grade or Bangalore Johnny.

At which Billy permitted himself a self-deprecating grunt.

"At the Academy, Mr. Cantillon, I flunked navigation."

The young naval officer was so startled, he forgot his manners to
blurt out: "But wasn't that a requirement for graduation, sir?"

"It was and is, Mister. Unless you were on the football team. They
cut a varsity football player a little slack. I always meant to bone up
later on navigation and the sextant, but ended up in the infantry and
said the deuce with it."

The Yale man in Cantillon decided no further comment from him
was required. Or even wise. While Bangalore Johnny, who understood

nothing of these arcane references to "the Academy" and to "football," but recognizing praise when he heard it, continued to preen. Henriques had been sparing with the compliments.

There were no complications clearing into the harbor at Tsingtao once the local harbor pilot had come aboard. Rumors of war had certainly cut into maritime commerce up here. Plenty of Japanese shipping, of course, both warships (mainly a half flotilla of gray destroyers) and freighters and a few tankers riding high in the water, empty. A couple of foreign tubs, at anchor, their skippers or owners waiting to see if a new war broke out before risking their vessels (and their own hides) on the high seas. The empty tankers, on the other hand, indicated maybe the Japs really were feeling the pinch and running short on oil, as their diplomatic bleats against the U.S.-initiated boycott claimed. A Japanese soldier on the pier waved at them, rifle slung.

Port had been to Tsingtao a couple of times and Rafter knew the town well, having been stationed here. For a provincial Chinese city, curiously, it was a very "German" place. Much of the architecture was heavy, dark, Teutonic. A few street signs were in German, remnants of the days when a German infantry regiment was garrisoned here. And you could smell the malt and hops of the big brewery where they manufactured a very good pale, light pilsner lager. The smell delighted Port, who for all his love of serious wine enjoyed a cold beer.

"Let's put on a little entertainment, Top, driving through the town. Show the flag, take the Bentley."

Rafter was accustomed to the occasional Billy Port flamboyance. Monsieur had, on orders, already affixed a good-sized American flag to the aerial and as soon as the stevedores had rigged an oversized gangway, he tooled the big car neatly down onto the pier where Chinese longshoremen goggled. Port squeezed into the back with Rafter and Leung, along to translate, while Buffalo, toting a Thompson gun, rode shotgun upfront.

"Monsieur, just follow Sergeant Rafter's directions and no speeding. We don't want to get a ticket."

Laurent caressed the polished hardwood steering wheel with a pleasure approaching the sexual, and pulled away from quayside, very slowly, the powerful engine growling in the lowest gear. He'd fled Europe in mid-1940, and hadn't driven a car like this since.

Port, enjoying himself, puffing at a good Havana, grinned.

"Drive on, Monsieur. *Allons-y.*"

Cantillon, left in charge but urged to consult with Federales when in doubt, saluted as they drove off. But then, so too did bored-looking Japanese sentries in their mustard-colored uniforms, who guarded the entry to the dock area from the seafront esplanade. Port returned the salute, and snappily.

Good for you, sir, the top sergeant thought, proud of Captain Port's crisply returned highball, all too familiar with his casual salutes.

The town—its factories, warehouses, and residences—looked weekday-morning normal. A little truck traffic, buses, private cars, most of them jalopies, mobs of Chinese men on bicycles going to work, women walking or waiting for the bus. Here and there passed a Japanese army truck and small detachments of marching Japanese, rifles slung but bayonets attached. Maybe they changed the watch at eight A.M. and these were simply the routine reliefs. No war nerves here, not that Billy could see.

"Turn here, Monsieur, on the right," Rafter called out. Laurent smoothly shifted gears, enjoying the car.

A few more turns and then Rafter said, "Here we are, sir. This is where the Marines bunk when they're in town." It was a small house with a gatehouse and a courtesy garden, a paved driveway, and a tall, white-painted flagpole, bare of flags.

As Rafter said, "No flag, no Marines, sir. They're supposed to run up the colors when in residence." A small plaque on the outer wall of the gatehouse proclaimed UNITED STATES OF AMERICA. And a date, too eroded to be legible.

What was clear, the lone Japanese soldier standing on the sidewalk to the left of the driveway. When Port got out, the man hesitated, but seeing the big car and the tall officer, pulled himself to attention and saluted.

"Good morning," Port said in English, returning the salute and striding past and up to the main house. Rafter had a key, thanks to HQ back at Shanghai, but when they let themselves in there was nothing, the house stuffy, as if it needed airing out. On a battered old table in the main ground-floor room was a ledger book used, apparently, as a log. The last entry, November 12, 13, 14. It was signed by a corporal. Rafter and Buffalo looked into all the rooms. No vandalism, nothing.

"Okay," said Port, "let's get out of here." At the American consulate they learned nothing. Almost everyone who wanted to get away had already left. The three diplomats who remained were sweating out what they thought were the last days of peace before they were closed down by the Japs and, one hoped, repatriated. An assistant consul got them coffee, served by a Chinese boy, and passed along the latest gossip from State back in Washington. All about which of the Dutch East Indies the Japs would grab first.

"The Brits and the Dutch pulled out last week. Small consulates, both. Not important enough to keep open."

Port didn't need small talk. He wanted to send a working party to the German brewery, take a few cases aboard, and get out of here. Cantillon had orders to take on fresh water, some fruit, milk, fresh bread, and the like. Unless the Japanese decided to be difficult, they might even clear tonight, round Weihai Point tomorrow morning, and make a hard a-port out of the Yellow Sea and into Bo Hai Gulf, straight on for Tientsin. That would bring them into the big port city with its Marine detachment on Friday, December 5.

After borrowing a phone to call Shanghai, but being unable to get through to the Park Hotel or Natasha, he thanked the consul for his coffee, and told Rafter, "No profit here, Top, let's move."

The beer was quickly aboard, the Japanese made no fuss, and at dusk they dropped the pilot outside the breakwater and set a course to the northeast. The weather held, another clear night. In a rust bucket like the *Virgin,* you didn't want heavy weather. Astern, in the gloom, they could just see a Japanese destroyer come out of its mooring and steam slowly after them, its course like theirs, set for the northeast. A flat sea and a starry night and except for the destroyer astern, it was hard to imagine there was a war on. But as swiftly as that destroyer reacted to their departure, it was becoming even more obvious he and his Marines, if they got away at all, weren't going to do it by sea.

On the bridge, watching Cantillon and Bangalore Johnny work, Rafter suddenly thought of something and called out, "Sparks, get Sparks up here on the bridge!"

When the radioman appeared, very calm and smiling (the moon was nowhere near full), Captain Port snapped, "Give me a traffic report, Sparks. What do you hear? Any hard news in English?"

"Aye aye, sir. Not much in English, something on battles in Russia and about peace talks in Washington. Plenty of Chink. Lots of Jap traffic, of course. But I don't understand a word of it. I . . ."

"That's what I'm interested in. Is it more Jap traffic now than say this morning or yesterday?"

"Yessir, I believe it's gone up considerable. Lot more than yesterday. They're jabbering away at a great rate the last twelve hours especially."

"Thanks, Sparks. Keep me up-to-date on any change in the level of Japanese radio activity, understood? Or anything you get in English that sounds interesting."

"Yessir, understood."

They steamed northeast through the night deeper into the Yellow Sea leaving only a luminous wake and their Imperial Navy escort.

18

President Roosevelt's personal appeal for peace is handed in to Hirohito.

SPARKS and his radio were taking on an importance Port hadn't anticipated. Not simply about the volume of Japanese radio traffic being meaningful, but keeping the tiny task force informed.

"Without you, Sparks, we're the blind leading the blind. Bad enough we're cut off from the regiment. Thanks to your radio, at least we know who's winning the ball game, who's losing, and who's been rained out."

At the captain's direction, Sparks scribbled a sort of daily summary of war news, not just the Far East and the Japs, but what was happening in Europe and North Africa. The men, it turned out, enjoyed the nightly reading of Sparks's report. Billy thought of doing the reading himself, or having Rafter do it, but in the end settled the assignment on Cantillon, when Sparks protested he was too bashful to read aloud.

Port tried to jolly the radioman along. "You might turn into a regular H. V. Kaltenborn, Sparks. Wouldn't be surprised after the war if you got a big job at one of the networks there in New York, rolling up to Rockefeller Center in your limo and reading the evening news at six. You and Gabriel Heatter taking turns at the mike."

"Yessir," said Sparks, grinning, "but I got me a hell of a time spelling them foreign names. And pronouncing them's worse."

"You're doing fine, Sparks. Just fine."

And while they thirsted for accurate intelligence about Japanese intentions, there was sort of a rooting interest about the rest of the war. Cantillon got considerable feeling into such items:

"British observers in Borneo report Japanese naval forces heading toward Malaysia and the Dutch East Indies. German Field Marshal von Rundstedt relieved of command for retreating from Rostov. (Billy wondered if that had been General Rostov's hometown.) A British Whitley bomber sank a U-boat in the Bay of Biscay."

"Where the hell's that, Lieutenant?" a Marine asked.

"Between France and Spain." Cantillon knew his geography; they were big on geography at Yale.

"They never send Marines places like that, do they?"

"I don't believe so."

It was a shame none of them spoke Japanese. There was plenty of that on the air and more every day.

Though there would have been nothing on Japanese radio about Emperor Hirohito's formal but privately held assent from the throne, on that very day, to his government's decision that Japan should go to war with America, Britain, and the Netherlands.

The radio traffic was mainly operational, though neither Port nor his radioman knew that, but could only surmise.

They got more substance out of English language shortwave intercepts, BBC mostly. Such as these nuggets December 4, a Thursday, and Friday the fifth:

Polish general Sikorski, head of Poland's government in exile in London, flies to Moscow to meet with Stalin, asking assurances that postwar Poland will govern itself without outside interference. Stalin cheerfully agrees and the two men sign a friendship pact.

Hitler permits his weakened forces in front of Moscow to go over to the defensive.

The Russians, in no mood to cooperate, immediately launch an offensive over five hundred miles of front, headed by General Zhukov.

President Roosevelt's personal appeal for peace to Hirohito is handed in at the palace by Ambassador Joe Grew. (There will be no reply, neither from the Emperor or the Tojo government.)

And then, almost miraculously, PFC Jones strolled onstage, and it was like breaking codes; suddenly they could listen in on the Japs.

Rafter hustled him up to the captain. "Sir, this is one of Federales's squad, name of Jones. Says he speaks Japanese a little. Understands it better. Put in two years at our consulate in Yokohama on guard duty. Had a Jap girlfriend. She taught him."

"That's fine, Jones. Why didn't you speak up sooner?"

"Didn't want to cause trouble, sir."

"Quite right, Jones," said Port, recognizing "a good thirty-year man" when he met one. Fellow like that doesn't get very far in the Corps. Then, neither does he cause difficulty. Jones had been in eight years and was still only a private first class. Rafter just shook his head.

"All right, you, Jones. Report to Sparks. He'll tell you what's wanted. On the double, you!"

"Aye aye, First Sergeant."

19

This freight's making all stops to Peking and the Forbidden City.

THE mood in Tientsin was different, really different. The Japs here were surly, throwing their weight around. Did even ordinary soldiers sense that regarding the Americans things were about to change?

"I don't think we'll take the Bentley," Captain Port decided. "Doesn't seem the time nor the place."

"Nossir," said Rafter, looking out at the heavy Japanese troop presence on the docks and along the Tientsin breakwater, the usual riflemen bolstered by sandbagged machine-gun nests at either end of the quay. No sentry here waved to them as the soldier at Tsingtao had done. To Rafter it looked as if they might have to fight their way off the ship and onto the beach.

Instead of Port's car, they winched up one of the trucks, and loaded a half-dozen Marines and one of the light machine guns for the drive to the Marine barracks. There was no trouble getting through the streets. But there were sure plenty of Japs, turning to follow the Marine truck with cold eyes. Plenty of Chinese civilians, too, but they seemed more intent on looking the other way and scurrying off without giving offense. To either side.

"Something's up, Top."

"Looks like it, Skipper."

The Marine guards at the barracks gate wore overcoats and fur hats against the morning cold, with cartridge belts, canvas gas mask bags slung, and toted Springfield .03s. No helmets yet, no tin hats, but those were the first gas masks they'd seen.

Port and Rafter left Buffalo and the half squad with the truck in the barracks courtyard and were taken in to the executive officer, Captain Jack White. Rafter excused himself and went off to visit the first sergeant and talk privately, top soldier to top soldier, maybe finding out things an officer couldn't. White poured the coffee, strong and black.

"Major Brown knows why you're here, Billy. But we're staying put. The major thinks our best shot is waiting for the *President Harrison* to get back from Manila and pick us up. We and the Peking garrison will make Chinwangtao overland."

There were thirty Marines at Tientsin and Port had expected this. He thought the major was dead wrong but it wasn't Port's call.

"Okay, Jack. The major want to see me at all?"

"He's pretty busy."

"Okay," Port didn't feel snubbed or anything. He didn't know Luther Brown and in a way was relieved not to have an officer who outranked him joining their little detachment. And he had plenty to do on his own.

"What's next for you, Billy?" White asked.

"Overland to Peking. By rail if I can get our trucks loaded. It's eighty miles and if we get snow the roads could be dicey. Are the trains running?"

"Depends on the day. And whom you pay off."

Port liked the sound of that. If it were simply a matter of money, he could do business.

"And after Peking?" Captain White asked.

"Playing it by ear. Couple of small, isolated detachments up north other side of the Great Wall. I'm supposed to pick them up along the way and get us out somehow. I'll pay my respects to Colonel Ashurst at the embassy barracks but I expect he and Major Brown are on the same page. Counting on the ship."

White nodded. "We're all counting on the *Harrison*. They say she'll dock in China December tenth at the latest. I sure hope so."

He looked gloomy at the prospect of waiting five more days and so Billy said, "Sure, Jack. Manila for Christmas, that's not all bad."

"Let's hope so, Billy. Hate to end up serving time in a Jap camp."

Rafter had gotten pretty much the same story from his sergeant pal. "He's jumpy. Worried the *Harrison* might be late. Or not get here at all."

"Well, that's their problem. We've got to rent a railroad train. Let's pick up Leung and the old exchequer and that PFC who speaks Japanese and get down to the rail yards."

"What do we do with the *Vestal Virgin*, Skipper?"

"I dunno, sell it back to them maybe."

They were about to get back into their truck when a plump, puffing gentleman in an overcoat and gray fedora trotted up.

"I'm the U.S. Consul, Captain. Name of Van Meter. Have you got a moment?"

"Nossir, I don't. We're trying to find a train to Peking. What is it?"

Van Meter, a diplomat, didn't take offense, but smiled his gratitude for small favors. After all, this was a Marine he was dealing with, not a fellow dip.

The Brits, he explained, had pulled out of Tientsin as well as Tsing-tao and the American was handling their consular affairs as best he could.

"We have a priest here who's very anxious to get out of China, Captain. A British Jesuit, Reverend Father Tertius Kean. Third son of a prominent Anglo-Catholic family which apparently spoke Latin over the dinner table. For a Catholic, he's got some fairly exalted Whitehall connections, I take it. Any possibility you might see your way clear to giving him a lift?"

"This could turn into a combat command any hour, Consul. Don't want any more civilians along for the ride."

"Well, it's a bit different for a man of the cloth, isn't it?"

Billy gave that idea short shrift.

"Nor do we need a chaplain."

"Shame. Father Kean's a considerable fellow. He served at Farm Street Church, London, baptized the writer Evelyn Waugh when he converted. He's a crony of Osbert Sitwell's and the darling of the Mitford girls, as well as an at-large curator of the British Museum, where they keep the Elgin Marbles, a world-famed paleontologist who..."

Van Meter was slightly intimidated by the Marine captain's wolf smile, but he'd promised Father Kean.

Port didn't want to be rude but was on the verge of looking at his watch.

The consul, giving it one final shot, plowed on.

"...made some extraordinarily notable finds in Mongolia. No better man in the field on dinosaur fossils. Speaks the local dialects. He..."

Dinosaurs? Mongolia? That triggered memory. Was it in a *National Geographic* story...?

"Mongolia? Isn't there some sort of dinosaur graveyard up there?"

"I believe so. The Gobi Desert. Father Kean could give you chapter and verse, I suppose. He's the expert, not I."

"You say he knows the Gobi?" Port asked, wanting to be sure.

"Did a lot of digs there, I take it."

"Is he fit?"

"Takes a sherry, but, yes, I'd say so . . ."

"When can I meet Father Kane, Consul? I've no time to waste."

"Kean, it's Kean. Father Tertius Kean, Society of Jesus, 'Tertius' being Latin for 'third.' "

"Yes, yes, and he knows the Mitford girls." This, impatiently.

"Curiously," the consul said, ignoring the sarcasm, "he happens to be in my office. Just across the square. Came by once again to see if I could plead his case. Matter of urgency, it seems . . ."

An Englishman who knew the Gobi? Where Port was supposed to track down some wayward Marines. And one route Billy Port might take in eluding the Japanese and getting out. Well, well . . .

Father Kean was sitting in the consul's office reading a week-old *Manchester Guardian*.

"Hello there, Father," said Billy, more enthusiastic than he customarily was with the clergy, and drawing a mystified look from Sergeant Rafter who didn't like Holy Joes. "And how are you this fine December morning?"

"Quite well, sir. Good of you to ask."

Kean was a tall, angular party in a bowler and a rather nifty black Chesterfield coat. Port guessed he was sixty.

"Nossir, sixty-eight next spring." The priest seemed enormously pleased to be taken for a younger man. Just then a large cockroach scurried across the floor and Father Kean was instantly on his feet, newspaper swiftly rolled, and with a crisp smash, the insect was dispatched.

"Can't let those fellows get away with their impudence, Captain. You know how they multiply. Worse than the Irish."

"Mmmm," Billy said, thinking fast. He liked the priest's agility. And looked him over more carefully, noting the extremely long arms, almost simian, and the smallish, cropped head, hawk nose, and big ears. And the eyes, lively, very keen. Except for the eyes, not really Port's idea of a "darling of Mayfair."

"Tell me, Father, what's the Gobi like in December? Can it be crossed by truck?"

"Oh, dear me, sir. If you're short of camels and can stay on the flat, of course. A gravelly sort of surface, quite drivable. I shan't recommend the hills. Despite the aridity, frequent blizzards and the grades are fierce. Steep gorges, rickety bridges over long-dried streambeds. Consul Van Meter, have you by any chance a decent map?"

When the map was spread on a table, Father Kean's long, elegant forefinger quickly limned out various routes across the desert, commenting knowledgeably as he went along. Unless the man was a charlatan, he certainly seemed to know his ground.

". . . it was at Flaming Cliffs, where Roy Chapman Andrews of your American Museum of Natural History in New York found those fossilized dinosaur eggs, a gorgeous place. Despite, as Mr. Andrews famously remarked, '. . . the brigands swarming like locusts, even up the walls of the cities . . .'"

Billy bounced to his feet.

"Consul, you've gotten your Father Kean a ride. Father, can you be ready to leave for Peking within the hour?"

Father Kean uncoiled his lanky body and grabbed Port's hand, the long fingers powerful.

"Packed and ready, Captain, and traveling light," he said, lashing out with one foot to kick an ancient carpetbag half concealed by the consul's desk. "You shan't regret this, sir. If it's Mongolia, Inner or Outer, and the Gobi, I'll help get you across, and point out tourist attractions along the way. God bless us all . . ."

The rail yards played about as well as the Marines could have hoped. There was actually a scheduled freight leaving at ten that night for Peking. For an exorbitant fee, they were willing to add a couple of flatcars to carry the four trucks and fuel trailers, plus the Bentley. And one empty freight car stinking of cattle manure (the straw could have used changing) in which the men could shelter during the cold hours of darkness. Billy called up Leung to haggle a bit, but in all candor he would cheerfully have paid twice the asking price.

"Let's have the old exchequer, Leung," he growled, miming resentment. The Japanese kept their distance. Chinese railway employees ran the system and the Japs provided security and that was it. You bribed the Chinese, you were polite to the Japs, punctiliously so. That was how it worked. The other way 'round, the Japanese would arrest you for bribery; the Chinese curse you as a foreign devil, and cheap besides.

Back at the harbor, the Japanese continued to look surly but made no objections, and the trucks came off smoothly. So, too, the Bentley.

"We'll take it as far as Peking, Monsieur," he told Laurent. "Beyond that, I can't promise."

Bangalore Johnny was called up. Rafter had composed yet another legal document, assigning the ship pro tem to "Captain" Bangalore Johnny, but stipulating William Hamilton Thomas Port of Pinckney Street, Boston, USA, as its lawful owner. The Malay mate was delighted at his promotion but seemed genuinely sorry to lose Cantillon, who made it a point to shake the hand of every crewman on deck.

"A most fine gentleman, sir. Excellent also at navigation and the art of the sextant."

"Yes, well," Cantillon muttered.

"I thought he was going to kiss you, Mister," Port said.

"Yessir, as did I," the naval officer said, composing his face.

"All right, you people," Rafter shouted, "let's get these here trucks off the dock and rolling. That freight train's making all stops to Peking and the Forbidden City and points west, and we better be onboard when she pulls out."

The ten P.M. freight to Peking got under way in a snow squall about one the next morning.

It was December 6, 1941.

20

There's an epidemic up there in the villages. Killing children.

LIKE Tsingtao with its German brewery and Shanghai with its cultural mix, Peking (also known, depending on the weather, as Peiping) was a big Chinese city with its own particular stench, especially in the heat of summer. French diplomats stationed there had a phrase for it (but don't the French always?). They called the capital "Pekin-les-Odeurs," "Peking of the Smells." It was the morning of December 6 and hardly summer when Billy Port's command on its freight train pulled into the gaunt rail yards east of town, and you could smell Peking already.

"Whoo-*whee!*" Billy heard one of his riflemen exclaim from the next flatcar. "Lemme back in that there cattle car. They ain't showered nor shaved lately in these precincts, if you ask me."

"No one asked you, hombre," Federales snapped, "and keep an eye out and your weapons at the ready."

"Yes, Sarn't."

Federales didn't cut them much slack, Port knew. That's why he had a good squad. And who knew what awaited them here in the occupied capital of China?

There was some bureaucratic nonsense at the yards with Chinese railroad men trying to get the flatcars unloaded and put back into useful service on another run and a Japanese noncom of a suspicious bent who wondered just why goddamned American Marine bastards were bringing weapons into Peking?

Leung, and a few dollars, squared the railroad men. While Port smiled winningly and waved Colonel Irabu's hastily scrawled document under the noncom's nose and after a brief scrutiny was given a more or less respectful salute. Yet, here again as in Tientsin, the mood was sulky, even more hard-edged.

Maybe they're just jumpy, he concluded. Maybe the 4th Marines marooned in North China weren't the only ones scared.

There was no way for Billy, or any of them, to know what U.S. Consul Richard Buttrick had just learned, that Japanese officials along the entire China coast had quietly cautioned their nationals to stay at home the weekend of December 7. Buttrick notified the Asia desk at the State Department in Washington by telegram but, receiving no reply, told no one else at the embassy or the Marine barracks on the reasonable grounds that he lacked instructions.

Once Billy got through the red tape it was a simple matter to get his little motorcade rolling out of the rail yards and into the busy streets of midmorning Peking.

At the Marine barracks, all seemed routine, no suggestion of bustle or hurry, only the usual sentry duty and a car or truck entering or leaving. The big compound was kept on its toes in normal times with sundown parades, band concerts, morning formation, and frequent inspections by Colonel W. W. Ashurst, a stickler and a traditionalist. Above the vast parade ground loomed the towering pagoda-like central building, which gave it the feel of a Hollywood movie back lot.

The night before, ignoring the stench of the rattling freight car, Port had briefed his people about the Marine barracks.

"Colonel Ashurst, who commands at Peking, is a fine officer but starchy. Goes by the rules. So, Top, I want you and Federales to fall out the troops in proper formation. Counting off, all present or accounted for, the works. Proper uniform of the day. And as for the civilians, Prince Yusopov, Monsieur, you too, Father Kean, and Leung, keep a low profile. The less explaining I have to do with Ashurst, the better. Once we're out of Peking and headed toward the Wall and Mongolia, we can all relax a bit. All we have to worry about up there is Japs, bandits, warlords, blizzards, and two Chinese armies at war with each other.

"Here in Peking we've got a bird colonel who goes by the book and loves reaming out innocent young company grade officers."

"Aye aye, sir," First Sergeant Rafter answered for all of them.

Everyone in Peking seemed nervous, Americans and Japs. Billy thought he'd better take the tension down a peg. It relaxed Marines to worry about the brass. And inspections. So he harangued them about proper formations and uniform of the day. Better they worry about the routine rather than about getting killed.

They stabled the detachment's Marines in the barracks and Consul General Buttrick took in their civilians. Rafter, as top sergeants do, bunked in with Peking's top soldier, First Sergeant Frank "Dutch"

Miller. Cantillon found a tame naval attaché who took him in. Port got a room at the BOQ where he washed up and shaved before presenting himself to the colonel. Ashurst waved a dismissive hand before his visitor could say a word.

"You can forget all that, Captain. The Embassy Guard will board ship at Chinwangtao when the *President Harrison* docks. You can go freelancing north and find those two detachments from Harbin. This command will get out by sea. I wish you luck."

It was obvious from Ashurst's smug tone that he believed Billy would need plenty of luck.

"Thank you, sir."

As Billy started to leave, the colonel motioned him to remain.

"Captain, your orders from Colonel Howard were to get out whatever unattached Fourth Marines you come across. There's no mention of civilians traveling with you."

Ashurst then fell into a disquieting silence. It was the question left unsaid that bothered Billy. Was he supposed to defend himself, deny all, or just what? In the end, he said nothing.

And it was Ashurst who blinked.

"Okay, Captain. You have your ways and I have mine. Which pass will you take through the Great Wall? Juyongguan's the closest, forty miles from where we sit."

"Yessir, but I've been hitting the maps and it's high. If we get snow, the trucks will have trouble in the mountains. I was thinking of heading farther west before crossing the Wall. Maybe closer to Mongolia. Our Harbin Marines are out there at Hohhot. Or should be. And it takes us away from Jap-held territory."

"You've never seen the Gobi, I take it," he said sourly. "But other than that, you make sense, Port. That route also brings you close to Datong and Jining. And since you've already collected a few strays along the way, I'd be much obliged if you could take along a few more. A Dr. Han and a small medical party. Health professionals on an errand of mercy..."

This wasn't at all the Colonel Ashurst Port knew. It was so unlike Ashurst, the colonel feeling the need to justify himself. "There's an epidemic up there in the district villages. Whooping cough. Sounds silly, a kid's disease, but the medics tell me it can run through every small child they have, from infants up to seven or eight, kill youngsters, damage their lungs, their throats, larynxes. There's a vaccine and by chance the big hospital here in Peking happens to have a supply. It's bandit country; not at all firmly under Imperial Army control. The Japs send out patrols and that's about it. Dr. Han and her team need an escort. Too dangerous to have a woman traveling alone. She..."

Port had now heard enough.

"Begging the colonel's pardon, but I can't take a woman where we're going. We may end up fighting our way out."

"You have a priest already. And some sort of Russian nobleman. One of the roles we play as embassy detachments is to assist the host country in time of natural disaster, flood, or plague. We won't fight their wars for them. But we sure as hell can provide humanitarian relief and transport Dr. Han up there to practice it. You're entitled to know as much about her as I do. She's married to a Nationalist general who's gone missing, dead or a prisoner of the Japs or jumped ship and joined Mao. All a bit vague. The doctor herself, part saint, part mad, and the finest physician in Peking. Maybe in North China. She's treated gravely ill or seriously injured Marines and they swear by her. You will escort Dr. Han north, Captain. That's an order."

"Aye aye, sir."

Colonel Ashurst smiled for the first time. "And we'll forget about your Chinese butler or valet or whatever the hell he is and the Frenchie driving your Rolls-Royce, eh?"

"Bentley, sir," Port said, knowing he shouldn't sass colonels. ("Chesty, forgive me," he breathed the pious prayer.) A woman, a damned woman. If he wanted a woman along he would have brought Natasha, who was no saint but then neither was she "mad."

Dr. Han indeed.

Consul Buttrick, a hospitable sort, hosted a small dinner at a very good downtown restaurant. Port, Cantillon, the prince, and Father Kean. Port thought it politic to leave Monsieur and Leung at home. Father Kean was very good, chatting on about the Great Wall in legend and lore. "In the third century B.C., a young woman named Meng Jiang walked halfway across China in search of her husband, a construction worker on the Wall, only to learn on her arrival that he had died years earlier of overwork, and been buried, while no one bothered to let the widow know. Meng wept such copious tears that a section of Wall was washed away and had to be completely rebuilt."

Billy drank sparingly. Buttrick, for the first time, mentioned the Japanese suggestion that its nationals stay home for the weekend.

"What d'you make of that?" Port asked, instinctively turning over his wineglass against a refill.

"Plenty of war rumors. Nothing new about those. But Roosevelt's letter to the emperor has been received. No reply yet."

"Will there be one?" Billy asked the diplomat.

Buttrick shrugged. "The only thing more impenetrable than the Chinese mind is the Japanese. It must be wonderful to be posted to an embassy in Rome, say, or Paris, where you take a cabinet under-secretary out to lunch, buy him cocktails or get him laid, saving your presence, Father. And he hands over the state secrets, in triplicate. The Orient, alas, keeps its mouth shut."

The phone exchanges were still working and Port took advantage of the BOQ's phones to call Shanghai. This time he got through and when the Park Hotel informed him Mlle. Natasha Rostov had checked out, he placed another call to Art Leavis at the American consulate, who, like almost everyone, was working late.

"Art, where is she?"

"Damned if I know how she did it, Billy, but your girlfriend got herself out of here somehow. I struck out, sorry to say, but Miss Rostov called me yesterday morning to thank me for trying, and to say au revoir. Said she'd found a ship bound for the Philippines and talked or bribed her way into a shared stateroom. Said to tell you she made some sort of suitable arrangement. Quite forceful young woman, isn't she?"

Yes, Billy agreed, wondering about that "shared stateroom," but inordinately pleased that she'd gotten away. "Quite forceful," that sounded like her, that sounded very much like Natasha. Or Meng Jiang whose tears washed away the Great Wall.

21

The hospital is canceling elective surgery, preparing for casualties.

HE didn't know how long he'd been asleep when Rafter was there, shaking him to wakefulness.

"Captain."

"Yes?"

"There's a Chinese woman to see you. A Dr. Han. Says it's important."

Billy wasn't thinking all that clearly yet. "Dr. Han?"

"I can tell her to get lost, Skipper."

"No, no. Let me get dressed."

There was a sort of lobby cum front parlor on the ground floor of the officers' quarters and Dr. Han stood there, very tall, a handsome face, short-haired, wearing well-cut pleated gray flannel slacks, a heavy gray pullover, and a short leather jacket such as aviators wore. On her feet, sheepskin-lined flight boots, and hung from a thong around her shoulders, big sheepskin mittens. At least she dressed sensibly for a truck ride in winter. If that's why she was here.

"I am Dr. Han, Captain. Are your men ready?"

"Ready for what?" Port was still groggy, not crisp. And compared to her, looking pretty cruddy.

"To leave Peking. The war, or the expansion of the war, is to begin within a matter of hours. I assume you don't want to be trapped here by the Japanese."

"The war's starting?" Billy was still fighting off sleep. "How do you know? Who told you?"

"My chief at the hospital is a Japanese. A fine doctor and a very good man. I believe him implicitly. He's been told to prepare the wards for casualties, to cancel elective surgery for the next few days. Send recovering patients home. No leaves or days off for staff. Need I go on?"

"But..."

"Yesterday we drew two hundred forty pints of whole blood, from two hundred troops of the Japanese garrison and forty civilians, Japanese who work at their embassy or in commercial or financial institutions in the city."

Billy wondered what the shelf life of whole blood might be. The woman went on: "And they need vaccine up at Datong and Jining. I can't afford to be delayed further. I'm aware the colonel proposed that I accompany you. There are children dying every day in those villages."

There was nothing emotional about this. The doctor was calm, soft-spoken, which made her even more impressive. He didn't hesitate.

"Well, we're leaving in the morning anyway." He shot a glance at his watch. Two A.M. He made his decision.

"Rafter!" The top was there, rocking back and forth, waiting.

"Yessir."

"Get Federales to roust out the men. We'll be rolling before dawn."

Then he turned to Dr. Han. "Get your people here. If the sentries won't let them into the compound, have them wait outside with their gear at the main gate. We'll pick them up in our trucks on the way out."

"Yes, Captain." She turned and was gone. No wasted effort with this one. Not very talky, either. But why did he believe her? Or was it that leaving a few hours early wouldn't cost him anything? While delay might mean captivity. Or his life.

Billy went back upstairs for a quick shower and shave and to get into proper uniform, including leggings, the tin hat, the two canteens of fresh water, and the cartridge belt, the holstered Smith & Wesson and leather holster. If we're going to war, Captain Port told himself, we're going to dress the part. Despite Sam Howard's strictures, there remained a touch of Annapolis in Billy.

He strode across the empty, darkened parade ground to the guard shack where he rapped loudly at the window and asked for the officer of the day. A middle-aged lieutenant appeared, skeptical and professionally smug.

"When you've been in Peking for a while, Captain, you'll realize these alarms are always going off. Someone has a friend who heard a rumor in a bar. A newspaperman needs a story for tomorrow's paper. It's how the Japs keep everyone rattled. Colonel Ashurst has very little tolerance for wild stories."

Okay, Port thought. He'd done the right thing. He'd told them as much as he knew.

The O.D. said he'd alert the main gate that Port's detachment would be departing early.

Then, having in effect written off the colonel, and to hell with him, Port did a one-eighty. "Lieutenant, call Colonel Ashurst. Tell him Captain Port's got to see him and right now. I'm on my way to his quarters."

The duty officer raised an eyebrow. But there was no mistaking Port's tone.

"Aye aye, sir."

Ashurst, as predicted, was not happy. He received Billy in his robe. "I told you you were free to go, Port. We're sailing on the *President Harrison,* on or before the tenth."

"Yessir, but today's already the seventh."

"I don't care if it's Christmas, Captain. This command is leaving China as an organized Marine unit, boarding ship as ordered. Now get the hell out of here and let me . . ."

"Colonel, I never met your Dr. Han before in my life. Not until two hours ago. Yet I'm going on her word that the Japs are about to start a war. She doesn't think you've got until December tenth. You know her. Would she lie about a thing like that? And why would the Japs be laying up two hundred forty pints of whole blood?"

"They're a prudent people, Captain. And civilians, even a fine doctor like Dr. Han, can be mistaken."

There was no budging him.

"Yessir," Billy said. "Sorry to have wakened you. We're leaving in an hour. Heading northwest. Thank you for your courtesies."

Ashurst just nodded. Then he said, "Godspeed, Captain. Find those Harbin Marines if you can."

"Aye aye, sir."

22

"Cruelty, too," said Zhang Yang, "has its place in a civilized society."

THE column that rolled out of Marine barracks, Peking, at four-twenty in the morning of December 7, 1941, looked different from the little convoy that arrived the day before by rail in the capital's train yards.

"I want the machine guns on their tripods, ammo belts threaded, rifles and BARs locked and loaded, and all canvas furled, Top."

Loaded weapons spoke for themselves. Furled canvas? You furled the canvas on trucks and drove them open to weather and the sky in a combat situation, to provide maximum visibility. If you expected a firefight, or strafing by air, you wanted to see what was coming, be able to fire back. The Bentley, too, would travel with its top down. The order of march would also change. Now that they were leaving the beaten track, the big cities and the railroad right-of-way, the column would be entering hostile country. At any hour, the Americans could be in a shooting war with the Japanese Army. After that came the warlords and the bandits. Port was now leading a combat patrol. Recon patrols went out looking for information; combat patrols went out looking for trouble.

Instead of the Bentley cruising out there jauntily ahead of the trucks, with Monsieur at the wheel, a boulevardier tipping his hat and signing autographs, one of the big six-by trucks took the point. Captain Port issued the instructions to Rafter.

"I want Federales out front as the point. He rides shotgun in that first truck with a good driver beside him. If Federales is our best scout, then he's better than you and better than me. Maybe he can smell trouble. And right behind his back in that first truck, set up a light machine guy with Federales's two best gunners. Drop the truck's windshield flat so it won't interfere with the gun's field of fire." Marine truck and car windshields could be lowered and bolted down, out of the way. The driver wore goggles and got scoured by grit and dust and damn near froze, but the gunnery was a lot more effective.

"Aye aye, Skipper."

"I'll ride shotgun in the second truck. Buffalo isn't the best driver I know but he'll do. And I like having him around with that Thompson gun. In my truck I want Sparks monitoring radio full-time and Whatshisname, the loverboy with the girlfriend in Yokohama . . . ?"

"PFC Jones, sir. The fella which don't want to make trouble."

"Yeah, he stays with Sparks to translate Jap.

"And you ride in the last truck, Top. You look for trouble from astern, check stragglers. And watch our ass."

Port checked his notes. There was more. "Leung stays with me to translate. Keep Prince Yusopov with you. He's been under fire. Issue him a weapon as soon as we're outside the Peking city limits. Mr. Cantillon? Let him ride shotgun, give him a taste of responsibility."

"He did okay helming the ship, sir," Rafter pointed out.

"Right, Top. Wisecrack withdrawn. Cantillon did fine with the *Virgin*."

"Yessir," Rafter agreed. He liked that about Port. You could call the captain on something, and if you were right, he'd back off and say so.

"And the Holy Father?"

"Tuck Father Kean in with Cantillon. They can have little chats. Discuss navigation. And Yale."

Billy rattled off and Rafter took down a few more truck assignments, very specific and in detail. Headed into combat, there was nothing more crucial than the approach march. You wanted the right people up front. "We can always changee-swappee later," Port said. Then:

"A two-minute piss call every hour, Top. Tell them do it by the side of the road. I know we've got women on board but to hell with chasing hedges to hide behind."

"Smoking lamp?"

"Lighted by day. Smoke 'em if they got 'em. At sundown, no more smoking. And we'll fly American flags from every aerial. When the shooting starts, we'll pull the flags and figure something else out. But for the moment, at peace with our Japanese brothers as we are, let 'em know who just rode into Dodge City. Don't be bashful. Swagger a little, okay?"

"We going to cross that Great Wall, Skipper?"

"Yes, Top. When it gets in our way. Then we'll cross the son of a bitch or knock it down. I don't yet know where."

When the column was formed up, Rafter fell out their Marines in formation on the parade ground and Captain Port ran through a quick inspection and took the salute.

"Might as well look like Marines," the top sergeant growled. Federales agreed. The men looked pretty good if he did say so.

"Right, Top."

Impressed, the Marines at the main gate, watching the motorcade form up with its odd mix of crew and passengers, stood to attention and snapped off salutes as the first truck rolled out into the street past Chien Men Tower toward the highway west. Above them along that side, so high it threw the street into shadow even at midday, was the Tatar Wall, along which bloody running battles had been fought between American Marines and Boxers during the Rebellion forty years before.

Billy Port snapped off a highball in response to the guards at the front gate, then, turning in his front seat, he called out to the radioman.

"Sparks, from now on, I want you listening twenty-four hours a day. And keep Jones there busy translating if it's Japanese."

"Yessir."

"Any news yet?"

"Not so far except them Russkis kicking shit out of Hitler at Moscow, sir."

"You might report that as 'the Russians are defeating the Germans,' Sparks."

"Yessir, like I said."

Leaving the city, there was a brief delay at a Japanese Army roadblock. But that was all it was, a brief delay. At the roadblock, machine guns were set up with a clear field of fire to sweep the road fore and aft, but no one was at the guns, only a few troops lazing about. If they were going to war, the news hadn't reached the outskirts of Peking. Port didn't even have to produce his phony pass from Colonel Irabu. In fact, once an NCO waved them ahead and the wooden crossbar rose, the three or four Japs saluted the Americans.

They might be the last Americans who would ever be saluted by serving Japanese troops. Rafter and Port, wanting to be every bit as proper as the adversary, saluted back.

Once they were through the city suburbs they began to see more and more Japanese anti-aircraft pits, machine-gun nests, and tented encampments. That was because they were getting closer to the front, such as it was, and farther away from the coast. The A.A. emplacements looked pretty useful. Chiang didn't have much air, few planes, and fewer good pilots, except for Claire Chennault's Flying Tigers, but for morale purposes and propaganda, the Chinese tried from time to time to bomb Peking, rarely damaging their enemies but cheerfully massacring big-city Chinese.

The country opened up now into farming acreage, trees bare of fruit, harvested fields, brown and dry except for some old snow in the shaded furrows, more lone farmhouses than villages now. Some of the farms were tidy, smoke rising from chimneys, the front step swept; others overgrown and slovenly, maybe abandoned. For all the arable ground, there were few farmers to be seen. But then, what could you plant in December, what might you harvest? Sometimes a kid or a woman waved. The men must all be in the army. Or dead. Occasionally, the villages they sped through were blackened and burned. There'd been some fighting north and west of Peking and someone had burned the villages to discourage people from aiding and abetting the enemy. Trouble was, from a villager's point of view, both Chiang and the Japs enjoyed burning a good village.

Japanese soldiers in the isolated posts gaped at the convoy with its bravely flying American flags. What were those bastards doing here? the soldiers asked each other. Where were they going?

The Marines, in a sporting mood, waved or called out, pleasantly, "Fuck you!" drawing a toothy smile and a wave back. Port wished he had some good Japanese curses but he didn't. And he didn't want to have to ask PFC Jones.

"Loverboy."

They were a couple of hours on the road when they saw the first eight men hanged. Six of them from one large tree with big lower branches, the other two from a telephone pole that didn't seem to be working, not with the wires dangling loose like that.

"Japs don't like it when you cut their wire," Rafter remarked.

"Don't blame them for that, do you, Top?"

"Nossir. An army don't need civilians cutting its damned wire."

No one took much note of the hanged men. Chinaside Marines, if they'd been here a year or two, had seen plenty of this. Dr. Han, well, maybe she'd seen as much of it as any of them. Only Cantillon, new to the game, stared, still seeing the dead, how they swayed in the soft breeze, how crows had eaten out their eyes and were working at other soft parts.

The convoy slowed but didn't stop and now it speeded up and Cantillon could no longer see the hanging men. The naval officer turned to Father Kean, hoping for a kindred spirit, perhaps.

"You mustn't become upset, Mr. Cantillon. There's a tradition of cruelty in this country, dating back to Qin Shi, their first true emperor, who ruled from 221 to 210 B.C. Wonderful fellow. Had the good sense to appoint intelligent advisers to key posts. One of them, Zhang Yang, who undertook important judicial reforms, also served his lordship by creating a system of appropriate punishments to dissuade lawbreakers. There's an excellent recent biography of the First Emperor by Luo Zewen translated by Dick Wilson. Grand stuff. Old Zhang didn't spare the rod nor spoil the child. He believed firmly in flogging, branding with irons, confiscation of wealth, deportation, beheading, quartering, live burials, cutting off the nose and feet, cooking in a cauldron. Much later, the Qing Dynasty adopted 'death by slicing,' cutting off first one limb, then the next, often after literally months of hideous torture. Compared to those days, hanging from a nice tree out in the country is devoutly to be prayed for."

"I guess," said Cantillon, not entirely convinced.

"Well, as old Zhang always said," Father Kean recalled cheerily, " 'Cruelty, too, has its place in a civilized society.' Interesting thesis, don't you think?"

Cantillon shook his head. "But who were those men? And who killed them?"

"Oh, they were Chinese," the Jesuit said, "little doubt of that. In this side the Japs win most of the battles and Chiang wins a few but whoever wins, it's mostly the Chinese who die.

"As for who did it, nobody may ever know. The Japanese because they caused trouble. The Nationalist Chinese because they collaborated with the Japs. The Communists because they were for Chiang. Or Chiang because they were Reds. Or some warlord because they didn't fall to their knees when his shadow passed."

Some thirty miles out as they came up over a low ridge and saw the first brown mountains rising, the higher crests already white, Buffalo called out, "There she is, Captain. There's the Great Wall of China!"

The kid was pretty excited, not having seen it before, except in pictures in magazines that his father had a subscription to. And Billy Port didn't blame him. It surely was something to see. He signaled Monsieur to pull over in the Bentley, and he climbed down from the truck cab and saluted Dr. Han.

"So far, so good?"

"Yes, Captain. Fine." She seemed very placid. Well, we'll see when the going gets a little tougher, Port thought.

"It's only another twenty miles or so to the Juyongguan Gate," he said, "but I'm giving it a pass. That's a popular gate with what I'd guess is a pretty substantial Japanese Army garrison. I don't want to have to fight my way through the Wall if I can slip through where it's more slimly held. We'll cross farther west. Do you know the passes west of here?"

"Reasonably well, some of them quite well, yes." And when he didn't say anything and she thought perhaps he doubted her, the Chinese woman rattled off the place names of gates yet to come: "Gate of the Mountain Temple, Gongzhen Pavilion, Temple of the Dragon King, Wanmen Pass, Temple of the Blue-tinted Clouds, Gate of the High Waters, Buildings of the Limpid Sea, Temple of Meng Jiang . . ."

"Okay, Doctor. You've convinced me."

"There is even, Captain, a Temple of the God of Medicine."

"Good, I may be asking for advice. Pick us a good one."

They all paused now, however, to stare at the mountains that held the not yet visible Juyongguan Gate in their grip, and along the crests of which the Great Wall wandered, snaking along, older than any of them, older than the Marine Corps, older than our whole damned country.

The day had dawned fine. The only clouds hung above the mountain range and the Great Wall to their north. There could be snow in those clouds and Billy didn't want to cross mountains in a snowstorm. Trucks could bog down and he didn't want that. Not with Marines out there waiting to be picked up and taken home. They started up again, drawing another five or six miles closer to the Wall before angling harder left. They could see the Wall in some detail now. The Juyongguan Gate, so-called, still masked by intermediate hills, was in actuality a very elaborate and quite substantial fortress itself, with inner and outer walls of its own, and pierced by small gates as the Great Wall was pierced on a much larger scale. There were passes or gates like this, some quite simple, others very complex, every twenty or thirty or fifty miles. But for almost every mile or two, tall stone beacon towers stood atop the Wall for its entire four-thousand-mile length. The idea was to pass signals from one beacon tower to the next by the simple act of lighting or extinguishing a fire. You could see the beacon towers easily, the highest points on the Wall. Juyongguan Gate would be coming up soon. Captain Port knew it from a touristy visit last year and from looking at pictures and schematic drawings in *Life* magazine. The same sort of artwork *Life* published of the Maginot Line, which turned out to be less impregnable than Joe Haynes's boss, Mr. Luce, had predicted, since the Germans didn't bother attacking it at all but simply went around it, and conquered France.

It was all very well for journalists, like Haynes or Harry Luce, to be mistaken in such matters. There was always tomorrow's edition or a fresh magazine coming next week. Men like Port, soldiers, paid a price for mistakes. They died.

23

*There are machine guns set up atop the Tatar Wall and
the Chien Men Tower.*

THE Marines camped by the side of the road, the trucks pulled off
into a copse of trees for concealment. No one was hunting them that
Port knew of, but why give people gifts? Get under the damned trees.
A few curious peasants wandered over to see the excitement but Leung
and Dr. Han spoke to them and they left, satisfied with whatever
they'd been told. Or maybe they'd been encouraged on their way by
seeing the three machine guns, set up and businesslike. Chinese peasants in this part of the country were accustomed to being shooed away
by soldiers of one army or the other and took no offense.

Rafter issued each Marine one bottle of German beer from Tsingtao
with the evening meal, eaten sitting on the ground around a couple
of campfires, the beer properly chilled from being in the open trucks.
"Save them empties," he ordered. "Up in the interior you can't never
tell when a few secondhand bottles come in handy to swap or use."
Billy thought of opening a bottle from his case of 1924 Château Latour
for Dr. Han, the prince, Father Kean, the Frenchman, and the rest of
what he'd begun thinking of, jokingly, as his "general staff," but
thought it was too early. Let the toasts wait until they had something
to celebrate, crossing the Wall, or getting into Mongolia, or catching
up with those long-lost Marines.

Twice during the night Sparks woke him.

"Damned radio's going crazy, Captain. Mostly Jap. Jones says he
don't understand all of it so they must be using code. But there's a
shitpot full of it."

"Anything important in English?"

"Nossir. Just the Russkis winning battles in the snow. And no answer yet from the Japanese emperor to Mr. Roosevelt's letter."

Billy was up before dawn, and had washed and shaved by flashlight
before six, prowling the little encampment, poking his head into
trucks, nudging a tired Sparks to wakefulness.

"Let's get cracking again."

"Yessir."

Jones was fast asleep, a beatific look on his simple, boyish face. Maybe he was dreaming of his girlfriend, the one in Yokohama.

Port stayed there until Sparks had the radio cooking. "Lot of Japanese?" the captain asked.

"Yessir, like last night."

"Okay, wake up sleeping beauty and get him on the job."

It was the morning of December 8, this side of the International Dateline, that is. In the States, including Hawaii, it was Sunday morning, December 7, 1941.

Rafter had coffee working so Port took a canteen cup, filled it halfway and made another circuit of their parking area, not wanting to sit still, unable to stay put.

A familiar feeling, not nerves as much as . . . what? Anticipation? Not a bad feeling at all. Almost a sense of relief, that, at last, things were going to start happening. Kind of how he told Joe Haynes last month after tennis, that if we were going to have another war, it was time for it. Halfway back to the truck he met Dr. Han. She too was walking off the night. Funny, he'd not thought of her as attractive. Tall, yes. Neat, placid, well spoken. But she was a damned handsome woman. Especially when she smiled, which she did now. A smile of apology.

"I'm afraid I may have been premature in my dire warnings," she said. "I hope I've not gotten you into trouble with Colonel Ashurst."

Billy laughed. "Doctor, when it comes to colonels, I'm usually in trouble. Story of my career."

As the convoy pulled out onto the provincial road, just before seven, the eastern sky was streaked with rose and lighter hues. Good day coming, Billy told himself. They could have gotten over the ridgeline at the Juyongguan Gate easily. No snow, no skidding trucks. Well, no sense regretting decisions made. Or unmade. Just give us a quiet day and another fifty or seventy-five miles and I'll settle for that.

He must have asked that final bit aloud.

"Sir?" asked Buffalo, his runner.

"Morning prayer, Buffalo. Nothing more."

"Yessir."

Buffalo was glad he was just a private first and not an officer. They were difficult to figure. Though he liked the captain.

Behind him in the truck, Port could hear the big radio crackling, hear Sparks and Jones tuning and turning knobs, discussing the short-wave traffic.

Then, urgently, Billy felt Sparks's hand on his shoulder.

"Captain, Captain. There's something now in English. I think it's the *Wake* sending."

The USS *Wake* was an American Navy communications relay ship anchored in Shanghai harbor.

"Give 'em your horn, Buffalo. Two honks."

Two blasts on the horn meant halt the convoy. Buffalo went deftly from the horn to the brake and the truck skidded on gravel to a stop. And the driver was out of the cab, his submachine gun ready, swinging it this way and that, in an instinctive perimeter defense mode.

Sparks repeated the message, reading off his scribbled notes: "Air raid on Pearl Harbor. This is no drill."

Billy was out of the cab too, and on the ground, crouched, ready for, well, whatever was coming next. The other trucks had also skidded to a halt. Men were jumping out of the truck beds, trotting up to where Billy Port stood.

"Captain! Skipper!"

"All right, Rafter, get 'em around. Everyone. We're all in this." Then, curtly, "Top, I want security out fore and aft. A hundred yards up and down the road, two men each. Now!"

Rafter nodded at two corporals and they moved off swiftly, with their weapons and men. The others settled down, circling Captain Port, listening as he spoke: "We have a radio report from Shanghai that Pearl Harbor has been attacked. And that this is no drill."

"Pearl what?" That was one man asking and Port ignored him. Chinaside Marines knew where and what Pearl Harbor was.

"Sparks, are you through yet to Marine barracks, Peking?"

"No, sir. Yessir! Now I've got 'em."

He handed the earphones to Port, who whipped off his tin hat and settled the radio-telephone hookup on his head.

Billy listened for a moment. Then he turned back to his men. "I got the top soldier, acting as Officer of the Day. Some of you know him, 'Dutch' Miller. Got an accent so I know it's Dutch. He says the Japs bombed Pearl Harbor. He says the Marine detachment at Peking has been put on the alert but confined to barracks. There are machine guns and mortars set up atop the Tatar Wall and the Chien Men Tower."

Both the Wall and the Tower loomed high over the Marine barracks and parade ground and the U.S. embassy. Billy could hear men's breath inhaled. They knew what this meant.

Port continued. "The machine guns and mortars 'ain't ours.' Repeat, 'ain't ours,' the first sergeant says."

"Any shootin' yet, Captain," a big BAR man shouted out, his tone not so much anxious as eager.

"Don't know."

Captain Port looked around. No one made a sound; they were waiting, all of them, just waiting. Okay, he told himself, give it to them straight.

And he did.

"I think we can assume the United States is now at war with the Empire of Japan. If those machine guns atop the Tatar Wall are Japanese, then the Fourth Marines are going to come under fire. And will be going into action.

"This is what we've all trained for. I don't know what'll happen back there at Peking. Or Tientsin. Or with the detachment at Chinwangtao. By now, I guess, it's too late for that ocean liner to get them to Manila. We know Colonel Ashurst and Major Brown will do the right thing.

"As for us, we're free agents, and we're going to join up with any other Fourth Marines we come across in the boondocks, and try to get out. Fight our way out if we have to.

"My attitude is, we're not trapped behind enemy lines, we're operating in their rear. We've turned the Jap flank.

"So I'm not going to worry about the Japanese Army. Let them start worrying about us. About the last Fourth Marines still loose on the Asian mainland, armed and dangerous and trying to get home . . ."

There was a low growl of approval from the Dog Company Marines, one or two shouts, "You got it, Skipper!" "Hell with them, Captain!"

As Port wound up, he was wondering if he might have said it better, or not at all, and whether he'd made sense. What would Chesty have said . . . ? Then Sparks called out.

"Captain, Colonel Ashurst confirms. War Plan 46 against Japan has been issued. Our country's at war."

Port tried to recall just what War Plan 46 *was*. He wasn't much for oratory; he'd made his speech. "Rafter, I want to see Federales and his corporals. At my truck, so we can monitor the radio while we go over the map."

As they gathered where the trucks were parked, even before they were all there and Port began to talk, there was a noise coming down the road from the northwest. An engine whine, high, almost a scream, not heavy as you get from a tank or big truck.

"Vehicle coming, sir."

Could the Japanese be onto them already? This quickly?

Another voice echoed the alert. "Motorcycle, Captain. With a side-car. Looks like Japs. Just the one bike."

Everyone had turned, weapons up and ready, eyes focused on the dusty, narrow provincial road. And here, by God, came a motorcycle with sidecar, coming fast, two men riding in their mustard-colored uniforms, accelerating now, coming even faster. They didn't seem to have any idea of peril, of Marines waiting. Just going someplace fast, flying a small flag from their radio aerial, a miniature Rising Sun. Port didn't hesitate. Just a couple of couriers, probably, but their radio aerial, that bothered him. With an aerial they could tell their buddies about Marines hiding just off the road.

"Federales, kill them."

"Aye aye, sir."

Their words still hung on the still winter air when a Browning automatic rifleman at Sergeant Federales's side fired off a short, violent burst. That's all you needed up this close with a BAR, a short burst.

The two Japanese soldiers were torn apart, dead before their skidding, tumbling bike stopped throwing up sparks and slid to a stop, twisted, smoking junk.

So it was on the day the Japanese attacked Pearl Harbor that Billy Port's Chinaside Marines went to war.

24

The first time a U.S. Marine command surrendered without a fight.

AND what of the other North China Marines on that same day? Colonel Dick Camp, USMC (Ret.), and retired Marine Captain George Howe remember:

The SS *President Harrison* was still at sea making for the port of Chinwangtao when she learned of the Pearl Harbor attack. The unarmed ship attempted to elude Japanese naval forces but was sighted and trapped off the China coast, where she was scuttled by her crew to keep her out of enemy hands. Marine hopes of escaping by sea were now ended.

At Peking at the barracks of the Embassy Guard, corporal of the guard T. G. Crews was told by a coolie speaking in pidgin, there were Japanese soldiers on the Tatar Wall, officially off-limits to anyone but Marines. Crews called out a couple of supernumeraries and told them to run off the Japs and report back. When they didn't return, he sent two more men. When they didn't come back, Crews rang the alarm. Outside the main gate the streets were curiously empty. And Crews had four missing men. Then his phone rang.

The officer of the day, First Sergeant Frank "Dutch" Miller, shouted that the Japs had bombed Pearl Harbor. He'd first called his commanding officer, Colonel Ashurst, with a message from the USS *Wake*. Ashurst told the top soldier to alert the men, but until the situation clarified to remain in barracks. As dawn broke, about eight o'clock, the Marines could see Japanese soldiers swarming all over the Tatar Wall and the Tower. And there were reports of "a hell of a lot of infantry" moving through the Peking streets toward them. When Consul General Buttrick, the senior American foreign service officer still in Peking, had a clerk phone the Marines to find out what was going on, the clerk said a flash had been received to implement War Plan 46 against the Japanese. All codes and confidential papers were to be burned.

By ten A.M. the diplomat had been told of notices posted in the city's streets warning all persons to stay away from the Legation Quarter and for residents west of Rue Meiji to evacuate, "if military action against the Marines" became necessary. In something of an embarrassing moment, Ashurst called Buttrick to admit he didn't know what the "flash" meant, since his plans were all "O" or "orange" coded. The war plans, it turned out, had been changed but no one had thought to provide a revised set to the commander of the Embassy Guard.

The two Americans talked for a time, agreeing that the Marines, with only 150 men and with no heavy weapons (they'd already been shipped to Chinwangtao to await the *President Harrison*), and completely surrounded by a much superior enemy force in the center of a crowded city, faced a suicidal position from a military stance.

After a second meeting, Buttrick phoned a Japanese diplomat who was a personal friend to ask that the Japanese consider the "special status" of Embassy Guards, and to afford the Marines all rights, privileges, and immunities, including diplomatic repatriation. The Japanese refused and at noon Colonel Ashurst drove to the Japanese HQ in a car with a white flag fluttering to surrender his command.

The Japanese were proper to the last, two sentries smartly executing a rifle salute as the American entered their building.

A "formal" surrender was set for one P.M. The Japanese refused to accept Ashurst's sword and the U.S. national ensign was handed back to him. But as Consul Buttrick noted, "He was heartbroken . . . a distinguished veteran of active service in the last war. This was a fearful blow to him."

At the big port of Tientsin, some eighty miles east, Captain Jack White, executive officer of the detachment, had his breakfast interrupted by a phone call from a Japanese officer speaking English. "The Imperial Japanese Army will take over the British Concession this morning by force. We do not wish any trouble with the United States Marines." White, a bit huffily, perhaps, said it was not the Marine mission to protect the British Concession. As soon as he hung up, a Marine dashed in with an urgent message from the Secretary of the Navy. "Execute WP 46 against Japan."

The Marines barely had time to feed their confidential radio codes and other papers into a coal furnace when the compound was surrounded by about a thousand Japanese troops with armored cars, while three aircraft circled overhead. A Major Omura drove up in a brownish sedan with Japanese flags and asked to see the C.O., Major Luther Brown.

Ushered into Brown's office, along with an interpreter and "the inevitable cameraman," Omura passed over a hastily handwritten note, "advising" the Marines to disarm voluntarily by one P.M. A written response was expected by noon. If this "advice" was not followed, "the Japanese Army shall be obliged to resort to arms and disarm you."

Though Omura and both Marines, Brown and Captain White, had all known each other for some time, the Japanese was blunt. Major Brown haggled a bit, saying he would surrender only if terms of the Boxer Protocol of 1900 were observed (calling for repatriation of the military forces of signatory nations). Omura called his boss, a general who said he would investigate the matter. The general was quoted as saying he was "personally guaranteeing the safety of the Marines."

Brown then dictated and signed a brief note of surrender, once again calling on the adversary to repatriate the Marines. After escorting his Japanese "visitors" back to their car, a distraught Luther Brown turned to Captain White. "Do you know this is the first time a United States Marine command has surrendered without a fight?"

At about one o'clock, thirty Japanese arrived to gather up the weapons of the little command, "seven pistols and thirty of their beloved .03 rifles."

In the Bo Hai Gulf port of Chinwangtao, about one hundred miles north of Tientsin, and the planned embarkation point for the Marines, the excitement began with a commotion in the squad bay. When the corporal of the guard looked in, he saw Marines gathered around a trans-oceanic radio on which an English-speaking announcer was saying Honolulu had been bombed. The senior NCO, Staff Sergeant Jack Bishop, was notified and took charge, ordering men to man their posts and retrieve heavy machine guns from the boxcars in which they awaited the *Harrison*.

Trouble was, the temperatures had been below freezing for days, and the cosmoline lubricant packing on the guns had hardened to the consistency of road tar. It took a PFC to come up with the solution, a hot shower. He burst into the room with a shiny gun in hand, shouting, "Hit the showers!"

The little (twenty-two Marines) detachment's C.O., Second Lieutenant Richard Huizenga, attempted to call Tientsin for instructions. By the time a radio connection had been made one hundred Japanese troops had surrounded the compound and Huizenga, accompanied by one rifleman, was haggling with four enemy officers through a civilian interpreter. When Gunner Bill Lee got the message from Tientsin, he sent out a runner to Huizenga. It ordered, "Do not repeat not resort to fire except in self-defense. Comply with demands of Japanese Army Forces." The senior Japanese, a major, rubbed it in by adding that anyone attempting to escape would be shot.

The Marines handed over their Springfield rifles, useless now, since every firing pin had been dumped into the compound's cesspool. Upon a command from Huizenga, the American flag was lowered, to a hand salute executed by the lieutenant's disarmed men. A Marine recalled, "As I watched 'Old Glory' descending in the chilled China air I faced conflicting emotions—anger at surrendering to a nation of 'toy makers' and some fear, for by reputation the Japanese tortured those they captured. It was simply unbelievable that this was happening to me."

At Peking, the Americans would endure a final humiliation.

Consul General Buttrick was handed the official letter by the second secretary of the Japanese embassy, which read in part: "The Imperial Japanese Government as from December 8, 1941, considers that the functions of your Embassy have ceased and that the Imperial Japanese Army will take measures to disarm the U.S. Embassy Guard and to stop the operations of the wireless telegraph and telephone apparatus located within your Embassy compound."

There was brief debate over just how the American flag should be lowered. Retreat was sounded, and the Marine detachment entered the quadrangle and fell in, NCOs checking their alignment, while what Colonel Camp describes as a "scruffy column of soldiers outfitted in mustard-colored uniforms [contrasted] sharply with the forest-green clothing of the men in formation."

Here in Peking, the Marines were still armed, and at a command, they slapped the wooden stocks of the old .03 rifles and executed the "Present arms!"

Now, as the main flag was readied to come down, the corporal field music, moistening his lips, raised his bugle and began to play the "Retreat" for a final time. "On the first note, the color guard slowly lowered the flag, keeping pace with the music, and as the last note sounded, the flag was gathered in and slowly folded. Standing alone, with tears streaming down his face, the field music stared at his instrument and then brought it crashing across his knee, destroying it."

25

Did the captain really mean that, that he could smell the enemy?

PORT's detachment knew little of this, of course. They had radio but with North China only a sideshow, the broadcast news was mostly of the damage at Pearl, the bombings at Clark Field, of reported invasions of Malaya and Luzon, of disasters afflicting our gallant Allies the Brits, of spunky Dutch subs sinking Jap ships all over the Indian Ocean, of a Yank named Colin Kelly whose B-17, with a single bomb, sank a Jap battleship off the Philippines. Not a mention of Peking or Tientsin. Or, God help us, Chinwangtao.

The little Marine convoy hadn't the time or leisure to weigh these injustices, but instead sped west by northwest in the shadow of the Great Wall, toward those empty spaces on the maps, the Mongol hinterlands in which Port hoped they might succeed in losing themselves.

They traveled now without flags and mostly by night or during foul weather, wary of Japanese air. And not just of Zeroes, the fighter planes that could chew up a convoy of trucks with their aerial cannon and machine guns. You didn't need heavy bombers to take out a truck and you didn't really need fighters. A single observation plane, the local equivalent of a Piper Cub, cruising at eighty miles per hour and sighting Port and his men, could provide map coordinates and distances and estimated speeds. So that at the very next crossroads at some nothing Chinese market town, a battalion of Japanese infantrymen, with a few tanks, could be there waiting. Port, with twenty men and three machine guns, wanted no part of tanks or infantry battalions.

The weather had begun to help, with cloud and flurries to screen the Americans. And they were enjoying a run of luck.

At Zhuolu just after a dawn fall of wet snow, coming unexpectedly on a two-truck Jap convoy of infantry, the Marines had their first actual firefight. The motorcycle couriers hadn't really counted.

You could credit Sergeant Federales with this one.

Federales had so far demonstrated enormous restraint in telling people about "Me and General Pershing." And now he and his point truck were out front, maybe a quarter mile ahead of the others, rolling at about twenty-five miles an hour, which for these rutted, mostly dirt roads was top speed, when Federales saw a truck, or was it two of them, splashing toward them through slush. His driver slowed, imperceptibly.

Japanese and American trucks at this stage of the war didn't look all that dissimilar at any distance. Sometimes, both sides were driving GM products. Or Fords. How could you tell them apart? Especially at dusk or dawn. Except that these approaching trucks showed Rising Sun flags and had their canvas up, not furled. Why shouldn't they? They owned this part of China, controlled the air.

Federales barked at the machine gunners crouched just behind him.

"Get ready, you peepul. I want you firing on my orders. Straight into that there truck. Short bursts. I don't want no barrels seizing up hot. After the first truck, you take the second if she's still coming."

"Aye aye, Sarn't."

Then, to the driver, "You give one blast on the horn, now!"

One blast meant "Enemy in sight." In their rear, presumably, Captain Port would hear the signal and take appropriate action.

Federales motioned the driver to resume top speed. They were closing fast, maybe two hundred yards from the lead Jap truck.

Which now, uneasy perhaps, was slowing to identify this truck hurtling toward them.

At a hundred yards, nearer to seventy-five, Federales shouted, "Okay, amigos, fire!"

The Jap truck's windshield exploded. Federales's driver thought it was already covered with crimson spray before it broke up. Maybe that was imagination. What wasn't imagination was how the truck swerved left, rocked once, and then keeled over on its side at damaging, destructive speed, plunging into a ditch and rolling, breaking off chunks of jagged metal and spilling Jap infantrymen, some dead, most still alive, all over the paved tarmac and the dirt shoulder.

Behind the first enemy truck the second braked, not sure just what to do but not wanting to end up as the first.

"Fire away!" Federales ordered. "Get this *maricón,* too!"

Not all of his men knew what a *"maricón"* was. But there was no misunderstanding the sergeant's intentions. By the time Port and the rest of the convoy had pulled up, both enemy trucks were off the road, one burning, the other battered and inert, while Federales's riflemen prowled the side of the road finishing off the last of the two or three dozen infantrymen.

"Well done, Sergeant," Billy Port said.

"Thank you, sir."

Port looked into his brown, old face.

"You knew they were there, didn't you, Federales?"

"Yessir, I knew they was coming."

The captain nodded. It was like a password, or a fraternity hand-shake, the ability to sense an enemy out there. Very few had the gift, but if they did, they recognized it in others. It was like that with Federales and Billy Port.

"I knew it. You smell them, don't you?"

"Yessir, I truly do. It ain't just smell, it's a kind of, I dunno, just knowing. You *know* they're there. I had it a long time, since I was a boy chasing Villa and them down on the borders. Me and the general, we used to talk about how I . . ."

"I understand, Sergeant," Port said, cutting him off. But respect-fully.

Because nine years ago in Nicaragua, Billy had also sniffed out an oncoming enemy for the first time, and remembered, with a strange pleasure, how good it was to be capable of doing that. And then, if you had to, killing men before they killed you.

Buffalo, cradling his Thompson gun, listened very carefully to this exchange, thinking he might learn from it, but said nothing. Did the captain really mean that, that he could smell the enemy? He could believe it of Federales, who was some kind of Indian and spoke funny. But Captain Port, who everyone said was rich and came from Boston?

War was a strange country, Buffalo concluded, and he hoped now the fighting had started that he would learn quickly and not be afraid and do his duty as the captain laid it out for him.

Dr. Han came up to Port's truck trailed by her nurse and orderly, all three toting medical bags. "May we be of help, Captain?"

"Thanks, Doctor. But we took no casualties."

"The Japanese in those trucks?"

Billy looked at her, his face hardening. He was aware from the sound of single rifle shots that his men had in all likelihood finished off whatever wounded Japanese there were. But more importantly, and he wanted no confusion on this, he was not about to start sharing his authority with anyone, certainly not a Chinese civilian.

"I'm not stopping to patch up enemy soldiers, Doctor. We're at war and in their territory. You're in a rush to get to those sick kids up at Jining and that other place. I just want to get the hell out of here and through the Wall before the Japs catch me. Please return to your truck. We'll be moving out."

"Yes, Captain," she said, her face as hard as his. But for different reasons.

As he watched her go, her back eloquently straight, Billy thought, Not very sporting, taking them in ambush like that. But then, neither was Pearl very sporting.

Both sides were playing hardball.

When the convoy drove off, wanting to get in another hour or two of driving before the skies cleared, behind them were the two Japanese trucks and all those dead infantrymen in the road or along the shoulders, and toward which local people, peasants and farmers, had begun cautiously to edge their way down from the low hills in order to scavenge. In rural China in the fifth year of war, even the dead had value. Boots, gold teeth, fountain pens, clothing, eyeglasses, knives. Rifles you didn't take; a Chinese peasant found with a Japanese rifle would be shot or strung up without discussion, never mind trial.

In his truck cab, Port ticked off the dead on both sides. Japs, almost forty. Marines, none.

Pretty fair scorecard. But they'd been lucky, too.

Old Rafter, the Dog Company top soldier who'd gone along with Port reluctantly, mulled their position. But only to himself:

They'd gotten out of Peking when Ashurst and his 150 Embassy Guards hadn't, including Rafter's pal Dutch Miller. Luther Brown and the Tientsin Marines put their money on the SS *Harrison*'s steaming into Chinwangtao harbor with bands playing. And they'd crapped out.

While Port, working off Colonel Sam's crazy scheme to drive overland, picking up stragglers as he went, and somehow getting into Mongolia or some damned place, was still a working Marine pulling down wages. As were his men.

While the others, nearly two hundred of them, had to bow their necks to the Japs and take it. Was there anything worse for a Marine? Well, Rafter concluded, maybe dying was worse. Dying was pretty bad. And up 'til now, he told himself, we ain't dead, we ain't took, and we done pretty fair.

A truck or two ahead, as they pulled away from the dead Japs and the burned and wrecked trucks, Lieutenant Cantillon turned to Father Kean. "That's the first real fighting I ever saw, Father. Is it usually like this?"

"Oh, yes, my boy," the Jesuit responded cheerfully, "except when it's worse."

26

The Japs gave them a scare. Two Zeroes came in low at last light.

IN the understandable and from a Japanese point of view entirely justifiable euphoria of that first week of the war, the incident at Zhuolo could easily be overlooked. Or put down to Nationalist guerrillas, a local patriot inflamed by some atrocity, or a madman.

Quite naturally, with thrilling victories against the U.S. and its Allies, officers of the Japanese military and Navy were beside themselves with excitement and pride. Of course they had been confident going in. But to have everything going *this* well? And against the great powers? After all, whatever their other weaknesses, the American Navy was first rate, and now at Pearl Harbor it lay largely on the bottom. The imperious MacArthur, one of the world's most storied generals, a former American Army chief of staff, had been caught with his pants down in the Philippines, his B-17s destroyed on the ground. Singapore's powerful artillery was aimed seaward, defying the Japanese Navy; but it was the Japanese Army slogging through the jungles of the Malay Peninsula that would take Singapore from the rear, despite its gallant Australians, New Zealanders, Scots, South Africans, and Indian Army regiments. Hong Kong was there for the plucking. The enemy, frankly, seemed in a state of shock.

Staff officers and attachés such as Colonel Jesse Irabu at headquarters in Shanghai had good reason to preen as they riffled through the daily battle reports stacked in the "in" baskets each morning. Irabu admitted his astonishment at how splendidly it was going. More parochial colleagues boasted of Samurai virtue and racial superiority, of humiliating Wall Street and Hollywood, revealing the posturing Americans as fakes. Irabu knew better but didn't argue with his fellow officers. They had a right to their enthusiasm. But he knew this was only the first game of the first set, and there was a long match ahead. But, hell! you couldn't deny what his Japanese countrymen had achieved so far. Not as noisy as the others, he indulged himself thinking of just how these Japanese victories were playing at Newport Beach, California.

Against such a background, what Port's detachment did at Zhuolo went unnoted until the report came in of Chinese peasants babbling of foreign devils, perhaps British or American, in green uniforms, swiftly and savagely destroying Japanese Army trucks and slaughtering Imperial soldiers.

Shuffling paper as desk-bound officers do, Irabu eventually came across the brief, one-sheet combat report from a provincial town of which he had never even heard, where thirty-six Japanese infantrymen had been killed in an ambush by "provocateurs," possibly (nothing was certain) Americans.

Pulling out a Chinese atlas, Irabu cross-referenced "Zhuolo" as northwest of Peking and just this side of and near the Great Wall.

How the devil could Americans spring an ambush in such an unlikely place, nearly two hundred miles from the sea, and at a time when their fleet was virtually powerless to transport and land even small raiding parties? Then Irabu, who as an officer was supposed to use his imagination, thought of Billy Port. When last mentioned in the daily and routine order of battle that kept HQ informed of just where "enemy" units were based, Port and his Shanghai Marines were reported as billeting overnight at the embassy compound in Peking. Where, Irabu assumed, they'd been scooped up on December 8 along with the garrison and were by now in a prisoner of war camp or, if the diplomats so ruled, headed to repatriation in a neutral country. Had Port gotten out of Peking before Japan snapped the trap; could Billy have ambushed those Imperial infantrymen?

Colonel Irabu was so intrigued by the possibility, curious as to Billy's fate and whether he might be involved in Zhuolo, that he placed a call to his patron General Nagata in Peking for information. The general said he would look into the matter and inform Irabu whether Port was a prisoner, which seemed likely, since nearly two hundred American Marines had without incident stacked their arms and surrendered.

"Obsessed by this fellow, Irabu? In war, obsession clouds vision." Nagata knew of the forces tugging at his young friend Irabu and admired how well he handled them. But this fixation on the Marine Port?

"Remember, Irabu, he was your tennis partner, not your brother. Don't get caught up in his adventures. He may be dead already, while you have a career ahead of you. Senior people are watching, you know. There's talk of you as 'our American,' a young fellow from whom even our Samurai can learn . . ."

"Thank you, General. I hope there's something to that. But I'd feel a lot better if I knew Port has been taken."

Or, improbable as it seemed, could he be still on the loose and causing mischief, somewhere in the badlands of North China?

During a firefight, a big one or just a skirmish like Port's killing of thirty-six soldiers that had caught Colonel Irabu's eye, Billy's mind never wandered.

There was only a crisply focused intelligence heightened by a natural tension and the adrenaline pumping. No thought of his own mortality, or refighting yesterday's battles, or thinking ahead to tomorrow's. Puller was like that, he knew. He was sure that their old C.O., Clifton B. Cates, was like that, so too Federales and Rafter. In a fight you were single-minded, fighting it and winning it. If you became distracted, you were dead.

Afterward, it was different. Following the postmortems and professional analysis, "we might have done this or that, or done it faster, or at another place," that kind of thing. Afterward, memory was okay, and so was consideration of tomorrow.

Now, the firing ended and the trucks again moving, he indulged himself, remembering Shanghai. A good three years: tennis with Lonsdale and Irabu, bar girls opening beers with their teeth, the whores waving good-bye at Bubbling Well Road, General Rostov before the suicide, Jimmy Jones when he was not only the city's assistant deputy marshal, but owned radio station RUOK, an amusement park, a dancing school, and the most opulent nightclub in Asia. Yet when he remembered Shanghai now, his memories centered on Natasha, dancing pressed against him, her body moving, her voice crooning in his ear, Tin Pan Alley à la russe. And where was she now? Was she safe, happy, had she found another "arrangement"?

It would be two more days of traveling before they got to where whooping cough raged and Billy had come up with a scheme that, if it worked, might enable the doctor to minister to the sick and yet not slow his trucks. Trouble was, Monsieur wasn't buying the deal. Billy informed the Frenchman he was lending his car to the good doctor and offering Monsieur's services as the best driver in Asia.

"Look, it's only a couple days, Laurent. You can easily catch up with the column traveling alone in the Bentley. Dr. Han needs a driver."

"You know me, Captain, trying to get to Dakar and join the Free French. I'm a wanted man by the Gestapo. Now you got me chauffeuring doctors around Mongolia with the Jap army after me. You're making sport."

He didn't lack for ego, did he? Port dropped his reasonable tone.

"Okay, we gave you a lift. You've got two days to think about a payback. If it comes to it, I'll drop you by the side of the road in the clothes you stand up in, with three days rations and a loaded .45. Use it on the bandits who come for you or use it on yourself, *mon vieux*."

"You can't do that, Captain, not to a fellow European."

"Just try me."

Now that the war had officially begun, Port resumed Cantillon's daily news summary based on Spark's notes. When they traveled by night and slept by day, the reports were issued at sunup, before the men started napping, four hours on, four off.

"Give 'em the bad news as well as the good, Mr. Cantillon. Marines are entitled to know what's going on in the world. And they don't need it candy-coated."

"Yessir."

That first wartime report certainly didn't spare the bad news. That's all there was.

"The Japs attack Hong Kong. The Brits have only six battalions and twenty-eight guns to defend the place. They have retreated to what they call their 'Gin Drinkers Line' and dug in. Japs land on northern Luzon. Wake Island bombed. Japanese infantry and tanks reported landing in Malaya. Brits have no repeat no tanks. More than half the British warplanes in Malaya destroyed on the ground in first attacks. What may have been a Japanese submarine fired several shells at oil fields at Long Beach, California, two nights ago.

"Long Beach? Ain't they got a helluva . . . ?"

Cantillon ignored the interruption. "Two big British warships *Prince of Wales* and *Repulse* steaming north to smash Jap fleet . . ."

"Well, hooray for our side," a Marine called out. "Until now, the Japs is pitching a shutout."

"Shut up, you," Sergeant Federales ordered. "Keep your mouth shut and learn something, okay, amigo?"

"Yes, Sarn't."

"And this final item," Cantillon wound up, "the Japs caught most of MacArthur's air force on the ground at Clark Field. Out of one hundred Flying Fortresses, only seventeen are operational."

The Marines didn't get that. After the Japs bombed Pearl, Mac-Arthur still had his planes lined up on the tarmac? They court-martialed officers for that. And wasn't MacArthur supposed to be this military genius?

Well, maybe it was all just enemy propaganda and things were really going better for our side. Port was still hoping that was the case but not believing it when he fell asleep.

It was late that afternoon when the Japs gave them a scare and almost caught them as much by surprise as those B-17s at Clark. Two Zeroes came in low at last light just as the Marines began to bustle about under the trees and crank up the truck engines and cook the "morning coffee" to be drunk at dusk.

Port had ordered no firing at enemy planes unless it became clear the planes had seen them and were coming in to attack. So when the fighters came in that low and that fast, there was only time to freeze, which everyone did, even Port's amateurs and women. And as quickly as it began, it was over, the planes out of there and away without having fired a shot, climbing to clear the ridges looming up ahead.

"They didn't see us," came from half a dozen exultant voices as a few others, impressed, murmured, "Damn! but they're fast!"

"They're looking for whoever shot up them trucks," Rafter said. And as if to confirm his thesis, from the south now came the drone of another plane, this one a spotter flying at about three thousand feet and heading their way, slow and high. Even from three thousand feet a plane like that might see men and trucks when a fast-moving Zero caught only a featureless blur of treetops and paddies. Which was what this country was, brown low hills, with rice irrigated in the low, boggy ground between, a scatter of farms with a pig or two rooting about and, but rarely, a skinny cow grazing on stubble no more nourishing than straw, a village every few miles linked by telephone poles (not functioning if the slackly hanging wires were to be believed) and the provincial road, alternately hardscrabble dirt and cracked, crumbling macadam.

In a landscape this dull, trucks and a score of men in uniform would stand out, crying for attention.

"Keep 'em down, Top. Keep 'em still. Smoking lamp out."

Rafter had already passed the word. Now, crawling, on hands and knees like an oversized spider, from one tree to another, he made the circuit, making sure everyone had gotten the message.

The observation plane made two lazy circles in the darkening sky and then, not wanting to be caught up there with full night coming, it broke off the second tour d'horizon and headed home, south and east. Had it spotted the Marines? Well, we'll soon know, Port concluded.

Within fifteen minutes their ride west by northwest had resumed. But for this leg of the journey Billy had Dr. Han and Father Kean in the truck with him, holding the largest scale map he had, using a hooded flashlight. Rafter took notes, with Mr. Cantillon summoned for his navigational skills.

"By my reckoning we're about one hundred miles west of Peking. By morning we'll be in the neighborhood of Datong, a pretty good-sized town where Dr. Han has reports of whooping cough. Is there a Japanese garrison at Datong, Doctor?"

"When I was there in March, no. But Japanese patrols came through every few days."

"After Datong, about ten or twenty miles out, we bump into the Great Wall. No skirting it any longer. We have to cross somewhere. After we get through, we swing due west, passing Jining on our right, another whooping cough hotspot. Drop off Dr. Han and her serums and expertise, this time for good, and roll at flank speed for Hohhot at the edge of the Gobi where we think Marines are holed up."

He put the map to the side. "Dr. Han, here's what I'd like you to do, traveling under your Red Cross credentials." The woman looked at him intently, not knowing just what was coming but clearly alert as to its possibilities.

"Take your crew into Datong with Monsieur driving [he said nothing about the Frenchman's reluctance]. Do your own work first. Assess the epidemic, visit the hospital, hand over your serums, see some patients. Spend as many hours as you need. Help them out. Be a good doctor. Then drive back to where we're bivouacked and tell me three things:

"Are there any Japanese troops in Datong? Any fuel and gas so we can top off? And from what you see, hear, know, or even suspect, which seems to you the best gate for us to get through the Wall. The smallest, quietest, least-patrolled pass in the neighborhood."

Dr. Han permitted herself a rare laugh.

"May I also do the marketing, Captain? Datong is famous for its soybeans and maize."

Billy did not normally welcome sarcasm at his expense. But he was asking this woman to put herself at risk spying and, in the doing, possibly to violate her oath. She was entitled.

"Especially if the maize is still on the cob, yes, Doctor."

He was rewarded with a small but genuine smile, the first since he'd kept her from treating enemy wounded.

After that he and Dr. Han and Father Kean went over the map again. The Jesuit had used two of the four nearest gates though not recently. But he did offer an encouraging word. "I'd say, Captain, that if you get through the Wall in this sector, you will have left the Japanese behind. Out there"—he gestured generally west—"you encounter the Gobi and Mongolia proper, the country of the warlords, of bandits, and eventually of Chiang Kai-shek or the Red Army. All of whom are perfectly capable of killing you for your boots, never mind your trucks, but at least you will have evaded the long arm of Tojo and his merry men."

"Sounds good, Padre," Port said.

It wasn't going to be that easy.

27

The battleship Prince of Wales *and the* Repulse
were sunk in ninety minutes.

MONSIEUR quickly saw the light. It was very simple. "Monsieur," said Billy, "give me any *merde,* and I'm leaving you here."

The Frenchman cursed a bit but when he drove off the next morning with Dr. Han and her assistants, he managed a sour smile. *"C'est la vie, mon capitaine."*

"C'est la guerre," Port corrected him.

Rafter, skeptical by nature, suggested, "He could just turn himself in and blow the whistle on us to the Japs."

"And get shot as a spy? I don't think so, Top. He'd desert if he thought he'd get away with it. But we're still too far from a friendly border."

Dr. Han and the Bentley were on the road to Datong by eight. It wouldn't be until eleven hours later, and full night, when they would get back.

To help keep bored men focused, Cantillon was whistled up. "Time for the evening news, Mr. Cantillon."

The young officer looked reluctant.

"There's one disastrous item, sir," he told Port.

"Well, go ahead. We want to know. Good, bad, or indifferent."

There was only "bad."

"On December tenth the British battleship *Prince of Wales* and the battle cruiser *Repulse* were both sunk in the South China Sea off the Malay coast in just ninety minutes by Japanese air and submarines. These were believed the last two Allied capital ships in the western Pacific."

"Oh, shit," someone groaned, half to himself.

Marines traditionally made sport of sailors (familiarly, "swabbies"), but were themselves "soldiers of the sea," and they understood what Cantillon's bulletin meant. First, Pearl, now this latest debacle, and professionals like the Marines, who respected the power and mobility of the great ships, knew that control of the sea had passed clearly to the Japanese. The Pacific now belonged to them. Whatever slim chance the Marines ever had of departing China by ship was finished; they were landlocked.

Trapped, hostiles all around them and maybe no way out.

"The hell with that stuff, you people," Port began coldly, realizing something had to be said. "We've been on our own since the regiment sailed. This just makes it a little bit more so. But I don't want anyone brooding on it. Just cheer up. We never did count on getting away by sea. I floated that as a cover story in Shanghai, that's why I bought the *Virgin,* to fool the Japs. The cover worked and we're moving on. Those poor Limeys are dead and I'm sorry as hell. And those boys at Pearl. And MacArthur's B-17s are shot up. But we're still alive and not doing too badly. Remember that and not the other damned stuff we can't do anything about."

Most of the Marines picked up on what their captain said, and with the few who seemed really down, he made an effort to get their heads up, lighting a good cigar and chatting casually with this man or that, joshing a big BAR man over the impressive number of ammo belts and loaded magazines he had draped about him, inquiring after a salty corporal's toothache of the day before.

"I got Doc to just pull the son of a bitch and pack it with cotton. Couple of APCs [what Marines called aspirin] and that bottle of beer didn't hurt."

"Good man," Billy told him, grateful for anything that might cheer a fellow up, "and if all's well, we'll have another beer tonight."

When Dr. Han and Monsieur got back, the Marines, idled all day long, depressed by news of the battleships, clustered around.

"Good news, Captain. Almost all good news. First, the epidemic..."

There was a little restlessness at that. The Marines didn't give a damn about epidemics. They wanted to know if they were going to have to fight tomorrow. If there were Japs at Datong. But she was a physician first, and Port cut across the murmuring, "All right, there. As you were..."

The men stilled and the doctor went on: "...the whooping cough here is not the worst sort. Datong, with the serum I brought, should be clean of whooping cough in a week or less. As for Jining, it was more virulent there but the epidemic has run its course, no further assistance required. Only twelve children died. I'd feared there might be more."

What a very "Chinese" thing to say, it occurred to Billy. A dozen kids dead of a single disease in a U.S. city would be front-page news. Twelve dead Chinese children? Nothing but a public health statistic.

Now she got to where the Marines sat up, and smartly.

"No Japanese garrison at Datong. A patrol drives through twice a week. They were there yesterday, an armored car and a dozen men in a truck. So the calendar is with us. Regrettably, Monsieur Laurent found no available petrol. I have information on the various local gates through the Wall. Several look to offer promise." After a moment, she added, "And we did the marketing. Fresh turnip, potato, and soybeans harvested this fall and stored in root cellars. Also, newly baked bread. I tasted the bread, so fresh I purchased a dozen loaves." That, if not the turnips, drew pleased grunts from the Marines.

When Dr. Han's party, including Monsieur, had been fed, they and the Marines chowing down enthusiastically on the bread and baked potatoes, the convoy would normally have moved off.

Not this night; they had to decide first where to cross the Great Wall. And whether to do it in darkness or at dawn. This was the first tactical decision Billy had to make since they skipped Peking. Rafter brought up the maps and they gathered around a low fire. It was very cold now, maybe down in the twenties Farenheit, coldest night they'd had. All the Marines were in their forest-green overcoats and a few sported fur caps until Rafter called them on it.

"We'll all wear tin hats until we got enough furs to go 'round. I don't like an outfit wearing different covers. Looks sloppy as the damned army." Nor did Rafter like the sound of that Jap armored car. A truck goes up against armor, the truck loses. He'd watched the captain's face during Dr. Han's report and he suspected Port felt the same.

Dr. Han and Father Kean took over the discussion of gates. There were four within reach: Daomaguan, Chajianling, Kiaguan, and Guan. The last two were getting into the Heng Shan mountains where the Wall crested at eight thousand feet in altitude. Too high; snow became a factor. No chains on their trucks, worn tread on a few tires. Dr. Han favored Chajianling which was only at four thousand feet. And which had other attractive qualities.

"The gatekeeper there is a man famous for his venality. He will sell his wife to travelers for the night and then beat her in the morning as an adulteress."

"We can do business with a fellow like that," Port agreed.

Father Kean, who "collected" sinners, nodded agreement. He also knew the gate of Chajianling. "For centuries it was celebrated as a horse market with Mongols fetching herds south to sell to the Han people. So there is an honored tradition of barter and trade. At places like this the Great Wall isn't so much a barricade as an open air market."

Dr. Han supplied the Jesuit with the name of Xian, the rascal of a gatekeeper.

A delighted Fr. Kean was barely able to contain himself.

"You're right! I'd forgotten his name. Two years ago he extorted me for traversing his gate with a carton of Holy wafers for communion. Said they were contraband and levied penalties. I customarily offer a blessing to people I meet along the route. In his case, I refrained."

Billy Port called his major domo.

"Leung, when we get to the Chajianling Gate, have the exchequer handy. I'll want you to haggle with this fellow and settle on a fair price."

"What are we purchasing, sir?"

"Only his undying friendship, though on a pro tem basis, Leung. We'll be bribing our way through his gate and into Mongolia."

Lieutenant Cantillon thought back wistfully to the ethics course Yale freshmen were required to take. Here were Marine officers and Jesuits chortling over the prospects for bribery.

It was decided to start early in full darkness at about three A.M., arriving at Chajianling Gate at daybreak. Dr. Han hung back to speak privately with Captain Port.

"Amid the good news from Datong there was something disturbing. I didn't want to say it before the men."

"What is it, Doctor?"

"The whooping cough epidemic seems to have jumped the Wall and settled in the closer villages of the Gobi as well as in Hohhot, where you hope to find your friends. For that reason, I wish to remain with your convoy that far. They'll need serum. I appreciate you'd like to see the last of us and concentrate on your own march, but is this possible?"

"Dr. Han, you saved our . . . rear ends at Peking. Of course you can stay. Was Monsieur cooperative?"

"Quite." She waited briefly, then added, "He is a remarkable driver, you know. Swift and most competent."

"I know about the driving. It's the man that bothers me."

"Captain, Laurent was fine."

When Rafter had posted the guards he and Port talked for a time. He felt pretty good. "We get through that Wall tomorrow, Top, that's a big leg up. That's maybe where we leave the Japs behind. Their planes and that armored car of theirs."

"Yessir, Skipper. Except we ain't through it yet."

28

"They got some dead people, Skipper. Hanging from ropes."

Nor would they be for a time.

They drove west with headlights along a road that rose steadily but at an easy gradient toward the hills and the Great Wall's gate, and there were no difficulties for the first few hours, only dark farms and sleepy villages to be driven through, a shaky bridge they crept across at a prudent five mph, a couple of drunken peasants riding an oxcart home after what must have been a considerable night on the town. Nothing more. Then, at about seven-thirty, with nearly full light and a clear day dawning, the Zeroes came in low and fast toward them, screaming at full throttle.

"Damn! Damn! Damn!" To get this close to the Wall and be caught by Jap air on an open road with nothing but a few spindly trees for cover.

Port and his sergeants didn't even need to shout at anyone. All four trucks and the Bentley instinctively veered off the road to right and left, bouncing and jouncing into the corrugated fields, hoping not to break an axle, dodging the paddies in which a big truck might bog down, and heading for the nearest hospitable tree. When a fighter plane strafed you, a lousy grove of trees was your best friend.

The planes, two of them, came out of the east and low, the rising sun just behind them and shining in the Marines' eyes. It couldn't be a better setup for the Zeroes, a worse for the Americans. Then over the sound of the engines came the stutter of machine guns and all the way out across the dry winter fields you could see plumes of dust spurting upward and then settling back as bullets tore into Pearl Buck's good earth. Then the planes were climbing steeply, to turn and come back for a second helping.

Did they know we were here? Was it last night's observation plane that gave the alarm? Or were they on routine patrol and just came across a target of opportunity? Port knew the Japanese fighter pilots were good. They'd been strafing the Chinese since 1937 and he'd seen their work against the Soviets at the Amur. So maybe these fellows had been hunting his Marines, getting back at them for the motorcycle couriers and the infantry trucks they'd cut up along the road out of Peking.

"Get those machine guns working!" Billy Port yelled. "The BARs, too! Aim twenty or thirty yards ahead of the prop!"

He was guessing, of course. Maybe it should have been fifty yards or a hundred. Billy had never been strafed before, the Sandanista rebels having no air force. He just wanted lead flying when the Japs came in again.

Now the planes were back and no time for speculation. Two of his three machine guns were in action and a couple of BARs as well. Most of the riflemen had their Springfields up and firing. Hitting a plane moving at three hundred miles an hour was by guess and by God. But you had to try, didn't you?

This second pass was a lot noisier, with the Marine gunners joining in and the Zeroes doing their share. Port hugged the earth to his thighs and belly, on his elbows and squinting up, could see chunks of metal and wood exploding and flying off a truck to his left. What truck that was, he couldn't tell. And in a manic moment, how was his Bentley making out? And were the Jap pilots puzzled at seeing *that* cruising around China in the middle of a war? Port had his Smith & Wesson out of the holster and fired off the six rounds. Some chance, Billy! he thought cynically. He was perfectly focused so not even the Bentley distracted him from what he was doing. Which was trying to kill an enemy pilot before the pilot killed him. Next to Port young Buffalo was sprawled sensibly flat on his back, the Thompson gun steadied in both hands, squeezing off bursts as the fighters screamed in, and yelling at the Japs, cursing them with a boyish, if vigorous, profanity.

And then, quickly as it began, it was over, with the two sleek little planes climbing steeply to settle again into level flight, heading home. Maybe they were out of ammo, so the Marines had been lucky. But if they'd come specifically hunting Port and his men, there could be other planes later in the day. It was unfair, how many hours it took trucks to cross fifty miles of rough country and how swiftly a fast plane could catch them at it.

"Rafter!"

"Yessir, I'm calling roll."

"Lemme know."

"Aye aye, sir."

Federales came up now.

"I lose one man. Dead."

The Bentley rolled up. They, too, had been hit.

"My orderly," Dr. Han said. "Wounded in the shoulder. The bone is broken but he will live. May I help your corpsman with the Marine wounded?"

"Yes, ma'am, please."

Good woman. She was cool as ever. But then, so too was Monsieur.

"I just kept moving, kept swinging the wheel to dodge them, Captain. This automobile, *très bon*. Corners beautifully. A shame about your fender."

There were two other Marines hit. One with a bullet hole in his leg, the other badly cut up by wood splinters from the truck bed that caught him in the face. Dr. Han said they'd be okay. "The leg wound, very nice. Didn't hit bone. Quite clean. Your corpsman Doc has already pulled the wood splinters from the other." She and her nurse had rigged a sling for their orderly.

"All the trucks are still running," the motor transport expert reported. To him, that was more significant than the casualty rolls. But then, that was the work he did, that was why Ford Motor Company promoted him to master mechanic.

Jurkovich had one additional comment.

"Don't worry none about those holes in the Bentley, Captain. A good body and fender shop'll fix them up good as new in no time. I'll do it myself if we come across a little foundry with a bellows and fire."

Rafter had the dead Marine, a rifleman name of Kenna, tidied up and stowed, wrapped in an issue blanket in the back of a truck.

"We'll plant him later," Billy Port said. "Don't want to stop now for burial detail."

"Nossir. We'll do him up proper t'other side of the Wall."

"That's well," Port agreed. Kenna was their first dead and they owed him a Marine's grave.

Rafter, like all of them, by now was fixed on the Great Wall of China, and the open country the other side of it where they might lose themselves, find friends, might eventually find a way out.

It was just short of ten A.M. when Federales, ranging out a mile ahead of the column in the point truck, spied the Chajianling Gate. He signaled a halt and came back to Captain Port.

"I don't like it, Captain."

"What it is?" Was Federales smelling trouble again?

"Nice big gate like that on a sunny morning there ought to be folks passing through, this way and that. There ain't nobody. But through the 7×50 glasses I see a little smoke."

"Cook fires, heating stoves?"

"Maybe so, Skipper. More like something went on fire and got put out. I dunno. Got a funny stink to it, too, the smoke."

When Federales was uneasy, Port took note.

"Why don't you close up to a quarter mile or so. Put your machine gunner on the alert and take a closer look. We'll wait for your signal."

"Yessir."

But instead of a signal, Federales had taken his closer look and then wheeled his truck around and sped back.

Port was waiting when the truck skidded to a dusty halt.

"They got dead people down there, Skipper."

"The Zeroes strafe them, too?"

"Nossir, these people is hanging from ropes."

Port didn't say anything. Sergeant Federales told you what you needed to know in his own style, unless he felt he had to quote General Pershing.

"Some of the wooden outbuildings up against the stone walls was burned out. There's bodies lying around on the ground, too."

Port couldn't resist asking.

"What do you think?"

"Looks like a raid in Indian country in the old days. That's how it looks to me, Skipper. Not like organized troops done it. Under the hanging bodies, someone built little fires, cooking 'em from the feet up, y'know."

Port called the NCOs together. And Cantillon, Father Kean, Yusopov, Leung, and Dr. Han. He briefed them on the basis of Federales's report.

"Looks to me that we stumbled on a massacre of sorts. And not by the Japs. But I don't like to pass this gate by and try for one farther along. Ground's higher there and maybe with snow. More to the point, it gives those Jap planes time to refuel, rearm, and hit us again. I really want to cross the Wall this morning. Since we don't know what's happened here at Chajianling, the whole command is going to drive up there, armed and ready and looking dangerous, and find out. Any better ideas? Rafter, Federales?"

Only Dr. Han spoke.

"Sergeant Federales mentioned bandits. There are plenty of those the other side of the Wall. For fear of regular army troops, they don't usually come through to this side. But perhaps with the Japanese now at war with America, and occupied on so many fronts, they become bolder?"

Father Kean nodded. "Makes sense, Doctor." The Jesuit knew a little about bandits.

Rafter briefed the men and within a few minutes the four trucks and the Bentley were rolling across the brown fields strung out abreast, to make more of a show of force, heading for the Great Wall, wondering if they were going to have to bribe an avaricious gatekeeper or fight a more formidable foe.

29

General Sin sent a few men out to be shot, to demonstrate the machine gun.

"I am General Sin. State your business."

A beefy man, gaudily uniformed, with a big, bland face punctuated by a stringy, oiled mustache, his chest festooned with decorations, cartridge belts, and bandoliers, and wearing a wide-brimmed fur hat of Mongol design, sat on an overstuffed easy chair with a useful-looking Mauser rifle across his fat thighs. The easy chair was set on bare ground before a small, open gate near the closed, and padlocked, main gate of Chajianling, and the general spoke to them in a Chinese tongue with which, fortunately, Father Kean seemed at home.

Billy Port just stood there, looking into the fat man's face, smiling pleasantly, indulging himself by considering the fellow's name, "General Sin." Who names these guys, the casting office at MGM?

But he directed his first words to the Jesuit doing the translating.

"Tell the general I greet him in the name of the United States Marine Corps and the Continental Congress. Tell him we are the advance guard of a column of ten thousand American Marines who will be passing through this historic gate en route to a great battle with the Japanese."

General Sin was the sort who got right down to cases.

"You got no cannons? How you fight the Japanese without cannons?"

"The main Marine column has many cannons. So many, their dust obscures the sky as they pass. Also flamethrowers and trench mortars. A terrible force, truly. Can we inquire just what has happened here? Why are these people hanging? Who are these dead? Are they Japanese?"

Port remembered parleys like this in Nicaragua. The longer you kept the bandits talking, the more time you had to count their guns. Sin seemed to have plenty, the nearest in the hands of a palace guard of a dozen or so armed men arrayed behind and to the great man's plump flanks.

"My army controls this province. I am much beloved by the people, all of whom respect my army and offer tribute. The gatekeeper here, a thief named Xian, failed to pay me the usual tributes. He's one of those hanging there."

Father Kean couldn't resist shooting a glance. His satisfied look told Port, yes, that was indeed Xian, the rascal who charged him for the communion wafers. His lower limbs were burnt black and smoldering but the face was easily recognizable.

"*Your* army, General," Billy said, stressing the personal pronoun, "my, my. This is wonderful news. My own colonel will want to meet with you when the main column arrives. To discuss tactics and longer-term strategy. Possibly a joint command with your army as the Marines march west?"

Billy maintained a stern face while peddling this nonsense.

Not General Sin. He swallowed some of it, leaning toward a youngster who seemed to be his aide de camp, a very neatly turned-out young officer with field glasses slung, and affecting a vaguely German General Staff uniform, with all manner of epaulets and pockets. Port took note of that. You always wanted to find an ambitious young commander-in-waiting. If he couldn't negotiate with Sin, and they had to shoot him, then maybe this fellow would be more amenable. It was like finding a Bangalore Johnny before pitching Captain Henriques into the harbor.

"Father, please ask General Sin how many men are in his army. And can we be of any service before we cross through the Wall?"

There were many, many men. Thousands, and more than thousands. Maybe as many even as five hundred, perhaps. All heavily armed. Ferocious, as well. Splendidly trained and to him, personally, as their general, faithful unto death. Just look around at all these bodies to measure their ferocity.

Port nodded.

"Please ask what is the tribute to be paid for passage through the Chajianling Gate. We wish to do the appropriate thing in dealing with the general."

Once again Sin turned aside to jabber with his right-hand man as well as with another, older gent, whom Billy took to be the paymaster.

There were shrewd looks exchanged. A sum was named.

Port turned without even an instant's hesitation, "Leung, bring up the exchequer."

The amount was paltry, though more than the venal Xian would have demanded, and when Leung, without even a flourish, handed it over in cash, General Sin made a mistake. Assuming these people dealt from fear and weakness, he got greedy.

"You got machine guns?" he asked.

Father Kean, unsure what game Port was playing, waited for the captain's lead.

"We have a water-cooled Browning .30-caliber heavy machine gun. On rubber-tired wheels."

When this was translated, General Sin looked very excited, his greed nearly sensuous. He had seen and admired such guns but never actually possessed one. And on wheels! His aides murmured their delight. Just think of it.

Port concluded, though without actually saying so, there wasn't that much difference between the bandidos of Nicaragua in 1932 and the warlords of today's China. While they boasted of living off the country, what they really did was loot the country. As well as travelers passing through, innocents like Billy Port and his slim command.

Captain Port called out to Rafter. "Top, turn your truck around and drop the tailgate so he can see the heavy pointing at him. And I want it pointing right at him."

There is something intimidating, even for a "general" like Sin, to be looking down the barrel of a working machine gun. But his admiration for the gun got the best of him, and with the help of a husky soldier on each side, General Sin was lifted from his easy chair and waddled, fatly, to the Marine truck where two gunners crouched behind the heavy gun, and called up to them in Chinese.

"He wants to touch it. Lift it down," Port ordered when he understood.

When the Browning was set down on the ground on its rubber-tired bicycle wheels, the two gunners resumed their place, one behind the weapon with his hand on the grip and trigger and the other gunner to the side, threading the ammo belt into the feedway. The warlord walked 'round the gun admiringly, then ran a hand over its lightly greased water jacket.

"Ah, such a weapon," he said.

A dozen of his senior officers gathered 'round General Sin, jostling each other to get closer to the boss, the young aide de camp prominent among them. Port shot him a grin and was rewarded with an enameled smile.

"This is your number two?" Port asked General Sin through Father Kean.

"Yes, Major Tang."

Then the general said, "Now that we are allies against the Japanese, and I rule in this territory, you will please supply me with a gun like this. With ammunition." Port noticed a small mob of Sin's men edging forward in a mass of uniforms and rifles behind and around him.

"Please, General, we don't want our machine gun damaged, do we? Please get those fellows back. Touching the gun is for you, sir, and not for common soldiers."

Angrily, Sin gesticulated and the mass of men retreated fifteen or twenty yards.

"You see, Captain, how my men love and obey me," Sin bragged. "And now, you can supply me this gun? Or one similar?"

It was time now for plain speech, Port recognized. No more feeling the merchandise with thumb and forefinger.

"No," Billy said, though still smiling.

"Oh?"

"We would first have to sign treaties. I would also have to consult with my colonel before turning over such a formidable weapon."

"I'm a general. Colonels are shit compared to generals." At that, more of Sin's men again pressed forward, as if to push the Marines back. Not only closing in on Port and Father Kean and Buffalo, his Thompson gun leveled, but fingering their weapons as if getting ready.

Sin was throwing his weight around. Port signaled to Leung again. "From my footlocker, fetch the sword." Then, to General Sin, "All Marine officers have swords, General. Do you?"

Sin was becoming bored. "Swords are fine. But I want to see the machine gun shoot. Here, I send a few fellows out there in the field. Have your men shoot them."

"Of course."

Leung held out the scabbard and Captain Port drew the sword.

"Send your men way out," Billy said, gesturing with the blade. "The heavy Browning has a tremendous range. A mile or more."

"Yes, yes," Sin said, enthusiastic once again, and waving three men out trotting alongside the Wall, already several hundred yards away.

"We don't usually wear our swords. Only on great occasions such as this," Billy was saying as he ran through the salute (very proper and deferential to General Sin, who seemed pleased) and then through several simple riffs of vaguely remembered sword drill, the polished blade gleaming.

Sin was torn, trying to keep one eye on the steel of a sword that would look very well in his hand, the other locked on to three soldiers trotting across a brown field in order to be shot. The machine gun or the sword? What a dilemma!

Then why not take both?

It was then Billy Port said, not to Sin but to his right-hand man, Major Tang, "I don't understand, sir, if the general is a general, why you are only a major. Shouldn't you be a colonel, at least?"

Father Kean translated and the young man's face lighted up.

"He says, Captain, 'That is a very sensible idea. But he is not sure General Sin approves.' "

Billy had the officer's sword in his right hand and, without turning, he called back to Rafter and his machine gunners at the truck.

"I'm going to show our friend here a little swordplay before he forces us to shoot his men. Keep the gun trained on him and his men here, not the three soldiers out there."

"Aye aye, sir." Rafter, too, had seen Sin's bodyguards edging in, weapons at the ready, had glimpsed other armed men on the Wall, in what was shaping up as some kind of move. The top also had caught a hand signal from keen-eyed Sergeant Federales, who knew his bandits.

Billy hefted the weapon and then, confident his Marines were arrayed behind him and on the alert, he flashed it back and forth very swiftly under General Sin's fleshy chin, before suddenly crying out, "Touché!" at which, with a horizontal, slashing blow, Captain Port cut off the warlord's head.

The fur-hatted, wide-eyed, mouth-opened head was still rolling when General Sin's squat body began to crumble, toppling sideways before collapsing heavily to earth on its back, gushing blood and with the warlord's ornately tooled boots gone toes up.

Even the soldiers still trotting across the distant field to offer themselves as targets could hear the stunned, communal gasp.

Port turned quickly to young Major Tang.

"Father Kean, tell this officer he has our congratulations. The major has just succeeded the late General Sin as commander of the army."

As the Jesuit addressed the young officer, Port jauntily saluted Tang with the bloody sword, adding in English, "Your servant, sir, as they used to say in the code duello."

Various soldiers were jumping up and down in glee, whether at Tang's promotion or Sin's death or just enjoying the show, you couldn't be sure. But they were all grinning at the Marines and shaking their heads in admiration at the dramatic swiftness of the general's dispatch. Billy Port grinned back, shaking hands, as in an aside to Father Kean, he said, not defensively, but wanting to make a point: "There are a couple of hundred of them. Twenty of us. I needed to get their attention."

"Yes, yes, Captain," the subdued priest murmured, uncertain after all his years in the East if he'd ever witnessed an actual decapitation before, "I'm sure."

30

A landing on Wake Island beaten off and two Jap destroyers sunk.

THERE was a good deal of celebrating on the part not only of the Marines, but of the late Xian's surviving family and friends, as well as among General Sin's army. The newly promoted "Colonel Tang," encouraged by Captain Port, and there on the spot, parceled out any number of field promotions from the ranks. As the majordomo Leung, instructed by Port, handed over to Tang an additional sum of cash, substantially more than already paid as a bribe to the late Sin, whose body had quickly been stripped of its cartridge belts and medals, and even his underwear and flashy boots, and tossed naked into the back of an oxcart to be disposed of by the locals of Chajianling, who had suffered under his tyranny. While his vast head was serving the children of Chajianling, a sportif crew, as a sort of soccer football.

"Tell the colonel he can now raise the pay of his men, Father. This will assure him of enormous popularity. At least until he becomes as much a pig as General Sin. I am also writing him a letter of introduction to the colonel commanding the main Marine column, which should be here by cocktail hour tomorrow, if not earlier."

Father Kean grimaced. Jesuits didn't mind the beheading of an occasional warlord, but they disliked untruths, and he was of course aware there was no Marine colonel, no ten-thousand-man main column. But he duly translated and handed over a sheet of paper drafted by Top Sergeant Rafter, and signed with considerable flourish by Port.

"What did you write, Top?" Billy asked.

"Said he would like his fellow colonel very much. That the two of them could talk colonel-talk and smoke a cigar. Crap like that."

"Well done, Rafter."

Tang was so pleased by his promotion, Sin's death, and the prospect of an alliance with the American Marine Corps that he marched through the Chajianling Gate at Billy Port's side, the two of them hearing cheers and receiving bows, and when they emerged into the sunlight on the other side, Tang had his several hundred men lined up in salute as the trucks and the Bentley car passed, the Marines shouting good wishes and tossing off cheerful highballs. Billy permitted himself the conceit that, back in Boston, this sort of adulation must be why people ran for mayor. Only a few hours earlier they'd been under fire, one of them killed, and now without further violence (if you excepted the unfortunate Sin), they were safely past the Great Wall and on their way to Mongolia.

Recovered from shock, even Father Kean was impressed.

"By Saint Sebastian the Martyr, Port, these old eyes have witnessed wonders, but never have I been so astonished as when you chopped off that fellow's head. You must have done such a thing before, to have carried it off so deftly."

"Well, I had intended to run him through. But he had so many medals, and with those cartridge belts crisscrossing his belly, I thought the sword point might simply bounce off. So I gave him the chop."

"But you had done it previously, sir, had you not?"

"Not quite, in Nicaragua we used machetes. Shorter, heavier blade, a lot more efficient than an officer's saber, I promise you, Father. And handy clearing undergrowth as well."

Lieutenant Cantillon, who a few months ago had been squiring debutantes to the officers' club at Pearl Harbor, was unable to say a thing.

While Rafter, who didn't excite easily, simply nodded.

"That was nicely done, Skipper. I'd have had Buffalo take him out with the Thompson gun, myself. But nicely done."

Only to his top soldier would Billy Port bother with explanations. "I thought of it, Top. But if we started firing, one of Sin's men was sure to be so nervous he'd fire back, and who the hell knew after that. The sword seemed like the thing to do."

Dr. Han, who'd busied herself with patching up wounded civilians at Chajianling Gate after General Sin's demise, expressed neither regrets nor scoldings. "Those men Sin hanged, they were tortured first, grotesquely so, and set afire. And Xian's wife, the one he pimped and then beat, she was raped by Sin's troops before they killed her. A nasty business, Captain. You did well to dispatch him."

It was now the afternoon of December 13 and they were through the Great Wall, where the threat of the Japanese should, at least in theory, be reduced. But Marine officers are supposed to think in terms of worst-case possibilities, and once they'd buried their dead Marine, John J. Kenna of Seattle, and Father Kean said the prayer and six men fired a volley over the place, they were back in their trucks, driving hard, intent on getting a few more miles between them and General Sin's army. Just in case Colonel Tang had already started to develop notions of grandeur, and lust after machine guns. Just after nine, full night and very cold, the hills higher with every mile, Port called a halt. Once the guards were posted and the meal eaten, Mr. Cantillon was called on for the world news.

"Well, sir, it's a combined account of the past couple days, while we've been busy. And except for a few bright spots, like Wake Island, it's pretty bleak."

"Go ahead, Lieutenant, we're all grown-ups."

The naval officer cleared his throat and began.

"Germany and Italy declared war on the United States (a loud "boo" on that one). Another Nazi retreat in a blizzard west of Moscow in the face of Soviet reinforcements fresh from Siberia. An attempted landing on Wake Island was beaten off and two Jap destroyers sunk [considerable cheering here!] by the Marine garrison of four hundred fifty . . ."

"Hell," someone called out, "they got four hundred fifty gyrenes there? We had four hundred fifty Marines here, we could go back and retake Shanghai."

Cantillon continued. "In Malaya the Indian Division retreated."

"What side was they on, Lieutenant?"

"More Jap landings in southern Luzon. At Hong Kong British forces withdraw from the mainland to the island itself. In Burma the Japs capture the British airfield at Victoria Point on the Kra Isthmus."

T' hell with Burma, it was that business about south Luzon that hit them. The 4th Marines were on Luzon and until now, the Japs were attacking from landing sites in the north. Now the south. Which put the regiment in the middle, didn't it? Men didn't like hearing stuff like that about their buddies.

Cantillon wrapped up the evening news with a stateside item: in California, for national security, because of sabotage and espionage, internment camps were being set up to hold Japanese-Americans, even those born in the States. Thousands of people might eventually be resettled in the Mojave, far from the coastline where they could signal Japanese subs.

There was little discernible reaction to that on the part of the Marines. "What the hell," Corporal Kress remarked, "they're all Japs, ain't they?"

Captain Port huddled in the cold around a fire with his NCOs and the others, pointedly including Cantillon, to discuss the route for the next day.

"By damn it's cold," Rafter said, who never complained.

"A harsh place, the Gobi," said Father Kean. "In summer the temperatures are known to top out at one hundred thirteen degrees. In January, the coldest month, it can drop to forty below zero Farenheit."

"Forty below?" Port couldn't resist repeating.

"Yessir, that cold. Course, we're not yet in the true Gobi, just at the edges. But January's coming and the north wind out of Siberia sweeps across these chalky steppes . . ."

Port cut him off with a clipped "Thank you, Padre." No need to get the men upset thinking about cold that bad. Better to concentrate on the chore at hand. If all went well, they could reach Hohhot by tomorrow or early the day after. Hohhot where there was whooping cough and, more to the point, where they might find a dozen Marines circuit-riding out of Harbin, fighting bandits, keeping American women from getting raped, especially those with relatives in Congress, and in general doing what Marines do so well, maintaining order and keeping the peace.

If all went well, that is.

31

"It's not as if Captain Port were important," said General Nagata.

THOUGH he didn't realize it, Captain William Hamilton Thomas Port, USMC, 051313/0302, was making a name for himself up in North China. The way gunfighters did out West after the Civil War in places like Dodge and El Paso or Abilene, where other gunmen, ambitious for celebrity, came after them.

As the Japanese Imperial Army now began to do in a modest but menacing way after Billy Port. Who, as it turned out when they re-checked their rosters, was *not* among the Marines who surrendered at the embassy in Peking.

Which would bring Colonel Irabu into it. Not that Port's laughably small command was in itself significant. But they'd killed Imperial Army couriers, destroyed truckloads of Japanese infantry, survived a strafing by Zeroes, somehow killed a Chinese warlord, and bluffed their way through the Chajianling Gate. So that without taking sub-stantial losses, Port's detachment had not only slipped out of Peking hours before the Marines were rounded up, but traversed a hundred miles of North China, and was already west of the Great Wall, headed for the trackless Gobi and Inner Mongolia.

In the East Indies, Malaysia, Burma, Hong Kong, the Philippines, even at pesky Wake Island, the Japanese were enjoying a grand run. Not to mention their triumph at Pearl and the sinking of those British dreadnaughts. But senior staff officers at General Hata's HQ didn't believe it was good policy here in China, where Japan had been fight-ing a war since '37, to permit a measly squad of Americans to freelance around the countryside, killing Japanese, impressing the locals, and, to indulge in the legalisms, defying terms of the formal Marine sur-render at Peking under which the officers and men of the 4th Marine Regiment were to turn themselves in. Or be shot.

General Hata put it this way: "It's a matter of face. You don't want enemy soldiers stirring up trouble in the interior and encouraging the Chinese resistance or Mongolian separatists."

"Face" was important, had been for a thousand years, dating back in Japanese literature to the "Seven Samurai" and "The Forty-seven Ronin." But beyond concern about face, Hata was the commanding general of a conquered hostile territory ten times larger than his own entire country. And for the most part these people were intimidated and placid. But like a parched field in the dry season, it could at any time burst into flame. Why give the damned Chinese the gift of fire? A few impudent Americans were nothing, unless they provided a spark to set the country aflame. With all the demands on Japanese manpower, Hata echoed a much earlier general, Napoleon, who advised Europe to "Let Great China sleep."

And when the Japanese Imperial Army's commander in chief in China expressed himself about "face," and followed up with warnings of a military and security nature, senior officers took notice and sent out inquiries. Shanghai provided HQ in Peking with Irabu's name as that of a man who actually knew the renegade Captain Port. An infantry general named Watanabe was assigned the job of running down Port and his Marines, and to that end he summoned Irabu to the capital and questioned him about the impertinent American's habits and tendencies for a full fifteen minutes. And then announced that a mobile force would be dispatched from the garrison at Peking to stalk Captain Port and his men on their ride across China. Stalk them and kill or capture them all.

"A simple affair. I won't need to bother you with it again, Irabu," said the general complacently.

"Yes, sir," said the colonel, relieved that Watanabe hadn't given him the assignment. And at the same time concerned that Watanabe was taking the Marine too lightly.

Irabu, who as a colonel of the Imperial Japanese Special Naval Landing Force, the equivalent of our Marines, was naturally outranked by Watanabe, so he shrugged off concern, saluted, and left. Since he was already in Peking for the day, he now made a call on a general of his own, the officer who'd earlier pushed the young colonel's career. This was Nagata, chief of intelligence for China, who did not outrank Watanabe but who, in this sort of matter, had considerable authority. Irabu told him the situation.

"Yes, I understand. Your continuing fixation with Captain Port. You don't like Watanabe's operation. I agree, Irabu. But it's his problem, not yours. Don't forget, Port is hardly even a sideshow. Pearl Harbor's a charnel house. The Philippines are rotten, decaying from within under that absurd MacArthur. Singapore is next. The Dutch can't hold. We're looking past Burma to India. With everything that's going on, one doesn't expend precious manpower on this fellow Port. The Imperial Army'll end up spread too thin if we go chasing rabbits."

"Port's no rabbit, General. But General Watanabe commands a division, thinks in terms of ordering out thousands of men at a time. This business calls for a small, fine-tuned operation."

"With you in command?" Nagata asked, smiling.

"Good God, no, General. The man was a friend. I'll leave it to others to catch Port before he gets into Russia."

"You think that's where he's going, Irabu?"

"It's where I'd go, General, if I were an escaping American and the Russians were my Allies."

"And if you did overtake him, would you bring him back?"

Irabu thought for a time. And then, quite solemnly, with no joy in it, the colonel said, "That would be best, General. But candidly, no, sir. To stop Billy Port, I believe one has to kill him."

"Well," General Nagata told Irabu, "don't waste time worrying about it. This is a big war. We'll get you out of drydock and onto something serious before long. It's not as if Port were important."

Irabu wisely held his tongue on that and General Nagata promised to keep his protégé informed.

Billy, naturally, had no knowledge of this, of discussions about him on the part of not one but two Japanese general officers, and of his friend Irabu's having declined to help run him down, if not to death. But despite all the things Port didn't know, he had already begun to think of his "impossible" task of getting out of China as becoming more "possible" every day they stayed alive. It was why he called in the radioman Sparks.

"Full moon's coming, Sparks. You going to be okay?"

"Yessir, Captain. Long as I don't do no drinking. If they got any bars in that there Hohhot where we're going, have the top keep an eye on me, Skipper. Maybe keep me confined to quarters for a few nights."

Port promised that he would. Not quite sure how you confined men "to quarters" when you were sleeping out nights under the stars.

That settled, there was the matter of making contact with his C.O., Colonel Sam Howard of the 4th Marines, fighting in the Philippines.

"I want to send the colonel a message, Sparks, nothing long. The Japs'll triangulate us to death if we give them time." Port knew that much about radio direction finders. "No hints where we are. Just a line or two for Colonel Sam from 'Billy from Boston.' Got it?"

"Yessir," Sparks said, without understanding a word of it, beyond the need to send quick and send short. With Rafter, Billy spelled it out, half embarrassed to admit neither he nor Colonel Howard had thought to arrange some sort of communications link (an actual code, of course, being exotically beyond Marine thinking in 1941).

"If we get to the border with Siberia, Top, and that'll take some doing, we then have a little problem. The Russkis are a suspicious people and there's been so much fighting with Japan over that border, they're touchy. I don't want to outflank the Japanese only to be shot by the Soviets, you know?"

"Yessir."

"It's why I'm trying to get word to Colonel Sam. If he knows what we're up to, maybe the State Department can square it with Moscow, diplomatic channels and all. So we can cross into Russia like 'The Saints Come Marching In.'"

"I get it, Skipper," Rafter said, though he didn't, not really. Even top soldiers were out of their depth when it came to "diplomatic channels."

So he and Port scribbled out a couple of simple messages, brief and in a homemade code, for Sparks to send. What they ended up with was: "Buying vodka for Boston saloons, Billy."

Port reread it, shaking his head. "Not very subtle. But then, is anyone listening?" Neither he nor Rafter knew what Colonel Howard was facing these days on Luzon, where the American-Filipino Army had begun to fall apart. The colonel might have more urgent priorities than damn-fool messages about "Boston saloons." With Christmas coming, Colonel Sam and what was left of the 4th Marines might be fighting for their lives.

As for Rafter, he decided on a tactful silence.

32

"The griffin is an imaginary creature," said the padre,
"half lion, half eagle."

By now Father Tertius Kean, Society of Jesus, had been thoroughly co-opted by the 4th Marines. Even to the extent of extending to him their familiar yet highly respectful title for any chaplain, that of "padre." To Marines it didn't matter if you were Catholic or Protestant; if you were a Marine chaplain, you were "padre." If there was a rabbi, or a mullah, serving Marines as chaplain, be assured he, too, would be "padre."

Father Kean was appreciative of honors bestowed.

Why was it, a Marine inquired of him that evening, as those not pulling guard duty sat around a small fire yarning over the day's single bottle of German beer (of which the "Holy Father," as Port christened him, also partook), that he had to get back to England? Especially with the German Blitz on and Londoners, or so Ed Murrow reported on CBS Radio, were sleeping in the Underground stations.

"Well, lads," said Father Kean, always ready for a tale, "it's because of the damned Blitz, you see, that I'm needed back there. For amid the nastiness Jerry is visiting upon us, the great British Museum has taken a knock or two, with several exhibits damaged. Including, and this must be held in complete confidence, that of 'the griffin . . .' "

Kean, teasingly, let the thought hang briefly in the air, as the young Marines leaned closer to the courtesy fire, and to the padre, all the better to warm themselves and to hear. Seeing this, Kean dropped his voice a register, and continued.

"You know, lads, that as well as being a priest, I am by training a scientist. A paleontologist, to put a point on it, the boy who goes out into the digs and comes up with the backbones and occasional rib of the odd dinosaur or wooly mammoth, and returns to write about it and put on slide shows for the ladies' clubs. And, of course, with the rare piece, to put the thing on public display at the British Museum."

Which had been the case with Father Kean's "griffin."

"What's that, Padre?"

Kean rubbed his hands with enormous relish. Like all specialists, he delighted in being asked about his field.

"In actuality," he began, "it doesn't exist, only in myth. The griffin is half eagle, half lion, a full-grown lion with powerful wings. Imagine the terror of ancient people even considering the possibility of such a beast."

"But you caught one, Padre?"

Mmmm, Father Kean thought, I may have to go a bit slower on this.

"No, lad. The griffin is an imaginary creature. What I found was the fossilized remains of something called a *Protoceratops,* a small, plant-eating dinosaur. What makes the *Protoceratops* unique is its shoulder blades that could, at first glance, be construed as vestigial wings. This fellow, quite probably, was what the ancients thought of as a half lion, half eagle, when they found its fossilized remains. A fully articulated *Protoceratops* is a rarity. And the specimen I found in 1922, pretty much all in one piece, preserved in a cave, its skeleton complete, in the Gobi Desert neighboring Siberia, is the very one that's on display today in London and which the bombs damaged. It's about eighty million years old, dating back to the Mesozoic."

"But there ain't no griffins these days, Padre?" a disappointed Marine persisted.

"No, sir. The Scythians may indeed have invented the whole notion of the griffin as the guardian of the gold in the mountains of the trans-Altai Gobi near Sinkiang. Either they created the myth out of skeletons they came across to keep people away from their treasure, or they really believed the monster existed. And that's the fossil I've got to patch up, like old Humpty Dumpty who fell off the wall."

"You'll be damned happy to get home, I guess," one Marine irreverently suggested. "And the hell out of China, Padre."

"For a visit, of course. But what better regions than these in which to die? Not boys like yourselves, but aging fossils like me, alongside the dinosaurs. And close by Everest, where monks chant, 'The jewel is in the lotus,' amid all the great religions, Buddhists and Confucians, and the Muslims to the west, and even a few Taoists and Animists, and Christians of every persuasion. Where do you get closer to God than here in old China, lads? Think on it."

It was at this propitious moment that Billy Port sought spiritual guidance.

"Padre, I'm asking Dr. Han to do another reconnaissance for me in Hohhot, looking out for Japanese. But this time, I'd like you to help."

"Don't know if I should, sir. It's a fine line, I grant you, but a priest doing military intelligence? I'm a Jesuit, you know, not a spy out of Hitchcock."

"No, Father. Not that. Our Marines, if they're there, went to Hohhot to save some American missionaries, place called Celestial Joy. I need to know where the missionaries are and if the Marines are still with them. I figure missionaries might talk more freely to another clergyman than to some soldier. That's all I need. The whereabouts of the Celestial Joy Mission and my squad of Marines."

"Then I'm your man, Captain . . ."

It gave the Marines an edge that Father Kean and, to a lesser extent, Dr. Han knew the territory. The country here, the people as well, was changing. Even on the fringes of the Gobi there were fewer trees, more dust, wind, the mountains with their snowcaps the only color against a monochromatic brown earth. Not sandy as in the Sahara but a chalky rock, almost a sort of driveway gravel back home. The people were different as well, not the true Chinese, the Han people, but distinctly Mongol in look, the cheekbones, the eyes, the browner skin. How swiftly the great country changed. The Chinese, farmers most of them, lived in clay houses built of the crude, local brick. While the Mongol nomads, who dominated west and northwest from here, lived in mobile felt yurts they erected and tore down in a matter of hours, or in tents called orgers. Less than two hundred miles from Peking and it wasn't really China anymore at all. Billy asked Dr. Han if she found the distinctions as startling as he did.

"Yes, go a few hundred miles anywhere in North China, and everything changes, the people, the culture, the architecture, the diet. From Korean to Manchu to Han to Mongol. Eventually to Muslim in the west and, in the north, Siberian. And, as well, the weather, the land, the crops, the religion, the language. Yet it is all one vast country. That's the wonder of this China of ours. And the mystery of it. You'll see it for yourself, so unlike the coastal plains where you were stationed."

Both the wonder, and the mystery, of her China and of Inner Mongolia to come, would have to wait.

That next day just east of the market town of Fengzhen, the first big snow caught them. They were rolling in daylight, secure that low cloud and flurries would keep the ranging spotters and strafing Zeroes grounded. The mountains here were hardly Alps but their maps showed passes as high as twenty-two hundred meters, about seven thousand feet, and their road climbing. So much so that when the flurries turned into a steady fall of big, wet flakes that stuck, and cut visibility, Port started thinking about bivouacking for the night. A farm, maybe even a small village. With the temperature hovering at freezing, the road still hadn't iced over, but he didn't like tackling a mountain pass with night coming.

"There's a market town shown on the map here, sir, this side of the pass, I recall as having an inn. Stayed there two or three years ago overnight," said Kean.

"I don't like it, Padre. Big place might have troops."

"Oh, not that big, Captain. Just where local farmers cart in their produce to sell in the market square. One narrow road through town from one side to the other might just take your trucks with a little to spare on either side."

The snow was getting deeper and Port decided to chance it, sending in one truck with a half-dozen men to scout around and Leung to translate. They were back in little over an hour.

"Looks okay, Skipper," Buffalo reported. "Not much of a place. But they got a hotel. And the people are pretty friendly. Mr. Leung says they think the United States invaded China and we're here to kick out the damned Japs and win the war."

When Federales and Leung confirmed, Billy took the risk. And when they drove into Fengzhen, Port saw what the Jesuit meant about the narrowness of the road. In fact, one Marine truck scraped a fender and lost its side mirror, annoying Jurkovich to no end. He hated to see a good vehicle damaged. It was near dark and with a foot of snow already on the ground when they were all inside the one inn and Leung had dipped into the exchequer to the satisfaction of an owner who had a little English.

"War be over yesterday now. You come, damn Japs go. Bastards."

"Well," Port told him, "it may take a little time."

"Sure, you got plenty more soldiers coming."

"I hope so." He didn't want these people getting in trouble with the occupying Japanese in their enthusiasm. Or giving them false hopes. But all through the late afternoon and early evening people kept coming to the ground-floor windows and the front door to gaze upon the Americans as conquering heroes.

There were only four tables in the small dining room but they squeezed in and with four Marines outside mounting guard, they took turns and made do. The meal ran heavily to rice, beans, and a choice of pungent sauces, and there was a good local beer. Rather saw to it that each man had a bottle with his meal, conserving the German lager from Tsingtao for the road. None of them had sat at a table to eat since the barracks at Peking.

"*Ma cher*," enthused Thibodeaux, "this is *très bon*."

"Nothing for you, Sparks," the first sergeant ruled. They were just a night past a full moon.

"No, Top. I understand."

It was also the first night since they left the Marine barracks that any of them had slept indoors, even if most of them had to unroll their sleeping bags on the floor.

In the morning the snow was ended but the sky was still low and gray, making enemy overflights unlikely. Dr. Han, Leung, and a couple of husky Marines went marketing in one truck while Laurent drove the Bentley with Federales and Buffalo east along their track of yesterday, taking back bearings to check on their rear.

They were soon back, a delighted Chinese boy of perhaps fifteen sitting on Buffalo's lap in the open convertible, grinning broadly.

"He says there's a Jap tank couple of miles east of here, Skipper."

A tank! Jesus, that was all they needed.

The "tank" with three Japanese crewmen and an accompanying truck with a dozen or so troops had stayed the night at the boy's family farm, sheltering as the Marines had done, from the snow. The boy said the talk was of chasing some Englishmen who were stirring up trouble in the countryside.

"Englishmen?" Port pulled out his pocket notebook and drew a few sketches on a blank page.

"Here, Rafter, show him this silhouette sketch. Is this what his 'tank' looks like? Or this? Leung, please ask him."

The boy didn't hesitate but quickly pointed.

"It's an armored car, then. Not a tank. Leung, ask him if it has wheels or tracks."

"He says wheels, Captain. He understands the difference."

"Okay, one armored car and a dozen troops. I don't want that armored car catching up to us on the open road. They've probably got a .50-caliber gun or even a cannon. They can stand off at a distance and shoot hell out of us. Our .30s can't match that."

"So we fight here in town, Skipper?"

"That's my thinking, Top, up as close to them as we can get; try to eliminate their edge in gunnery range. What about you, Federales?"

"I think so, too. Let them drive into town and hit them on the narrow piece of street where our trucks got stuck and that Jurkovich went loco over the busted mirror."

Yusopov, who seemed at times to be mute, spoke up now. And surprisingly.

"Captain, you have petrol. Thanks to the prudence of the first sergeant, you have empty beer bottles. I dislike even using the man's name, but the so-called Molotov cocktail proved an effective weapon in the hands of Soviet partisans overrun by the Nazis in those first months of the war. It's crude but simple. If you can get sufficiently close to this armored car, well . . ."

Billy was reseeing that narrow street coming into Fengzhen. Put a couple of men inside the houses and shops bordering the road, maybe on the second floor (no house in town could boast of a third!), they could get this armored car. And then take care of the accompanying infantry on their own terms.

"Okay, Top. You and Federales, get at it. Yusopov, do you know just how the partisans rig these 'cocktails'?"

"I do, sir. Fill the bottle with petrol, fashion a wick from a gas-soaked rag stuffed into the neck of the bottle, light it, and toss. If I can be of service . . ."

"You can, Prince." Within moments the Russian and Federales and four or five men were kneeling on the snowy ground next to a gasoline trailer siphoning gas to fill beer empties and fussing with greasy rags from Jurkovich's stock.

Federales, the nearest thing Billy had to a guerrilla fighter, seemed delighted at learning another dirty trick.

"Armored car and a truck coming, Skipper!" A Marine lookout gave the alert.

"Okay, let's go," Port cried out. Then, to Leung and Father Kean, "Try to keep the local people back. I don't want to kill anyone but Japanese."

"Yes, sir," Leung said, adding, "but they dearly wish to see you killing them."

"Sure," he said flatly. Then, more forcefully, "Dr. Han, stand by for casualties, please. Here in the hotel restaurant, you can clear the tables and work there."

"Yes, Captain." She didn't smile but there was no reluctance, nothing dating back to when they destroyed those enemy trucks.

Outside, in the freshly fallen snow there were kids and Port snarled, warning them off. The children giggled and retreated a few steps but no more. Everyone wanted to see these Americans fight the Japanese. Damn! He didn't want to get kids killed.

"Chase those kids, Buffalo! Scare 'em off!"

"Aye aye, sir."

It wasn't that cold, and with no wind, it was a nice morning and Fengzhen was pretty as postcards.

Well, that wouldn't last, Port knew. And it didn't. He and Buffalo found an open door and were through it and upstairs and opened a window giving out onto the narrow street.

In less time than anyone would have thought, Federales and Yusopov had prepared maybe twenty Molotovs, and had a relay of Marines carrying bottles up the stairs to the second floor of buildings on either side of the road. By now, the enemy armor was close enough they could hear it coming. Four Japanese infantrymen, riflemen, were out there in front, wary, moving slow, looking this way and that, the way good infantrymen walk who've been at war for a while.

"Don't anyone take out the riflemen," Port whispered to himself. If they did, they'd lose the armored car; it would be backing up and out of here too fast. Armor, even tanks, let the infantry clear the way. It was their tactic, their technique.

And Molotov cocktails? Credit Yusopov and the Russian partisans. Except that now, in Fengzhen, the U.S. Marines had lifted the idea and without paying royalties.

It was easy, really. They let the four riflemen enter the narrow main street and when they'd gotten thirty or forty yards past the windows where Port and his men crouched waiting, the armored car nosed into the street, rolling easily ahead, slightly slimmer than the American trucks that had scraped the walls on both sides, a small cannon and a big machine gun facing forward, jutting from the turret. The car was buttoned up, the topside hatch closed. Well, good for them, it limited the crew's vision to either side or ahead through the narrow observation slits.

Twenty yards into the road the car paused, considered the position, the possibilities, and then again moved ahead. It was at that moment that Billy Port snapped his Zippo lighter and held it to the wick before tossing the first beer bottle onto the turret of the enemy vehicle. All along the alleyway Chinese windows flew up and a half-dozen other bottles followed, full of gas, smoking at their mouths, to land with a smash atop the armored car. The driver, understandably alarmed, hit the accelerator and the heavily armed vehicle leaped ahead, slamming into one building in its haste, before bursting into flame and greasy smoke. It was then that they popped the hatch and one of the soldiers scrambled upward trying to climb out but Buffalo caught him with a burst from the Thompson gun. The man slumped back, twitched, and sagged, his uniform now aflame, jamming the escape hatch and trapping his crewmen inside.

The reek of the burning Japanese machine, and now of the burning men themselves, reached Port on the upper floor of a shabby shop in a Chinese town no one ever heard of.

And for an instant, as the screams died off, he remembered the stink of men burning to death in Nicaragua ten years before, roasted over open fires while they were still, at least for a time, and for too damned long a time, alive. Men who'd been his friends.

Seeing their armor destroyed, the Jap infantry ran. But not far. The Marines cut them down, the four out front and the six still behind in the truck, also burning now from a spare Molotov cocktail someone had left over.

33

*"There was about twenty bandits, drunk and carrying on,
and we flushed 'em."*

"FIRST Sergeant, casualty report?"

"No casualties, sir. Ten enemy infantry dead. One armored car destroyed and the crew cooked, sir."

"Well done, Top. Let's move 'em out."

The Americans left Fengzhen in a hurry. It wouldn't take long for the Japanese to realize an armored car had gone missing and Port wasn't hanging around to be questioned by homicide detectives. It was already bad news for the town and its inhabitants that Imperial soldiers had been killed there. Someone would pay for that. It wouldn't do anything for the townspeople for Port and his men to be caught. If the Marines ran, maybe the Japs wouldn't spend too much time burning the town or hanging Chinese, but get after the Americans.

They crossed the pass without stalling despite the deep snow and descended onto the flats leading to the Gobi. Once through the pass Billy dropped from his truck to ride with Dr. Han and Laurent in the Bentley, picking up a conversation broken off the previous day.

"And what do you know about the American mission in Hohhot?"

A distracted Dr. Han did not answer. Maybe she too was remembering the smell of the dead in the armored car. Then, shaking her head, "Sorry, Captain. You asked?"

She knew little beyond its name, Celestial Joy. Operated by an offbeat American Protestant sect. "Quite a small place, apparently, more an orphanage than anything else, I take it. But while I'm at the hospital seeing about the epidemic, perhaps Father Kean might nose about?"

"That's the idea. Even if confronting Protestants with Jesuits is dicey business, Doctor." He was essaying a small and not terribly funny witticism and the doctor seemed to appreciate the effort. No need to be depressed; not as fortunate as they'd been so far. What they'd pulled off with that armored car in Fengzhen was pretty good.

"Well, we'll try, Captain; you must not despair."

"No, I won't."

Billy wondered about this woman. She'd been machine-gunned, coped with epidemics, charmed the cynical Frenchman, run recon patrols for the Marine Corps, offered to patch up wounded Japs, and she was comforting *him?*

He thought of Natasha Rostov, also to be reckoned with. If she ever got to Boston, he wondered, would she actually charm his old man into a flyer on Russian vodka? She just might.

They halted early that afternoon in a snowy draw sheltered from the clearing skies by a few trees, slim and leafless and the only trees in sight. Nothing was coming up behind them, not that they could see. Ahead, nothing. But Hohhot was a much larger place than Fengzhen (there was even a small airport shown on the map) and Port wasn't about to risk his column without first sending a recon patrol. That was Dr. Han's role, abetted by the Jesuit, with Monsieur driving. From this distance, everything looked placid. But you never knew until you went in and took a look.

There were low hills to north and east, whitened now by yesterday's snow, and a road, dirt but oiled and graded, leading directly into Hohhot, with little traffic. The fields, too, were empty. But then, whatever crops they grew here were long since harvested and spring plowing was months ahead. There was finally a thin sun.

Port caught up on a little sleep and then, just before dusk, Buffalo wakened him. "Skipper, the Bentley's back. Not the doctor but the padre and Monsieur."

Port dashed cold water into his face and ran his fingers through his hair before putting on the helmet and the gun belt, the revolver bouncing on his hip, and trotted off to see Father Kean and the Frenchman. He could feel the cold coming as the weather cleared.

"Well?"

"Pas de Japs," Monsieur said. "No Japs."

"But a real epidemic," Father Kean put in. "Dr. Han's staying there overnight. There are a few dead children already and she and the nurse are busily inoculating. She'll report more fully in the morning."

"Okay. And the Marines? The missionaries?"

Father Kean gave Captain Port a look. "The mission's on a rise of ground three or four miles outside the town. I have precise coordinates and could easily guide you. The Marines are still there and well. Or so I'm told. The missionaries too. But there are complications."

"Oh?" Billy said. What the hell did that mean?

"They're an odd bunch."

"Odd?"

"Yes, a Pentecostal sect. Holy Rollers, in fact."

"Well," Port said sarcastically, having recognized the snobbery in the Jesuit's manner and tone, "that explains everything, doesn't it?"

"Yes," the priest said, prim and disapproving.

In the morning they followed the padre's directions, skirted the town on its right, and drove into a patchwork of low hills, until, on a bit of high ground, they saw the mission.

"They got a steeple, Captain," Buffalo said, "at home, churches always got steeples."

"I guess."

They had more than steeples. They had Marines.

"Advance and be recognized," called out a smart, but very young enlisted man with a tin hat, leggings, and a Springfield, all very proper, but with a homespun sort of three-quarter-length lambskin and fleece coat tightly belted with a standard-issue web gear gun belt. Federales in the first truck drove up to a sturdy timber barricade a few hundred yards this side of the famous steeple.

"Fourth Regiment Marines under command of Captain Port," Sergeant Federales announced. "Stand aside, amigo."

Marines don't really need passwords or documents, not when an NCO speaks with authority.

"Pass on," the boy said, lifting the heavy barrier rail and snapping off a very proper present-arms with the rifle as a salute.

Federales gave him an approving look (except for the fleece coat, on which he was withholding judgment). "That's well, Marine."

Celestial Joy, for this was it, stood atop a small, rounded hill with a dandy 360-degree prospect of the surrounding terrain. Good field of fire; nice position to defend. As Port drove in, he noted the white-washed stucco wall surrounding the mission compound, scorched here and there by fire and riddled with bullet holes, holed in places as well by larger caliber shells.

"Looks like they had theirselves a firefight, Skipper," Buffalo offered.

"That happens," Billy agreed.

Without further argument, the heavily timbered main gate swung open.

"I am Reverend Dr. Hopkins," said an old man, bright-eyed and sporting a long wool scarf in scarlet and a herringbone tweed overcoat that had a few years on it. At his side, a tall, plain, big-boned young woman in a shawl over a heavy cardigan sweater and gum boots. "My daughter, Miss Rose."

Billy tossed off a salute.

"I'm Captain Port, sir, ma'am. Here to be of service if we can. May I please see the Marine in charge?"

"Of course, of course," said the reverend. "The man's our savior. Sergeant Brydon. I'll have him sent for."

Brydon was swiftly there, snapping off a brisk salute and reporting himself by name, but togged out in the same sheepskin coat as the sentry. What the hell was this?

The Marines had been here since early September, Brydon said, and were billeted in what was once the one-room schoolhouse, with cots set up on the classroom floor, facing the blackboards. A Marine brewed coffee while Brydon briefed the captain, Rafter, and Federales.

"When the bandits hit and killed them people, sir, Harbin got a wake-up and hurry-up from Headquarters Marine Corps to send a patrol down here and clean 'em out and do whatever we could for the 'Rollers.' I mean, we ain't supposed to call 'em that. Nice folks, the reverend doc and Miss Rose especially. It took a week or so for news of the attack to get to the States and for orders to get back to us. Then a couple days to get here and by the time we did there was a dozen dead, some kids plus two males and one female, a Miss Janet, she was the lady got raped, sir, also the mission organist. Miss Rose and the reverend doc, only reason they escaped, they was down in Hohhot doing the marketing that day. There was only about twenty bandits and when we got here they was all drunk and carrying on, living it up here at the old Celestial Joy, and scaring hell out of the kiddies. But we flushed 'em out pretty quick. Killed eight or nine, put the others under arrest, and turned 'em over to the authorities in Hohhot."

He paused. "Sir, from what I seen so far of the authorities, them bandits made bail pretty quick and lit out for God knows where.

Maybe I should of kept them locked up here. But with only a dozen men myself, I figured, let the local precinct cops have the pleasure."

"You did right, Brydon," Port said. And meant it. Guarding prisoners was wasteful, took manpower.

But Brydon had more to say. Consulting a little notebook, a kind of log, the sergeant said, "Then early November, the ninth, the bandits come back. We beat 'em again but it was close this time because they wasn't drunk. I lost one man dead, one wounded, and four kids and an amah, that's a nurse, got killed. Now we hear talk at the market in Hohhot that they'll come onct more before hard winter. So I was real glad to see you come rolling up in your trucks, Captain. I knew the Corps wasn't just gonna forget us. These is fine people. They say Miss Janet was the best and nicest of all. They ain't Rollers exactly but they get into a frenzy when they pray and there's considerable thumping of Bibles. They're also big on hymns and the organ. All the little kids got to sing in English; it's a rule, 'Nearer My Guards to These' and such. All the grand old songs. And they're learning them the lingo at the same time as the tunes."

Port nodded, impressed by the sergeant's sincerity, but more interested in these Marines of Brydon's and of the other, still missing squad.

"Did Harbin or anyone contact you about a 'warning of war'?"

"Nossir, not in no definite way. I didn't have a radio but there was a phone in town and I called 'em back in Harbin a couple of times and they told me things was getting hairy and to stay in touch. Then, about ten days ago, when I called in, all I got on the phone at Harbin barracks was someone jabbering Jap. I didn't understand a word but it sure weren't no Marine. I got Reverend Hopkins to check with his Chinese pals in town and they told him there was rumors the war was on and we was in it. So I suppose our boys at Harbin barracks either scrammed outa there or got took. Plenty of Japs in Harbin, sir. It's one of their regimental HQs."

"Ten days ago" was about when Pearl was bombed.

"No sign of Japs here?"

"Nossir. Not a one since we come to town. I don't think they like coming this deep into Mongolia. No fighting here except with bandits."

Nor did Sergeant Brydon know the whereabouts of that second

flying squad of Marines sent out by Harbin in November. "They could be anywhere, Captain. I swear, I dunno. Travis, the squad leader, he ain't my idea of first team all-Chinaside Marine."

Rafter picked up on that. It wasn't like one Marine sergeant to rip another in front of an officer.

"What does that mean, Brydon? Speak out straight now."

"Well, Top, it ain't no secret. Back there last summer Travis he was up before a captain's mast. Caught him buying and smoking hashish with the locals. They got some pretty fancy opium dens up there in Harbin, good-looking women and good-smoking dope, and Travis couldn't resist the one or t'other. Busted him back from staff to buck sergeant and fined him a month's pay."

And then sent him off unsupervised on independent patrol into bandit country, Port thought. Whose brilliant inspiration was that?

Oh, yes, there was one more thing.

"Those sheepskin jackets you're wearing, Sergeant? What's that all about?"

"Yessir, well, we come down here without our issue overcoats, sir, 'cause the September weather weren't cold yet, and by mid-November, we damned near froze in our utilities. So we bought these locally. Warm as hell and short as they are, you move better than with long overcoats."

Brydon wasn't sure if he were being chewed out or just questioned. So he said, a bit tentatively, not knowing if he were bragging on these coats too much or if this captain really wanted to know, "Should I pass the word to the men about them, sir?"

"No," Port said amiably, "but where do you buy them? And have they got any more in stock?"

Rafter, even more than Federales a stickler about the uniform of the day, pursed his lips.

34

They hung a bedsheet and ran a movie. Stan and Ollie.
Or Shirley Temple.

PORT's command had been on its own ever since the war began, but Sergeant Brydon's squad, lacking radio, was almost totally out of touch. The Marines knew little more than the abandoned children of the orphanage. That evening as the troops relaxed in the compound of the Celestial Joy Mission, Lieutenant Cantillon briefed these newly attached Marines, and the American missionaries, on Pearl Harbor and its consequences. Port admired how articulate he was, how poised for his age.

Reverend Dr. Hopkins and Miss Rose sat transfixed, as if hearing of events in other galaxies. Hong Kong attacked, the Philippines invaded, the American fleet sunk, two famous British warships gone, Singapore threatened, the Dutch East Indies, the Germans at the gates of Moscow, America in the war against not only Japan but Germany and Italy.

These Marines of Brydon's were most particularly concerned with the fate of their pals, the 4th Marines who'd shipped out to Manila.

"So the Japs are there, too, Mr. Cantillon?"

"Yes, north Luzon and more lately south Luzon as well. Manila bombed. MacArthur's air force destroyed."

He gave them a fairly accurate but rather dramatic account of Marine heroics on Wake Island. That roused the boys, you can be sure.

Then one of Brydon's men, a southerner, asked a pertinent question: "How'd you all get through the Jap lines into Mongolia?"

As several of Port's men vied to tell war stories of the dead Japanese couriers, the trucks they'd shot up, of being strafed by Zeroes, the decapitation of General Sin, Top Sergeant Rafter silenced them with a growl. "Couple of skirmishes. Nothing big. We stayed cool and got lucky. Remember that, you people. That's how it goes when you serve under Captain William Port." Pause. "And me."

"Right, Top. Right," men murmured. Then Sergeant Brydon walked Rafter and the captain around the perimeter, showing where he had his three BARs placed, where they mounted guard duty. Port listened, approved, told him to add their light machine guns to the mix, pointed out where he wanted them placed, and asked if Brydon had anything else.

"I mentioned the talk in town, Captain, that them bandits really is coming back a third time. You see a fellow on a Mongol pony out there a ways off, maybe a mile, and he's watching us. The minute I put a fire team out there in his direction, he scoots. But they're out there. Like how these Gobi wolves keep their distance, circling a campfire."

In the late morning Monsieur and Dr. Han returned from the town.

"How was it?" Port asked. For the first time, Dr. Han looked tired.

"Better at the end than when we arrived. The serum and a few trained hands make all the difference. The hospital of Hohhot had two doctors, one quite elderly, a handful of nurses, no serum, and more than four hundred sick children. Hundreds more ill at home. We've seen most of them at least once. My nurse is holding the fort for the moment. And my orderly's arm is better so I may be able to send him in, too."

"And Monsieur?"

"Do not misjudge this man, Captain. I know your feelings about him, his selfishness. But I have seen him now at close range in a variety of situations. Do you know he was with us yesterday and today, scrubbing up and working in the wards, taking temperatures, changing bedsheets? Even wiping shit off their bottoms and being gentle about it. Which even the best nurses are not always, the job being what it is. Whatever he was competent to do, he tried to do."

Laurent playing nurse? Billy believed her. But still. And when later he encountered Monsieur with no one within earshot and asked how it had gone, the Frenchman shrugged.

"I killed very few patients. And those were going to die anyway."

"I hear you were pretty good."

"*Pas mal,*" he conceded, "*rien mas* . . . nothing more. Don't get the idea I enjoy this *merde,* Captain." Clearly, Laurent didn't want to be thought of as going soft.

To Billy Port, the Frenchman was incidental. They'd gotten this far and found the first dozen of the Harbin Marines. Fine. Now where was the other bunch led by a sergeant who smoked hashish? Should they invest the time and energy into looking for Travis? Or hang a right to Jining and pick up the provincial road due north through the Gobi and into Mongolia proper? From there, only three hundred miles to Mother Russia.

Which was how Port, a registered Republican who'd voted by absentee ballot for Wendell Willkie, had begun to think of the Soviet Union. If only Colonel Sam could get our State Department to put in the fix with the Kremlin. How great would it be for the last of the 4th Marines to drive into Russia with Prince Yusopov translating, Cossacks dancing, gypsy violins, caviar and vodka for all hands.

Then reality obtruded. It was still a long way from here to the Soviet Union. Sam Howard was up to his ass in Japs. And the commies in Siberia would probably shoot Yusopov on sight.

Port brought Brydon in for another chat. "We can't just loll around here, Top. There's an airfield, not much of a one, but where there's an airstrip there could be Japs flying in. The telephone exchange is working. We could have a battalion of enemy troops rolling up the road from Chajianling Gate any hour now. And if the reverend and Miss Rose want to come along, hell, we've already got a Jesuit and a woman doctor. Join the parade; it's a Radcliffe College mixer as it is. In the meantime, we don't have a clue where those other Marines are. And that bothers me. The rest doesn't, but that does."

"Sit down, Brydon," Rafter told the squad leader.

Port walked up and down the mission room they were using. But he didn't waste any time.

"I want to get out of Hohhot and quick. There are too many roads in and too few out. But I don't want to leave Mongolia without Travis. Now where the hell do you think Travis is? You've been circuit-riding out of Harbin for a couple years now. You know the man. *And* the country. Give me an educated guess."

"Captain, he's gotta be north of here. But beyond that, I don't have a clue. If he went back to Harbin then he's been took. The place's crawling with Japs."

Port shot a look at Rafter, a canny man with a look on his face.

"You, Top, any ideas?"

A moment passed and then the first sergeant said, "Yes, I do, sir. You, Brydon, just where in Mongolia is it they sell the best hashish?"

Miss Rose and the reverend doc were gracious hosts. That evening after the meal they trotted out the little kids to serenade the Marines. Brydon gave Rafter an aside.

"The kids like music and they got storybooks with colored pictures. And crayons for scribbling and coloring on blank paper. I don't think they're much for the holy rolling, the Chinese kids, I mean. Or the Bible reading. And they tell me Miss Janet, she was the lady got raped, she was more better on the organ than this one, Miss Rose."

Despite her marginal talent for the organ, Brydon was clearly intrigued by Miss Rose.

"Woman like that, ten thousand miles from home, taking care of little Chink and Mongol kids she never saw before. And not afraid of bandits, neither. You gotta admire a woman with spunk like that, Top."

Rafter just shook his head. He didn't believe in encouraging good sergeants to go bad, falling in love, getting married. In the Old Corps they didn't have women. Or orphans or Holy Rollers and Jesuit priests. Or people inventing new uniforms out of sheepskin. It was a good thing Chesty Puller sailed home before all this came down. He didn't believe Major Puller would have been happy. The Japs and bandits, you signed on for, but not all this.

Reverend Doc sketched out Celestial Joy's history. "We go back to the time of the Boxers. Then about eight years ago, Pearl Buck came by. She'd heard of our work, took notes, not for *The Good Earth* that they made the movie of, but another book she was writing. Took notes, spoke to individual orphans and staff, offered the children sweets. Quite a lady, unspoiled for all her fame."

The big excitement these days at Celestial Joy was the movies. "One Saturday night a month," said Reverend Doc, he got hold of a film. There was a sort of circuit, one missionary sending the can of film on to another, via a passing traveler in a motorcar or by Mongol courier on a pony. Miss Rose hung a bedsheet against a wall in the courtyard and the kids sat on the ground and watched. Laurel and Hardy were the favorites. Since the film was in English, and the children spoke either Mongolian or Chinese, some of the nuances slipped past. But Stan and Ollie did their best.

"I wish you could stay for the next film, Captain. It's due any day now. Rose runs the projector far more smoothly than I ever did. With very few breakdowns. Sometimes we get a Shirley Temple. The children love her. The blonde curls astonish them. I'd be honored if you could attend. Last spring we had *Wizard of Oz*. Oh, but that was splendid."

Reverend Doc had one final request, if the captain didn't mind.

"Let's have it, Reverend."

Well, sir, the children saw your machine guns. They wonder if they could see you shoot yours. They'd like to see it, Captain."

Billy Port considered saying he would take it under advisement. But the reverend seemed to want some sort of a thrown bone. So Billy, who understood schools and teachers, tossed one.

"Please tell the children that Sergeant Brydon's truck, having seen better days, will be cannibalized by Sergeant Jurkovich for spare parts we can use on the other four trucks. Your children may never have seen a GM truck cannibalized, Reverend. Believe me, firing machine guns is as nothing in comparison."

The missionary looked at him for a moment and then said, "Oh, yes, I'm sure, sir. The children will be thrilled."

All Port really wanted was to get out of here. He didn't like Hohhot; had a queasy feel about it. Brydon and his men were too comfortable here. When Marines got comfortable, you knew trouble was coming.

Reverend Dr. Hopkins just stared as the Marine officer walked away. Wondering if watching men tear a truck apart would entertain, or terrify, the little ones?

35

"Captain Port sees through the crap. He kills people. Remember that."

At first light Brydon woke the first sergeant.

"Top, that Mongol horseman. He's out there again. The fellow I told you about. I got the feeling he's sizing us up, that something's coming."

Rafter took it in. Then he grabbed Brydon physically by the arm. "I don't wake up the skipper without a reason. You tell him about this guy on the horse."

"Top, believe me. The guy's out there. But never this early. He . . ."

"Tell the captain. And no bullshit. Captain Port sees through the crap. He's got the Navy Cross. He kills people. Just remember that, Brydon."

"Top, I been a Marine eleven years now. I know about Billy Port. Him and Puller and what they done down there killing all them Haitians."

"It was Nicaragua where he killed people. Remember that. And then you just speak up smartly when he asks you something."

When they shook Billy awake, he took the 7×50 glasses.

"I see him. This the same man, Brydon?"

"Yessir. I know the way he sits a horse."

Port didn't waste time. "Top, get Federales here. Right now."

When the Mexican came up, Billy handed him the field glasses.

"I see him."

"Take the Bentley and a couple men. Drive out fast and bring him back before he gets out of range. I want him able to talk, savvy?"

Federales didn't say a word. Just nodded. General Pershing's name never came up.

This was just after dawn. By quarter to nine, the Marines were back. Port lighted a cigar, enjoying himself, and went out to meet them. It was times like this when all those damned field exercises back at Shanghai paid off. Small-unit tactics, that's what Marines wanted, not clicking your heels and rendering the rifle salute.

Sergeant Federales had the Mongol horseman tied up, strapped across the hood of the big car. The man had a bullet hole through his right arm. No one was doing anything about the bullet hole. The Bentley's hood was hot and he was strapped tight.

"We killed the horse. I don't want a lousy horse drifting back to tell no stories."

"Good," Port said, drawing on the cigar. By now he had Leung and Father Kean there with him.

"This boy, he talkative?" he asked Federales. "I want him talky."

"If he's smart, Skipper. But I don't get the lingo. You want me to work on him? Kick him on the arm where he's shot? That might signify."

"No, just keep the engine running. I want that hood hot. Leung?"

Buffalo, the Thompson gun cradled easily in his big hands but zeroed in on the prisoner, stood by on the alert, as Leung began the questioning. The majordomo tried their captive in Cantonese, Mandarin, and something else.

"No good, sir."

"Padre?"

The Jesuit said something in another language to their prisoner. The man spat in his face.

"Hey, shithead!" Buffalo snarled, raising the wooden stock of his Tommy gun.

Father Kean held up a hand, "No, no, my son. But if he striketh my other cheek, hit the little bastard."

"Aye aye, Padre."

The Jesuit resumed, and this time the prisoner, appreciating how much he had already gotten away with, jabbered a defiant response.

"Yes, he understands. His name is Lao. He says they're coming to kill us all. Rape the women, steal the children, take the Celestial Joy movie projector and the Laurel and Hardy film."

"Thank you, Father," Billy said, smiling. "They keep close watch, don't they?"

"They mentioned the organ. They want that too."

"Wouldn't you?" Billy asked. "Out here in the Gobi, how much organ music do you hear?"

The prisoner, at least part Mongol by the look of him and from what Father Kean took from his dialect, flexed his sore arm from time to time but otherwise remained stolid, unafraid, and unmoved.

"Leung, fetch my sword, please. Let's loosen this boy up a bit, Father."

"Well, I don't wish to be a party to . . ."

"Don't worry, Padre. I just want to scare him."

"Oh, well, then . . ."

"Please tell him we are going to cut off his hands and feet with my sword and then cook the rest of him in a large iron pot over a slow flame."

Billy gave the man a huge smile as he spoke.

"Oh, I say," the priest objected.

"Please, Father. Just tell him."

Kean did as he was bid, Jesuits having their pragmatic side. Port, warming to the task, tossed in a few variations on the theme having to do with the man's tongue, ears, and private parts, as Leung brought up his sword and handed it over.

"Sorry, Padre, but in Nicaragua we found that last threat especially persuasive."

"Yes, yes, quite," Kean said hurriedly, wishing he were anywhere but in the compound of Celestial Joy. It was what came of decent Catholic priests mingling with Holy Rollers.

The Mongol caved in swiftly after that.

"He says he was born and raised locally," Father Kean began, "in a village between Hohhot and Jining, was drafted into the Nationalist Army, but was homesick for Mongolia so he deserted. He joined the bandits last spring. Most of them are deserters as well but he's the only one from around here. So they use him as their scout. He's got a girlfriend in Hohhot and sneaks in to see her whenever he can."

"Does him credit," Billy said. "Local boy makes good."

There were about thirty men in this gang and they had, the prisoner said, somehow acquired what he called "a big gun."

"He says they will blow down the mission walls with this gun," Father Kean said.

"What do you think he's got, Brydon?" Port asked. "Any artillery around here that you know of?"

"Can't imagine, Captain. Can't be that big. Not and be transported around on ponies."

The plan, the prisoner Lao said, was to close up that night after sundown, occupy a small height of ground about a mile north of

Celestial Joy, and to open the bombardment with their "big gun" at dawn. Then, when the compound walls crumbled and Marine resistance was broken, to assault the mission in a gallant charge on their Mongol ponies and massacre everyone (well, perhaps not the women).

He looked quite pleased to be giving this account. "Okay, Rafter. Get Doc up here and patch up the fellow's arm. If he's told us the truth, he rates that much. If he hasn't, we can always get that iron pot on the boil."

Then he called Rafter, Federales, Brydon, and a few others to a council of war to discuss things the Marines were really going to do. Lieutenant Cantillon, by now routinely permitted to join the grown-ups, sat there, taking mental notes and wondering what it might be like to do this sort of thing for a living. And thinking how wise he'd been to avoid the draft by joining the Naval Reserve at Yale. And not these people.

36

Brydon's Marines, charging over the hill, firing and tossing grenades . . .

At dawn the first shell whistled over the Celestial Joy compound.

"Pretty nice for a ranging shot. They must have a gunner over there. Might have killed somebody," Rafter reported. "They got themselves a field gun. I figure 37mm tops. But a nice weapon." The first sergeant had an appreciation for professional gunnery, even from the competition.

"Okay," Port said. "Now let's give them the mortar."

Toward dusk Billy had them set up their 60mm mortar inside the mission compound with an observer on the stucco wall to direct fire. They'd fired three ranging shots, with the keen-eyed Federales tracking the hits in the gloom, and correcting up or down for range.

They'd lucked out on a mortarman. Rafter found one among Brydon's squad, a PFC Dixie. "He ain't Lou Diamond, Skipper," the top admitted with a requisite bow to the legendary Marine Corps mortarman. "But there's a good feel to him. He's got that mad glint in his eye all them fellows got."

It was true, Port thought. He never had known a good mortarman who wasn't slightly mad.

Dixie also got shells out there in a hurry. There were three in the air before the first one hit the enemy hilltop.

"Left twenty-five yards," Federales called out, a perfectionist, "fire for effect!" Mortarman Dixie made a quick adjustment and three more shells chugged out, one, two, three!

As they hit, the dust and clods of frozen earth were still settling from the first concentration.

"Give 'em three more and send Brydon in," Port ordered.

The final three mortar shells were on the way when Rafter fired a signal flare into the brightening morning sky over the compound wall. At which Sergeant Brydon and his squad burst out of a shallow draw on the south side of the bandit position to assault the little hilltop. Port's light machine guns, set up as a base of fire, at the same moment hit the bandits with overhead fire, the tracers easily visible in the smoke and brown dust hanging over the hill's crest.

It didn't take long.

Brydon's charging Marines swept over the hill, firing as they ran, then tossing grenades, until, after no more than a minute or two, the sergeant lifted his Springfield in triumph and called the "cease-fire."

The bandits never did fire a second shell from their "big gun."

Port and Buffalo and a fire team trotted out to cover the fifteen hundred yards to the enemy position while behind them in the compound, First Sergeant Rafter took down the time and the date and such data, as top soldiers do. When the count was complete, he got a crew to work swabbing out the mortar tube and securing the ammo. "Nice clean job, Dixie," he told the smiling mortarman.

"Thanks, First Sarn't." The gunner clearly enjoyed his work.

Brydon came down the captured enemy hill to meet Port, who had lighted a fresh cigar.

"Sir, I report the taking of this here hill, whatever it's called. Our casualties, one man slightly wounded but walking. Twenty-two dead bandits, most by mortar, the rest by machine gun and our small arms and grenades. About eight or ten of them got off, but some of them was hit for sure. We shot their ponies when they retreated. So if it please the captain, we could go after them, tracking by the blood. They're afoot in the Gobi, which ain't what you want to be out here in winter, Captain."

"No, I think we'll let them limp off. Good report, Sergeant."

And it was. It was Brydon's men who defended Celestial Joy in the first place and they deserved the honor of assaulting the enemy hill. Federales's squad could have done it. Maybe better. With Federales, Port didn't think eight or ten would have gotten off. But it was the right thing to give Brydon the job. A good Marine NCO appreciated recognition.

Billy did not mention or comment on the odd fact that there were no bandit wounded still on the hill. Only the dead. It was unlikely all the wounded had been carried off by their fellows but the captain didn't pursue the matter, not wishing to inhibit aggressiveness. Or get into another debate with Dr. Han.

Then, as the Marines came off the hill, several of them lugging three or four rifles, not wanting to leave anything that might call out to the fleeing bandits, drawing them back, along with the Marines came his highness, the Prince Yusopov, dusty but still elegant, a nice-looking Luger in his belt and three captured rifles slung, and a slightly embarrassed look on his face, a caught-playing-hooky look.

"Please don't blame the sergeant, Captain. He didn't know I was tagging along until we got to the top."

Port knew that was bullshit, that a patrol leader ought to know if he's got a stranger trailing him. But the prince was so modest, so apologetic, how could you get sore?

"You leave the sergeant to me, Prince. And the fighting, as well, please."

Yusopov lifted two hands in plaintive helplessness.

"It's been so long, Billy. I couldn't resist."

"And?"

"Gunsmoke smells the same in any language, Billy. By now, I should know that. But it's been a while."

Port nodded. He understood. But he was commanding a detachment of United States Marines in hostile country. This wasn't the company picnic. He couldn't let people, even one as battle-hardened as the prince, go off freelancing. He kept an iron grip on his Marines; it didn't pay to do less with civilians. Even Father Kean or Dr. Han. You don't coddle people, not if you command.

Rafter sent out a working party with a truck to retrieve the bandits' "big gun." It was indeed a 37mm field artillery piece, Czech-made by Skoda. Stolen from Chiang, most likely. Or sold by one of his officers. They did that in the Chinese Nationalist Army where an officer might miss the occasional payday and made up the difference with a little free enterprise.

"Rafter, stow this cannon somewhere safe. Along with its ammo. You never know, do you?"

"Nossir, not ever."

They were back at the compound before noon where Miss Rose and Reverend Doc had all the children, and their skeleton staff, lined up in tribute and to raise an enthusiastic, if a bit garbled, "Yip, yip, 'ooray!" Brydon's wounded man was looked at and then Rafter asked what they ought to do with the prisoner.

"Well, after a poor start, Lao provided good intelligence, Top. So I guess we can't parboil him after all."

"Nossir."

It was a grudging "nossir." You had the feeling Rafter didn't like releasing prisoners nor taking them along. But what the first sergeant thought was one thing; the Geneva Convention something else.

Port looked down at the ground for a bit.

"Okay, Top, let him go. Have Doc change the dressing, give him a meal, and kick his ass out of here. Let him walk into town. Maybe he really does have a girlfriend."

"Yessir."

That, too, was grudging. Putting the enemy on probation, assigning him to a parole officer, that was a helluva way to fight a war. PFC Jones, the "Loverboy," had a girl in Yokohoma, this Lao had a woman here, Jurkovich's missing driver was "shacked up" in Shanghai, Sergeant Brydon was making eyes at Miss Rose.

"Women!" the first sergeant said, regimentally indignant.

It snowed again that night, this one a fluffy, lighter snow. Too dry for a heavy fall. But it was snow and it was cold, by Reverend Doc's thermometer, down to fifteen degrees Farenheit, the coldest night yet. Which convinced Port, as hurried as he was, and fearing the Japanese behind him, to invest one more day here at Hohhot.

"We need cold-weather gear, Top. I know you don't like it. But you heard Father Kean. Forty below in January. Christmas is next week. Marine issue overcoats aren't going to get us to Siberia. Those sheepskin coats just might, if anything does. Hats as well, and mittens. Maybe fleece-lined boots if we can get some big enough for American feet. Unheated trucks, canvas-furled, tents but no stoves. And it's five hundred miles to Russia.

"We need that gear, Top. Take a fire team into town, plus Leung and the exchequer, plenty of cash money. Take Lieutenant Cantillon to try on for size, being our tallest man. Pick a little fellow, too, use him for sizing as well. Take Brydon. He knows who sells the stuff. Buy a dozen extra of everything in case we catch up with Hashish Travis. Empty out the stores. If Macy's runs out, try Gimbel's. See if they've got a Filenes."

That went right by the top, who had never been to Boston. Dr. Han had rested and was also on her way back into Hohhot.

"If we can, we're leaving tomorrow," Port told her. He was rough as a cob with his first sergeant, gentle with her.

"Will you be coming with us, Doctor?"

She shook her head.

"If only I could stay. I still have sick children. Their mothers can't cope. Their fathers? Who knows where they are? And the bad cold is coming. It will kill the virus. But it will also kill weakened children."

"What can I do, we do?"

"I understand you can't stay here. The Japanese. You have now twenty-five or thirty men. Maybe if you find this fellow Travis, another dozen. To lead them out of China, that would be a miracle."

Captain Port gave her a look, just slightly self-conscious.

He agreed to wait for her decision until the last possible hour. The illness here at Hohhot pulled at her; so did the very real possibility the epidemic might be even worse farther north, where Port was headed. And then, unexpectedly, that placid man, and by-the-book noncommissioned officer, Sergeant Brydon, threw him a curve.

37

"If the plane is big enough, take it. Grab the pilot. Kill the rest."

RAFTER, Cantillon, Brydon, and a fire team had just returned from town with an impressive stock of assorted sheepskin apparel, coats, hats, mittens and gloves, felt boots lined with fleece, the produce market scoured, and the local fuel depot emptied of diesel and gasoline into a fuel trailer and several drums, the whole business settled by Leung with Port's cash, when Brydon approached.

"Sir," Brydon began, somewhat tentative. More than tentative ...

"You got the cold-weather gear. Good."

"Thank you, Captain. But I got something else to say, sir."

"Go ahead," Port said, a bit impatient, wondering why Brydon hadn't taken it up with the first sergeant.

"I'd like to be detached from your command, sir, and stay here at Celestial Joy," Brydon said. "No way of telling when those bandits will be coming back. Miss Rose and old Reverend Doc and a couple of converts and forty kids. We can't just leave 'em here like this, can we?"

"Well ..."

Port was usually on top of things; this was something new.

"I mean," Brydon went on, "if it ain't bandits, Captain. It's the Japs. Or Chiang. This whole damned country ..."

When Billy didn't say anything, the sergeant went on. Unable, really, to stop.

"What I mean is, everyone hates everybody. Nice, gentle folk like this, they're just asking for it, sir."

"Yeah, I know."

"They need a fellow like me can handle a gun. If you could spare one of them BARs, Captain, and a dozen magazines. I could help them keep this place going 'til winter closes down the fighting. Then by next spring, maybe the U.S. will be back on top, and ..."

Billy Port cut him off.

"You're a good man, Brydon. Good NCO. But you've got to get something straight in your head. This country, I mean, our country, is at war with the Japanese. You and I are United States Marines. And we're trying to get out of China and somehow, somewhere, hook up with the regiment and get back in the war. Not chasing Mongolian bandits but as U.S. Marines against the Empire of Japan. The folks who bombed Pearl and are trying to take Wake and are killing Fourth Marines on Luzon. You get me, Sergeant?"

"Yessir, Captain."

Brydon wasn't really focused on what Port was saying. He was thinking of Miss Rose, how awful she played the organ, how much the children loved her. Port, of course, didn't know this or that the sergeant had in effect tuned him out.

"All right, then, Sergeant. You're dismissed." He expected Brydon to renew the argument but he didn't.

"Yessir."

Early that afternoon, the snow clouds gone, high in a dazzling blue sky, if to remind everyone of just whom they were fighting, they saw the enemy plane.

"Get down. No firing. Freeze!" Rafter called to the working parties in the mission compound. "Don't do a goddamned thing!"

The assumption, this was an observation plane. A Zero would have come in low and firing, strafing anything that moved. That's what Rafter thought, that's what Billy Port thought as well. Maybe a Zero would have been better. Not all fighters carried radios. A spotter plane surely would. And the Marines, from Port and the top soldier down to the lowliest private first class, knew it was radio that could bring the Japanese infantry after them, not just ten men and a careless armored car this time.

Now the plane had passed over, dropping in altitude on its approach, headed generally in the direction of Hohhot, four miles away. Perhaps this had nothing to do with the Americans. Maybe this was a civilian transport carrying a medical team to check out the whooping cough, or accountants to collect the taxes, incidentally inquiring of the local authorities if any crazy foreign devils had been seen. Except that there were no local authorities. Bandits ran this place, if anyone did. The Gobi and most of Mongolia, ever since war broke out with Japan, had been a no-man's-land with warlords in between.

And now a couple of dozen Marines out on a limb.

The plane (with the Rising Sun emblazoned on its wings and fuselage) was a small transport that landed gracefully at Hohhot Aerodrome, the aviation hub of the Gobi, fully equipped with a single dirt runway, one adobe hut, and a tattered windsock.

"By damn! They're landing here!" said a startled Marine. Even Reverend Doc was impressed. "We haven't seen a plane arrive here all month."

Port summoned his top people to talk over what it meant. By now the plane was down and had taxied to the 'dobe hut. In the clear, crisp Gobi air, four miles was nothing. From the height of Celestial Joy, even without field glasses, the Americans had a ringside seat. But before Billy could even begin to assess this new situation, his top soldier had an idea:

"Skipper," Rafter said, "do you think that there plane is big enough to carry twenty-five Marines the hell out of China?"

Billy stared at him.

"Well, now, Top, that is just about the most sensible question anyone's asked since we left Shanghai."

They broke out the 7×50 glasses to check out the plane more closely and passed them to Federales, keenest eyes in the outfit.

"What do you think?"

"I don't know much about planes. But at this distance, I don't think it looks that big, Skipper."

"Well?"

"Why don't I go into town and take a look?"

Then Billy Port thought of something.

"Have we got anyone that can fly a plane?"

Lieutenant Cantillon, seeing Port's eyes sweep toward him, hurriedly shook his head. He was getting to know how Marines think, if the guy can navigate a ship, maybe he can fly a plane.

"Nossir, not me," he said in some alarm.

Rafter interrupted this line of thinking. Quietly, to the captain, he said, "Of course we ain't yet got Travis and his people."

"I know." It was exasperating. If they really did find a plane to fly them out of China, should they scrap the opportunity? Just go on looking for another few Marines? Where and when do you cut your losses and go, just go?

"Well, let's get the plane first and then argue about it," Port said.

He sent Federales and a fire team. "Leung, they can't speak the language. Will you . . . ?"

"I'll accompany them, sir."

The truck rolled up. Federales waited his orders.

"Get the size of the plane. If it's big enough, find the Japs and grab the pilot. Kill the rest. Throw a guard around the plane, see that it's fueled, and signal me. If it's too small, or if the Japs see you, kill all of them. Then blow or burn the plane. First check to see if there's a working radio. We need to know if we've been spotted."

"Aye aye, sir."

Port racked his mind. Was there anything he hadn't thought of? Maybe sending in Federales with a combat patrol was a mistake, that they would be better off just lying doggo, up here, keeping an eye on the airstrip and the town. Do nothing, and let the Japs have a meal and fly out again, none the wiser.

No, some big mouth in town was sure to spin a tale of free-spending Americans window-shopping for Christmas, buying winter coats and trying on hats. A tale these particular Japanese could be relied upon to carry back to Peking or wherever they were based, to enlighten the Zeroes and the infantry. No, the Japs had to be killed and their plane either confiscated or destroyed.

It did not occur to Captain Port that such a violent act might bring down a terrible retribution on the American Mission of Celestial Joy and its enrollment of innocents.

38

Both Japanese pilots had been beaten to death by a murderous mob.

IT turned out that even had Port and his men done nothing, the enemy plane held the potential for tragedy.

The men from the Nakajima eight-passenger two-engined Army transport were civilians, bureaucrats dispatched from Harbin to assess supply and production data from provincial towns and small cities in North China, Manchuria, and Inner Mongolia, sleepy places like Hohhot. With winter coming on and airports shutting down by snow or fog, this might be the last visit until spring. And with the countryside at war, it was considered sensible to have officials travel by army planes piloted by military aviators.

Except that in this instance one of the two pilots, both of them wearing sidearms, had a favorite place he wanted to visit while they were in town. It was there after a third round of drinks, sake and chilled Asahi beer, were on the card, the pilot, who considered himself a hell of a fellow, thought he discerned impudence on the part of one of the bar's patrons.

The proprietor was summoned, demands made. The five bureaucrats attempted to calm the irate aviator. The "impudent" patron, a young Mongol, had objected to the pilot's swagger and ogling of his wife. Japanese officers do not take gladly to civilian criticism even from other Japanese. To be "insulted" in this manner by an inferior people was intolerable. Tensions swiftly escalated when the pilot ordered the bar owner to eject the "impudent" Mongol or have his establishment shut down by order of General Hata.

All this might have ended as just another barroom brawl except that once the first punch was thrown, the drunker pilot pulled his revolver.

Before the mischief was over, a half-dozen Mongols, including one woman, had been shot and both Japanese pilots and the five civilian bureaucrats had been beaten to death by a murderous mob. Fights broke out every Saturday night in bars around the world; this one would have consequences.

Sergeant Federales knew nothing about it. His men were at the airport, sheltering in their truck behind the adobe hut, while Leung, being an Asian and wearing civilian clothes, was sent out to case the Nakajima.

"Well," Federales asked when the Chinese returned, "not big enough for twenty-five men, is it?"

"No, Sergeant, the door was unlocked so I went inside. Eight seats only. And those close together without additional space. But they have a radio. I don't know how it functions. No weapons to be seen."

"Well then, Captain Port wants that there plane burned or blown and the crew shot, amigos. So we'll wait for the Japs to come back from lunch." He called out to the Marine stationed on the side of the tarmac nearest the road from town. "Anything?"

"Nothing, Sarge. No vehicles, no one walking. Some farmer out there way off in the field with an ox or a cow or something."

"You ain't no farm boy, are you? Don't know a cow from an ox," Federales said sourly.

"Hell, Sarge, I'm from Cleveland."

"Don't you sass me, you. Just keep watching."

"Aye aye."

It wasn't long before they heard the low, rising growl of the mob, punctuated now and again by a klaxon or a shot, coming toward them from the town. Being an NCO accustomed to making decisions, the Mexican made one now. To the driver, he snarled, "Crank her up. Trouble's coming. And this ain't our fight."

Federales knew nothing of the dead Japanese or the riot they'd ignited. Only that it was heading this way. Hundreds of people, making a lot of noise. Men returning to their own plane would have come quietly. Not like this.

The Marines cleared the airstrip before the first Mongols arrived. As Federales sped away, a mob burst out onto the tarmac in trucks and old cars and what looked like a scrapped school bus, plus some on ponies and one fellow atop a camel, all of them bound for the Japanese Nakajima with sticks and tools and a few ancient rifles and fowling shotguns.

The Marines pulled into a gully and halted to look back. The plane, the Nakajima transport they'd hoped might carry them safely out of China, was already on fire, but even as it burned, dozens of men tugged at the wings, trying to rip them off by sheer force, as others atop the wings jumped up and down in a heavy rhythm, intent on breaking them off even before the flames completely took hold.

"Well, we didn't get around to smashing the radio," one of Federales's men remarked. "But I guess it's okay."

Federales kept shut. He understood there was no way the plane's radio would survive all this. But the skipper told him to destroy it and he hadn't. And Captain Billy Port had a way of coming down hard on a man, 'specially an NCO with a few years on him. Well, too late now to brood on it.

He wondered where the Japs had disappeared. And what started the riot? When he asked Leung what he thought, the Chinese shrugged. He didn't know, either.

When the first explosion erupted on the tarmac, the men and boys on the wings leaped for their lives. It must have been one of the fuel tanks. The entire plane was burning and the crowd backed off to a safe distance, still jumping up and down and dancing, but staying clear of the flames and the exploding fuel. Federales could see the interior skeleton of the plane glowing red as the fabric burned away. Then another explosion as the rest of the fuel went up and suddenly there was nothing left of the aircraft but a twisted, skewed pile of blackened metal and the stench of burned rubber from the tires and insulated wiring and seats.

"All right," Sergeant Federales said quietly, "let's get out of here and smartly."

What they didn't know, none of them, was that a sense of dread had begun to come over the Mongols of Hohhot, recognizing that the murder of Japanese officials and destruction of a Japanese Army plane would not go unpunished. Most Mongols had observed such punishments meted out, and had no illusions about their severity or their inevitability.

It was a man called Lao, with an injured arm in a sling, a fellow of no standing nor reputation, who came up with the idea of a scapegoat. Suppose the Japanese could be convinced this atrocity had not been committed by respectful Mongols, but by foreigners. The savage American mercenaries they called "Marines," who cared only for killing and were camping out at Celestial Joy.

Mongol elders understood the logic of protecting Hohhot from Japanese vengeance by blaming someone else. The "someone else" in this instance would be innocent outsiders. What did that matter? That was what "foreign devils" were for, to be blamed. Wasn't that the way of the world?

Lao, preening, agreed that this was so. He was thinking, not only of his rough-handling at the hands of the Marines, but of the mission at Celestial Joy, which had defied him and his friends. Let the Japanese provide vengeance. Lao told himself he was truly a descendant of the great and wily Genghis Khan.

39

"On this occasion, we will have a movie: Laurel and Hardy in Saps at Sea.*"*

ON what would be the Marines' last night at Celestial Joy, Port asked Cantillon to give the troops and their missionary hosts a final briefing on the war.

The young naval officer was apologetic.

"Not much of a report, tonight, sir."

"Well, do your best, Mister. If you've got any useful accents, you might try them."

"Accents, Captain?" Cantillon was a literal sort who wanted to know precisely what he was being asked to do. He understood that Port had his reservations about him but he didn't want to be made a fool of.

"Well, you know, a German accent, a Japanese, a Brit, an Italian. I mean, if you feel you can carry it off. The troops enjoy being entertained."

"Yessir."

Being young and a Yale man, Cantillon gave it an energetic try.

His first item was typical. "December nineteenth and twentieth on Hong Kong, British counterattacks are unsuccessful. Bad luck, old chap."

"Hitler removes Brauchitsch as commander in chief of the German Army. 'I can do it better myself,' says the Fuhrer. *Jawohl! You schweinehund.*" This he accompanied with a very serviceable Nazi salute.

"Hey, Lieutenant, that's pretty good," a Marine called out.

"Danke," said Cantillon, getting into the spirit of the thing.

"Bitte," shouted someone with a little German.

"Back home, the Selective Service Act is amended. As of now, all American men twenty through forty-four years of age are liable to be drafted."

"That mean we gotta go in the Army, Mr. Cantillon?"

Cantillon assumed a stern pose. "There is that possibility."

Considerable booing. Then, less buoyantly, "More Japanese landings in the Philippines. The latest, on Mindanao."

As his audience fell silent, Cantillon roused them once more. "In Germany, Herr Doktor Goebbels urged civilians to donate winter clothes to the German Army in Russia."

"Hey, send 'em some sheepskins."

There was a brief final item that Cantillon played straight. "The internment program of Japanese-American civilians in California was marred by violence. As the first internees arrived, they were stoned by onlookers. National Guard troops restored order."

Reverend Dr. Hopkins had permitted the children to stay up late and Miss Rose played the organ while the children sang. They were off-key and Miss Rose didn't help much. Though you wouldn't know it to look at Sergeant Brydon. Then, to an enormous cheer, Reverend Doc announced, "On this very special occasion, we will also have a movie. Laurel and Hardy in *Saps at Sea*."

As the film ran Dr. Han beckoned Billy Port.

"Captain, the epidemic here seems under control. If you agree, I will continue north with your column. Is it agreeable that I retain use of Monsieur Laurent and your Bentley?"

"Of course. Only both of you keep watching for air. There are very few Bentleys in the Gobi and the Japanese aren't stupid. That plane today gave me a scare."

"No, Captain. You may have been surprised. Or worried. But if you permit me to say, you don't 'scare.'"

In the morning, much to First Sergeant Rafter's annoyance, the Marines fell out for the first time in their sheepskins, self-conscious, looking down at themselves. Port took the trouble to get a thermometer reading from Father Kean that might justify this highly irregular uniform of the day.

"Twelve degrees Farenheit, Captain. But a fine, overcast day."

"Thank you, Padre."

He had Rafter announce the temperature, just to rub it in a bit. You didn't want to do it too often, but a captain had the right to needle a top soldier on occasion.

40

A place known for the beauty of its women, the quality of its hashish...

AFTER Jining on a north by northwest course along the track ("road" being too grand a word) for Bayan Har and then Sonid Yougi, they would be in the true Gobi Desert, no more than one hundred miles from the border of Outer Mongolia itself.

"From here on, Padre, we're very much in your hands," Captain Port told the priest. On their first night out of Hohhot (a low ceiling permitted them to travel in daylight and now darkness halted them just south of Bayan Har), Billy asked Kean to give the troops an appreciation of what lay ahead.

"A brief lecture to the lads? Of course, Captain. Show me the Jesuit who won't climb into a pulpit."

Rafter posted perimeter sentries and gathered the rest of the party around several small fires cobbled out of brush and ignited with a liberal dose of gasoline. The men were in their sheepskins and glad of it. Before Kean began to speak, he'd sneaked a look at his thermometer.

Nine degrees above zero at eight P.M. with a wind rising.

"Well, lads, here we are in the old Gobi. The name itself is Mongolian for 'place of no water.' And it is one of the emptiest places in the world, fewer than three people per square mile. The desert itself stretches in a sort of arc, a thousand miles in length and three hundred to six hundred miles in width, across North China and Mongolia to Sinkiang in the west. And unlike what you may have seen in the cinema, films like *Beau Geste,* most of the Gobi isn't a sand desert but chalky rock. For vast distances, in fact, you can drive an auto with little difficulty despite the lack of actual roads. I've been the length and breadth of it. The people, nomads mainly, are quite friendly. All but the bandits and renegade soldiery. And with temperatures falling, we'd be well advised to make a few friends. Their nomadic tents, felt affairs called yurts, are very cozy, and if we are offered hospitality, Captain, we'll be fortunate. Some of the smells may be a bit off-putting, yak butter used as hair dressing, for example, and dried cattle droppings burnt as fuel, but one becomes accustomed.

"There are several mountain ranges, nothing like the Himalaya, or the Greater Khingan Range behind us to the east; much more in the modest range of five to seven thousand feet. We'll get some snow. The area of the Gobi we're crossing is called the Ala Shan."

Marines like a good yarn but aren't too fond of lectures. And now one of Federales's BAR men called out: "They got any Japs up there in them Shans and yurts, Padre?"

"Generally, no. The Japanese sphere of influence is from Peking east. But in wartime, one never knows."

Port took over at that point.

"Depending on the situation and the personality of the commanding officer, the Japs can be expected anywhere. They patrol west out of command posts such as Harbin, where Sergeant Brydon was stationed. Brydon, you agree on that?"

"Yessir, Captain. Weeks would go by with no Jap patrols toward Mongolia. Then all of a sudden, they'd be going out every few days. Like us, mostly in trucks with a few sidecar motorcycles. And maybe an observation plane."

"Padre?"

"Just winding up, Captain. You won't find much petrol out here. The nomads have their Mongol ponies and some Bactrian camels, those are the fellows with the two humps. There are almost no rivers but with a rainfall of eight inches per annum, there are underground streams you can reach by shallow drilling. Useful to remember that if you get thirsty. Could save your life."

Rafter, a practical sort, heard that and wondered: How in hell do you know where to drill, Padre?

Port thought he was finished when the old priest said, "Most of the region dates to the Cenozoic Era but the central and northern Gobi, where you find absolutely the best dinosaurs, preserved by the extreme aridity, dates back to the Mesozoic. And, I'm concluding now, Captain Port, I assure you, the areas of greatest cultural interest are the Buddhist cave-temples near Tun-huang. We can thank the geographer Aurel Stein for his discovery in 1907 of the famous Cave of the Thousand Buddhas. If you have the leisure, sir, I commend the frescoes, startling in their freshness."

Billy Port was aware of the crank in most of us, so he shut up Father Kean by promising to keep the famous cave in mind.

It was just a few days short of Christmas and for the Marines a bleak time, as Lieutenant Cantillon brought them the bad news via Sparks's radio:

"Two Jap aircraft carriers, the *Hiryu* and *Soryu,* joined the battle for Wake Island on December twenty-first. Just before midnight on the twenty-second, a Japanese landing force succeeded in reaching and crossing the beaches. Although the garrison continued to fight, on December twenty-third they were compelled to surrender."

Wake Island gone!

And what was that, "compelled to surrender"? How many of them were left by then? No one knew, no one said.

But to Port's Marines, every bit as isolated as the Wake Island garrison, surrounded not by the Pacific but by Asia, this was devastating. First, the 4th Marine surrender at Peking and Tientsin. Then, word that the Japs had flanked the Marines on Luzon. Now the fall of Wake Island.

As one of Federales's fire-team leaders put it, "You expect the Limeys to lose Hong Kong and the swabbies to get surprised at Pearl and MacArthur to get his ass kicked. But to have United States Marines wave the white flag, Christ! I never thought we'd see that, boys."

It took Federales, the Mexican accent never more prominent, to cut that kind of talk short.

"You shut your damned face about stuff like that, hombre. We ain't got no white flags here in Mongolia. You loco, or something? What we got is three machine guns and Captain Port and the best top soldier in the regiment. And we got my squad and another squad and a trail behind us of dead Japs and bandidos and warlords. And we're out here on the famous Gobi Desert, swaggering around like we owned the sonovabitch. So let's have no more talk about no damned surrenders!"

"Okay, Sarn't. I ain't saying no more."

"You better not, amigo. Or I run your damn ass up to the captain."

With NCOs like Federales around, Port knew, an officer didn't have to make flag-waving speeches. It went down better when it came from the sergeant, anyway. Unless, maybe, you were Chesty Puller.

Even Rafter, still sulky about these new sheepskin uniforms, thought Federales did just fine. And, he had to admit, the sheepskin was a lot warmer than the issue overcoats. And didn't weigh you down so much or trip a man up.

On Christmas Eve, they bunked in for the first time with nomads, sharing their yurts, with the farm boys among the Marines enjoying being around livestock, the sheep, goats, ponies, camels, and the large-horned cattle the Mongols herded along from one waterhole to the next. And a good thing, too, since that night the glass fell to zero Farenheit.

"It'll go lower, Captain," Father Kean promised cheerfully.

"I guess," Billy agreed. The Jesuit had been right about two things: the yurts were warm, and they stunk. At Billy's orders Leung paid out the coins to the nomad leader. It must have been sufficient because the man, closemouthed until now, babbled his gratitude.

"Sir," Leung reported, "he says he has seen such coinage before."

"Sure," Port agreed. Throughout much of the Orient, American dollars were recognized, even prized tender.

"From other men in green uniforms such as yours, sir."

"Other Marines? When? Where?"

Leung and the nomad spoke at length, with Father Kean summoned to translate and belatedly joining in.

"He says four weeks ago. A red-haired officer and twelve or fifteen men, heavily armed. They passed through and spent a night with his family and their herds. They were accompanied by some Mongol horsemen our friend here did not like. Men with a bad reputation in the region."

"And they were with the red-haired Marine?"

"Yes, sir."

Port called Sergeant Brydon. "What color hair does Sergeant Travis have?"

Brydon stared in confusion.

"Well, sir, bright red, close-cropped but definitely red."

With Kean interpreting, Port questioned the nomad more closely, unfolding a map, but to little effect. The man knew his terrain but could not make the adjustment from three-dimensional country to two-dimensional paper. As far as Leung and Port could make out from the nomad's description, and the pace at which his herd moved, they'd encountered Travis near Naran Bulag, about 150 miles north of Jining, quite close to the border of Outer Mongolia.

"You know the place, Padre?"

"Not well, but the general area, yes. Done a good dig not far off. Found some splendidly fossilized dinosaur eggs."

"Ask the man if Travis was settling into winter quarters. Or on the move somewhere else?"

Port was accustomed to giving orders and having them obeyed. And now, with the first suggestion Travis and his men might be in reach, he quite forgot he was addressing a Jesuit priest and not one of his enlisted men.

"Quickly, Padre. There's no time to waste. I've been ordered to bring that man and his detachment back."

Kean ran through a catechism. At the end of which he turned to Billy Port and smiled.

"He thinks they were headed for Baruun Urt. That they would winter there."

"Baruun what?"

"Baruun Urt. Another market town. Caravans pause there for supplies. It is a place known for the beauty of its young women. And, or so this fellow says, the availability of good-quality hashish."

Port didn't like it. Women and drugs, the place sounded too popular for his tastes. "We want to give big cities a pass, Padre. If a town has a lamppost, we keep right on going, take a detour."

"These market towns aren't much, Captain. Primitive places, really. The nomads have a way of exaggerating when it comes to the beauty of their women, the grandeur of their cities. I wouldn't guide you into anything perilous, sir."

"I'm sure not, Padre. But I'm paid to ask."

When they left the nomads the next morning, Port shook the headman's hand and Leung paid out a bonus. For information above and beyond the call, about a redheaded rogue sergeant called Travis.

But when they'd saddled up and were about to move, Rafter came up, visibly shaken.

"That Brydon, Skipper. He lit out in the night. Stole a Mongol pony. Left a note for you. I read it. Didn't want no delay."

"It's Celestial Joy, isn't it?"

"Yessir. The mission and that Holy Roller woman, Miss Rose. That's where Sergeant Brydon's went on us."

Port nodded. "Who's his senior corporal?"

"Fella name of Young, Skipper. I'll go find him." Rafter started to go for Young but stopped and turned, his face hard.

"That Brydon, I could send Federales after him. Bring him back hog-tied across the hood of a truck, under arrest for desertion in the face of the enemy."

"No, Top. Just find Young and tell him he's got Brydon's squad. And if Young does the job, he'll be earning another stripe."

"Aye aye, sir."

41

On Luzon MacArthur realigned his forces across the neck of Bataan.

THEY no longer traveled with canvas furled on the trucks or the top down on the Bentley. Port grumbled but it was just too cold, the men risking frostbite. Christmas Day they made only ten miles. One of the trucks broke down and in temperatures near zero the master mechanic, Jurkovich, worked bare-handed to get it moving again. They still had some built-in redundancy in trucks but if they found Travis, they'd need the capacity, and this was no time to start leaving wheels behind. You never knew when there'd be another truck breaking down. Or being shot up in a firefight.

"Good man, Jurkovich. Walter Reuther and the Ford Motor Company both can be proud of you," Port told him, noticing how the blood from skinned knuckles on his right hand had already coagulated, frozen brown against the skin.

"Hell with that, Captain. Just let me thaw my fingers before they start dropping off one by one."

"Take care of him, Rafter," Port whispered. "Get Doc to patch him up. We don't want to lose this fellow." Hard to accept, but an officer knew that in a pinch there were men that were expendable. And then there were men like Jurkovich. Like Sparks. Like Doc . . .

"Aye aye, sir."

For all their woes, Port was feeling a little better about getting this far and eluding the Japs.

Its enemies tended to think of the Japanese Imperial Army as this enormous monolith, irresistible and ferocious. The fact was, and this realization was coming to Billy Port, that as 1941 was ending, the Japanese in China were spread thin. The men who captured Hong Kong, drove relentlessly down the Malay Peninsula to menace the great British bastion of Singapore, who cornered MacArthur on Luzon, seized Thailand and crossed into Burma and eastern India, rolled up the Dutch on Java, who stormed and captured Wake, those troops didn't materialize out of nothing.

No, they were drawn from the North China garrisons and even from General Hata's main field army.

The Imperial Forces, and as a soldier Port had to admire them, had taken on themselves a mighty task over one-seventh of the world's land mass. The wonder was, this smallish island people with few natural resources, but with their Samurai warrior tradition, was not only waging a sprawling, complex war but they were winning it.

Though in places like Mongolia, the widening war left them undermanned. Port recognized this, counted on it. So that, in a way, even Cantillon's nightly news with its litany of Jap victories and Allied disasters was encouraging. The farther the Japanese advanced in Southeast Asia and the Indian Ocean and the Pacific, the better it was for a detachment of American Marines attempting to slip through the enemy net and get away.

That night, being Christmas, they passed out the last of the beer from Tsingtao (none to Sparks), thawing it first so that it could be swallowed and not just chewed. They built up the fires and sat on blankets on the ground. Port, who still had a supply, passed out cigars to men who said they really smoked cigars, not to boys who'd "sure like to try one, sir."

"No chance of that, lad. Cigars like this are serious business. They're not Lucky Strikes." He lighted a cigar of his own but, though he thought about it, hadn't yet gotten into the Château Latour '24. The wine really ought to wait until Siberia, if and when. And then, being Captain Port, he made a quick tour of the sentry posts, wishing each man a good Christmas and shaking hands. Only one sentry took him up on the cigar but they all seemed pleased that he'd come out into the cold to be with them. Good company grade officers did that; they walked the perimeter.

Cantillon, who had a voice, asked Billy if he could arrange a sort of Christmas musicale.

"A few popular songs, perhaps. The usual hymns, sir. Most of the men probably know the words. It'd be nice. And Father Kean could give a blessing."

"Good idea, Mr. Cantillon," Billy told him, but first, Port had Cantillon read the news, get the ugly stuff out of the way. Then they could sing "Jingle Bells" and "Home on the Range" or whatever else they had on the program.

"Okay, now listen up," the top sergeant growled, when the detachment had gathered, bundled against the cold and closing in on the small fires. Port thought he felt a few lazy snowflakes drifting down, lightly touching his face, but in the dark he couldn't be sure. Well, Christmas . . .

It sneaked up on you, didn't it? There ought to be some snow, shouldn't there? Cantillon began his report.

"On Luzon General MacArthur orders a realignment of forces across the neck of something called the Bataan Peninsula."

"Is that a retreat or an attack, Lieutenant?" someone called.

"Not sure. We'll get back to you on that in the late editions."

"Ha!" There were cynics in the Corps.

"On Hong Kong, the British surrendered."

Silence. The Marines enjoyed poking fun at the Limeys. But most of them knew Hong Kong as a favorite liberty port, remembered the tall buildings, the towering Peak where the rich lived, and grandly, the bustling harbor, the race track, the bars and restaurants, the good tailor shops where you could get a custom-made uniform for ten or twelve bucks. And the women, the beautiful Chinese and Eurasians, the well-dressed Englishwomen passing, cool lovelies pretending they didn't see the young Marines. But seeing them. To have a great city like Hong Kong, Brit for so long, fall to the damned Japs? And in a matter of weeks?

"In North Africa, the German and Italian retreat continues and the Allies take Benghazi."

"On the Eastern Front, one German Army commanded by General Guderian is down to forty tanks."

"I thought we was the 'eastern front,' Mr. Cantillon," one of Federales's wiseass corporals suggested. "We're east of Russia, ain't we?"

"Good point, Corporal. We'll keep that in mind. And now, a very Merry Christmas to all, courtesy of the United States Navy and the Pacific Fleet."

That drew a hoot. There wasn't that much of a Pacific Fleet left, was there? But then, in a hastily arranged chorus, led by Father Kean, Dr. Han, Prince Yusopov, Monsieur, Leung, and Cantillon, they sang a medley of Christmas tunes, "dedicated," said the Jesuit, "to the United States Marine Corps, in which we, at least temporarily, have the privilege and honor of serving."

Considerable cheers.

Except for young Cantillon, Dr. Han, and the Cajun Thibodeaux, who also had a voice, the music wasn't very good. But what it lacked in quality was made up for in enthusiasm, especially when the Marines joined in.

Monsieur was something of a revelation, impulsively breaking into popular French songs Port recalled from the Folies Bergère of a few years back. And he could carry a tune, winning applause and a "bravo!" from placid Dr. Han.

"A regular Maurice Chevalier you are," Billy told Laurent in an aside, meaning it as a compliment. Only to be surprised by the race driver's snarled anger.

"*Merde, mon capitaine.* You know that bastard still sings in Paris. At all the big music halls, entertaining the Germans and their whores."

"Not Chevalier," Port said.

"I assure you, sir. But then," this less aggrieved, thoughtful, "if the Boche permitted a running of the twenty-four hours of Le Mans, would I not be there, behind the wheel of a racing car? Would not the Parisians, and especially the Parisiennes, come out to cheer? We French, we adapt, we accommodate. When you are invaded every twenty-five years, you learn to live with defeat. Oh, yes, we learn well."

Father Kean, not to be outdone by a Froggie, and a bit low about Hong Kong, offered a rousing chorus of "Soldiers of the King Are We," and Cantillon recalled Yale with a fine "Whiffenpoof Song." Dr. Han, to a chorus of demands, stood shyly to sing a small, sweet song of her childhood, and then blushed away compliments, as Sergeant Federales, having enjoyed his beer, performed a very nice "Cielito Lindo," with numerous choruses of "Ay, ay, ya, ya," in which the Marines, especially his own squad, loyally joined in.

Then, on a quieter note, Father Kean led them in the Lord's Prayer. But not before a brief sermon, reminding them that whatever church they attended at home, it was in a chill desert land very much like this one, that Christ was born, while nearby shepherds watched over their flocks of sheep and goats and, yes, their camels.

The Marines stood. And most of them prayed. Including Billy Port, surprising himself a bit.

And then, a cappella and without notice, tall Mr. Cantillon took center stage unasked, stood there all alone in the campfires' ring of light and, quietly at first, and then soaring in power and depth sang:

"Silent Night, Holy Night,
All is calm, All is bright.
Round yon Virgin, Mother and Child,
Holy Infant, so tender and mild.
Sleep in heavenly peace, Sleep in heavenly peace."

When it was ended there was a hush. And Father Kean, standing near Port in the flickering light, said, but only to Billy: "In France in 1914, I was chaplain to a battalion of the Irish Guards, and on Christmas Eve, or Christmas night, I forget which, the boyos in our trenches sang that song, feeling sorry for themselves, I suppose, being away from home and at risk. And the final chorus had just faded away in the dark when from the other trenches, in the original German, those fellows over there responded, the same hymn, the same tune, but with the words in German.

"And you had the feeling that perhaps, just perhaps, both sides would come to their senses and call off the whole bloody massacre. And, of course, we didn't. Neither Jerry nor ourselves. Too stubborn, too proud, too . . . I don't know. And the war went on for three more Christmases with God knows how many boys dead on both sides in the trenches . . ."

Impulsively, Port took his hand and shook it.

"A good Christmas to you, Father."

"Thank you, Captain. And a happy Christmas to you."

How many Christmases would this new war last? the priest wondered, but did not say.

42

They saw their first wolf pack. Tough customers for a man afoot.

Boxing Day, December 26. The padre, recovered from the fall of Hong Kong, took it upon himself to explain to the Americans just what, and why, Boxing Day was. But this Boxing Day would also signal a change in their luck. The Japanese, thought to have been left behind, would shortly reappear, very much onstage.

Port was more interested in Father Kean's knowledge of the neighborhood than the origins of Boxing Day.

"So we're now officially in Mongolia," Billy remarked the next day as they drove, in a chill sun, north by northwest through brown rolling uplands (no recent snows here) covered with closely cropped grass, grazed down to the roots by the goats and sheep, he supposed. Father Kean and Yusopov were riding with him in Billy's truck, both men good conversationalists but when Captain Port's mind was on other matters, knowing enough to shut up.

So the Jesuit limited himself to answering questions.

"The genuine article, Captain Port. Han China is behind us and ahead lies the true Mongolia. As large in square miles as Western Europe, the Gobi alone the size of France. I make it from here five hundred or so miles to Siberia. All of it across Mongol land on both sides of an invisible border dividing Chinese from Russian-influenced Mongolia, Inner from Outer. A large and empty place with nothing of much use but wild ponies and nomads, killing cold and a cutting wind, and God help the man without a yurt in which to hold back the night. A stark and terrible place in winter."

"But beautiful, as well," put in the prince, the steppes of whose native Russia had many of those shared characteristics.

"Any hunting up here, Padre? We could use some fresh meat."

"Surprisingly so, Captain, considering how arid it is. Not that all the local fauna is fodder for the pot, but they're out there. Mongol tiger, brown bear, hibernating in all likelihood. Some leopard, the rare snow leopard among them. Gazelles, long-legged rats, musk ox. Wild upland goats. Wolves. And of course the famous Mongol ponies. The nomads rope and break them to the saddle. Legend says it was on just such ponies that Genghis Khan conquered half of Asia and Europe as far west as the Dnieper. Wait 'til you see them in their galloping herds, sir. Thick-necked, stocky, more like zebra without the stripes than the horses we know in England or your Wild West."

The Jesuit wasn't just talking for effect. Before the morning was half gone they saw their first wolf pack, big, heavy-bellied, useful-looking brutes, eight or nine of them grouped up, loping easily along in the rear of the column, maybe two hundred yards back, no farther, cutting across their track, perhaps hoping for a straggler. They'd be tough customers for a man afoot.

Prince Yusopov was a hunter, and recalled with zest, even after all the years, the great hunts of his youth on the family estates near Sverdlovsk, the Pripet Marshes with their flights of duck and goose, the pine and spruce forests on the Polish border. He'd read Turgenev as a boy and had reread his hunting tales again and again in exile. "Billy, I've fetched along a couple of good, light hunting rifles, Mann-lichers. And a 20-gauge shotgun for birdshooting. If we come up on any game, I could get out there a couple hundred meters off the track so as not to spook them. Bring back some of that fresh meat you mentioned."

Port enjoyed a hunt himself but a good hunt took time. You moved quietly, which meant slow. It wasn't sporting, he realized, but it would be a lot more efficient to turn a couple of his BAR men loose to shoot game from the moving trucks. Not wanting to shock the prince, he limited himself to remarking, "I think we might do better trading with the nomads for a couple of fat sheep. Or turn Leung loose and deal for cash."

An eagle circled overhead, tracing big, lazy arcs. Except for the wind-driven cold and a chalky dust the tires kicked up, filming everything with a fine grit, even your teeth, it was nice country, if stark. When he said so, the runner Buffalo, who rarely spoke, said, "Pretty short on trees, Captain."

No one argued that.

About noon they caught up with a big herd of several hundred sheep and goats, a few camels, and some ponies, chivvied along by maybe thirty men and their yipping, hurrying dogs. These were the first working herdsmen among the nomads they'd seen up close and

Port slowed a bit, despite himself, to have a better look. The headman, who had some English and enjoyed showing it off, was a cheery fellow Father Kean thought he'd met years before, and with the midday meal due, he hustled up several shy women who might have been wives and some giggling and quite pretty younger girls, and slim boys togged out for riding, who were surely children, or perhaps grandchildren. Dr. Han, who seemed never to need rest, was already chatting with some of the mothers and looking down children's throats, her nurse, the rapidly improving orderly, and Laurent trailing dutifully with leather satchels.

"They've suggested we join them in a meal, sir," the padre told Port. "He seems to know who I am and is very impressed by your splendid trucks. They're staying here for tonight, setting up their yurts and the women cooking, and he asks if we would do him the honor of sharing the meal?"

"I don't want to take their food, Father. Or do they have plenty?"

"They seem to, right down to cheese and lashings of cream butter. He said they'll butcher a few goats. If you paid them something for their trouble, I'm sure they won't take it amiss."

"Fine. Perhaps they know something about the country ahead. Whether there are any Japs. Or crazy Marines with red hair."

"He said the only excitement they've had was last night when a wolf pack took one of their lambs and they had to chase them off. But I'll keep him talking, Captain. We might learn something."

During the meal and then after, over steaming tea, the young girls danced and men strummed stringed instruments. It was all very nice. "They're fine people, Father," Cantillon said. "Are they all like this?"

"Well, yes, Mr. Cantillon, except for those such as we've met who'll cut a man's throat for his boots.

"But it is a dear, sweet place. My reasons are partly parochial; 'a paradise for paleontologists,' they call it. And in fairness, much of the trouble is stirred up by foreigners, not the Mongols. Did you ever hear of Baron von Ungern-Sternberg, Captain Port?"

Port hadn't. Nor even Dr. Han. And certainly not Mr. Cantillon who couldn't recall his being mentioned at Yale. The Jesuit, delighting in a good yarn, rubbed his hands.

"The baron was a German Balt called 'The Mad Baron' for his wild eyes and hair, for some reason a psychotic hater of Jews who, in 1921, booted out the Mongol warlord Little Hsu, and ran the country for five terrible months, torturing and slaughtering so enthusiastically that wild dogs grew fat in the streets of Ulan Bator gnawing at the corpses. It took Mongolia's 'national hero,' Sükhbaatar, in July of that year, to invite in the Red Army, overthrow the baron, and expel the Chinese. Mongolia went lefty there and then, declared itself the world's second Communist nation, and ever since has cosied up to the Soviets. Splendid people, even when sorely put upon . . ."

Cantillon assumed Father Kean meant the Mongolians and not the Soviets.

After reviewing the maps and from what the nomads said, they were 540 miles from the nearest of the Siberian rivers, one of which they would have to cross to get safely into the Soviet Union.

Port attempted to pin down the only one of them who'd passed this way before.

"At fifty miles a day, Padre, that means ten or eleven more days. But does the country get rougher than this? Any real hills? Marshes? Or is it all pretty much like this, rolling grassland and chalk steppes?"

"It gets hillier," the priest said. "But no real mountains. The Altai are their big, snowy mountains but they're south of us. Nothing higher along here than fourteen hundred meters, about four thousand feet where it's cut by the gorge at Hongor. Then up ahead, beyond the gorge, there are marshes and lakes as well. Finally, some hilly cave country. I've dug there, some nice finds. You shouldn't have trouble."

"Good," Billy said.

"Unless we get snow. Dry as it is here on the steppes, at below zero temperatures, snow will reduce your traction, Captain."

Billy grinned. "That was a nice thing about Nicaragua; it very rarely snowed."

"I daresay."

After lunch and the music, and some bashful flirtations between the Mongol girls and the young Marines, the nomad horsemen, several as young as twelve, mounted up and galloped out onto the steppe toward some dust. "They've sighted a herd of wild ponies out there," the Jesuit said. "They'll try to bring them in. Though I think they've got plenty of horses already and just want to show off a bit for their visitors in front of the women."

"Not much different from the way men act in Boston, Father."

"Or in London, sir."

The roundup was dusty but effective, the Mongol "cowboys" using loops of rope not as lassos, but fed through an eye at the business end of long poles, forming loops to snare the wild horses around the neck.

Some of the Marines were Westerners who knew their way around horses, and they nodded admiringly at the Mongol horsemen's work. Though they didn't think that much of their ponies.

"Built like barrels, they are. Not a speed horse in the field."

Yusopov and Rafter, with two Marines as escort, strolled out into the country for a mile or two and brought back some of what looked like grouse and a small antelope ("gazelle," Father Kean corrected them) for the pot so that Captain Port was able to return the favor and invite the nomads to dinner that evening. There was more dancing and a little local liquor Father Kean warned them about. And as Port posted his sentries that night he sent Buffalo off to ensure none of the friskier Marines planned to spend the night in Mongol yurts with girls or young women who belonged not to them but to Mongol nomads who might take offense.

"Cold as hell," Billy told himself as he slipped out of the stinking yurt and the snoring to unroll his sleeping robe and fall asleep looking up at the stars in a sky as deep as any he'd ever seen.

They hadn't yet had a day as fine as this one. And he felt pretty good about it. A raggedy-ass Marine on hostile ground takes what small pleasures he can and is grateful for them.

But they hadn't put on much mileage and ought to be up and moving early next morning. You never get back the day you lose. Port's margin of error wasn't all that generous. Not as he reckoned it.

In the morning the padre's glass read twenty-one below zero Farenheit and things were about to change. And not for the better.

43

Not difficult to track us, is it? Just follow the graves.

I⊤ was a couple of Zeroes. Maybe the same two planes that hit them earlier, maybe not.

It might have been keen-eyed Buffalo who shouted the first alarm. Whoever it was, he wasn't fast enough. Not for the Marines, not for the nomads moving in roughly the same north by northwest direction, even if more slowly and a mile aft of the trucks to stay out of their dust.

The Zeroes came out of the east and low, very low, the perfect strafing posture for the hour. By the time the Marines saw the red balls on the tan wings of the planes it was too late. Port heard and saw the machine-gun fire from the first pass rip up the brown earth in front of his truck as the driver simultaneously slammed the brakes to the floor and spun the wheel, turning the vehicle toward the oncoming planes, trying to provide them a smaller target than a broadside. All around them you could hear the incoming rounds hitting the ground or, in too many instances, the Marine trucks or the nomads' herds and mounts and bundled felt yurts lashed atop camels.

Adding to the din, the sound of Marine guns firing back, machine gunners and BAR men swinging left to follow the Zeroes as they passed overhead and then climbed steep and fast, getting swiftly out of range, before turning in a large, high semicircle, heading east once more, to come back again out of the rising sun for another run.

It was this run that did the damage. This run that caught the Mongol ponies.

Ordinarily, Japanese planes ignored the nomads. There was no profit in shooting up a yurt or killing a camel. But these nomads were fair game. Traveling, or at least in parallel, with four trucks of marauding American Marines, cruel and ferocious men who'd already in their bloody march killed Japanese soldiers and fired at Japanese planes, to say nothing of killing Mongolians and Chinese.

If the nomads had joined up with the Americans, they, too, were the enemy. That the two disparate parties had done nothing more sinister than share a meal, a song, and catch a few wild horses didn't signify.

Port, flat on his belly on the cropped grass, stubbornly, stupidly, firing a single-shot Springfield rifle as they came in on the second run, over the clatter and rip of the guns, could hear the terrible screams of dying horses even before the planes had zoomed in, fired, and climbed out again. And though he did not know it yet, mingled with the death cries of the horses and camels and herded animals, he heard the agonized human yelps and shouts of fear, of pain and anger, from the Mongol children, the women, the men of this harmless little perambulating village . . .

And then, and then . . . a rare shout of exultation.

"He's on fire, the bastard! He's burning. Oh, look at him burn! Oh, baby! Look at that son of a . . ."

Someone, no one could say who, had hit the second of the two Japs, hit him mortally . . .

Now, on the frozen Mongol steppe, no matter the dead and screaming, thrashing, pitching, spasmodically jerking, wounded man and beast, eyes swept upward into the high blue sky where one Zero had just about vanished triumphantly into the distance, while the other fell behind, slowing, shuddering, rolling, burning, smoke streaming from first its tail and then from the entire ship, the engine no longer pounding efficient as a metronome, but growling, its cylinders irregularly hitting and then missing, as it choked on its own smoke, on its own bodily fluids, the liquids themselves burning, all smoke, all flame, the pilot dead or wounded but unseen, his own blood by now boiling and burning, a young man trapped in his flaming airborne coffin.

What used to be a man.

A few yards away Port could see Rafter, still firing, tracking the dying plane, squeezing off the single shots, coldly intent on his target, intent on his death.

"It's okay. Top. It's okay. He's dead. You got him. Someone got him . . ."

He understood Rafter's hate. Aircraft were so impersonal. Infantrymen killed each other on the ground where they lived, where they fought, where they would one day be buried. Pilots, well, now, they were something else again. Who knew how they died? Nor could anyone promise them burial, no modest, decent few feet of hallowed ground.

Billy wanted war to be personal. He realized he resented their planes more than he hated the Japs themselves, hating the plane more than the man who flew it. In a spasm of righteous anger he squeezed off one final, useless, out-of-range shot of his own in the vague direction of the dying Zero.

"Bastards!" He was as bad as Rafter.

By the time the wounded Japanese crashed, First Sergeant Rafter was already under control, on his feet, his rifle slung, and checking rosters. It didn't take long.

"One dead, sir," he reported. "Three hit, none of them bad. That's what Dr. Han and Philo say. Our trucks are all still working. Got a flat tire or two and a leaking radiator. One fuel trailer holed but no fire. They're patching the holes. Jurkovich is working on them. The Mongols, well, they got it pretty bad. Dr. Han and the Frenchie went over there to help out."

Port asked who the dead man was and thanked Rafter.

"Write up the casualties, Top," he ordered. "Stow the body in a truck."

"Aye aye, sir."

The dead Marine, Fiore, had been in Dog Company, Port's company, for three years, and the company commander just nodded, hearing the man's name, and thanked his first sergeant for a good report. That was all; no tears, no gush, no muttered regret. Rafter permitted himself to issue a small, and decidedly private, judgment on his commanding officer.

"He's a cold one."

It wasn't criticism. Simply a commentary, and in ways, an admiring one. Back at Shanghai, so went the barracks gossip, so went the more measured and mature talk at the Staff NCO club, "That Port's a piece of work." Well, Rafter thought now but did not say, if Billy Port brings us through this shit and gets us out of China, gets us back to the regiment, then, to hell! Who's going to question the man who gets us home?

The captain was already visiting the Mongols. Talking to them in a lingo few of them knew. Or to the headman who did. Gripping an arm here, stroking a child's head, taking a weeping man's hand. All about him, dogs yipped and howled mournfully, one or two of them nosing at their own dead. Women wailed, small children sobbed or crouched, silent and shocked, their eyes huge, blank and unbelieving, young girls fretted with their hair, lips trembling, not knowing what to do and lacking proper words, but trying to reestablish some sort of tribal and family order out of murderous chaos, a familiar routine that might begin with something as simple as pushing back into place a straying lock of glistening black hair.

After you've seen your family machine-gunned around you, how do you get back to the routine, repair the breakage, return to normal?

Captain Port had his ways of telling the Mongols how sorry he was. His dead and wounded Marines, well, that was different; they were on the job, this was their work. The nomads had just gotten in the way.

The people were bad. The animals, especially the horses, might have been worse. What were those drawings Goya did, *"los desastros de la guerra"*? Billy remembered seeing the show at the big art museum in Boston. The horses of Mongolia were like those drawings.

Dozens of them were down. Not all dead. The dead, well, they were dead. The wounded, their legs still kicking and twitching, some of the legs broken, and with the shuddering kicks, the big broken leg bones were tearing through their own flesh, the sharpened, jagged, and splintered bone ends cutting into muscle and fat and internal organs, tearing their own bodies to pieces.

Federales, moving amid the carcasses, didn't hesitate.

"Shoot them. If they're moving, shoot 'em. Through the head."

"Aye aye, Sarn't."

You could hear the single, merciful shots. No echo on the plains. The nomads, perhaps fearing the planes had come back, looked up, startled. Then they saw what Federales was doing. And understood. They were horsemen. They'd killed horses themselves. A pony with a broken leg? You didn't leave him limping across the Gobi for the wolves to run down, snapping, biting, and gnawing at his entrails while the horse was still standing there, shocked and unsteady but still alive.

By early afternoon the Marine trucks had put on a little speed and pulled away from the nomads. Why expose them to more punishment? The Japanese had picked up their trail. How difficult could it be to track us? Port thought angrily: Just follow our graves. Read the obituaries. Give ear to the first sergeant's report.

Before they left, Dr. Han told Port she and Monsieur would stay here for a few hours. They had work still to be done among the Mongols. Billy imagined what sort of grisly work it would be. Amputations, the setting of bones, cauterizing wounds. "We'll catch up to you before dark, Captain."

"Fine," he said. Too many things were happening too fast to agonize over what seemed a sensible arrangement. The woman had common sense aplenty, enough for the both of them, Laurent and herself. Then Leung was dispatched quietly to the headman to hand over a substantial purse. Along with a ritual apology Port had attempted to make with gestures, delivered by Leung in appropriately flowery terms.

How do you pay for three dead children, one dead mother, two dead men, one pretty teenaged girl without a right leg, nine others hurt, and God knew how many beasts of the field? You don't. You provide Dr. Han and temporarily Doc Philo, and whatever medical assistance you can, open the exchequer, and say you're sorry.

And then get the hell away from these people. Put some miles between you and them before you kill them all.

Father Kean, sensitive to mood, trotted up to Port's truck. "May I ride a while with you, sir?"

"Sure, Padre. Give me your hand."

When the priest was hoisted into the truck with him, Billy gave him a crooked grin.

"Fast planes and slow horses. Hardly fair, is it?"

"Soldiers' calling, Captain. Neither fair nor unfair. Just the way things are."

"Easy to say so. But I should have chased them off at daybreak. The Japs wanted us, not them."

The Jesuit nodded, not saying anything. Port didn't need to be preached at, not in this mood. Let the man talk it out if he wanted.

"Well," Father Kean said, so as to give Billy a small out, "it's a hard trade."

Billy knew he ought to respond.

"I don't mind the killing itself when it's a fair fight. Killing Japs or bandits or General Sin or shooting down that Zero, frying the pilot, that's the work we do. Taking out that armored car with a bottle of gasoline, no strain. It's the innocent bystanders that eat at me. The nomads and their kids. That girl who lost her leg. What kind of life does a kid with one leg have in the Gobi?

"I've always prided myself on being a good Marine, a good officer. But at times like this, I wish I were more like Dr. Han. Or even Sergeant Brydon. Trying to help out. Instead I'm the boy causing the trouble."

Kean, but gently, protested.

"Think on this, sir. When you kill a warlord or shoot down a plane preying on the innocent, haven't you been every bit as useful as if you'd been giving inoculations? Think of it that way, Captain."

"I suppose," Port said, "but in China there's always another warlord or fighter plane or another bandit. You kill one and another pops up. The inoculation saves the kid. Maybe forever."

44

"Irabu, this is General Nagata. I have dreadful news."

No one thought it would be easy, getting the last of the 4th Marines out of China. Now it got worse.

Their old friend, the spotter plane, was the tip-off. When it closed, dropping down to three thousand or so, the Marines knew this wasn't just another overflight. The Japs knew what they were looking for, the criminals who destroyed their Nakajima "Storm Dragon" on the tarmac of Hohhot and murdered its pilots and passengers.

The Zeroes were just shooting up a target of opportunity; they hadn't connected the Marines and their nomad pals to the killings at Hohhot. The observation overflight was different, this was calculated. Japanese intelligence had put two and two together and come up with Billy Port.

A man called Lao had gone to the Japanese investigating the atrocity and said it was Americans. They were the ones who committed the outrage, not Mongols at all, but foreign devils. Men in forest-green uniforms, who had a base of operations at the Celestial Joy Mission. If Lao knew about the Lindbergh baby, he would have pinned that on Billy Port's Marines.

The Japanese who questioned Lao, having gotten everything they considered useful, then tied Lao to a straight chair and shot him, on the reasonable grounds that a man who betrayed others would, if given the opportunity, betray you as well. And then they began to settle scores.

A flight of Kawasaki light bombers (code-named Lily) was sent to bomb Celestial Joy and any Marines who remained there, to punish the missionaries for consorting with the enemy, and to impress local people yet again with Imperial power.

Sergeant Brydon, who had reached Celestial Joy on a stolen pony only the night before, was still trying to set up his Browning automatic rifle to fire at the Japanese planes when the first bombs hit. He was wounded and the organist Miss Rose and fifteen of the children died on the first run. In the chapel, into which he had herded a dozen kids, Reverend Doc was caught by the second run, which took off both legs, and with the children dead or dazed and not knowing how to help or what to do, Reverend Hopkins bled to death in one of the pews. Six of the mission staff and eighteen children survived. Most would not live through the winter.

Brydon, who fastened his web belt around his thigh to stop, or at least slow, the bleeding, took two days to die. Willpower, mostly, and his issue morphine kept him going that long. He had one of the kids bring him a school composition book into which he wrote a detailed report of what had happened, appended his formal apology to Captain Port for having deserted, and summoned the strongest and most sensible of the surviving mission workers, a Mongol carpenter.

"Let the others bury Miss Rose and Reverend Doc and the children," Brydon ordered, to the end a good sergeant. "You take my horse; my canteen, my Smith & Wesson, and this money. Ride like hell north and find Captain Billy and give him this notebook. He'll reward you and report to the mission authorities back in the United States what a grand fellow you are. You understand?"

The man said that he did and Brydon, comforted at having done the right thing, promptly died. Three days later, the Celestial Joy carpenter caught up to the trucks with his report of the Japanese attack and of Sergeant Brydon's death.

The bombers reported no trucks in the area of Celestial Joy so it was assumed the Marines had left before the bombing attack and therefore escaped just retribution. Therefore, an observation plane was sent to find the Americans. All of this information was passed on to Imperial Army headquarters in Peking to be assessed by the intelligence section.

General Hata, the Japanese commander in China, was already out of sorts, having just been stripped by Tokyo of another two infantry divisions and an air wing, reinforcements for the Japanese Army fighting in the Philippines and Burma. And this at a time when Hata had Chiang's Nationalists again on the run near Changsha and thought he might keep right on going to threaten Chungking. But not with winter closing down the fighting, and not with a depleted air arm and without those first-line divisions. Now came this irritating business about Marines still loose and making trouble in the Gobi.

Hata called in General Watanabe for a rocket.

"I thought you were taking care of it. That you were sending out a small force after the Americans and assured me that would be that."

"I underestimated the difficulty, General," Watanabe admitted. He didn't think it was the moment for going into detail, his decision to mount a pursuit on the cheap, using ordinary garrison troops, and the subsequent ambush at Fengzhen, for example. "But there's a colonel named Irabu who actually knows this Marine captain. With your permission I'll contact the Special Naval Landing Forces and have him seconded to HQ. Irabu warned me Port was a tricky fellow. I should have listened. We'll give Colonel Irabu the task and do it properly this time."

General Hata respected a man who confessed error but hated liars and makers of excuses.

"See that it's done then. We don't need such distractions when all else is going so well." It was Hata's troops who'd stormed Hong Kong, winning for him that highest of praise, a message from the palace manifesting the Emperor's pleasure.

In Shanghai Irabu got the call. It might take a few days but his transfer would be coming through and when it did, he was to report to General Watanabe in Peking and organize a punitive expedition, tracking down to capture or kill the Marine force commanded by Captain Port. Watanabe, stung by Hata's rebuke, followed with a phone call of his own, coming down heavily on a junior officer with all the righteous power not only of the Imperial Army but the Samurai tradition.

"You're the one who knows him," a clearly irritated Watanabe said after having been informed Irabu had asked for a pass on the assignment. "How he thinks, how he reacts. Remember, this is China, not California, a war, not a tennis match, Colonel. You've got your orders. *You* catch him, *you* kill him."

Jesse had a temper, something to which his tennis pals, ironically including Billy, could attest, and it very nearly erupted now. It was a cheap shot, Watanabe's tennis crack. But what options had Irabu? It was clear his assignment had already been approved by Hata, which meant even his patron, General Nagata, was powerless to intercede. Agonized, Irabu mulled the position. The professional killer in him, honed at the Amur River, ought to welcome such assignments. Watanabe was right; Irabu was the one Japanese officer who knew Billy Port best and was the most formidable foe the Marine would encounter. From a purely military point of view, Irabu ought to be clicking his heels and saying yes, sir. But to set out coldly to kill a good guy and a friend who was just doing his sworn duty? Suppose he accepted the job, though with mental reservations, going about his task so methodically and thoroughly that Billy surely would be out of the country before Jesse caught up with him, rendering the problem moot? Could he get away with that sort of halfhearted effort? His reputation was one of dash and determination, that of a resolute and deadly warrior. Watanabe would see through a sham. So, too, surely, would Hata, a more subtle man.

When he was opening the mail that next morning in his office, the phone rang.

"Irabu, it's Nagata."

Now they were really ganging up on him.

"So you're in it, too, General? I'd hoped you wouldn't have to involve yourself..."

"Irabu, I'm not calling about that rogue American. I have dreadful news. Your parents are dead."

When Colonel Irabu had gotten himself under control, the general told him the story. "Our sources read a report published in the local California newspaper. Knowing its significance, they had someone check further with the police. It's true. Your mother burned to death, their home destroyed by flames. Your father, burned less severely, died later in the hospital at Fresno."

"Of the burns?"

"No, he committed hara kiri out of guilt for having failed to save your mother."

Irabu groaned, unable to form the words, and General Nagata went on.

"It's worse, my friend. The fire that destroyed your house was set. Arson."

"The police did this?"

"Not that we know of. Apparently a committee of vigilance of some sort. Civilians, local people envious of your parents, their wealth, their success, perhaps even of your own achievements. Also resentful and angry about Pearl Harbor. Actual neighbors, perhaps. Long-time friends, even. Your father and mother had agreed to be interned in a camp being set up in the Mojave Desert to house Japanese-Americans relocated from the seacoast and other areas the federal government in Washington felt too sensitive to have the Japanese living next door. Even American citizens of Japanese origin."

"Vigilantes?" Irabu repeated dully, his head spinning, vague and unfocused. Such things happened in movies, not on successful farms in the San Joaquin Valley, the richest agricultural spread in the world. And now his parents were dead, his home burned, the house where he was born and lived for the first eighteen years of his life. Nagata understood his anger, his stupified confusion.

"Your parents protested but in the end said yes. They would go. Leave their land, their agricultural business, their home. But they were still making arrangements, seeking to set up a trusteeship over the property with their bank and a local lawyer, and had not yet vacated their home. There were people anxious to take over the property, greedy people who grew impatient. There have been other such attacks on Japanese-Americans by local people. Even the American press joins in decrying them . . ."

"Who were these bastards? I want their names. Our intelligence has sources, General. I must know which of our friendly California neighbors killed my mother, shamed my father."

He and the general spoke for a long time and then Nagata said, trying to cool his protégé's fury, his appetite for vengeance, "You can ignore Watanabe's directive. With a personal tragedy like this, I assure you, everyone will understand. Take a long leave. Go back to Tokyo, rest, distract yourself, and recover from your loss. They'll find another officer to go after Port."

Irabu said something that Nagata didn't quite get.

"What did you say?"

"I said, *don't* find another officer. Tell General Watanabe I'll take out the patrol myself. I'll find Port and his Americans, find them, bring them in or kill them. I'll be leaving in the morning for Harbin and the Gobi, General. This is something I can do. And now, something I *have* to do . . ."

Jesse Irabu was an orderly, efficient man who knew what he wanted and usually knew how to get it. To track down and kill United States

Marines you wanted the best men you could get, you wanted Imperial Japanese Marines of the Special Naval Landing Force. Before flying north from Shanghai he spoke to General Nagata again and the general issued certain orders on his young friend's behalf. Colonel Irabu ordered up four big scout cars, strong and powerful, riding on oversized solid rubber tires, with machine guns mounted on their hoods, one of the guns a .50-caliber lifted from a Zero fighter and remounted. Each car to carry four to six Japanese Marines, the men fur-clad from head to boots. Irabu knew Manchuria and its winters better than he knew Mongolia or the Gobi, and he'd been warned that the Mongol winter, farther from the sea, might be even worse.

The orders Irabu issued no longer envisioned a methodical, half-hearted tracking operation but a sprint, fast, close, deadly. It did not at this stage involve air strikes. Not with an entire air wing being taken away from Hata's China command to fight in the Philippines, leaving Zeroes at a premium. Well, then, this would be a fight between foot soldiers, Japanese Imperial Marines in pursuit and United States Marines on the run. An earlier two-Zero flight had attacked Port's trucks plus some Mongol mercenaries, losing one plane but scoring a number of hits. Irabu knew there were four trucks, no more, because only weeks ago, he'd seen Captain William Hamilton Thomas Port load four big Marine trucks onto a tramp steamer of Portuguese registry at the waterfront of the Whangpoo River. The trucks, the surviving Zero reported, were on a heading generally north by northwest through eastern Mongolia, probable destination, the Siberian border along the Amur River or, more likely, in the Onon River marshland to the west. A route that would take the Americans through or close to the Mongol market town of Baruun Urt.

From that time on, even in the vast emptiness of the Gobi and Inner Mongolia, Irabu had Billy Port in his sights. "I don't need Zeroes but I do want a daily observation overflight," he told Nagata. "I want to be kept informed how much of a lead they have on me, just where these Americans are, and where they're headed."

45

It turned out that Yusopov had a brother who was doing penance and good works.

As Port's Americans neared Mongolia's forbidding Hongor Gorge, beyond which in the villages of the Gobi proper it was said epidemics raged, Prince Yusopov, in the top's words, "began paying his way."

At first, the Russian had been reluctant to impose himself on Billy's friendship, Port being younger but also in command. Nor, as a foreigner and their guest, did Yusopov want to seem to be questioning or ordering Marines about. Not yet, at least. The Molotov cocktail he taught the Marines how to fashion and use was clever sleight of hand. Once they neared or crossed into Russian territory, then, Yusopov knew, he could be of real value.

It was again very cold as they set off at first light but they'd grown accustomed to that. What was odd, here in the high desert, was the chill humidity. "Not quite wet enough to rain or snow," Father Kean remarked, but it was sufficient of a freezing mist to reduce visibility and coat everything in ice. "Better alert your drivers, Captain," the priest warned. "They're the lads to bear the brunt of this. And unless I'm mistaken, the road rises from here. You don't want skids, not at the Hongor Gorge, with sheer cliffs falling away on one side and occasionally both. Compared to the flats we've been crossing, this is the roughest patch we're likely to see in eastern Mongolia."

"Hongor?" Prince Yusopov said. "Place with a deep-cut gorge, rope bridges, and a ramshackle old monastery sprawled above?"

"By God, sir, yes. Odd, mystical sort of affair. Not a proper Roman Catholic monastery. Or even one of those lama-ridden monstrosities that plague the traveler in Nepal or Tibet, ten-year-old monks shoving the begging bowl at you and turning prayer wheels. Don't know quite how to characterize this place."

"I can tell you, Father," said the prince, "it's a Russian Orthodox monastery, named for Saint Grigori. I know one of the monks, if he's still here, still alive."

"My dear Prince, I didn't mean to offend . . ."

"No offense, Father Kean. It's my brother who's the monk, not I."

Well, thought Port, this was news. With the émigré White Russians you never knew what was coming next. You tended not to think of them as having relatives, actual families, exiled and cut off as they were from hearth and home, perpetually living "abroad."

"My older brother," Yusopov elaborated. "Doing penance for our family's having done away with the Starets."

"The Starets?" Cantillon said. "Who are they?"

"Rasputin, whom they called 'The Starets,' the mad monk who was the tsarina's most intimate adviser and, except for Kerensky, probably the individual who did the most to bring about the downfall of the Romanovs and eventually the Bolshevik Revolution. It's a familiar story in Russia, though perhaps not in America. My father and several other nobles conspired to murder Rasputin, to rid the tsar and the country of him. Brother Anatole inherited all the sanctity in our family and much of the guilt as well. He's been wearing a hairshirt over Rasputin since 1916. Though most of our set think good business was done that night in the Petersburg cellars, when they poisoned and shot the fellow, and then flung his body into the Neva."

"Top Sergeant," Port called out impatiently. This was all very well but he knew about Rasputin and had little interest in penitential hairshirts. But only wanted to get the column on its way, especially with the weather souring.

"Yessir."

"The road's getting worse and Father Kean says the uphill grades start here, with steep drop-offs coming on both sides. Who's your leading driver? Jurkovich?"

"He's got the lead truck, yes, Skipper."

Port walked briskly up the unpaved road, feeling the steepening gradient in the calf muscles of his legs.

"I'll come with you if I may, Captain."

"Sure, most welcome, Prince. You've been here before?"

"Only once and that ten years ago and not in winter. The road then was dicey but passable. I spent a week visiting. My brother and I correspond, though not often."

"And he's been here since 1916 when they..."

"No, he joined the Church later, during the Civil War. Thought it might be possible to pray away the Bolsheviks if we couldn't defeat them in the field. Left the White Army to enter an Orthodox monastery and do penance in eastern Siberia. Then packed up and moved down here to Mongolia and the Hongor Gorge when the Reds captured Siberia in '22 or '23. Since besides being a monk, he was also a prince and a White Russian officer, he and a few others thought they'd better get out while they still could. This is a backwater of a place, Saint Grigori, dating back more than a century, still on the Julian Calendar and consequently running about a fortnight behind the rest of the world. The abbot here was formerly the Metropolitan of Vladivostok. Saintly old gent, famous for lashing himself bloody on holy days, of which the Orthodox Church has a multitude."

"Not much fun being an abbot," said Billy noncommittally. He was more interested in how they were going to get through the gorge on an unpaved road in an ice storm without losing their trucks or killing themselves.

"Tell me about the road. How bad does it get? Can trucks handle it, do you think?"

"It gets pretty steep, as I recall. Not bad when dry, of course. Ice'll be tricky."

They discussed the road and the weather for a time and Yusopov offered to ride shotgun in the lead truck with Jurkovich.

"I might remember something about the road, its twists and turns, and if we encounter one of the monks, I can communicate with him. They don't have motorcars themselves. Just donkeys and Mongolian ponies."

"Are they allowed to speak?"

Yusopov gave Billy a look. "Just try to keep a Russian silent. Even those who've sworn vows. They'll take a drink, as well."

The freezing mist, if you didn't have to travel through it, was beautiful, coating surfaces and the men themselves in glistening ice. You couldn't have staged *The Nutcracker* more dramatically.

Beauty, unfortunately, eluded the first sergeant, eluded most firsts. Watching the ice form, not only on the trucks, the road, the slopes above and the cliffs below, but on the tin hats of the Marines, their sleeves and shoulders, icicles hanging and dripping from the noses, ears, and chins of the men, the top shouted, a first sergeant and not an art critic: "All right, you peepul. You will cover up them there weapons so they don't get iced up in their moving parts, you hear me."

"Aye, aye, Top," came the murmurs, as men obediently moved their rifles and BARs about, out of the mist, under their sheepskins and ponchos, attempting to shelter the hardware if not themselves from the Mongol ice. Marines were good about that; the weapons came first. You could afford to be reckless with yourself.

Not with your weapon.

Even this early in the climb with the grade and the glaze of ice, it was very slow going in lowest gear. The first soldier took advantage of that in throwing out a point.

"I want two men up front on foot, you, Buffalo, with the Thompson gun. Hundred yards forward of the first truck. And a good BAR man, Federales. Pick one."

The trucks, grinding laboriously up the grade and skidding, the wheels spinning, were moving so slowly that a couple of foot soldiers, lugging weapons, could easily walk ahead, cautious, cagey, aware, looking about. The work infantry soldiers did. Sure, you could lose a good point man this way. Better that than a truck carrying ammo and tents, rations and fuel, and a couple of men. Besides, a man sniffed out the road ahead; a truck, stinking of diesel and rubber and lubricating grease, couldn't. Animal instinct, that's what you wanted.

Port thought about it as he plodded uphill through the mist alongside the prince. Good soldiers have a nose, can smell danger. Could have used that at Pearl, couldn't they? Or in the Philippines, where MacArthur lined up his B-17s? As a professional soldier Port shook his head. When this war sorted itself out, there would be general court-martials a-plenty. How could a man of MacArthur's intelligence have been so careless? Laziness, fatigue, arrogance, the burden of years?

War? It was simple. Kill the other guy first and you win.

Politesse? That, too, lost battles, had no place. Remember Wolfe and Montcalm on the Plains of Abraham? "Pray shoot first, gentlemen of France."

"Mais non, tirez d'abord, messieurs les Anglais."

Both Montcalm and Wolfe, two celebrated generals, two fatheads, died that day at Quebec City. Port, who was not a famous general, had no intention of dying. Not here. Not in some lousy little hill-country pass in Mongolia. He pushed his command ahead, up the gorge through the ice storm, kept them going.

Hongor Gorge was longer, tougher, colder than any of them expected.

Yusopov rode from time to time in the lead truck next to Jurkovich, staring through the windshield, advising him what might be coming next, straining to see. The visibility up there wasn't very good and Jurkovich's charms were limited to driving competently and his conversation to the merits of various makes of truck. So he got down again. "I'll walk along with the point men, Sergeant, if you don't mind."

"Better you than me, Prince. Cold enough inside the cab."

Yusopov set off striding along with Buffalo and the other young Marine, enjoying the walk, remembering other climbs. As a young man before the war he'd climbed Mount Elberus, tallest peak of the Caucasus, and enjoyed a summer doing the usual tourist ascents in the French Alps. Buffalo was pleased to have the Russian beside him, very impressed that Captain Port's detachment had its very own prince, and that they were slogging along there side by side at the point. Never believe that back home, having a prince walking with you, exchanging the time of day. You didn't come across many princes in Erie County.

"You ever in the army yourself, Prince?"

"Yes, during the World War and then in our Civil War. In the Preotrazhensky Regiment."

"That anything like our Marine Corps?"

"Yes, actually. An elite regiment whose members were personally selected by the tsar. And swore fealty to his person."

"He was the king, right?"

"Yes, king, emperor, and autocrat."

"You ever see him, the tsar?"

"Many times, Buffalo. And visited often at the Winter Palace where he lived."

Wow! Next time they got someplace that had a post office, Buffalo was going to write home and put all this in there, about the prince knowing the tsar and going to the palace and all.

Then, abruptly, he broke off.

Just to their rear the lead truck, with their best driver, Jurkovich, at the wheel, had skidded almost sideways across the narrow, iced dirt road, and Jurkovich honked, then waved at them through his open window. "Get the captain the hell up here," he growled. "These trucks ain't gonna make this grade. Not with the ice."

Buffalo ran back downhill and soon returned with Port. Jurkovich, out of his cab and standing with them on the road, was explaining things, apologizing.

"Not your fault, Jurkovich," Port said.

"If we had some burlap sacking for under the wheels, Captain . . . give them a little purchase."

Then Laurent was there. It was comforting to have experts on hand.

"What do you think, Monsieur?"

The Frenchman shook his head.

"God himself, or Fangio, couldn't get up a slope this steep with ice. I'm surprised your trucks got this far."

The four Marine trucks with their fuel trailers attached, and the Bentley, had all come to a halt, stalled here and there down the mountain road for a couple of hundred yards. One truck, third in line, was tilted halfway into a ditch where the shoulder pinched out.

"Well, we don't have burlap sacking," Port said. "And there aren't any big enough trees along the right-of-way that we could winch ourselves along with ropes."

"Captain," Yusopov said.

"Yes?"

"We've got three, four hours of daylight. If you'll let me take Buffalo, we can hike up this road to the monastery. Check out the grades, how bad it gets, and maybe find a monk and borrow donkeys. Otherwise, it'll be a cold night sitting out here waiting for tomorrow and the road to open up."

Port looked at the top. First soldiers usually had good sense. How they earned those six stripes, three over and three under, on their sleeves.

"Top?"

"We ain't making money just standing here, Skipper."

"Okay, Prince. Buffalo!"

"Yessir, Captain?"

"You and your BAR man go along with Prince Yusopov."

"Aye aye, sir."

A half hour later, maybe a mile up the road, the visibility even worse with the icy mix still falling and the afternoon gloom deepening, Buffalo froze.

"Someone coming," the runner hissed at his BAR man and the prince.

The BAR man smartly hit the deck and had his weapon leveled even before Buffalo was off the road to the right, the Thompson gun ready. Yusopov, taking his lead from the two young Marines, crouched, a revolver in his gloved hand, staring into the falling mist.

"It's one of the monks," he said, seeing more clearly now an approaching rider and his mount.

The monk, a plump man swathed comfortably in furs and mounted atop a smallish donkey that didn't really look up to the task, cried out a cheery Russian response to Prince Yusopov's Russian greeting.

Turning to his two Marines, Yusupov said, "This is Father Valentin of the Monastery of Saint Grigori. The monks traditionally give shelter to travelers overtaken by night or the weather. He says that if Captain Port wishes, he will guide us the rest of the way. And when the storm ends, they can supply draught animals and rope."

"Why, yessir, Prince. I'll double-time back there and tell the skipper." Then, to the monk, "Hi, there, Padre. We got a Jesuit with us already but we could sure use some donkeys."

The monk, who spoke no English, blessed Buffalo with the sign of the cross. Then the Marine sprinted off downhill to where Port paced impatiently alongside one of the stalled trucks.

The ice storm kept up and with darkness falling, Billy and all of them trekked up the road to be met by Father Valentin, who led them across a rickety footbridge suspended perhaps five hundred feet above the gorge, to where the monastery perched on a promontory overlooking the Hongor. Prince Yusopov had already crossed once to arrange things and now returned to greet them.

"We're in luck, Billy. My brother Anatole is not only alive and well but has been elected abbot. They'd be honored to have you as guests. There was a bit of a flurry when I told them about Dr. Han. They're not keen on women but can always use a doctor. At the moment there's one broken arm, two cases of influenza, one suspected hernia, and a molar to be extracted. Most of the monks have some age on them and a few are falling to bits and pieces. She'll be busy."

The monks parceled out the Marines to various stone cells (Father Kean, being a fellow practitioner, was provided an actual room and Dr. Han a virtual suite).

The first sergeant posted sentries on the road below the monastery where they'd parked their trucks and through the night every two hours fresh sentries could be heard moving across the creaking suspension bridge. Port, who didn't trust monastic engineering, forced himself to tackle the bridge twice and come back. The men always knew it when an officer shirked.

There was a communal dinner, a good, hearty borscht, some wonderful fresh bread, an entrée long on grains and vegetables, somewhat short on meat, but the monks broke out a passable red wine. And plenty of it. So much so that the top sergeant made a positive thing of keeping an eye on Sparks, while trying to recall the phase of the moon.

There was also prayer. Tertius Kean, S.J., as a courtesy, was asked to deliver a blessing.

"Grand stuff," one of the older Russian priests judged Kean's effort. "You used to hear it in the English church in Petersburg before the war. Before the . . . Revolution. As a seminarian I sneaked over there on a Sunday. Ah, those English Jesuits . . ."

"Most gracious, Father," said Reverend Kean, clearly moved. "Was Farm Street that prepared us, and well."

The abbot, Father Prince Anatole Yusopov, presided. The guilts, he admitted, in reference to Rasputin, were still working at him. But not overly so and he enjoyed running a monastery and was fond of his fellow monks.

"God is good," he announced.

"Yes," Prince Yusopov agreed. A shame poor Rostov never found this sort of peace instead of shooting off the side of his head.

Over a brandy trotted out after dinner, Anatole and his princely brother swapped yarns. That, too, was grand stuff.

"I miss it, you know, Nicky," the abbot admitted. "Music, theater, society, women. We had everything there in Petersburg and tossed it away. You in exile, me a monk in sandals."

"But no hairshirt?" his brother asked, half in jest.

"Damned things itch," declared the abbot.

"But it must be peaceful here," Port remarked enviously, "except when the Marines drop in."

"Oh," said Father Anatole, "you're hardly the only uninvited guests. We get the odd warlords seeking tribute, convinced our chalices are studded with rubies and emeralds, and our tapestries priceless . . ."

"No Japanese?" Billy asked, always avid for a little useful information.

"Six months ago a Japanese patrol looked in on us. When the border wars with the Soviet Union were on, their attentions were more frequent. They were convinced we were sending military secrets direct to Stalin by carrier pigeon. We cursed Stalin out as the Antichrist, spat contemptuously at the mention of his name, and we were finally accepted as reliable counterrevolutionaries not on the Kremlin payroll."

Billy explained there was a new war on, between Japan and the Americans and Brits.

"Are we in it?" one of the Russians asked, apologizing that they had no radio and the mails were slow.

"Only against the Germans, not yet the Japs," Port said.

"That's curious, isn't it?"

Port agreed that it was. No one at the monastery seemed excited that another war had broken out a month ago without their knowledge. Monsieur, crabby at this enforced idleness, a postpartum separation from his beloved (well, Port's) Bentley, groused, asking if the weather was always this beastly.

"No, Monsieur Laurent. This ice storm is a freak and very rare. But cold. No denying the cold. It should clear by tomorrow or the next day."

The monks did some low-pressure converting of nomads and nearby villagers in summer, but with temperatures to forty below, "there's precious little proselytizing in winter." They traveled mostly by donkey but, said the abbot, "occasionally we take the train."

"What train?" Port demanded. This was news to him.

"Oh," said Father Kean, "there's a train all right, running east-west from Harbin to Ulan Bator. Occasionally as far east as Mukden and, before the war, Vladivostok. Only trouble is, people keep blowing it up, stealing the rails and, for building and firewood, the sleepers."

"Sleepers?"

It turned out "sleepers" was British for ties.

Nicky and Anatole Yusopov compared notes on missing friends. Most of the people they mentioned seemed to be dead or exiled or "in the Lubyanka."

"What's that?" Port asked, after his wine and brandy feeling entitled to ask.

"A prison in Moscow. Stalin puts his enemies there. Dreadful place."

"I see." He didn't, really, but it seemed serious business to the White Russians and he dropped the subject so as not to intrude.

Father Anatole and the monks prayed over them all again (being particular about mentioning the souls of the tsar and tsarina and the children, including that persistent Romanov wraith, Anastasia), and, loudly, "the late but not lamented Grigori Efimovich Rasputin."

"Who's he again?" Rafter whispered in Port's ear, not wanting to appear nosy.

"A political monk, some time ago. The abbot and the prince's daddy bumped him off."

"Oh," the top said, befuddled; but nodding understanding. First sergeants prided themselves on never seeming shocked by anything.

Dr. Han had been busy, healing the sick and removing molars, and she gave the abbot a summary. "The hernia was a groin pull, happily." Buffalo asked how close to being proper Roman Catholics these Russian monks might be and was politely exhorted to read up on the subject when he got home. While Federales found a monk or two who would listen to his tales and told them how he and General Pershing hunted down Pancho Villa, and later whipped the Germans. The monks knew about the Germans but needed to have Villa explained. It was all quite jolly. They kept pouring the wine and the wary top kept watching Sparks.

On the second day the storm ended. But with the road still sheathed in ice, they had to call on the monks, their donkeys and their ponies, amid considerable prayer from the clergy and curses (from the Marine Corps), to string ropes on the trucks and winch them up over the crest and then cautiously downslope on the other side of Hongor Gorge, without losing them to gravity coming or going, not with five hundred miles still to travel.

"Couldn't have done it without you, Prince." Billy meant it; they could have died there on that iced-up road, frozen or starved, or just sheer frustrated to death. Or caught by the damned Japs, somewhere out there behind them. He knew how lucky they'd been so far. "We owe you, Prince. You and that holy brother of yours and his troupe of drunken monks."

"Nonsense, Billy. Just good fortune that Anatole found religion."

Jurkovich, from Hamtramack, remained surly. "I'm a Polack. I don't like Russians very much." Most of the Marines felt different, after a night in a real bed, bare as it was, indoors with heat and a meal, some wine. Buffalo and most of them might have echoed Doc Philo. The corpsman put it simply: "Except for the crappy soup and all the praying, them Russkis is fine people, Top. You think they're like that up ahead in Siberia?"

"I reckon. Folks is much the same wherever you find them, the good, the bad, and the ornery."

Port hoped so, too. But he didn't forget what the brothers Yusopov told him about the Lubyanka, where Moscow put its prisoners.

46

Hell of a nerve, chasing them instead of capturing Rangoon.

Now Dr. Han once again would come to the Marines' assistance. Just before leaving them forever.

She, her nurse, the patched-up orderly, and the Bentley, her "faithful cavalier" Monsieur at the wheel, ranged north and west of the column, day after day, visiting the few actual villages and ministering, especially to the children and pregnant wives of the roving herdsmen.

Through word of mouth, the mysterious bush telegraph of primitive peoples, came news of a much more lethal sickness than whooping cough plaguing the region: diphtheria. Beyond the Hongor Gorge, whole villages were being visited by pestilence.

It was Monsieur, the race car driver, and not Dr. Han who told Billy Port of diphtheria and begged favors.

"Why didn't she come herself?" Billy demanded. "God knows, I'm in her debt."

"She's shy, cher Port. But also, doesn't want to owe you. Even dislikes being in debt to a rogue such as myself. *Sais pas.* When I meet the first woman I understand fully, I'll inform you and instantly, *mon capitaine.*"

"Yes, I know." Port felt like that, too, about women. Even Natasha, just a kid, but forever surprising him.

The Frenchman and Dr. Han had been out all day on their rounds through snow squalls and with a falling thermometer. Monsieur's lean face, pale and slack in Shanghai, had over the weeks browned and tightened, and in his sheepskin coat and heavy mittens and whipcord riding britches with the scuffed, dusty riding boots, he looked more the adventurer than the Paris boulevardier. Was that a consequence of wind burn and being on the wagon? Or was it the influence of noble Dr. Han?

None of my damned business, Billy told himself. Then, abruptly, not wanting unsought confidences, he snapped: "Okay, what can I do?"

"She wants to leave the column, to stay here in Mongolia. Curing the sick, raising the dead, the usual thing."

"Here? But there's nothing here. A few herds, some bandits, barely a dirt road or hut, and the wind is nine parts sand."

"What I told her, Captain Port. 'This place is *merde. Zéro à gauche.* Forget it. Mongolia is nothing. They got sick people in much nicer places you could work.' "

" 'I'm here and so are the sick children, Monsieur Laurent,' she told me. 'They need me. Captain Port's Marines don't. In a week or two they'll be among allies, and can get on with their war. That's their business; mine is being a doctor. I can practice here without limitations amid a people with no alternatives. In Siberia, what would I be, another unwanted Chinese who claims to be a physician. Better expel her, put her in a camp. With such émigrées, you can never be too careful . . .' "

Her sarcasm was right on, even as the Frenchman aped her tone. Port nodded agreement. "On that, she's probably right."

Monsieur lighted a Gauloise. "Oh, there's another thing, *mon capitaine,*" he said, keeping it casual. "Can you let her keep the Bentley?"

"The Bentley? She wants my Bentley?"

Monsieur was enjoying himself, seeing Billy Port disconcerted.

"Well, *she* didn't say that. Dr. Han thinks she can make it with a couple of Mongol ponies. Maybe a camel, filthy beasts! Spitting at you. Bite your damned face off as well. Your Bentley was my idea, Captain Port. Much more efficient than ponies. And can you imagine me sitting a camel? The Bentley's the very thing. Just as a loan, you understand, until the war is over and we can return it to you better than ever. Your sergeant can make out the papers as you did when you purchased Captain Henriques's garbage scow, remember? She continues to debate but I believe I'm convincing her."

"Mmmm."

Laurent knew he hadn't yet closed the sale. "And of course, you know the car's in the best of hands with me. Those hack Soviet mechanics, *mon dieu* . . . to hand over to them a vehicle of such pedigree! Scandalous!"

In the end Port agreed. What was left unsaid was that the Frenchman was staying in Mongolia as well. Billy could envision Dr. Han giving inoculations in a Gobi yurt, snipping umbilical cords, setting bones. It was beyond him to see the Laurent of the Grand Prix de Monaco in that setting.

So to be sure he understood all this, Port said, "But you're joining the Free French. To help de Gaulle defeat the Boche. No?"

"It is my most ferocious wish, sir."

"Well, then. I understand Dr. Han's motivation. But yours?"

"*Mon capitaine,* I have experienced an epiphany. Today I think primarily of the sick. The *petites enfants.* Of my own ambitions, my *espoirs,* nothing. I abnegate self and focus on the children. Memories of checkered flags, *la vie sportive,* belong to the past. Glory and France are the future and can wait."

"Yes," Port said, uneasy in the presence of such piety, "very noble, I'm sure."

Especially when Monsieur capped his demand for the Bentley with one more request: "Sir, this is most difficult for me, but I must inquire. Could your man Leung advance me a few francs from his purse? I dislike being a burden to Dr. Han, even in this fucking wilderness, with all her other concerns. A loan, of course, between gentlemen."

"A loan?" Billy said. "You're the most famous deadbeat in China!"

"Absolutely a loan! My honor does not permit me to accept gifts or donations, sir."

Billy finished by giving the driver a thousand in cash, U.S. dollars. And when Laurent attempted to press a promissory note on him, Billy gave him a look. "Let's be realists, Monsieur."

Dr. Han came to thank him (for the car; neither man thought it appropriate to mention the cash). She was perhaps forty and looked thirty, so bright-eyed and happy she seemed.

"I can't tell you how . . ."

"Doctor, don't even try. The miracle isn't that I'm giving you my car . . ."

"Lending . . ."

"But this spell you've put Monsieur under."

She smiled. "He is devoted to the children. Such a selfless man . . ."

"He's never been devoted to anyone but himself. Then you happened along, Doctor. You've redeemed a sinner. God bless you both. You'll need it."

"You don't resent that I'm abandoning you and your men?"

"Marines are pretty self-reliant. And we've got Doc Philo."

"He's a fine man, your doc. I have learned much from him. The setting of compound fractures, alone. After the war, please see to it that he goes on to medical school? Never again will I slight a doctor of veterinary medicine."

They talked over timing, details of her departure, once the column passed through the rough country coming up. Then Billy dropped the bantering tone. "Dr. Han, regarding this epidemic, have you had diphtheria?"

"Never, but I've been vaccinated against it."

"And Monsieur Laurent?"

"He knows about the epidemic but didn't comment on it, Captain. He strikes me as the kind of man who is unkillable. Recall his car crashes. Of which he has favored me with numerous colorful accounts . . ."

She smiled her proud, though thin-lipped smile, then turned and went off to busy herself with chores and preparations.

It was, thanks to Dr. Han and her driver, a Mongol herdsman who provided the final clue to the whereabouts of Sergeant Travis and his lost patrol. This was at Conagol, after they came down from the heights of Hongor, perhaps eighty miles east of Baruun Urt, and just inside the border of Outer Mongolia, a place where caravans and herdsmen paused because there was water. They filled their water tanks and bought beans and root vegetables to flesh out their canned beef and pork, while Port encouraged Leung and the padre to mingle with the locals.

But before they learned anything, it was Dr. Han who broke the news.

She and Monsieur had left shortly after first light, heading west deeper into Outer Mongolia, only to return not ninety minutes later, at a crisp thirty miles an hour, about as well as even Laurent could do on the trackless chalk.

What happened, Port asked himself as he saw their dust plume coming fast, they couldn't find the epidemic? People are keeling over from diphtheria and Monsieur lost the way? A Marine corpsman could find a damned epidemic!

"*Mon capitaine,*" the Frenchman called out, cheered to be driving and quite excited. "We encountered some damned shepherds, stupid, stinking fellows. They tell of a crazy man with red hair and green uniform a two-day ride by horse or camel north of here. In low hills. This man rules there as a warlord might. Nomads and the innocent give the place wide berth because of his madness and violence, a band of foreigners terrorizing the district north from Conagol. The doctor and I thought instantly of your *monstre sacré,* the outlaw sergeant Travis."

My God, Billy thought, had Travis gotten himself elected general?

Dr. Han filled in details, maps were pulled out, and Father Kean fetched. The difficulty in getting to where Travis might be was that the border between Inner and Outer Mongolia was so vague and indistinct. This side, the Japs still had territorial rights, the other side, the Mongolian Republic. Port had no desire to be interned as an alien and sit out the war for straying across a line he couldn't see. Precisely where along the border would they find Travis? Dr. Han, unable to answer but having done her little bit, earned a handshake.

And then, as she got back into his Bentley, Billy topped that with a most enthusiastic kiss on both cheeks, and a clutching of her hands, startling both of them. After which, Dr. Han resumed her humanitarian journey as the Bentley roared off in a cloud of chalk dust and a vigorous sounding of horns by the Frenchman, the thousand bucks burning holes in his pocket.

"Dammit, Top," said Port, "that's a hell of a woman."

"Yessir," said Rafter, his enthusiasm controlled.

From Conagol on, not wanting to be surprised by either Travis or the Japs, Port sent two trucks scouting ahead, one commanded by Rafter, the other by Federales; the vehicles manned by four or five Marines and heavily armed, each truck with a light MG and a couple of BARs. Once either of them contacted Travis, if they did, they were to get back fast to Port. That damned Jap spotter was up there again. Keeping an eye on them for the Zeroes? Or was infantry on their trail? It was a hell of a note, the Japanese Imperial Army wasting so much time on a handful of Marines when they could be giving glory and honor to the emperor by capturing Singapore or taking Rangoon.

There was also a bright side. Siberia was no longer just a distant fantasy. So if the Japanese were to prevent their getting there, they had no time to lose. New Year's Eve was coming. And Billy recalled Father Kean's weather report: in January in Mongolia, forty below zero. Could you fire up the engine of a Zero, would infantry on either side fight effectively, in such cold?

Billy thought enviously of the regiment sweating it out under palm trees in Manila. The officers' club at Cavite Naval Base probably served a wicked Tom Collins. If the Japs hadn't yet taken Cavite, officers' club and all.

Late that afternoon Federales came back at flank speed.

"We found Travis, Captain," the Mex shouted. "Crazy bastard took a shot at us. They're up in some low hills with a touch of forest. Saw smoke, so they got wood to burn."

That was good news. No wood out here on the plain and for two nights they'd been sleeping cold.

"You sure it was Travis?"

"Yessir, him or one of his men. Wearing Marine issue overcoats. None of these crappy sheepskin jackets."

"Red-haired fellow?"

"Dunno. Had a tin hat. But it was good shooting, just a warn-off. Kicked up dirt ten yards in front of the truck."

"Why would Marines scare off a Marine truck?"

"No idea, sir. Maybe they're loco, maybe alerting us to bad hombres in the neighborhood. Bandit country like this here, you can't never be sure. Like fighting against Villa. Come back here in a hurry with the map coordinates."

"That's well," Port told the scout.

He got the command moving, shouting the orders himself in Rafter's absence.

"Saddle up, saddle up!"

They rolled until full night and then bedded down, thankful for the down sleeping bags. "Man, it's cold." They'd paused toward dusk on encountering a single big tree which they cut down with Rafter's axes and saws and Billy had them build a large fire. Not only for the heat, but to draw Rafter and his truck back to them. The enemy observation plane didn't fly by night and the local Mongols already knew where the Marines were. Sure, there were risks, but in this instance, Port thought them manageable. He didn't want men freezing to death, or tangling with Travis in the dark; let that wait for morning.

Rafter came in about nine. "No sign of Travis, Skipper. Couple of nomads think he might be northeast of here."

"Federales found him. Saw a man in a tin hat and proper-issue Marine overcoat. Squeezed off a warning shot."

"Hmmmm." The top didn't understand that one, either.

Captain Port and the first sergeant had them awake and on the trail before dawn. Too cold to sleep easy, anyway. Father Kean's handy-dandy pocket thermometer said eighteen below. Hell of a country. Spit crackled before it hit the dirt. Men wondered what must it be like north of here, up there in Russian Siberia? How bad could Luzon be, even awash with Japs? They had palm trees down there, sunshine, and local gals.

"Here we got cold *and* Japs."

The top went from man to man, issuing orders. "Work your weapons in the trucks without cartridges. See that the action works. If you've got gun oil, keep it light. Slather it on heavy and your damned action'll freeze. The machine guns, too. Light oil only. And not much of it." Federales and Rafter made the rounds, checking individual weapons, making sure. Telling them to work their bolts while he watched. Even with good troops, you check.

"Long way from Manila and the regiment," men told their buddies. "No shit, Mac?"

Cantillon had told of rumors that Manila might be declared an "open city," open, that is, to the enemy. Could that be so, an "almost" all-American town like Manila occupied by the Japanese, with 4th Regiment Marines herded behind barbed wire? Maybe it wasn't so bad here in the ol' Gobi after all.

Sunup came just after eight and it was near ten when Federales signaled back to Port in the second truck.

"It's up there, sir. Them trees on the forward slope. It was uphill of them trees that hombre shot at us."

There were no warning shots this time but as the trucks ground their way uphill in low gear, some men who were clearly American Marines came downhill toward the trucks. Port's men fell immediately into a skirmish line with weapons at the ready to wait for them. Were Marines going to have to shoot it out with Marines?

Port walked up the hill toward the new men, Buffalo with him, the Thompson gun ready.

One of these new Marines must have seen Billy's railroad tracks, and he snapped off a salute, the others following. Port answered their salute, then called out: "I'm Captain William Port, Fourth Marines. Is this Sergeant Travis's patrol?"

Two of the Marines looked at the other, the one who seemed to be the leader, with two red chevrons on the sleeves of his overcoat.

"Yessir, good morning, sir. Corporal Joe Gang at your orders, Captain."

"And your sergeant?"

"He ain't here, sir. He got kilt."

"Killed? Who killed him? The Japanese?"

"Nossir," said Joe Gang, "I kilt him my own self."

47

*"He asked if he could smoke hash but I said no.
He could have a last cigarette."*

THAT stopped Port cold.

"You killed your sergeant, Corporal?" No wonder they fired a warning shot; they were mutineers.

"Yessir. Had to do it, sir. He went crazy. Smoking hashish up in the hills with the Mongols and some Chink deserters. He was talking to God and asking where Sam Houston was."

"Sam Houston? What in hell does Sam Houston have to do with it?"

"Sergeant Travis is a Texan, sir. Claims he's a great-grandson or something of the Colonel Travis that commanded at the Alamo. He went nuts, sir. The opium or the hash or whatever, we had to call him 'Commandant Travis,' and take oaths to the Republic of Texas. Kept sending for Jim Bowie and Crockett and issuing orders that we had to kill all the Mexicans. They was all bastards couldn't be trusted . . ."

"No Mexicans here, Corporal, except Sergeant Federales."

"The nomads, sir. He thought them was Mexicans. Told us to shoot 'em down like dogs. Had the blood lust, he did."

Federales wasn't happy with the line of questioning.

"Listen, you, Corporal, I won't hear more of this crap. Not about Mexicans and not in front of me, hombre, you hear?"

Joe Gang lifted his hands helplessly. "I ain't saying it, Sergeant. That was Travis. He hated Mex. But he's dead."

Port thought the sensible thing was to turn Gang and his men over to the first sergeant. He wasn't getting anywhere and it didn't pay to have an officer looking mystified. It upset the men. That's what sergeants were for, to figure things out and report back.

"Fall 'em in, Top. I want every man questioned. What they saw, what Corporal Gang told them, what Sergeant Travis did and said. We're going to have to turn in a report. Maybe convene a court of inquiry."

That was how Marine officers thought. Even a thousand miles from the regiment, even in hostile badlands, surrounded by enemies. The rules were the damned rules. "Rocks and Shoals," that's what they called the regulations for military justice, for courts martial.

"Aye aye, sir," said First Sergeant Rafter, as if they went through this sort of thing every day before lunch.

That was how top soldiers were, too. Acting as if they'd heard just about everything before.

They walked uphill through the trees to where Gang and his men lived, in a log cabin of sorts with a sod roof and chimney, through which smoke was rising. "Some Russkis built this place years ago," Gang told Rafter, "used it as a hunting lodge. Wolves, mostly, and bears, local people say." When Rafter had gone through the eight men and taken notes, he gave way to Port in the questioning of Joe Gang. Port, Rafter, and Federales took him outside, despite the cold, so Gang could answer up freely without being overheard.

"Tell us about it, Corporal. I want to hear your side and check it against what the others say. About why you had to kill Sergeant Travis."

"Aye aye, sir. We was a squad of Marines up here in Mongolia. The war wasn't on yet and we was just patrolling east out of Harbin and supposed to head for Hohhot and Brydon's people. We had no officers, no radio, no nothing but Sergeant Travis. And then our damned truck went down. Couldn't get it running, no way. Ever since we been using Mongol ponies we bartered for with the nomads. And Travis was going bad. He'd just been court-martialed back in Harbin about drugs. When Travis wasn't on the stuff, he was a good NCO, ran a good squad. But when he was stoned, he got crazy. He found some fellows up in the hills. Said they might help find us another truck. He started spending a lot of time with them. Planning strategy, he said. But I think it was just the opium and the young girls. He was up there with the Mongols and some Chinese they had with them, like he was king o' the hill. They was a little afraid of him too, that's how crazy he got. Then word came that the Japs and us was in the war. A nomad had a radio and he told us. Said the Japs invaded Hawaii. Maybe California, too. And Oregon. So we knew we was cut off.

"At first Travis made sense. Said a squad of Marines on their own had no chance up here. If we could tie in with the Chink Army, hell, they was our allies now. Between us we might be able to do something.

But Travis kept yelling about killing the nomads. That they was Santa Ana's Mexicans. But, hell, Captain, if we was ever to get out of here with winter coming and Japs all around, we'd need these local people, not kill 'em. Mostly Travis was whacked out and I was trying to think for both of us. I said, we gotta have friends, Travis. To trade with and for guides and such. He kept saying they gotta be killed before they came over the walls and captured the Alamo. It was a shrine, and sacred, and we had to defend the son of a bitch.

"I was only one corporal out of three. So I talked to the others and told 'em, if we hoped to get outa here, we couldn't be killing Mongols. And we gotta do something about the sergeant."

" 'Like what?' they asked me."

"Like we kill him before he kills all us."

"You couldn't arrest him, bring him up on charges?" Captain Port asked.

"We was living in tents and yurts with no locks on the door or bars on the window. That was before we found this old hunting lodge and moved in. And who the hell was going to sit up all night listening to Travis yelling and cursing? He was telling the younger fellas there was a 'dobe church up at Baruun Urt that we got to fortify on orders from Stevie Austin hisself, an old Spanish mission, he said. So we could stop the Mexicans at San Antone.

"I said, Sarge, there ain't no Mexicans. Only Mongol herders and nomads. And how we gonna live off the land if we shoot the folks own the land? You know what he said?"

"No," Rafter said.

"Travis said Sam Houston was counting on us to save Texas."

Federales didn't say anything, but looked as if he was considering it.

"So when I heard that," Gang said, "I said, okay, we got to kill him."

"The other two corporals, they said, 'Hell yes, if you do it, Joe.' "

Joe Gang fell silent. Then, calmer, he said to Billy Port: "Captain, this was wartime. You got to have someone to lead. You know that, sir. So I said, okay, then I'll lead. I'll kill Commandant Travis.

"And I done it, sir. And I was right to of done it, sir."

Billy Port weighed what he'd heard, convened a captain's mast right there on the spot, with Rafter and Federales and Lieutenant Cantillon serving, the latter as recording officer and in defense of Joe Gang. Cantillon, saying nothing, wondered if an officer could do both.

They built a fire and sat down around it on the ground. Even Corporal Gang. Rafter posted sentries and chased away the curious and Port got them started. "Mr. Cantillon, please take notes. We'll have to write up a report when we're back with the regiment."

"When" they were back, not "if." Port made a point of it and Cantillon found his stubbornness on the matter irrational, but comforting.

"Okay, Gang. Just tell us how it was and what happened. From the time you all first talked about killing your sergeant. Why and when and who was there."

Joe Gang looked uneasy. Port wasn't starting off very supportively, was he?

"Well, sir, like I said, we three corporals agreed it had to be done and I volunteered. There was some talk among the men—we told 'em what was up—of shooting him while he slept. 'Cause the men was scairt of the bastard, I mean Sergeant Travis. But I said, hell with that! This ain't the damn army. If we're gonna shoot a noncommissioned officer of Marines, we're gonna do it proper. So when he was shaving one morning two of the boys jumped him, tied him up, and they hustled him out in front of the squad.

"I fell everyone in and told off the charges against Travis, trafficking in drugs, consorting with bandits, threatening to kill civilians, endangering the command, being whacked out on dope, everything I could think of, including selling weapons to the enemy. He just cursed me out. Called me a rodeo cowboy been thrown too many times. And he wasn't far wrong there.

"But in the end I told him he was gonna be shot and asked if he had any last wills and testerments and such. And he just said, 'Don't miss, Joe, 'cause if you do, I'll come back and get you.'

"Well, I had to laugh. 'From thirty feet with a Springfield .03, Travis, I ain't gonna miss.' So we tied him to a tree and gave him a minute to pray if he wanted, and I called the squad to fall in and stand at attention, properlike. Then the sergeant cussed us some again and asked if he could smoke some hash and I said no. A cigarette, but no dope.

"Then I stood out there in front of the men, facing Travis, and I said, 'Here it comes, Sarge. I promise it'll be quick.'

"And he looked me right in the damn eye and he called out, not loud: 'God bless the United States Marine Corps. And Semper Fidelis, you sons o' bitches!'

"I shot him then. Pretty a shot as you'd want, square through the chest. And finished him off with a .45 slug in the head. Too bad we had to do it, Captain. When he was sober, the sergeant was a good Marine."

48

Marines, being sensible folk, did not like advancing under enfilade fire.

THEY found Corporal Joe Gang not guilty on all counts and Port promoted him on the spot to buck sergeant and squad leader.

Cantillon thought they might have pondered the verdict for a while, if only for appearance sake, but everyone else believed it was properly done. Especially Joe Gang.

Top Sergeant Rafter, who liked to know his NCOs, got the newly minted sergeant aside and talking about himself. Gang was thirty and had been a Marine eight years. "Before that I was a rodeo rider in the Northwest, Pendleton, Cheyenne, as far north as Calgary for the Stampede, and onct I went east to ride at Madison Square Garden there in Noo York. Worked out of a small cattle town in eastern Oregon, place called Joseph."

"They name you for the town or the town after you?" Rafter asked, manifesting a rare wit.

"Nossir, Top," Gang said somberly, "they named that there town after a great American, and a great soldier, Chief Joseph of the Nez Perce tribe. Back sixty or seventy years ago he led the U.S. Cavalry a merry chase in and out of the mountains of Oregon and western Idaho and up into Canada even. Best guerrilla fighter there ever was. Even the Army said that when he wasn't ambushing and killing 'em. Finally, when Chief Joseph knew he was outgunned and wasn't never going to win no matter how long he fought, but only lose all his people to starving and freezing to death, he brought the tribe in and signed the peace. That was when he made that famous speech of his, promising the Army, 'I will fight no more forever.'

"Chief Joseph was a great man who kept his sworn word and later on they named the goddamned town for him."

Master Sergeant Rafter had read the commendations and knew what young Billy Port had achieved in the jungles of Nicaragua ten years earlier alongside Chesty Puller. And was tempted to remind Gang there were Marine officers who also knew a little about guerrilla fighting.

Instead, he held his tongue. Gang would find out soon enough how good Port was in a fight, how efficiently these Dog Company Marines and their captain trafficked in death.

That day was January second of 1942. A new year, second year of the new war as well. But the world news didn't get much better. Mr. Cantillon reported the Japanese had occupied Manila after it was declared an "open city."

Manila? Where their buddies in the 4th Marines had evacuated to and landed just a month or six weeks ago? Port's Marines looked at each other. Maybe they weren't so bad off here in freaking Mongolia after all. One Marine asked what that meant, "occupied"?

"That mean the Japs had to fight their way in, slaughtering and butchering, Mr. Cantillon? Or our side just plain quit?" The naval officer felt discretion was called for and said he'd get back to them on that.

And Billy Port, knowing he shouldn't, permitted himself an additional and quite private sense of loss. All the stuff Major Ridgely took to Manila for him aboard ship to keep from the Japs: his books, the Waterford and silverware, the uniforms tailored by Poole's, his civvies, the vintage Bordeaux. And then, and only then, he thought of poor Ridgely and where the major might now be, if anywhere.

"Damn!"

Sergeant Joe Gang was sent for. "Get your squad squared away tonight, Sergeant," Port told Gang. "I'm moving north at first light. Siberia's not much more than a few hundred miles as the crow flies." He'd not yet grasped that his new buck sergeant had a mind of his own.

"Trouble is, Captain, we ain't crows," said Gang. "North of here is where Commandant Travis's old *compadre* Tarif hangs out. And that boy is mean. He's from Sinkiang out there in the wild west of China near Afghanistan and he's as much Afghan as Chink. Like Travis, he enjoys a toke at the old hashish, too. And he's got a few hard boys along with him, mostly Nationalist deserters that Chiang would cheerfully hang if he had them back. And some Mongol bandits that's even worser. There's twice as many as we got here. They make a living ranging way out into the country, robbing herdsmen, raping the girls, rustling the ponies, and dropping in on a merchant driving through or a village that looks promising. Then they scoot back to their hidey-hole with their ill-gotten gains where it's tough to get at them. Even if you had enough men."

"Why's that?" Port asked. The answer was, to a Marine, a familiar one.

" 'Cause they hold the high ground, Captain."

Tarif had been Travis's pal, with a mutual interest in hashish and profit, but after Joe shot Sergeant Travis, relations went downhill.

"Tarif knows I don't trust him and he sure don't trust me, Captain. I killed his *compadre* Travis and I don't smoke dope or rape young girls, and in his book that puts me down as trouble. And I suspect he got wind of Pearl Harbor and what you told me about the Japs kicking hell out of us, and he thinks that means he can bully us around some, being that we're Americans. We had a friendly firefight or two with them boys already. And a few that weren't so friendly. So to get past Tarif we got to detour east a bit or fight him here on his ground. Don't see no other course. We leave 'em alone and untouched and they just might start tracking us. They'll see we got trucks and weapons that would look mighty good on Tarif's mantelpiece. I wouldn't like that, lookin' back over my shoulder at them boys, and sleeping scairt."

"And I don't like detouring 'east,' " Port said flatly.

East took them back toward the Japanese. Not a clever idea. Not the way that pesky spotter plane was haunting the column. So that left a fight.

"How many men has Tarif got," Port wanted to know, "and what weapons?"

"About forty Chinese, all of them been soldiering a couple of years so they know the work. The rest, maybe twenty or thirty more, they're local talent, Mongol. Joined up for the profit, to see the world, and get in a little rape on the side. They ain't soldiers really, just bandits, but they got their nasty side."

Well, so did the Mongol bandits at Celestial Joy, killing and raping. Since Father Kean was forever prattling on about what a peaceful, placid, amiable folk the Mongols were, Billy now inquired sourly of him about the paradox. The Jesuit conceded the point: "I did mention brigands back there in Tientsin, Captain, and don't forget Genghis Khan was a Mongol."

Joe Gang relieved Port on that. "This Tarif ain't no Genghis Khan nor cousin Kublai neither. But he's camped out on the high ground straddling this road we got to use and got some entrenchments dug in case we come after him. And by now he's sure to know we got reinforced. His boys swap the news with the natives and keep up-to-date pretty good. They got to know about you and your command, Captain."

"Weapons?" Billy asked.

"He got some Springfield rifles old Chiang issued them back at boot camp and a rusty old Maxim. Plus our Browning light machine gun that Travis traded him for dope and a couple of frisky Mongol girls."

"Sergeant Travis was selling your guns?"

"Well, swapping's more like it. And before I kilt him, that USMC machine gun was sure one of the items in the indictment, you might say, sir."

Despite Kean's failure to mention Mongols who didn't behave like Little Lord Fauntleroy, he knew the country and Port didn't, and so the priest was again called for consultation.

"Tarif's force, maybe sixty, seventy men, is here, Padre," Billy pointed out on the map. "And we're here. I don't want to avoid them by swinging east, leaving us vulnerable to the Japs. Especially by air, strafing and bombing. We don't need any more of that. Our route goes right through him. Do you know what the country's like in Tarif's precinct? Sergeant Gang says he holds the high ground. I need to know more about the terrain, where Tarif's people can fight with a secure rear if I attack."

"And you have to attack?"

"I'm not leaving sixty armed hostiles in my rear, Padre. They could shadow us all the way to the Russian border. And that would be a hell of a note, us in a firefight with the Japs up there and Tarif coming up on us from behind. I'm not fighting on two fronts. No, I've got to deal with them here."

Father Kean, though not enthusiastic, nodded agreement. It made sense, and as both a Catholic and a scientist, he took some things on faith, but not all. So he said, stabbing a finger at the map, "Get me up to this height of ground, sir. From there through those marvelous binoculars of yours, I may be able to fashion you a more detailed topographical map. I did a dig not far from here in '34, a velociraptor vertebrae that had its novel features."

Federales, the scout, and Gang, who'd been there, drove the fifteen or so miles with Father Kean and four Marines. They were gone for about six hours. And when they returned they had the best of all possible intelligence sources; they had a prisoner.

"Well?" Port asked Sergeant Gang and Federales. But it was Father Kean who in response handed over what looked to be a reasonably detailed and marked-up map. Then he answered a question that hadn't been asked.

"This Tarif chap's no General Sin, Captain. He won't stand there and be decapitated." The priest sounded impressed despite himself.

"Sergeant Gang?" Billy asked, seeking enlightenment.

"They got the high ground on a ridgeline that runs roughly east and west. Being on top, they can shift around and defend against people coming at them from the north. Or fellows like us coming up the road from the south. It looks like they've dug in some, Skipper, but shallow with the ground froze solid. And they ain't got no bob wire. They live in big yurts on the reverse slope. From where we was we could just see the tops of. This fellow we brung back's an amigo of Tarif. One of his Chinese Nationalists. Claims his boss Tarif's not just another bum, but was a major in Chiang's army, pretty good one. Got cashiered for corruption. His boys brag about him with considerable respect."

"Chiang's army, corrupt? Next thing, they'll be discovering whores on Bubbling Well Road."

Rafter grinned. He knew Port's sarcastic bent, had suffered it himself on occasion. Now the captain called on his scout.

"Federales, this map gives me their position and deployment. But where are their automatic weapons?"

"Don't know, Skipper. Their right flank is the shoreline of a small, frozen lake. Their left flank's anchored on the ridgeline and dug in. Ridgeline runs about three or four miles to the east before it falls away and dies. But from where we was, we didn't see no automatic weapons."

Joe Gang pitched in again. "The prisoner says that before Tarif deserted Chiang's army, he swapped a field gun, French 75, to the Reds for cash. His men hadn't been paid in three months and he used the dough to pay the rent, buy a little rice and some baby lamb. It was a pretty old gun, dated back to the Battle of the Marne."

Port laughed. He recognized that, given the circumstances, he might have done the same for *his* men. But he wanted a little precision here about the enemy, not colorful anecdotes. Good! They had no artillery. Marines don't need French 75s shooting at them. He asked again about the automatic weapons.

"Where is our light machine gun that Travis gave them? And the Maxim, where's that? We've got to know."

In a frontal assault it wasn't riflemen that slaughtered you but the machine guns.

They hadn't spotted them even with the glasses, and Federales and Gang admitted they were only guessing. "Got to be on both flanks, for enfilade fire."

"Enfilade" meant catching the advancing force from the side, cutting them down in rows and not singly, which you did firing head-on.

Marines, like sensible folk anywhere, did not like advancing under enfilade fire, so Port called up his mortarman, the one they called Dixie, and pointed out on the padre's map where the enemy machine guns might be, out on either flank, and what the range looked like.

"When the game starts, you hit their right flank first, pour it on 'em, then the left flank. You've got to knock out those guns or we're going to lose Marines going up that forward slope. Sabe?"

Dixie, a corporal and an old-timer who'd been on Haiti and fought in Nicaragua, nodded.

"Skipper, if them machine guns is where they're supposed to be, I'll get 'em for you."

49

When a BAR shot takes you through the body, you're done, you are.

TAKE the high ground, the Marines preached. In their Bible, that was the first commandment. After that you praised the Lord and didn't covet your neighbor's wife nor bear false witness. But taking the high ground, that came first.

How many times had Billy Port gone up a hill against armed men? And now he would be attacking a ridgeline at dawn against sixty or seventy troops of various persuasions with no artillery or barbed wire and only two machine guns that might not be all that well maintained. On that basis, and even outnumbered, Billy had to like his chances. You didn't need Chesty Puller to conduct the dress rehearsal. Or Clifton B. Cates, Chesty's icon, a colonel who looked like a swell—sleek, chinless, and smoking an elegant cigarette holder. A dandy who was an instinctive killer and very cold, who men said would one day be commandant.

Funny, but as good as Port was, and as self-confident, he had no such lofty ambitions. Let Cates become commandant. Or Chesty—though that was doubtful—given that Puller was only marginally less rebellious than Billy himself.

"Rafter, we'll attack at precisely eight-fifteen A.M. from the southeast. I've been timing the dawn and that'll give Tarif the low sun in his eyes and we'll be coming out of it into his blind spot."

"Aye aye, sir."

You didn't have to be commandant of the Marine Corps to figure out sensible little moves like that, Port told himself a touch smugly; just a good infantryman. He thought about dragging out the captured Skoda 37mm gun but didn't have an artilleryman.

"Hell with it, Skipper," Rafter concluded, "we'll probably just blow our own selves up." Infantry first soldiers didn't really believe in artillery.

Billy tried to leave Yusopov and Father Kean behind, giving them a transparent sob story about needing to secure their base, their supplies, and the petrol trailers. The prince raised an eyebrow but agreed; the Jesuit wasn't buying.

"I'll be going along, sir, thank you very much. The boys count on their chaplain being with them in the time of duress, and besides, you may need a little interpreting done after the battle's won."

They didn't actually take Tarif completely by surprise. One of his Chinese, up early and wandering down the forward slope to take a piss, saw the Marine trucks pulled up and parked ominously on the flat ground out front. But instead of giving the alarm he buttoned his trousers and stood there staring out down the slope at the flat below, squinting into the sun, attempting to figure out just who around here was wealthy enough to own four trucks and what they were up to. Then, being a dim sort, he turned to trudge slowly up the hill wondering what his corporal might say when awakened and told about trucks.

And by the time this military genius realized better to wake the corporal and be slapped around than not to tell him and be shot for letting the enemy surprise them, the whole matter had become academic.

The first .60mm mortar rounds began hitting Tarif's right flank where, it was assumed, one of his two machine guns was sited, at exactly eight-fifteen.

By then, two dozen Marines were humping their weapons and themselves up the lower slopes of the ridgeline, firing as they went, not at actual targets, for no Chinese were yet visible, but getting into the spirit of the thing and keeping heads down. While above the advancing Marines came the comforting overhead fire of Port's three machine guns from near the parked trucks, hitting the top of the ridgeline with sustained volleys, so that the Marines coming up the slope could see the brown dirt kicking up, could hear the occasional ricochet off metal, and now, for the first time, the cry up there ahead of them of a man being hit. One of "them," not one of "us." But that meant Tarif's boys were quickly out of the yurts and getting up into firing position.

For the first half minute or so, it was all quite pleasant, a good morning's shooting party in the sun. The sound of your own guns is always encouraging; the sound of theirs, well, less so.

Then, as the Marine mortar shifted its aim from the right flank to the left and started to pump out another concentration on where they thought the second machine gun ought to be, the first Marine was hit and went down. Port knew instantly the enemy machine guns hadn't both been silenced. Not yet. The gun they thought was on the far left flank wasn't. Instead it was closer to the center of the line, and just a few feet down the forward slope nestled behind a hillock so nearly not there, they hadn't noticed it. Or realized it just might shelter a gun and its crew.

It was the old Maxim. And old as it was, its crew was good and got to it fast, so that with its very first burst it took down two advancing Marines from the side. It wasn't perfect enfilade fire, not far enough in front of the line to be that, but it was pretty effective. All around Port men dropped to earth, crawling uphill or firing prone in the direction of the Maxim, trying to get its crew before it got them. Port was down, too, low as he could get on one knee, needing that little edge in height to see what was happening. Behind him Rafter was waving frantically at the mortar crew to adjust fire from the flank, and bring it down on the Maxim.

"Get him! Get him!" Marines were shouting. The mortar crew picked up the hand and arm signals but couldn't hear them. That wasn't why you shouted in a firefight, anyway. You shouted to be doing something and not freeze up, get too scared to fight.

Then one of the mortar shells hit close to the Maxim and by now the American machine gunners seemed to have targeted the same little hillock. You could see the .30-caliber shells slamming into the earth, the chunks and clods, the plumes of dirt, could hear the dull thud. Then another mortar shell hit, still closer this time. Port tried to differentiate between the sound of the Marine machine guns and the Maxim, to determine if the Maxim was still firing.

He jumped up then and yelled at the Marines to both sides, "Let's go. They got the Maxim. Come on, go! Go! Go!"

Port himself was going now, hard as he could, and not straight ahead but veering right, dodging and running low, toward where they'd sited the Maxim.

He was passed by a young Marine he thought was Buffalo, running even faster.

"Hit them with a grenade!" Port shouted, reaching to his belt for a fragmentation grenade of his own. When you got close enough, that was when you went to grenades, a concussion grenade if you had one, to stun them, knock hell out of them. Then you finished them off with shots.

Which was what was happening now, perhaps thirty yards farther up the slope.

"We got 'em, Skipper," someone yelled. It was Buffalo. Standing half crouched on the ridgeline itself.

Port turned his back to the enemy to signal Rafter. "Move the mortar and machine-gun fire the other direction now, Top. Keep pouring it in. We'll secure this flank."

Rafter nodded his understanding and also turned to give hand signals to the base of fire near the trucks. When Port reached the ridgeline he saw the Maxim, on its side and badly twisted, with a couple of Chinese irregulars splayed out on the ground, not looking very perky. Meanwhile two Marines with BARs, lying prone, were paying back the enemy with enfilade fire of their own, hosing the entire length of the ridgeline over and over, pausing only to slam home a fresh twenty-cartridge magazine.

Someone to his left shouted: "They've broke, Skipper. They've broke and they're runnin'!"

And they were. There were Marines all over the ridgeline now and the BARs shut down, not wanting to hit their own people with friendly fire.

Port moved left, his Springfield at the ready. There were bodies sprawled awkwardly everywhere on the ridge, none of them Marines. But as far as he could see, all Chinese or Mongols, in their bloody furs looking like dead bears piled up after a hunt. The overhead fire of the machine guns and the mortar concentrations had done most of the damage. The BARs and grenades and the riflemen did the rest. All the enemy still on the ridgeline were dead, no wounded, no prisoners. In a firefight if a man was down but still moving, the Marines kept shooting. A moving man was dangerous. So you made sure he didn't move anymore.

To the north down the ridge's reverse slope, he could see men running, a few of them not well but lurching, cockeyed, sort of. These were men who'd been hit; the captain wondered if Tarif was among them.

"Bring up the light machine guns. I don't want them getting away."

He wheeled and saw Joe Gang. "Sergeant, get your BARs pulled down on those men running. I want them dead. Get as many of them as you can. Get 'em all."

"Aye aye, sir."

Captain Port looked at his wristwatch. Eight thirty-five. They'd jumped off at eight-fifteen. Twenty minutes. Not bad; they'd worked fast. Around him Marines lying prone had set up their BARs and were using the automatic rifles on single-shot mode, all the better to pick off individual men fleeing into the distance, three hundred, four hundred yards out now, and growing smaller. But still within range, still being hit and spun 'round, still going down clutching at their guts and rolling around. It was too far to hear them scream but you knew they were screaming. When a BAR shot takes you through the body, you're done, you are.

Rafter, a top soldier in a firefight or out, was calling for head counts, inventorying equipment. The firing was still going on but he was checking things.

"That Browning machine gun Sergeant Travis swapped for. I want to see that gun."

"Got busted up, Top. Mortar shell hit it."

"I want it anyhows. Need the serial number. It's checked out to Travis's squad and poor Joe Gang don't need courts of inquiry asking about how a perfectly good machine gun got lost."

"Aye aye, Top."

"And them enemy Springfields you collected, pull the firing pins and throw them the hell away. I hate to leave a usable weapon just lying around."

A dozen men along the ridge continued squeezing off shots. It was easy shooting on a landscape with so few features except for the fleeing men. It helped, too, that the sun was higher now. You could hardly miss. The Marines kept firing for perhaps another five or six minutes. By now it was a turkey shoot, men calling out to their pals, calling the shot. "That guy far right. He's mine! I'll take him."

By now, it was target practice.

When there were no more targets, Port called for the cease-fire.

50

"I'm like the lepers of Molokai. Whatever I touch, dies."

As first sergeants do, Rafter was checking the roster, toting up casualties.

"Two dead, Skipper. Six hit, one of them through the lungs pretty bad, and we may lose him. Doc's working him over. That's one time we could of used that she-male Chinese Dr. Han, I can tell you. The others will make it, walking wounded except for one fellow broke his leg. Oh, yeah, Father Kean got knocked out."

"And how in hell did that happen?"

"We left him back with the trucks and the mortar but he got curious and came strolling up the hill. Looks to me like a ricochet hit him. Or a chunk of rock. Got a nasty bruise on his forehead and a little bleeding where it broke skin. He's out of it. Doc'll fill you in."

"Not until he's taken care of the bad wounded, Top. Who are the dead?"

One of them was a new man from Joe Gang's squad. Rafter wasn't quite sure yet of his last name. The other was Jones from Federales's squad, the kid who'd pulled consular guard duty in Yokohama, who'd learned Japanese from his girlfriend, and who translated for Sparks.

"Loverboy."

"Yessir," the first sergeant confirmed. "The Maxim got 'em both. Body shot, stitched 'em both. Enfilade fire from the Maxim."

Port shook his head angrily.

"That damned gun was in the wrong place. Tarif should have had it way out on his flank, not snugged up to his center like that, damn him. The mortars would have taken it out if the Maxim was where it was supposed to be."

Rafter, too, was angry. That was the trouble with wars. You did all the right things and lost good men because the other dumb bastards made a tactical mistake and *you* paid for it.

"Okay, Top, write up the casualty report. We'll bury the dead here and patch the wounded."

"Yessir."

Rafter knew better than to ask about writing people up for decorations. That was parade ground stuff. Or for when they got back to the regiment. He never even brought it up. Instead they moved on to tidying up the ground, counting the enemy dead, and going through their pockets. Maps, orders, service record books, how much ammo they had, looking closely at their weapons, whether they were cared for, or had pitted barrels, if equipment and uniforms were in a good state of police. Marines were finicky on the details. You learned things about the enemy that way, things that could give you an edge, even when they were dead. Of course, with irregulars like these, you got a mixed bag.

After the cease-fire, Joe Gang took a fire team out north of the ridgeline for a half mile or so, tracking the retreating enemy, checking the remaining dead. Among them they found Tarif. The chief cut-throat survived the actual firefight and had gotten off the ridge alive; it was as he fled that Tarif was killed.

"You sure?"

"Yessir, Captain. I met him with Travis. Head shot. Neat as you'd want, from behind. Six hundred yards range if it was a foot. Bullet took everything north of his nose from the inside and blowed it out the front. I wouldn't of known him except for all them medals that he awarded hisself. And by the lower half of his face, the gold teeth and Dr. Fu Manchu mustache. Pretty shot."

Some of Tarif's men did get away, maybe fifteen or twenty of them. But from the blood they left behind and the weapons discarded, they were no longer much of a factor.

Not a bad morning's work, Port concluded. They'd eliminated another obstacle between here and the Siberian rivers. Too bad about losing two men. Damned Maxim gun, placed improperly, when a man experienced as Tarif should have known better. Billy looked over the ground one more time, fixing it in his mind, and reminded Rafter to write down the map coordinates in case he ever had to write a report. Then he gave the order and the trucks drove back slowly to their little base, such as it was, close by one of the nomad villages.

Father Kean drifted in and out. Concussion, that's what Doc said. Port hoped that was all. Concussion, he understood. It would be nice if Dr. Han were still with them to check out the priest. Even if Doc did his best.

"Father?" Cantillon asked. He'd taken on the Jesuit as a personal concern, sitting by him in the gloomy yurt, chatting when he was awake, soothing his forehead with a damp cloth, helping him get down the tea Mongol women kept fetching. And now when the wounded man moved slightly, opening his eyes and trying to squeeze out a smile, asked solicitously, "Can I read to you, Father? Or would you prefer that I just shut up?"

"Yes, my son."

Not knowing what that meant, the young lieutenant patted Kean's hand. Cantillon had seen the fight that morning, from back at the trucks, under orders from Port to stay there. Still, he'd once again heard shots whining overhead, seen men hit, men die. He felt better spending time with the priest, like himself an onlooker more than a warrior, than alone in a yurt with his memories of the morning.

So Cantillon changed the subject. To the attractions and wonders of Mongolia. It was below zero, snowing, they had taken casualties, more hard fighting loomed, and they were sheltering in a stinking felt tent. Curiously, their less than glowing surroundings seemed to energize the old man.

"Ah, yes, Mr. Cantillon. Did I tell you of the Cave of the Ten Thousand Buddhas?"

"I don't believe so."

"A shame Captain Port's course missed it out. One of the splendors of Asia. An archaeological marvel. Oh, my."

Then Billy Port came in to the yurt, shaking snow from his fur hat and the sheepskin coat.

"What marvels are those, Padre?"

"The Cave of the Ten Thousand Buddhas, sir. Dating from as early as the fourth century, anno Domini, well preserved in the desert air, the texts and frescoes truly unmatched. The Brittanica devotes several pages to the subject. I commend it to your reading, even as an amateur."

"Thank you, Padre."

Port told Cantillon he'd take over sitting with Father Kean. When the young officer had gone, the priest said, "A delightful boy. Not at all your calloused professional warrior."

"Not at all," Port agreed in a growl.

The Jesuit, who just minutes before was unconscious, was fully alert and heard the growl under the words.

"I didn't mean that as a reproof, sir."

"Well, men are different. Some better than others."

"Tut, tut, Captain. You're a career soldier. Mr. Cantillon's only learning."

"Thank you. And speaking of which, I don't want you getting into any more firefights, Father. Some of us do it for a living; I don't want to lose you on a whim."

"Mea culpa, Captain. I'll try next time to behave. But I began going over the top with the Tommies in 1914, and foolish habits are difficult to break."

"Well, I guess you'll survive."

"Thank you, Captain Port, for putting up with me."

Then, as if he'd been thinking about it, Billy asked, "Would it tire you to talk for a bit?"

"Of course not, Captain. With the well meaning, such as young Cantillon, I doze off, lapse into comas, just to shut them up and get a little peace."

"Well, I'm not all that well meaning, so please tell me if you get bored."

"I shall, sir," Kean said with a grin.

Billy Port began his confession, not knowing precisely how to do it.

"I realize it'd be nice if we were all more like Dr. Han, concerned with the children, the suffering we glimpse as we pass, curing and saving. But I'm at war, trying to survive. To get myself and my men out of here and across the river into Siberia. And then a boy like Cantillon looks at me cow-eyed and disapproving. When it comes to war, I know he's wrong and I'm right. But there are the residual doubts."

"We all have doubts, Captain Port. Saint Augustine had doubts. Jesus once asked that a cup should pass."

Port shook his head.

"It wasn't like this back in Nicaragua in '32. Chesty and I [in trying to make his point, Port didn't bother to identify Puller further] didn't agonize. All that poverty and sickness and the horror of a civil war in a primitive land. And we just kept the railroad running and killed bandidos and tried not to get roasted over fires ourselves. We fought, we lost men, we fought again. We were on the side of the angels; the other fellows were the baddies. There were no doubts. None! And I was a kid, Cantillon's age, a year out of the Academy."

"And now you're an old man?" Kean said, smiling at the unintended irony.

"Thirty-two years old, ten years a soldier."

"And with doubts."

"I know there shouldn't be, that I'm doing my sworn duty. We killed thirty or forty men this morning, men who would have killed us. I lose no sleep over that. So I don't think I'm confusing guilt and doubt. What bothers me is the decent, helpful little things I might have done between firefights. Things left undone along the way . . ."

"And except for an old Jesuit who just happened along, whom do you tell? Is that part of it?"

"Yes, Father."

Billy had the feeling he was making a fool of himself, confessing sin he wasn't even sure he'd committed to a Catholic priest.

"Go on, I'm a listener. Not a judge, Captain."

And you're a shrewd old bastard, Billy thought. But he did go on.

"Okay, Padre. It's just this. If we hadn't passed this way, how many people would still be alive? From General Sin to mad Travis and his pal Tarif plus a couple of Marines and some Japanese soldiers. It's the innocent bystanders that bother me, Miss Rose and Reverend Doc and the children of Celestial Joy, the nomads they machine-gunned. Like the lepers of Molokai, whatever I touch, dies. You always know where Billy Port passed; just count the dead.

"And then I tell myself that's rubbish. Hell, China's been at war for a thousand years, give or take a time-out. Someone else killed Travis, someone was bound to do away with General Sin. And I know we have to fight the Japs. They started it. I really believe we have to finish it."

Father Kean coughed and Billy handed him a stale cup of Mongol tea.

"It's cold, I'm afraid."

"Fine, Captain. A frog in my throat. The tea loosens it."

"I guess I'm making an ass of myself."

"No, you wouldn't be as good a soldier if you didn't understand duty. Nor as good a man if you didn't have doubts."

Buffalo came to the entrance of the tent then. "Top sergeant has to see you, Skipper. Shall I tell him to come over?"

"No, I'll be there. Thanks, Padre. Let me know if you need anything."

"I'll sleep now for a while, thank you, sir. But think on this: why don't I stay in China and minister to my flock? Instead of hurrying back to London to glue together some old bones that fell off a museum wall?"

"Perhaps you're not the only fellow with a few doubts."

Maybe it was a good thing they had the old priest. Otherwise, Billy thought, he'd be peddling this crap to the first sergeant. Who might not understand.

The man who was lung-shot died, Archer, that they called "Bones" on account of he was "just skin and . . ."

No muscle nor gristle but a good man. Billy went to see Archer where Doc Philo had him and Archer seemed to be at peace and not in pain. So Port held his dry, skinny hand for a time, and when Archer asked who it was there at his side in the gloom of the yurt, he told him, "It's me, Archer, the Skipper."

Bones died with Port by his side and still holding that lean young hand and Billy was glad Archer knew he was there. Rafter rigged a gasoline fire to thaw out a patch of ground they could dig into with picks and spades and plant their dead. By some miracle Father Kean was up and about and able to say a few words over the graves. That night, still pale and a bit shaky, he joined them for dinner in one of the yurts. Concussion was like that. It came in a hurry and often wore off fast.

"Strange, Captain, but when I woke I was so hungry, I thought I might as well get up. People suddenly lusting for a good meal probably aren't dying after all."

There was some chat about the firefight with Tarif and then more general war stories, Yusopov weighing in with a few good anecdotes about fighting the Austrians in 1914 and '15, then the Germans, still later in the Civil War, battling the Red Army. Cantillon mostly listened, not having had a prior war, while Federales told of the wild and strange men who rode with Pancho Villa. And even wilder men chasing them under Pershing. Billy tossed in a few Chesty Puller stories but otherwise kept shut as a commanding officer ought to do.

Then the padre suprised them all again. By taking up the thread of conversation and running with it in ways you didn't expect. Not that any of them were bored, far from it. Just they'd not seen it coming.

"When I got that knock on the head," Father Kean began, "I was pretty woozy and for a bit there thought it was a quarter century or more ago, that once again it was the summer of 1916 on the Somme. I'd been in France since the first year and by now had a respectful appreciation for the trenches, and the cover they gave you. But these new fellows, the City Battalions of men raised by Kitchener, volunteers all, the best that Old England had, really, were impatient. Afraid the war might end before they had their time up at the wicket. They were professional men, university men, lawyers and journalists and wool merchants from Bradford and textile buyers from Manchester, county cricketing stars from Liverpool, and bank clerks with futures in Threadneedle Street. They had scant understanding of what was coming, and they couldn't wait to get out of the trenches, damn them. Couldn't wait to get at Jerry, to be part of The Big Push.

"You wanted to take them by the shoulders and shake them. I recall how fine the weather was, the smell of the crushed grass under our boots and of trees in fruit, and how it was on the approach march up to the jump-off, through a lovely French countryside that hadn't yet been fought over. I can hear still the sound of the new battalions, confident, brave young men, the Welshmen singing and the Scots piping, fellows sure of themselves and their strength, eager to have a go at Jerry, at the Hun.

"You couldn't tell them anything, of course, they wouldn't have listened, wouldn't have believed you.

"And then at dawn, that Thursday morning, the first day of the Somme, the Tommies went cheerfully over the top, the new men, the City Battalions, walking slow and steady as they were trained to do, toward the Germans, toward the wire and the machine guns and the shells, into a low sun that blinded them, and at day's end, by the time darkness called halt to the slaughter, sixty thousand of us were down, sixty thousand British soldiers hanging on the wire, dead or wounded or prisoners or just vanished in the shellfire.

"It was there on the Somme that an entire generation lost its innocence, lost its confidence, and the strong young men who lived through that damned day never forgot it, and turned into Neville Chamberlain."

Port lay awake briefly that night, still hearing the Jesuit's voice, recalling the quiet in the yurt, when Kean stopped talking and at last fell silent.

Well, it might be bad here, a few orphaned Marines in a strange and hostile land, scheming and fighting and trying to get away before the Japs got them, but it sure wasn't the Somme in 1916, thank God.

And, for all their cares and woes, the last of the Chinaside Marines in mid-January of 1942 were surely closing on the final leg of their long ride. Siberia no longer loomed as some bleak, cold emptiness of exile and despair, but was beginning to sound like Eden, a promised land flowing with milk and honey, and not that far off.

It was perfectly natural and even healthy for Port's Marines to be feeling pretty good about themselves. They were not yet aware that Colonel Irabu was coming after them.

51

*The night is worth a million reinforcements. So went
the Imperial Army mantra.*

MEN who knew Irabu, who'd served with him in the Amur River
fighting, or later at Shanghai in diplomatic circles, noticed the change;
narrowly focused, impatient, driven. With all his gallantry under fire,
his ferocity in battle, there had always been about Irabu a sort of, what
was it, nonchalance? Imperial Army friends, his peers, put it down to
his California roots, and were permitted to tease him about it, to make
small jokes about having their very own Yankee Samurai.

This was a different Irabu. You didn't tease, you didn't make jokes.
Shallow men theorized he yearned for the pleasures of Shanghai, resented being ordered about by an infantry general like Watanabe, or
bridled against this new assignment, running down a handful of renegade Americans. Or speculated that General Hata himself had rep-
rimanded Irabu for some unspecified dereliction. Others, more astute,
felt that could never be the case with Irabu. But he was surely a
different fellow, they agreed on that, disagreed only as to his motivation. Was something eating at him, a goad that drove him? Perhaps
a loss. Had a friend died fighting in the Philippines? Or in the Malay
jungles? Was killed assaulting Hong Kong?

Colonel Irabu issued no explanations, made no apologies, took no
one into his confidence but his patron Nagata. And just went about
preparing for his mission and hurrying along his men, chiding, snapping at them, driving them.

Irabu's modest detachment of one lieutenant, two sergeants, and a
dozen Imperial Marines in four big Mitsubishi scout cars fitted with
oversized tires (ideal for the chalky Mongol steppes) departed Harbin,
Manchuria, early on January 9. Though he did not know the precise
location of Billy Port's detachment at that moment, the last observation
plane sighting put the Marines about six hundred miles west of the
Irabu task force and maybe three hundred miles short of their Soviet
Union sanctuary. Irabu's scout cars rolled onto flatcars in the Harbin
yards and traveled the first two hundred miles west by train, the
Harbin-Ulan Bator leg of a line that here in Manchuria was pretty

secure, but which in North China and Mongolia was chancey and often cut. With the next hundred or so miles on good Manchurian roads, Irabu reckoned he would swiftly halve the gap between him and Port. After he closed, of course, there would be more to it than a pursuit race; when he caught up, they would have to fight.

It was also on January 9 that British General Wavell's forces protecting Singapore, mainly Australian and Indian units, fell back across the Muar River to the south bank, where a new, and not very successful, stand would be made against the Japanese Imperial Guards Division. And it was the day General Homma on Luzon opened his campaign against the Americans and Filipinos trapped on the Bataan Peninsula, a ninety-day campaign that would end April 9 with the surrender of seventy-five thousand men, twelve thousand of them Americans.

As a Japanese and an officer, Irabu was interested in these far-flung campaigns, but always before him as the real target were the fleeing Marines. Two days of hard driving west as he left Manchuria and crossed a chunk of North China found Irabu in Inner Mogolia skirting the Gobi and intent on Hohhot, the last fully documented location of Port's men. Plane spotting had them traveling due north of there by a couple of hundred miles but Irabu took little on faith and was intent on questioning people face-to-face who'd actually seen the Americans. He stopped for an hour at Fengzhen where he inspected the burnt-out armored car. How could they have been so careless as to drive into a trap like that in a village alleyway? No wonder Port was still at large if that was the quality of his pursuers. Irabu also questioned townspeople, who lied, of course, he realized that, but were not very clever at it and he drew conclusions. And drove on. At Hohhot Irabu recruited local assistance, one Mongol scout who claimed (the Mongols were infamous among the Japanese as braggarts) to have explored every mile of ground between here and the Siberian border, and a schoolteacher who hired out as an interpreter. He didn't really believe local stories blaming Port for killing the Japanese officials and destroying their plane. Billy, trying desperately to get out of China, was too clever to waste time bumping off a few bureaucrats and bringing down the wrath of the authorities. Irabu briefly poked through the ruins of Celestial Joy for clues as to Billy's plans and found none. The people running the place now, a few surviving Mongol converts, and the handful of shocked kids left, confirmed Port and the Marines had been there, saved them from bandits, and departed. Beyond that, they gestured vaguely north. It was then that Irabu also turned north for Jining and Mongolia proper just beyond, and the Siberian sanctuary he was convinced was Port's goal.

At this stage of the chase, Irabu was fueled by anger, an avenging angel responding to the slaughter of his family. An intelligent man, he understood Port wasn't to blame. Other Americans were, probably farm country rednecks who resented his family for its wealth, or just for being "Japs" in "God's country," and enjoying the place too damned much. There were a few like that even at UCLA and in intercollegiate tennis. Since the actual killers were out of reach in California, Port's Marines were the sole available targets for his righteous fury. Only twice before in his thirty-five years had Irabu been as intensely focused: during the fighting on the Amur River when he and his men drove off Zhukov's armor; and when he lost the Newport Beach girl he was going to marry, who'd suddenly become untouchable.

That Port's command had killed other Japanese was an act of war. Now their contest had become personal: was he or was Port the stronger, were the Japanese or the Americans the superior people half-way through the twentieth century? A month ago, Irabu would have laughed off as rubbish such Nietzschean racial theorizing.

No longer; now the Japanese colonel had to know.

None of this did he communicate, no suggestion of vendetta, as he drove his men. They were professionals and this a campaign. He channeled his fury into an even greater efficiency of effort, a crisper sense of duty, a clearer objective. He knew the men were good soldiers; he wanted them better.

"Fall them in, Lieutenant. I want their weapons checked twice a day. Before we break camp mornings and before we sleep at night. Any rifle or machine gun the sergeants find unfit, any man they find shirking, I want to be told instantly. We could be in action against the Americans at any hour. Day or night. No one is to relax; I want this command constantly ready for combat."

"Yes, sir."

Colonel Irabu knew that soldiers everywhere, even the Japanese, spoke occasional rot. Such as that stuff with which they mocked the

Russians, chiding them for having "a despicable urge to live." But if he cringed to hear such foolishness uttered in the terrible fighting at the Amur, he held dearly a more serious and hard-learned mantra of the Japanese infantryman: "The night is worth a million reinforcements."

If he could catch Billy Port after dark and surprise him, Colonel Irabu reckoned, the Japanese would surely win. He didn't think the Americans, not even their Marines, liked night fighting. But if Port somehow learned Irabu was on his scent, and they met by day, the American would be a formidable foe.

As if to impress upon his men the seriousness of their mission and his own demand for taut discipline, when the Mongol schoolteacher from Hohhot hired as an interpreter was caught pilfering, a sergeant ran him up to the lieutenant, who approached Irabu about the matter.

"Two pairs of good wool socks, sir. His feet were cold and he worried about frostbite. He was envious of our socks," the lieutenant concluded with an amused superiority.

"Bring him here."

"Yes, sir."

When the schoolteacher was brought up and shoved to his knees on the frozen earth in front of him Irabu said, "The Japanese soldier does not tolerate thieves." Then, to the nearest sergeant, "Take your sheath knife and cut off the top joint of his right thumb. He won't be as light-fingered next time."

The schoolteacher was still conscious and still screaming as they cauterized the wound and bandaged his hand.

Port, far to the north, having worked off his own philosophical meanderings on patient Father Kean, was again the practical soldier, stalking the perimeters of his latest campsite, checking on the sentries and chewing at the men to keep their weapons from freezing. They'd be needing them again soon enough. And last night, the mercury had fallen to twenty-five below.

Siberia was now less than two hundred miles from where they slept.

From Jining north, Irabu found the going cold but the trail heating up. His two-way radio brought a single report from marauding Zeroes that thought they saw or had actually strafed a short column of trucks that might be Port's. They had the coordinates (being fighter pilots, the numbers would be approximate at best) and provided them to Irabu. The spotter plane promised him was only rarely in the air, grounded by visibility or the extreme cold. From such slim data he attempted to puzzle out and plot Port's course.

"Siberia, of course," Irabu told his men. That much he was sure of. You didn't have to be a genius to opt for the only allied country within a thousand miles. Siberia literally cried out to be the Marine sanctuary. The last remaining questions were of timing and precise destination: When would Billy try to cross the frontier? And just where, at the Amur? Or farther west over one of the Onon River bridges? Sniffing the air, poring over the map, calculating in the air sightings such as they were, questioning nomads, or coming across the dead from Port's skirmishes, Colonel Irabu tended toward the Onon rather than the Amur River. Too bad; he knew the ground better along the Amur.

But perhaps they would catch Billy while still in Mongolia and before he reached the line of the rivers. If he failed to overtake the Marines Irabu would no longer be the same man, or the same Japanese. Vengeance drove him, so did professionalism and pride.

"We'll be on the trail one hour earlier from now on, Lieutenant," Irabu ordered.

"Yes, sir," the young officer said, bowing. And asking himself, not for the first time, was it true that the colonel was born in California? What was California like? he wondered. In motion pictures it looked gorgeous but with film, they could conjure up tricks.

Earlier that day the Japanese column had seen its first wolf pack working along the edges of a small pine forest. The mercury fell to fifteen below and there was the feel of snow coming. The arid Gobi had fallen behind them and the country ahead looked rougher, low hills rising, treed here and there. That night, toward two A.M., there was an alarm as one of Irabu's sentries fired a shot.

He was a young man from Osaka, a city boy, and except in the local zoo, he'd never seen an actual brown bear, and had panicked, squeezing off a round.

52

*A man who charged Zhukov's tanks wasn't going to
dodge the lousy cavalry.*

THE brown bear was nothing, an incident, to be laughed off and sport
made of a young soldier. And Irabu was making good time, better
time than Port, and at least in part satisfying his competitiveness and
natural impatience. The first few hundred miles by rail helped, and
then the Japanese had been able to cross the Hongor Gorge on dry
roads, speeding past without hesitation the Russian monastery where
Port lost almost two days. It was near Conagol, a hundred miles or
so east of Baruun Urt, where Irabu hoped to gas up and take on
supplies, that he encountered an obstacle, the first on the road north.
His observation plane alerted him.

"Colonel, I passed over Ulanhot about an hour ago on a bearing
270 degrees West. And this side of Conagol, maybe thirty-five miles
to the east, there's what looks like a cavalry detachment, thirty-five or
forty men mounted, traveling on a course that may cut across your
route."

"Cavalry? You don't mean trucks? We're tracking four American
military trucks," Irabu said, knowing how stupid it sounded but impatient with this pilot. Damned flyers, American or Japanese, heads
in the sky instead of concentrating on the job. The flyer, disdainful of
infantry, answered right back.

"Colonel, I know horses from trucks, sir."

"Could it be a Mongol tribe on the move, ponies and camels and
their yurts?"

"Colonel, these are mounted troops, on horseback and riding
formed up and in columns of twos, trailed by a half-dozen heavily
laden camels. Looks like their supply train. I've seen plenty of nomads
from up here, strewn out and spread all over the place, pretty slovenly
too. These men are uniformed and riding in formation. I just don't
know who they are."

Irabu questioned him more precisely about bearing and distance
and then he ordered the four scout cars to a halt while he and his
lieutenant and the two sergeants unrolled and went over the maps.

None of the four had heard mention of enemy cavalry since the first year of the war.

"Wait a minute. Could they be Mongolian Republic troops patrolling the frontier? It's their country, after all."

The Mongolian Army was something of a joke but who knew? Japan wasn't at war with Mongolia. Why bother, their country nothing more than a very large and sparsely inhabited nothing, a buffer zone between the great powers? If this really were Mongol cavalry, Irabu and his men would exchange salutes and roll on, making an elaborate show of staying on their side of a frontier so vague no one, not even the Mongolians, knew exactly where one country started and the other left off.

To be sure, they woke the schoolteacher, dozing in one of the vehicles, and slapped him into wakefulness in case they needed an interpreter. His hand seemed to be coming along reasonably well and he was surprisingly affable, probably fearful not to be, and realizing how easy it would have been for this fearful Japanese colonel to have had him shot.

The Imperial Army had its own cavalry but none anywhere near here. Irabu was sure of that, having studied Japanese displacements all over North China before leaving Harbin. It was awfully far from Chiang Kai-shek's lines for it to be Nationalist cavalry. Then one of the sergeants, who'd fought at the Amur, asked: "Could it be the damned Russians, Colonel?"

With the Soviets, anything was possible, and they had entire divisions of mounted troops. But wouldn't they all be off fighting the Nazis and if not, how could they have penetrated this far south of the border without someone having raised a diplomatic screech?

In the end Irabu decided to continue en route to Conagol without changing course, taking the precaution of sending one car out a couple of miles ahead as point vehicle, with instructions to radio back in when the horsemen were actually sighted. He wasn't sure he really believed there were any horsemen. But he wanted to be careful in this godforsaken and often hostile country.

It was a prudent decision.

No more than forty minutes later the radio crackled into life.

"Cavalry sighted, Colonel. As the pilot said, maybe fifty or more. There're not Japanese, sir, but I don't recognize the uniform."

"What formation are they in? Column of twos or fours or in line abreast?"

Irabu didn't know much about cavalry tactics but he had the impression that if mounted troops intended to charge, they spread out abreast.

"They were in column but they're moving out now on either side."

"Range from your car?"

"About half a mile, sir."

"All right, return to me on the double."

The scout car was soon back in sight and Irabu waited. "If the horses follow, I'll fight them here. We've got the advantage of a slight rise that'll slow horses as they come up the slope. Lieutenant, unlimber that .50-caliber and the other machine guns and get the riflemen prone on the ground. No firing until you get the order. They may see us arrayed up here and think better of it and go home. Wherever home may be."

"Yessir."

With fast scout cars like these, the lieutenant knew, Irabu could easily avoid a fight entirely, outflanking the cavalry, whoever they were, and with a slight detour continue the march north.

That he'd rather fight against forty armed men with his dozen or so was typical of what the younger officer knew of the colonel. A man whose infantry charged Marshal Zhukov's tanks across the frozen Amur a couple of years ago wasn't going to dodge a few lousy horsemen.

Or so the lieutenant told himself, slightly nervous and perhaps wanting to get his own martial juices flowing if it came to a fight.

Irabu wasn't nervous at all. He'd not been in a firefight for almost two years and rather welcomed the prospect. Neither did he really worry about the odds, forty against twelve. When it came to machine guns versus horses, as they used to say back at UCLA when facing a team they knew they could whip, "You're playing with house money."

"Here they come, sir."

"By God," Irabu realized, "they are cavalry and they are coming."

Over a distant rise, maybe a mile north of their position, there was the mysterious cavalry coming on at a nice trot. Smallish, long-haired horses, ridden by what seemed to be big men. To him, the horses were clearly Mongol ponies, the men looked Chinese, not Russian or Mongol or, remembering a favorite film, Brits in *The Lives of the Bengal Lancers.*

The approaching cavalry was stretched out abreast covering a front of maybe two hundred yards, and coming on now at a slightly faster trot. There was a thin sun and Jesse Irabu could see glints off what seemed to be swords. Now he could also see they carried heavy saddle-bags and packs, as if they'd come a distance, and had carbines slung, short cavalry rifles. With their sheepskin jackets and fur hats and bandoliers crisscrossing their chests, they looked like irregulars, except they rode not only well but kept to formation in what was an apparent and disciplined response to orders. You didn't see that much with bandits such as thrived here in the badlands. Or with the North China warlords.

And then, galloping alongside what seemed to be their officer, a horseman broke out a guidon of sorts, topped with a kind of regimental or unit flag. A red flag!

"It's the Chinese Communists!" the Japanese lieutenant said in mild astonishment; "Mao's Red Army."

The horses were less than half a mile off now, and coming faster. Unless they were bluffing, and there was no sign of it, they would shortly be on them if the Japanese Marines didn't fire.

Irabu, so decisive usually, was a bit puzzled. The Reds fought pretty well against the Imperial Army when they had to, but they seemed to prefer fighting Chiang. Now here they were picking a fight against Japanese Special Landing Force Marines armed with machine guns who boasted a terrain advantage.

In a steady voice, Colonel Irabu now called out, "Aim at the riders with your first shots, then if they keep coming, shoot down the horses. On my command: Fire!"

It didn't take long. Most short-range firefights on open ground don't. Difficult to miss. Perhaps twenty of the Chinese Communists and several horses fell on the first volley. Then, with four machine guns firing, the rest of the horses started being hit, wheeling out of line, lurching or sprinting away, depending how bad their wounds, this way and that, plunging and bucking, then limping off or falling sideways to the brown, frozen earth.

"Keep firing," Irabu shouted. A few dismounted riders with their carbines unslung and lowered sprinted toward them up the little slope, until they, too, were caught by machine-gun fire and fell heavily, or staggered about for a time before dropping.

"Call the cease-fire, Lieutenant, but have the men remain at the ready."

"Yessir. Cease fire!"

There was no corpsman with the Imperial troops and they wouldn't have wasted his time tending to enemy wounded in any event. But as the Japanese advanced on foot down the hill, they kept their weapons on the bodies, several of which were still moving, though not in any deliberate or rational way, just twitching and rolling this way and that. Some of the wounded were yelling but the Japanese didn't understand the words. Nor did they really care. One of Irabu's sergeants grabbed one Chinese by the collar of his sheepskin and was dragging him upslope toward the colonel.

"This fellow's alive, sir. Do you wish to question him?"

He dropped the man's jacket so that he fell back onto his back, looking up at Irabu.

"You," Irabu called to a corporal who spoke a little Chinese.

"Yes, Colonel."

"Ask him who they are and why the hell they charged Imperial Army machine guns? We meant them no harm."

The wounded man listened and then he said, blood running from his nose and one eye apparently shot out, "A long-range raiding party from the Fourth Chinese Route Army. We didn't know you were Japanese."

"Who did you think we were?"

"Chiang's men, Nationalist sons of whores, of course."

They'd crossed the friendly People's Republic of Mongolia, living with nomads in their yurts along the way, and into Inner Mongolia and the Gobi, looking for Nationalist garrisons to surprise or roads and telegraphs to cut. Maybe even bump into their new allies, the Americans. There were rumors American soldiers had been seen disembarking from ships at Vladivostok to attack the Japs from the rear. Mao's men didn't think the Japanese customarily ventured this far west. As he wound up his doleful account of a promising mission gone disastrously wrong, blood bubbled from the wounded man's mouth and he choked on it, unable to say more. And then died.

One Imperial Marine had been shot in the upper arm by a carbine bullet and after his sergeant swabbed the wound and bandaged it, the man groaned aloud as they stuffed the arm back into his fur parka lest he freeze. A mile or so to the front Irabu could see the pack camels and their drivers. He was about to order one car up there to finish them off but then said, to hell with it; he had his eye on the ball, on Billy Port, and mustn't let a couple of camels distract him further.

"Almost noon," Irabu told the lieutenant. "Let's get moving. These fellows thought we were someone else. Their mistake stole two hours from us and I want to get to Conagol before dark and get that fuel."

"Yessir."

He recalled a Cossack charge one muddy morning two years ago in marshy country near the Amur, not forty horsemen coming at them but six hundred. What a slaughter that was. He probably should have kept right after Port, and driven around these Chinese, but he didn't yet know these new troops of his, and wanted to see them under fire.

You can tell something about a man when there's a little shooting.

They resumed their drive north leaving behind them about forty men and a like number of horses on the slight rise of land, most of them dead but a few still crying out or moving slightly. Two horses, apparently unhurt, stood apart from the dead grazing the dried brown grass. And before the four Japanese scout cars had vanished over the horizon, the first wolves could be seen trotting toward the killing field, sensing a free lunch.

53

"I don't want Jap regulars on my ass, Gang. If you catch them, kill them all."

A hundred miles to the north Billy Port's detachment shivered through their coldest night yet, twenty-seven below. If luck held, in another few days, the Marines would reach Russian Siberia.

It was the next midday when Federales approached First Sergeant Rafter.

"Someone's coming, Top."

Rafter, who no longer doubted the Mexican's mystic powers, didn't ask Federales to justify himself. And not wanting an anecdote about General Pershing, he only asked, "Which direction and how many?"

"From the south. Coming up behind us, Top. I don't know yet how many."

"I'll tell the skipper."

"Ask him if he can stop the trucks. Keep the men quiet. Maybe I can hear something."

When the first sergeant got to Port's truck, Billy looked at his watch as if to emphasize the need for haste, but nodded. "Stop 'em just in the lee of that next hill. I don't want to be sitting out here in the open for the planes."

Beyond that, Port said nothing. He didn't have to be convinced of Federales's worth.

Once they'd parked the trucks and shut down the engines Federales clambered to the roof of his own truck's cab with the 7×50 field glasses and, standing to gain additional height, scanned the ground to the south, sweeping back and forth over an arc of perhaps ninety degrees. Not that he expected to see much but there was always a chance. Dust rising, smoke, something like that. If you had nothing better, you could take a bearing on a wisp of airborne dust from activity you couldn't hope to see over the horizon.

But there was no dust, no smoke. Nothing. Federales dropped lightly to the hood and then to the ground, trotting out onto the flat ground where he fell to his knees and very carefully brushed away at the dirt with one hand, smoothing a small place on the ground, dusting it free of loose grains. Next he pulled a bayonet from its sheath, wiped the blade clean with a filthy pocket handkerchief, ran a practiced finger along its honed edge, and then, with a swift jab, powerfully drove the first two inches of steel blade into the frozen Mongolian hardpan. He left it there quivering slightly for an instant, before crouching even lower and, with his head turned to one side, opened his mouth and clamped down his teeth on the cold blade.

"What's he doing?" Cantillon asked Rafter.

"Quiet, if you will, sir."

"Sorry."

When, after a minute or so, Federales raised his head, Rafter answered Cantillon, still speaking low.

"He was listening for hoofbeats. His teeth pick up the vibration through the blade in the ground. He says it's like hearing, only better, using your teeth."

"But it's only for hoofbeats. Not engines?"

"He can get vehicles, too. But hoofbeats is best, on account of the vibrations are like telegraphy. Every telegraphic man has his own 'hand,' or so Sparks tells me. It's like that with Federales; every horse has a distinct gait, a vibration of its own."

Cantillon just shook his head. "Cars and trucks as well?"

"No, Lieutenant. I don't believe Federales claims that of vehicles. Maybe he can tell a Ford from a Studebaker but I don't think he goes beyond that."

Sergeant Federales had heard no hoofbeats. No horses coming after them. Nor camels either. But he had heard something through his teeth and he hurried now to Captain Port.

"I got vehicles, Skipper. Several of 'em, not sure what kind or who. They're behind us, maybe only fifteen miles. Maybe twenty. Coming on, too, moving pretty fast. Faster than us, I reckon. Automobiles like your Bentley. Or light trucks. Nothing big as we got, not that I can tell. Smaller and lighter in weight. Horsepower, too."

"Bandits? Or Japs?"

"Don't know, sir."

"Any guesses?"

"Engines sound nicely tuned. Nice smooth carburetion. Hitting on all cylinders from the vibration."

"Which means what, Japanese?"

"From what I seed of how these Mongol bandits and North China warlords mistreat their camels, and the few vehicles they got, I'd say, yessir. Sounds like proper soldiers coming. And the only proper soldiers they got up here, except for us Marines, is the damned Japs. General Pershing always use to say . . ."

"That's what I think, too, Sergeant," Billy said, cutting him off, "I think you got us some Japs."

The captain turned away and stalked over to where Rafter stood, waiting. "Officer's call, Top. In three minutes. At my truck."

By now Port's "staff," such as it was, had been defined. The first sergeant, Federales, and Joe Gang, and Corporal Young who'd taken over Brydon's squad, Prince Yusopov, and Cantillon. Not Father Kean, so as not to compromise a man of peace.

Port told them what Federales said. "So we think it's Japanese coming, in cars or light trucks, probably. No tanks, nothing heavy he says. I don't intend that we get ourselves squeezed between whatever Japanese are coming up from the south and the Japs north of us manning the river line to Siberia. These boys behind us are moving pretty fast, probably faster than our trucks, so they could come up on us any hour now.

"I don't like that, them catching us. So I'm going to hurry things up a bit, ambush them first."

"The whole column?" Rafter asked.

"No. It doesn't show on the maps but the padre tells me about an hour north of here there's an east-west ridgeline where the track passes through a natural little gorge, nothing as deep and rough as Hongor. But that little gorge could give just enough cover for a few good men on the hillsides above. At least, that's what the padre says. What we're going to do is drive up there now. And if the ground looks like Father Kean says, drop off a few BAR men and maybe a machine gun. Catch these people as they drive past."

Sergeant Joe Gang would lead the ambush, Captain Port said.

The ground, it turned out when they got there, was pretty much as the padre had said. Federales, Rafter, and Port climbed the hill with Gang to check it out, calculating where the sun would set if the Japs got here before dark, blinding men coming into it in the little gorge.

"If there's an edge, you want it," Gang said, agreeing with the others on positioning his men, and doling out rations enough for one night, and their sleeping bags. No fires tonight; not for Joe Gang's men. When Gang mentioned this, Port snapped at him. "I know it's going to be cold, Sergeant. Don't tell me what I know already. It's only one night."

Port was tough with Joe, chivvying him, hurrying him along, not wanting to have his entire command caught here in daylight.

Only Federales looked uncomfortable. "Yes?" Port asked, hearing the objection still unspoken.

"I don't like dividing the command, Skipper. If they come after dark, maybe they could outflank Joe Gang and three men. Maybe we should all set up here, ambush them with everything. The whole command."

"I don't like it, risking everyone, Sergeant. Let Joe Gang hit them first and then we come back fast in the morning and finish the job."

Port looked to Gang, the raw meat he was putting out there on the pointed end of the stick.

"Are you okay with this, Joe?" he asked. The squad leader nodded. That's all Port needed. If two of his top NCOs objected, he might have been persuaded. "We'll set up a strong point a couple of miles north of you, Gang. That way, we'll hear whatever shooting there is. We'll come back for you at daylight. You hang in there until dawn and we'll be back. Remember that, Sergeant. We'll be back for you. Just get those Japs. Get 'em all. I don't want Jap regulars on my ass when I get to the river. Get them, Gang. Get them all."

"Aye aye, sir. We'll do our best, Captain."

"I know that, Sergeant."

They did their best. But Colonel Irabu's hired Mongol guide was as knowledgeable as Father Kean and also knew about the little gorge. Which would, as the sun fell and day faded, assist Irabu and his friend, the night, to outflank the Marines waiting to kill them.

54

Arrogant? Port had been outsmarted, as bad as MacArthur,
the brass at Pearl.

PORT lay in his sleeping bag, waiting for something to happen, not
really asleep, when he heard the firing. It was just before midnight.
He sat up in the bag, feeling the cold, and crawled out. The sentries
had been walking their posts and were of course up already, but all
around him, his men were doing what he did, scrambling free of the
bags, pulling their weapons closer to hand. When you heard shots in
Indian country, you grabbed for your rifle. There was no wind, at
least. This cold was bad; with wind it would be terrible.

"It's Joe Gang," awakening Marines told themselves. "Joe snapped
the trap on them. Oh, but it's sweet."

"Listen to those BARs. They're cranking 'em out. Joe's getting
'em all."

It was all good. The trap had worked. The damned Japs, wow! Joe
Gang caught them by surprise, those bastards. Good for you, Joe!

The firing went on. After a time, it went on too long. If Gang's
ambush really had worked, by now the enemy would all be dead or
running and the firefight would be over.

Port knew it. He called for Rafter.

"Top, we're going back there soonest. I don't like a firefight that
lasts this long."

"No, sir. That first volley should of got them all. Got 'em or chased
'em."

"Well, I told Gang we'd come for him at daybreak."

"Yessir. I don't like doing it in the dark."

Port knew Rafter was right. Maybe he'd lost Joe Gang's people.
That was bad enough. Losing the rest of his command in confusion
and the night would be worse.

Then the guerrilla fighter in Billy Port spoke. "Get Federales. I'll
send him and Buffalo. Maybe two more. And on foot. It can't be more
than three miles. Four at most. There's starlight, they can follow the
road. If the Japs expect anything, they'll expect trucks. If the Japs

wiped out Joe Gang, maybe they'll be asleep. Maybe they'll be celebrating, the sons of bitches."

"Yeah, Skipper," Rafter said, thinking what Port was thinking, that the Japanese wouldn't know about Federales, coming for them in the dark with a knife and a couple of good men. Jesus! but it was cold. Could a man wield a knife at twenty-five below?

Captain Port's orders to Federales were more precise than that. "I want to know what happened tonight. It's one A.M. Even in the dark, you ought to be there in an hour and a half, two at the most. It's dark until after seven. If you find Gang and his men, ask them. If they're still alive, bring them back without another firefight. If they're dead, I want to know it. If you have to fight, kill as many Japs as you can without getting your own patrol wiped out. If Gang's lost, I don't want to lose you, too. This is recon first, Sergeant. Unless you have to fight your way out, understand? I need you back here telling me what happened. Vehicle tracks, how many, and what type. Foot tracks if they show on frozen ground. Tell me where the enemy is, and how many."

"Yessir, I understand my orders, Skipper."

"Good. Take Buffalo and you pick two more men. Travel light, no packs, no sleeping bags or rations, just weapons, canteens, and ammo. We'll be there by daybreak with your gear. I'll be there, Sergeant. You can count on it."

He'd made that same promise to Joe Gang, hadn't he? But he didn't agonize over it; in combat you go crazy second-guessing yourself.

"Aye aye, sir." The scout was smiling. Or so it seemed in the firelight. Billy thought again how Rafter had to convince him to take Federales when Port himself thought the sergeant was too old.

Billy was glad it was the Japs and not Port's command that the Mexican was coming after in the night.

Of course Port didn't know the men he was sending Federales to reconnoiter, and perhaps to kill, were commanded by Jesse Irabu, or that Irabu's command consisted of the best the Japanese had, their own Imperial "Marines."

They moved fast, Federales and his three men, the little noise they made masked by a wind that came up late. The terrible cold drove them to vigorous exertion, so that, even with scouting the ground ahead, not wanting to fall victim to whatever happened to Joe Gang, by three in the morning the patrol reached a position from which they could just discern, by starlight, the loom of the little ridgeline and the gorge that pierced it. It was up there in the gorge that they found Joe Gang.

He lay, bloodied and shivering, in a dip in the ground, sheltering and hurting, fearing that it would be the damned Japs, and not Federales, that would find him. There were Japs there, all right, two of them, lying dead around him. Tough and hard and proud as he was, Gang was hiding. He was scared and cold and in pain. Thank God for the morphine in his first aid pack, not recognizing the irony of needing drugs, the man who executed Sergeant Travis.

"Joe Gang?"

That was Federales, his distinctively accented voice hushed and husky.

"Yeah. It's me, Mex."

Federales didn't like being called "Mex," but this was hardly the time and the place to say so.

"Joe, you bad hit?"

"Yes, I'm bad hit. And two of my boys is dead. I don't know about the third."

Federales squirmed toward Joe Gang on his belly, surrendering no profile as hostage to the starlight, staying out of sight. As he had years back along the Rio Grande on night patrol in the dancing shadows of Villa's campfires. On a night patrol you crawled, you slithered, got low and stayed low, the dirt your best friend. He got to Gang and reached out a hand to touch his arm. Even in the cold, Gang's sleeve was warm. And wet.

"Half my arm is gone, Federales. And maybe one eye. Them boys over there ain't no virgins . . ."

Federales wanted to comfort the wounded man but remembered Captain Port's orders. To get out of China, Port needed to know what he was up against.

"How many is they, Joe? What weapons they got?"

"I dunno. Not that many of them. They got automatic weapons. They got grenades. And they're smart. Except I killed one of them, maybe two. Slashed his damn throat and then used the knife to chop off his epaulet to get the insignia. Figured the captain might know it." He paused. "Oh, shit but it hurts. Hurts where my arm was."

Federales took the blood-soaked fabric with its metal decorations. "I'll get it to him, Joe."

As promised, Port and the rest of the command were there at dawn. The Japs, realizing they were outgunned, and hearing the trucks, had fallen back. Taking their dead and wounded, it seemed, as none were to be found on the bloody ground. Even the bodies circling Joe Gang had vanished. Doc Philo worked over Sergeant Gang. "That hand's got to come off above the wrist, Captain. Ain't enough there to save. Cauterize the stump and he'll be fine. Give him a nice stump, a useful metal hook. The right eye's gone. Otherwise, if shock and the frostbite don't kill him, he might make it."

"Okay, can I talk to him?"

"He hurts, Skipper."

"But can he talk?"

"Yessir."

Maybe rodeo riders had a superior threshold of pain. Or maybe the backup dose of morphine Philo gave him had kicked in.

Joe Gang seemed anxious to reassure the skipper.

"I'll be okay, Captain. Doc's taking good care. Your Mex found me just in time."

Billy wasn't there to enjoy a good conversation. "That's fine, Joe. But I need to know what happened. You were going to jump the Japs. But they jumped you. What went wrong?"

"Yessir, I'll take the blame all right. But they was smart. Come at us from above, from the other side of the hill. We was halfway down the slope where you left us. Our weapons zeroed in on the track below. They must of took the high ground and got above us and behind us. I never heard 'em. Didn't make a peep. All that crunchy gravel and chalk underfoot, not a sound. Marines don't move that quiet, Skipper. But those boys did. When one of their vehicles rolled into the gorge ripe for the picking, we jumped up and we hit her with everything we had. And then, behind and above us, they hit us. The damned ambushers got ambushed."

"Who were they, Joe? Jap regulars?"

"Yessir. But not Jap Army. Uniforms got a different look. I brung back some insignia. Mex got 'em."

"Federales doesn't like to be called 'Mex,' Joe," the captain said gently.

They brought him the insignia.

"I've seen 'em before," Port said. He had. On the epaulets and uniform collar of an officer of the Special Landing Naval Force, the Japanese equivalent of the United States Marines. On the uniform, specifically, of Colonel Irabu.

"Jap Marines, Joe. Best they have. There's an officer I know from Shanghai, a Jap colonel," Port said. "You hear any shouting, anyone calling the name 'Irabu' during the firefight?"

"Nossir, I was too damned busy not getting kilt. And don't know much Jap anyways, just 'Make mine beer' and 'Get the hell out of my way,' up in Harbin."

Port had sent those four Marines up there to lay for the Japs and the Japs had been smarter than he was, than his Marines were. They moved a long way, and quiet, in the dark and the cold. That took march discipline, took good men, good officers. They'd killed two of his men and probably the third and crippled Joe Gang and Billy Port could still admire them as professionals. And could still assess his own performance, and find it lacking.

He also puzzled over just why the Japanese Army would detach such crack troops and send them after a couple of dozen Yanks just trying to get away? What kind of priority was that? Japan was busily conquering the Pacific and half of Asia, and they wasted good officers and trained men on a wild goose chase after a short platoon of United States Marines?

That, too, was pretty dumb. As dumb as he'd been not taking Federales's advice and sending too few men for the job. There was consolation in knowing the enemy brass could also fumble the damned ball.

Maybe Billy was going to get himself and his men out of North China after all. And then a chilling thought occurred: was it possible out of pride or some other reason that Irabu was conducting a vendetta?

In full daylight they found the third Marine. He was dead, too. Knife wounds. He'd been the Marine highest on the hillside in Gang's defensive position, the Marine the descending Japs must have come upon first, and killed without a sound. As Joe Gang put it, "We are not playing in the Sally League."

Billy didn't spare himself. Puller used to rip him about intellectual arrogance. And here he was, losing good men because an enemy officer outsmarted him, as happened to MacArthur, to the Brits at Singapore with their big guns pointed seaward, as befell the brass at Pearl.

With Rafter writing up the report and noting the map coordinates of this place, they buried the three Marines in chalky ground the other side of the little gorge and by ten that morning were again rolling north. With two keen-eyed Marines in the last truck manning the heavy machine gun and Rafter scanning the track behind them with the 7×50 glasses. Federales was in the lead truck, staring toward Siberia. Captain Port had already been ambushed once and didn't like it, not a bit, and he wanted the best eyes they had watching out for strangers. Both fore and aft.

For strangers. Or, just possibly, for a man named Irabu.

55

"We're like those old Western gunfighters," said Puller.
"Our time is past."

THE Siberia bridges. They'd become their fixation. Not many miles ahead, fifty, forty, maybe less. Their passport to Mother Russia; their farewell to Japanese-occupied China. As long as they could stay ahead of their pursuers, that is. If the Japanese caught up to them in sufficient force from the rear, you could forget bridges and passports and just about everything. But let's think positively, okay? Billy told himself.

All we need is one bridge, one intact bridge, Port kept thinking, kept telling the rest of them. "One working bridge that can carry a couple of trucks."

He harped on it so much, even Rafter was grinding his false teeth. And that wiseass Marine Thibodeaux, though not in Port's hearing, had the men in his truck reciting, "Over the river and through the woods, to grandfather's house we go."

Problem was, the Japanese had aerial reconnaissance, and Port didn't. All he needed was one friendly Flying Tiger to tell him about the bridges to Siberia. "Dear General Chennault, Sir: May we please rent one P-40 for the day at the usual rates? Much obliged, William Hamilton Thomas Port, 051313/0302, USMC."

The map showed plenty of Onon and Amur River bridges but who knew which of them had been blown during the 1939 fighting and repaired? Or not repaired. Which had collapsed of age and poor maintenance, or had been washed downstream by the spring floods? Which bridges were heavily defended at this, the southern or Chinese bank of the river? Would the Japs in the midst of a brand-new and bigger war still be that paranoid about the Russians? Which of the bridges might have nothing more than a sentry with a rifle and a semaphore gate of the sort you'd find at a midwest grade crossing? And which might be a nest of machine guns, tied in with wire, ringed with mines?

After the firefight between Joe Gang and the enemy Marines, Port got out of there as fast as he could. Irabu, if it were Irabu, was bad enough. But suppose he called for air? The Zeroes were worse. Didn't matter how clever Billy was, how canny was Sergeant Federales. The planes traveled at three hundred miles per hour and could kill them all in a single pass. Courage, marksmanship, discipline, were all fine. But not if the planes caught them in the open. And on the Mongolian plateau, virtually everything was "the open."

Billy and Puller and other infantry officers used to talk about air power, how it changed the rules of the game. They knew what the German planes had accomplished in Poland and France, what they'd done to the Russians in the summer of '41, thought they knew what air could do even to the finest and best-led infantry in the business, their own Corps. "We're like those old western gunfighters," Chesty once remarked. "They knew their time was past. The Colt and the Smith & Wesson finished. The planes and tanks are taking over and the best man doesn't necessarily win. Maybe the time for infantrymen is past. Our time. A damned shame, too."

"I guess," Port had said, not as gloomy as Puller, not having thought it through as deeply. He was thinking on it now.

Urged on, chewed at by Port, the Marines drove hard all that day and into the dusk. The roads were awful and even at these temperatures Jurkovich sweated-out broken axles and what in the hell was he supposed to do about those? You didn't lug spare truck axles around Asia, y'know. The going was hard, too, on Joe Gang, whom Port had to question, wanting more detailed information about the sort of vehicle the enemy had, that first car that came into the gorge, that Joe opened fire on, the only one Joe had actually seen and might describe.

"Joe, I know it hurts. But I've got to ask. Try to remember what exactly you saw."

"Like a big, open car, Skipper. Like your Rolls-Royce I heard about but twice as big. With a big .50-caliber machine gun mounted on the hood. Not a truck like we got. Just a real big automobile." Billy didn't bother to correct him about the make of his Bentley. Joe's wounds kept opening with all the jouncing over the uneven, irregular gravel. Doc Philo gave Gang a look when Port finished grilling him.

"If you can stand it without the morphine, Joe, that'd be best. The shots kill the pain, but they ain't no good for you long-term, savvy?"

"It ain't that bad, Doc," Gang said, "just the throbbing. And the itching where my hand used to be. And one eye ain't working too good."

"Good man, Joe." Philo's bedside manner didn't extend to telling rodeo riders they were shy not only of half an arm. But an eye.

Port knew damned well what the road was doing to Joe Gang but he kept them moving, chasing darkness, wanting someplace to hide. They started to see more trees, and that cheered them. You can conceal trucks if you have a few trees. Night's our friend, too, Port told himself, unconsciously echoing Irabu's mantra. "Trees and the dark," he kept telling his men, that's what war often came down to. Trees and the dark and maybe a spit of high ground. Rafter understood, and most of all so did Federales. "A poor soldier don't need much, amigos, but he needs cover."

That night, in an actual little forest, they made what might turn out to be their last or their next to last encampment on enemy territory. Port posted twice the usual number of sentries. To be caught this late in the game would call for a general court. Then Cantillon was called upon for the first time in days to read the evening news. He gave Port a look.

"Sparks doesn't have too much, Captain. Since Jones was killed, we don't get the Jap reports."

"Well, do your best, Mister."

"Aye aye, sir."

It wasn't award-winning stuff.

"General Wavell rallies the troops at Moulmein, Burma."

"Which side he on, Lieutenant?"

"Ours. The great Rudyard Kipling once wrote a poem about 'the old Moulmein pagoda/looking eastward to the sea/And a Burma gal a-setting/And I know she thinks of me . . .'"

"No Burma gals around here, Lieutenant."

"Correct," Cantillon agreed, allowing himself a small humor, "setting. Or standing."

Then, continuing, "The Japanese invaded the Dutch East Indies." Pause. "The Dutch are on our side."

"Hitler fired another field marshal, fellow named Leeb. The Brits bombed three German cities, Hamburg, Emden, and Bremen."

Then Cantillon sped hastily over the next item. "Admiral Kimmel and General Short are found guilty of dereliction of duty at Pearl Harbor. In North Africa, General Rommel captures Benghazi. General Rommel is a German."

Brief interlude of boos at this.

When they woke next morning the temperature was eighteen below and a light snow was falling. Snow, too, was good. The Zeroes wouldn't fly through snow, nor would that observation plane that was dogging them.

Trouble was, this close to Siberia, when a "light snow" fell, it had a way of turning into blizzards. By midmorning the trucks were already in difficulty. Port went up to ride with Jurkovich for a time.

"Those Jap scout cars, Jurkovich, if that's what they're called, will they handle deep snow better than our trucks?"

"Captain, if I could go over one of them, get a close look, I could tell you. What's their clearance, how good are the tires, how many low gears, are they four-wheel drive or what?"

Port looked at him narrowly. "Well, if you can't coax any more speed out of our trucks, and they catch up with us, you may have a closer look than you want."

The motor transport NCO kept his mouth shut. Damned officers, chewing you out for no reason.

Port sensed it.

"Okay, Jurkovich. you didn't rate that. I guess we're all a little edgy about the Japs on our tail. I know I am."

"Yessir."

"Anyway, how deep does the snow have to get for our trucks to stall?"

"If it stays level, another six inches. If we get hills, damn them, we're in trouble. We can't cut steep hills when there's a foot of snow, sir."

That was when Port dropped from Jurkovich's cab and walked back to his own truck. The snow was coming down even heavier, and to Billy, despite the marginal visibility, it seemed the road was climbing. Not steeply, nothing dramatic like the gorge at Hongor, but it was going up. Rafter trotted up heavily to talk to him.

"Skipper, the padre says he knows this country. Says it was near here he found that griffin he's forever jabbering about, the lion-eagle."

"Get him!"

Kean was very excited. "If memory doesn't play tricks, just along the road here, on the right side halfway up the hill; there are some big caves. We found a few bones in the diggings, but the best preserved fellows, they were in the caves. I spent three months here in 1922, but God bless you, Captain, that was twenty years back. Give me that map of yours and I'll try to puzzle it out. Lot of caves along here, or should be, a few you could drive a truck into, most of them so small that you crawl inside, but they'll provide shelter if that's what you're thinking."

"The hills get much higher?"

"No, sir. Of course, in snow, hills have a way of growing taller."

As the priest scrutinized the map and cast glances about him, squinting through the flakes for his precious caves, Billy wasn't thinking shelter. He was wondering if this might be the ground on which to surprise their pursuers.

And kill them.

When the priest volunteered to scout ahead, Port sent him off with three Marine huskies.

It wasn't an hour later that Father Kean, moving like a man half his age, hurried back to the convoy plastered with snow but exultant.

"The padre found the damned caves!" Buffalo shouted. "He found the bastards!"

"About a quarter mile ahead, sir!" the priest called out. "Up there, you'll soon see the first of them. They're smallish at first, but where there are small caves, you'll find the occasional big one."

And they did, just barely. That's how fast the snow was falling. There was no chance of getting any farther before night. Billy sensed the Japanese coming, right on his heels, with his trucks crawling at maybe a mile an hour. While Irabu's scout cars could be making much better mileage. It was eerie, the recurrent nightmare of running up an endless staircase with someone behind you and coming closer. Could you be claustrophobic in a vast emptiness?

By three in the afternoon they'd pulled into the woods to hide the trucks, their tire marks and footprints soon to be drifted over.

Inside the first of the big caves they huddled out of the snow, and then sent out security, rotating the men every hour, to warm up and dry out by the big fire they'd fashioned in the padre's cave.

"Not mine, really; the *Protoceratop*'s cave. Where we found him, twenty years ago. He didn't object to trespassers, having been dead awhile, eighty million years."

One of Federales's squad poked Thibodeaux. "That's older than the sarge," he whispered.

Port and his sergeants went over the maps with the priest and Yusopov and then Billy got up impatiently.

"Come on, Top. You, Federales."

Outside it was snowing as hard as ever, a foot or more down by now. More coming. The Mexican peered through it, saw nothing. Brushed away the snow with his hand to drive his bayonet into the ground again. Felt nothing. Did heavy snow muffle vibrations? And then he said, "Skipper, we gonna try to outrun these hombres all the way to the border?"

Billy shook his head. He'd been pondering the same question and it didn't take him by surprise.

"I don't think we can do that, Sergeant. Their vehicles are faster. They can call in air. And if they catch us out there on the open road, they can pound us to pieces with that .50-caliber."

"Yessir," Federales said, "that's what I think, too."

When Port didn't say anything, the Mexican went on: "That's why I think we oughta fight 'em right here, Skipper. We got to wait out this damn snow anyway. When it's finished, in the morning, whenever, and the Japs come along that same road we just followed, they got to be coming slow. I don't care how good cars they got. From these caves closest to the road, we could hit them when they come up. Hit them hard . . ."

"I like it," Rafter put in. "And there's one good thing about snow this deep. The Japs ain't gonna be able to outflank us by climbing the high ground behind us, like they did with Joe Gang."

Port didn't say anything. He wasn't sure. He'd laid one ambush already for the enemy and all he did was lose three good men and Joe Gang's arm.

Confidence had never been the problem; if anything, it was arrogance that got him into trouble. But the ease with which Irabu ("if" it were Jesse) turned the tables on his Marine ambushers and killed them had shaken Port. Until now, his ride had gone so well and so far, the enemy outwitted and outrun and confounded, so that Siberia, and sanctuary, were just beyond that next bend in the Mongolian road, just over that next Mongolian hill.

And now?

There was a schoolboy poem he'd learned by heart at Boston Latin, by Gerard Manley Hopkins, all about a "hound of heaven" who hunted the narrator "through the nights and days/down the labyrinthine ways..." Something like that, and the "hound" was really God.

Of course he didn't share the poetry with his sergeants. Not bloody likely. But to himself he admitted doubts. Had the relentlessly pursuing enemy gotten to him?

Then, standing there in the snow while his men waited, he made conscious effort, and shook off the mood, and went back to doing what soldiers are paid to do and at which they are supposed to be good: to make a plan. And then to carry out that plan and fight, and defeat, an enemy.

"Is this the right ground to fight on from our point of view?" he asked.

Rafter, not the instinctive warrior Federales was, shuffled his feet. "Well, we got the high ground, and..."

"You ain't gonna get no better, Skipper," Federales said.

I'll go with Federales, Port told himself.

"But with a difference..."

Both sergeants, not having heard his unspoken decision, waited, not sure what the captain was saying.

Billy let them wait. Then, "These people are professionals. I learned that with Joe Gang; I learned my lesson. I'm not dividing the command this time. No sending out three Marines and Joe Gang. This time a full Marine rifle platoon takes them on and we hit them with everything we have. We win or we lose right here. Okay?"

"Skipper," said Rafter, a practical man with snow piling up on the back of his neck and drifting wetly down inside his uniform collar, "let's get us outa this damned snow and inside that cave and plan this here operation."

"Let's do just that, Top."

It was Father Kean who gave them their theme.

"So you'll fight them here," he said, sounding gloomy about it, not happy that a place sacred to him, and to his precious fossil on display at the British Museum, was about to become just another killing ground. Not only was there nothing he could do about it; it was he who'd led the Marines up here, thinking it was for shelter.

"Yes, Padre. If they come."

"Oh, they'll come, sir," he lamented. "I believe they will. This is the griffin's graveyard; this is where the dinosaurs came to die. Why not a few men?"

56

Joe got them to rig him a holster so he could draw the .45 cross-handed.

THEY came. At midmorning. And this time, the Marines were ready for them.

The snow ended around daybreak and by nine a winter sun had turned the road, the hillsides, and the trees where they hid the trucks into a winter palace, the fresh powder snow lying deep and mostly untracked. Above them a gloriously blue sky, not even a puffy fairweather cloud. "Five above zero," the thermometer read, or so reported Father Kean, who'd prayed away disillusionment in the night and was, if not precisely cheery, less glum.

Rafter fretted busily over that pristine snow, and kept after men to brush over their tracks. A half mile back along the road to the south, along which their pursuers would have to come, Federales and three men lay under trees in snow on the hillside watching, listening, sniffing the air. Federales had no vibrations this time but they had their eyes, their ears, and were ready to drift silently back through the evergreens to alert Port and his thirty men, armed and waiting, the three squads combined, very nearly a regulation rifle platoon. Even Rafter was reasonably content.

"I seen worse, Skipper."

"So have I, Top."

It was just past ten when they saw Federales coming, running doubled over and fast, despite the deep snow, with Buffalo and two others panting in his wake.

"We got engine noise, Skipper. Three, four vehicles. Maybe a mile down the road, maybe less, coming this way, grinding along in what sounds like low gear. Them Jap scout cars, gotta be. Nobody else in town that I know about."

Port grunted assent, reminded Rafter and Federales yet again to let the Jap vehicles get well into the trap before they hit them, "Like at Fengzhen," swiveling his head around, checking once more the three machine guns, the mortar, and his BAR men. Out of sight, but out there on his flank, he knew, were Prince Yusopov and three Marines seconded to him as Molotov cocktail specialists. He liked it that he couldn't see them. Nice work, Prince, we'll make a Marine of you yet.

Then, to Rafter: "Get me Joe Gang if he feels up to it, Top. I'd like him here telling me just how the Japs came at him the last time."

"Aye aye, sir."

"Help him into that sheepskin, too. He'll need it if they keep us waiting."

The enemy didn't keep them waiting.

Joe Gang lay next to the captain on the little steep pitch from which Port planned to direct the fight. "How's the arm, Joe?"

"It hurts, Skipper. Otherwise, okay. I got them to rig me a holster on that side with the .45 loaded. That way I can draw cross-handed. Little practice, I might get good at it."

"Can you load a clip one-handed?"

"Not too good. Got to hold the clip between my teeth and shove in the cartridges. But I'll learn. And I can still shoot a little."

They could all hear the engines now. Billy looked at his watch, pushing back the sleeve of the sheepskin and the cuff of his mitten. Ten-nineteen. He looked around again to both sides and behind. Then Joe poked him with his good arm, nodding his chin toward the road.

One Japanese scout car was coming up the snow-covered road toward them, maybe seventy-five yards away, moving slow. Port looked toward Joe Gang, eyebrows raised.

"Yeah, Cap. Same as with me. One car come in. But that one had a big machine gun mounted."

Port nodded. This car carried only two men, with room for maybe six, and had no mounted fifty.

He knew then this car was bait, and that the other cars weren't coming right behind it. Not yet, they weren't . . .

And then the firing began.

"Japs! Japs, up on the hillside left! Watch your left, amigos!"

Damn! They had been flanked again!

By now everyone was firing. Including at least one machine gun. And the first of Yusopov's cocktails had blown on the road halfway down the hill. Next to him Joe Gang was talking fast: "The same damn curveball they threw at me, Skipper. Send in one car, then hit you on the flanks. They must of come around us, moving on foot quiet through the snow."

By now the lead vehicle was past him and going fast, as fast as it could with the snow, but it wasn't doing so well. Not with all that Marine firepower targeting it. By now the driver was dead and the other fellow a probable and the car had lurched off the road out of control, hit a tree, and bounced.

"Forget the car!" Port shouted. "They're finished. Get the others on the hillside and down the road."

Well, you didn't really have to be told that. A promising little fire-fight was under way, punctuated by grenades (whose? you couldn't tell) and by Molotovs (ours, a Yusopov exclusive). And in broad daylight, with sun and a high blue sky, except in the trees, you could see it all. Way down the hill, there must be two or three more Jap scout cars and their rear guard.

And by now, it had to be obvious the fight wasn't going their way. "Gotcha!" Billy snarled. "You reached too far and I've gotcha!"

He and Buffalo were sprinting through the woods downhill toward the fighting, Joe Gang, surprisingly nimble, keeping up, the .45 out of his holster and clutched in a mittened hand. How he was going to reach the trigger, Port was not able to imagine, but wasn't agonizing over it.

Rafter trotted up to them.

"We got most of them, Captain. Prince Yusopov burned up a couple and our riflemen got the rest. Maybe four or five ran. They're still running . . ."

"Keep after them," Port ordered, "get them all if you can."

He came up now to the side of the road where two Jap cars stood, riddled with bullet holes, one of them burned black by a Yusopov cocktail. In that one, two Japanese were dead, one still inside the car and burned, the other lying in the melted snow next to his vehicle, one foot and leg still inside and grotesquely twisted, as if he'd been trying to get out when it burned but had gotten stuck.

"Well, Captain, you got 'em," said Joe Gang. "They walked into it, and you got 'em."

"Their officer made the same mistake I did with you, Joe. He tried to do too much without enough men. Sending a dozen men to take on and outflank thirty Marines. Just can't do it."

"Well, he won't try it again, Captain."

When they'd tallied the score and Rafter made his report, there were nine dead Japanese Marines, three scout cars destroyed, one scout car escaped with what various reports said were four or five men, at least some of them and perhaps all wounded. Or so the Marines concluded from the blood on the snow.

One American Marine was dead of gunfire and two wounded. One of Yusopov's people had a burned hand from a Molotov cocktail that went off before he could throw it.

"Jesus," Rafter complained, half to himself, but also shouting at the burned Marine, "how dumb can you get? Light the damned thing and throw it. Don't stand there admiring your handiwork. Throw the hell out of it!"

Sympathy was not Rafter's strong point.

"Yes, First Sarn't, yessir."

Colonel Irabu's body was not among those they found and tallied. Could he have been in the car that got away, the one with those wounded men, the one with the .50-caliber mounted up front?

57

You improvise in war, like in jazz. But a band doesn't take casualties.

THE dead man was Corporal Kress. "Old Fat Ass Kress," Rafter said thoughtfully. "That boy sure had a keister on him. You don't see a keister that size on many infantrymen. Usually, they run it off, march the damn thing off."

Port agreed that you didn't see many like it.

They thought about burying Kress, but with Siberia so close, and no chance in this cold that he'd spoil, Rafter said why not fetch him along in a sleeping bag and give him a proper send-off across the border in old Russia?

"Might be a consolation to his folks, Captain. People appreciate knowing where a fella's planted and maybe someday even coming over to see the place and lay a wreath."

"You think Fat Ass had folks, Top?" a BAR man said.

"Everybody got folks, lad. Even Kress. And don't you forget it and disrespect your corporal."

"Okay, Top," Port said. "We'll take Kress to Siberia. You handle it."

"Yessir."

It didn't cost anything, Billy thought, and it might save them an hour. Even more if the padre decided he had to say a few words over Fat Ass.

And even with the bashing they gave the Japanese up there in the snow, Billy wanted to be on the road. He didn't like that bright blue sky they were featuring today that just beckoned the Zeroes. Within an hour of ending the firefight, they'd tidied up the caves and gotten back on the road, moving slow with all that snow but moving, which was the important thing.

If he had the luxury of time, and no Jap air, Billy would have gone after that last scout car. You don't wound an animal and then leave it still alive behind you in the underbrush. But he didn't have the time nor, with the snow ended and the sun out, did he have weather on his side. So they'd saddled up quickly and he kept them on the road until night.

If all went well, their next to last night in China.

They posted the usual sentries and then, at Port's insistence, posted a few more. To their rear. Federales, as cautious as anyone, looked at Rafter.

"The skipper must of got a feeling about that Jap colonel, Top."

"They used to be pals in Shanghai. Played tennis and such. So we'll just let him be, Federales. The captain don't need no advice from his sergeants unless it's about soldiering. If he wants to brood on his old buddy a bit, the man's entitled." Then Rafter grinned. "You know, like you do about General Pershing sometimes."

Federales shook his head.

"You know it, amigo. All these years later, I find myself remembering how it was over there in old France, me and the general at Soissons and them places . . ."

It was a quiet night with the temperatures, which had warmed during the snow, again plunging, and except for sentry duty, just about everyone slept well. You come through a good firefight and do well at it, you usually sleep fine. Billy Port did.

In the morning they closed up to within about eight miles of a big river that separated Mongolia from the Soviet Union. This was the Onon.

After posting a machine gun in woods to their rear, Port sent Federales and the prince, plus three BAR men, off in one of the trucks to reconnoiter the near bank of the river. "Get as close as you can, but don't be seen. If they see you, we're blown."

"Aye aye, sir," Federales said. Yusopov said nothing, thinking instead how close he was after so long to his country. They were back by early afternoon. Federales saluted and began his report.

"Hold on, Sergeant. They didn't see you, did they?"

"Nossir. That part of it went smooth."

"Okay, we'll have officers' call so you'll give your report only once."

He kept it tight, himself, the top, Federales, Joe Gang despite his wounds, the third squad leader, Young, Father Kean because he knew Mongolia. And Prince Yusopov, their house Russian. Then, impulsively, for in combat, Port was a creature of impulse, he said, "Find Mr. Cantillon. I want him here, too."

He saw the question in Rafter's face.

"Well?"

"He's a swabbie, Captain. It's not like we need him."

"He's a commissioned officer, Top. Been with us since Shanghai and stays cool. You can't say he doesn't." These were almost the same words with which Rafter had once defended the young lieutenant to Port.

Rafter moved his upper plate around in his mouth but didn't say anything more.

What Billy was thinking but didn't say, Suppose I get it. He's the only other officer you've got.

Federales wanted to defer to the Russian in giving the report but Yusopov shook his head. "Your patrol, Sergeant. I was along for the ride." Port wondered, had there ever been as odd a couple as these two? The Indian tracker who'd shadowed Villa and the Russian aristo whose daddy bumped off Rasputin.

"Go ahead, Federales."

They'd found a vantage point overlooking the river and had cobbled up a rough map. There was only the single road heading to the river-bank and the mile-long wooden bridge. "Nothing fancy," the sergeant said. "Just a good, solid flat bridge on four sets of piles. Looks strong enough to carry tanks but it's barricaded halfway across.

"You could see a coupla miles in each direction, upstream and down, and that's the only bridge we seen. We counted Jap heads, Skipper. Saw eight or nine boys lolling around. Not looking too sharp. Garrison troops, I'd guess. They got a hut for sentries to shelter in, and a half-assed little bunker that might have a machine gun. Too small for much else. Out at midspan is that barricade, Captain. Logs mostly. Put there to stop the Russkis. And that looks like our problem."

"We'll get back to that, Sergeant. Were there any Jap Marines like the bunch we just killed? Jap Marines with anchors on their collars?"

"Nossir, not at that distance, leastwise."

"The river frozen solid?"

"Looks like it."

Port was thinking maybe they could finesse the barricaded bridge and cross on the frozen river. Who was that escaped across the ice? Someone in *Uncle Tom's Cabin*? Was it Liza?

He asked questions about the steepness of the bank on the near bank, on this side, and whether the ground was marshy leading down to the water's edge. That was important. Did the marsh freeze up this early in the year? Did a drivable road parallel the river on this bank? "No," to that. Not in either direction. Port turned to Yusopov. "See anything?"

"No more than Sergeant Federales."

"That ice hold a truck?"

"I'd be guessing. Later in January, surely. Now, I don't know. These Siberian rivers run swiftly. That means whatever the temperature, there could be air holes, soft spots where a truck could bog down."

Port nodded. Then, again to the prince: "See any Russians on the far shore?"

"No. Some smoke. One midsized wooden building. Might be a farmhouse. Or a barracks. No vehicles."

"Steep bank on that side? Can trucks climb it?"

"Looks like an easy gradient."

"No barbed wire or tank traps. No ditches?"

"None we could see."

"Good," Port said.

Then Yusopov said, "I agree with the sergeant. The Japanese troops I saw looked second-rate."

In a firefight, not everything goes as planned. In the chaos and the noise and the fear, and with men you're counting on going down, you improvise, instinct takes over, the "natural" in you comes out.

Or it doesn't. So you tried as best you could to prepare. Which is what Billy did now.

He got them to redo the map, to work up something more precise, tried to get exact distances, roadbed width, how much cover, if any, would the bridge superstructure give the trucks if they crossed under fire and tried to blow their way through the log barricade. Billy Port wanted to know more about the ground, on paper and in his head: the high ground, the little dips and draws in which you, or the enemy, might be concealed. Where the mortars might reach with their vertical fire, but not the machine guns. You wanted to know about the odd building or hedge or grove of saplings, if there were railroad tracks laid, where the ground was spongy and where hardscrabble. What kind of mature trees grew here—wood splinters from shellfire could kill a man as surely as steel fragments.

A good soldier tried to memorize everything and then, when the shooting began, to improvise on top of the set piece, the way musicians did when they sat in on a jam session, playing riffs off the theme, and playing off each other. All this was more difficult in war than in jazz, where all of your players were usually as alive at the finish as at the start.

In the end, with two hours of daylight still, he drafted Federales and the prince and two others and returned to their vantage point near the river.

"I need to see the ground for myself," he told them, not used to giving explanations. At the rise of ground, Federales and Yusopov lay prone next to Port just below the ridgeline, indicating this feature or that, as he swept his glasses back and forth, looking at the bridge and the adjacent ground and taking mental notes until the light faded. Then, satisfied, he finally grunted, "Okay, let's go home," and they made their way back, wriggling the first few yards backward on their bellies, and then rising to break into a small, swift trot back to the truck.

The bridge wouldn't work. The barricade was too weighty, too complex, even for their demolitions. Use enough explosive to blow the barricade, you blow the damned bridge.

"So we'll cross on the ice," he said, the decision made, the uncertainty fled, *"Hans Brinker and the Silver Skates."*

Federales looked at him, puzzled. As did the prince.

"Never mind," said Billy.

That night, their last in China, gathering his little command around several small fires for less than thirty minutes, just before sentries took their posts and the others slept, Captain Port issued orders for what in all likelihood would be the last battle ever fought on the Asian mainland by the 4th Regiment of United States Marines.

Then, satisfied they knew the plan, he went over it one more time. To be sure.

58

They were all dead by now. Their eyes and ears blown out by concussion!

THEY would hit the bridge at dawn. That was when troops, especially garrison troops with comfortable billets, were slower in their instincts, their reaction time. And the light wouldn't yet be all that good. Having made his plan, Billy fell asleep almost immediately and slept well.

The night passed quietly and they woke him at four A.M. He shaved in the warm dregs of a canteen cup of black coffee Buffalo fetched (if they got into Russia, an American officer ought to look smart), brushed his teeth, gnawed at some stale bread, slurped down a can of peaches, and pulled on issue field shoes (fleece-lined felt was warmer but you fought in field shoes) and leggings, and got into his web gear and gun belt. He picked up the loaded Springfield rifle and stowed a canteen inside the wool undershirt next to his body to thaw, as he prowled the area like one of those Mongol wolves that stalked the column.

No snow, a very cold night of stars glimpsed through broken cloud, three hours before first light. Rafter called in all but two rear guards with their machine gun, and they joined the others, thirty men in all, gathered and standing easy around Port, the way a football team does before the kickoff around their coach. As he tended to be before a fight, Billy was cheerful. He'd laid his plans, they knew what they had to do, they were good men. So he didn't make a speech.

"Give me a weather report, Padre!" he called out.

The old Jesuit, slipping easily into Port's mood, replied chirpily, "Two above on my glass, sir, which qualifies as a January thaw. With snow flurries promised in Siberia, Captain."

"Let's hope it doesn't thaw the ice, Father. Leung, the old exchequer ready for customs and immigration on the other side? Passports and documents in order?"

"As is customary, sir."

"First Sergeant, your report, please." Billy was punctilious with senior NCOs.

"All present or accounted for, sir."

"Buffalo?"

"Truck number one squared away, Skipper."

The plan was pretty straightforward. Only four trucks, their canvas furled, with fuel trailers hooked up securely, and carrying heavily armed men. But Buffalo would lead the parade and Billy wanted to be sure of him.

Truck number one, Buffalo driving and lugging a Thompson gun, with three men and sacks of grenades, that was their assault group. Buffalo would drive hell-bent for the sentry hut and the little block-house the instant the first Marine mortar hit. That was the signal for the jump-off, for Buffalo to ram his truck into the hut and then, if it was still running, into the bunker, before jumping out hurling grenades and firing from the hip. After killing whatever Japanese were there, they were to secure this riverbank while the other trucks rolled past them and downhill to the river and out onto the ice. As the rear guard, Rafter and the heavy machine gunners would cover the other trucks as they made their way onto the frozen river and started for Siberia. Rafter and the heavy gun would then move out last, with the gun leveled toward anyone coming after them. Billy and Yusopov, leading the way across the ice, would take the first truck into Russia.

As Billy admitted, "Not very complicated, Top."

"Nossir," said Rafter, who'd once put in a tour at the Washington, D.C., Marine barracks, at Eighth and I Streets, and consequently had an appreciation for pomp, "it sure ain't a funeral parade with John Philip Sousa leading the band."

Billy watched them climb into the trucks for the approach march. It began well, all the trucks turning over nicely, and even the wind was favorable, coming at them head-on out of the northwest.

"That's well," Port told people as he walked from truck to truck, wishing them luck. "Downwind of the Japs, they won't hear the trucks until it's too late. Nor smell us, either," he added, drawing chuckles from men who hadn't bathed regularly.

They were less than an hour's drive from the river, and from departing hostile country, the last lap of Billy Port's long ride. In the third truck, they'd set up the 60mm mortar on its steel base plate and, to save time, would fire from right there on the truck bed instead of the ground. Dixie, the mortarman, had loaded a white phosphorous shell (what they called "willy peter") for the first volley, to provide masking smoke at the bridge when Buffalo's truck came rolling down on the Japs. The two light machine guns were in Port's truck. And in the rear came Rafter and the heavy gun.

Just in case it's Irabu back there, Billy told himself, but did not share the information lest he spook anyone. When men are going into a fight, they're already thinking all sorts of things, some of them scary. These were good men. But why push it?

They rolled north at six and pulled up by seven just short of the river, sheltered by darkness and a dip in the road, all four engines idling so there'd be no ignition failure or risk of stalling when they jumped off. Port walked ahead to Buffalo's first truck, whispering up to him in the cab. "We'll go about seven forty-five. First light. Wait for the willy peter to hit and then go like hell."

"Going like hell" on ground like this might be fifteen miles an hour, both men knew.

"Aye aye, sir. See you on the other side."

"Yes, you will, lad."

In those last few minutes, waiting, Billy tried to imagine what the prince was thinking, couldn't, and turned back to stare ahead. Next to Port, the driver, Jurkovich, their master mechanic, chewed on an unlit cigar. Not one of Billy's, Jurkovich having a stash of his own.

"I like a good cigar, Captain."

"Yes, so do I."

That was all. They had other things on their minds. Men talked idly, or chewed on a cigar, or cracked a poor joke to hurry the passing of time. Which was odd, Billy realized. Why would you hurry what might be the last few minutes of your life? But soldiers always did.

He checked his watch. Seven-forty. Not long now. They would know one way or the other pretty soon. Impatient, and wanting to give his four trucks a final check, he jumped down from the cab to the snow-covered ground to walk back for one last word with the top about watching their rear.

"Don't leave without me, Jurkovich."

"Nossir."

It was then, with the first gray of morning hinting at the day to come, and a brief snow squall passing through, in the half-light and falling snow, the sounds of their approach masked by the Marine trucks' idling engines, that the enemy caught up with Billy Port.

The big Japanese scout car came up on and violently tailgated the rear of Rafter's truck so abruptly that Irabu very nearly got himself killed in the collision and in the startled first volley of fire that followed. And instead of surprising the Marines in the predawn, stunned and shocked himself, knocking his already bandaged forehead against the windshield, as his driver, also badly shaken, instinctively threw the big car into reverse and spun rubber backing up and off the road. While Top Sergeant Rafter, recovering quickly, shouted, "Japs! Dead astern! Hit 'em! Hit 'em!"

They all heard that first heavy *rrrippping* sound as Rafter's gunners fired on his order, getting their gun into action first while the Japs were still scrambling backward, blood running down Irabu's face, blinding him, and the concussion blurring judgment.

Billy Port, on his feet abreast of the front hood of Rafter's truck, as shaken by what happened as any of them, stared through the snow to where the big enemy vehicle was spinning its tires as it turned in a violently short radius not thirty yards from where he stood, trying somehow to scramble out of there and get away. The din was deafening, everyone firing now and up ahead the mortar prematurely chunking out the white phosphorous shells, as drivers hit their horns and stepped on the gas.

The scout car was now headed directly away from the column but in its front seat, standing, hanging on to the windshield and a roll bar, was a fur-clad figure with a bloody face looking backward, wild-eyed as if in shock, trying to gauge whether he and his men were going to get out of this alive or be gunned down here on the riverbank.

Not able to stop himself, Billy Port raised a hand to attract attention as he shouted, "Jesse! Jesse! Give it up, man! Give it up!"

The Jap vehicle kept going and within seconds had vanished into the squall and was gone.

Billy Port turned, sprinted toward the head of the column, shouting for the mortars to keep firing. Two trucks ahead, in all the excitement, Buffalo had just hit the gas. They were all rolling within seconds, and when Port leaped onto the running board of his own truck, Jurkovich shifted so quickly into gear that he rammed Buffalo's rear bumper while its tires still spun, screaming, trying to gain traction on the frozen earth, and then went roaring straight downhill for the enemy positions guarding the Onon River bridge. For both sides, the Marines and the Japs, the fight was beginning as a total screwup.

"Jesus!" someone shouted. "That's all we frigging need!" Japs in front of them, Japs in their rear!

Port had no idea who was shouting but he heard the *chunk chunk chunk* of another three mortar shells coming out of the tube, one, two, three! and the mad, furious sounds of firing up ahead and just behind.

Billy's truck leaped ahead. Could be worse, he told himself; there are always screwups. Just stay cool. He was talking aloud now, not to Jurkovich but to himself. "We got started a few minutes early is all. And now we know who it is that's coming after us."

Behind him the firing continued, short bursts from the heavy gun, other weapons answering. He wished he knew who was getting the better of it, us or the Japs?

The top was too busy to make a report. What had happened was his first burst from the Browning took out the Jap windshield and killed a man riding in back. Colonel Irabu, wiping away blood blinding one eye, was firing his Luger at the Marine truck, but missing wide as his driver spun the wheel in a tight, violent U-turn. The gunner manning Irabu's .50-caliber machine gun hadn't yet gotten it into action. When Irabu shouted at him the man groaned. So he was hit, too, and Irabu was stripping off gloves to get at the gun himself. Rafter, seeing the enemy car reversing in confusion, and trying to turn, ordered the gunners to squeeze off a few more bursts and shouted ahead to the driver to go for the river. And then for good measure and to slow pursuit, the top tossed a couple of grenades tumbling behind them along the track, blowing one after the other.

By then, Rafter couldn't see the enemy car anymore. If they hadn't killed all the Japs, maybe they could outrun them. By God, but them boys took some killing, didn't they?

One Marine lay bleeding on the floorboards, knocked silly by the collision and nursing a broken nose and some smashed teeth, calling for a corpsman. "Shut up, you back there," Rafter shouted angrily, "you ain't even shot yet." Doc Philo was in another truck and in this one, the Marines were too busy firing the machine gun and looking around for Japs to patch people up. "Go, go, go!" Rafter shouted, knowing the wounded could wait a bit and the dead were in no hurry. Up front at the riverbank, Port was already out of his truck and on his feet, waving men this way and that, using his Springfield to direct them. There was still some firing from the little blockhouse but the sentry hut had been demolished. There were men all over the ground, in mustard-colored uniforms, most of them. Buffalo and his boys must have done a job on them. Bringing up the rear Rafter yelled again at his driver, "Go like hell!"

Not his fault, but Port was frozen into inaction. He wanted to order his trucks down to the riverbank and out on the ice. It was an order he couldn't give until he got a signal from the first sergeant that their rear was secure and until Buffalo broke off his own firefight, and could get away.

No one was just standing around. There were Japs all over the place, some of them wounded but firing back, men injured when Buffalo smashed their hut, but fighting on. Not the blockhouse; there the firing had stopped. PFC Schaefer, a smart boy, coolly dropped grenade after grenade down through the damaged overhead vent of the blockhouse. They were all dead in there by now, their ears and eyes blown out by concussion in a tightly closed space, blood running out of their mouths and noses.

Billy had the field glasses up. Out on the ice everything looked clear so far. No problems out there if only the ice held. "Come on, Rafter! Hurry it, hurry it!" Of course the top couldn't hear him. But he knew, as Port did, how urgent this all was.

Now finally Rafter was there looking down at his captain from the truck and Port shouted at him again. "Where are the Japs?"

"We hit them, Skipper. Back there in the woods."

"Dead?"

"I dunno, some of them."

If his first sergeant wasn't sure, then they'd better get a move on. You know Marines, after a firefight, they light the smoking lamp, take a coffee break, talk things over. The hell with that!

"Watch me, Jurkovich. When we go, we're going fast."

"Aye aye, Skipper."

"Buffalo, finish those bastards. There's some of them still alive."

The runner heard him and nodded, trotting off, yelling for Schaefer. Mad Red Donnelly had a BAR and was taking down Japs trying to escape on foot out on the ice. He was firing single-shot not automatic and the enemy soldiers went down, one after another.

Then Rafter waved a hand, signaling him ahead. "We must be clear now. Skipper! I can't see nothing coming."

"Okay! Head for the river!" Billy shouted, "Follow me onto the ice! And watch our back!"

But would the ice hold?

59

The Japanese scout car with the .50-caliber was closing and closing fast.

COLONEL Irabu, who was definitely not yet dead but with a bloody face and a hole through his left thigh, sat upright and painfully in the front seat of his vehicle in the forest overlooking the riverbank, and using field glasses could just see the river through the trees and falling snow, and he, too, was wondering about the ice. His lieutenant, that promising young man, was still alive and functioning. As for the two enlisted men, the machine gunner was gut-shot and not much good. The man in the backseat had no face anymore and you could forget him. The Mongol schoolteacher with the bad thumb had, wisely, jumped out and run away when the firing began. As for the scout car, lacking a windshield and one fender, but with the engine working, it still had that big .50-caliber machine gun mounted on the hood, which meant it was still a player.

Now, for the first time, Irabu saw at a distance the first and then the other two American trucks. Two were still loading men and their weapons from the firefight but the first of them was easing its way downslope toward the river. Seeing them, Irabu, out of fury and frustration, was cursing and swearing, trotting out every vulgarity and four-letter word he'd ever known, or even imagined. Trouble was, with the concussion he suspected he'd suffered, he was unaware he was cursing in English.

"Colonel, I'm sorry, but if you could tell me in Japanese what you want..." the lieutenant offered.

"Sorry."

"Might I put a dressing on your head, sir? Keep that blood from running into your eye?" The lieutenant didn't know about the hole through Irabu's leg.

"Time for that later, Lieutenant. You drive and I'll handle the .50-caliber and let's move!"

"Move where, sir?" The lieutenant assumed that as badly wounded as Irabu was, that their battle was over.

"Down to the river and out on the ice. Our car is faster than their

314 · JAMES BRADY

trucks. From a few hundred meters behind, we can hit them with the .50. No cover for them, no vibrations to disrupt our aim. We can shoot out their tires, kill their engines, and catch up."

The lieutenant was game but he wondered if Irabu could see well enough to hit anything. Or with his own wounds, how well he could drive. Between them they tugged the machine gunner out of the front seat and tossed him onto the snowy ground at the side of the road. The man in back without a face wasn't in the way and they left him sitting there. For the first time the lieutenant saw the blood spurting from Irabu's muscular thigh.

"Colonel, your leg."

Jesse ignored him. "Clock's running, Lieutenant. The damned Americans will be on the ice. Let's roll."

"Yes, sir," he said, getting back behind the wheel. The colonel wasn't a man you argued with.

Well, Irabu told himself, considering I probably have a concussion and have a few other holes in me, we might yet catch Billy Port. And cheered by the possibilities, he rethreaded a belt of ammo through the machine gun with cold fingers but without difficulty, and fired off a short burst.

"Fine, it's still working. Let's go, Lieutenant. Let's go catch those American bastards."

He wasn't aware that he was talking English again, or American, but his lieutenant understood the tone of command, and throwing the big car into gear, headed through trees toward the shoreline and the river.

Down at the water's edge the last Marines were boarding trucks. Yusopov, who'd done his share of the fighting at the bridge, scorched and smeared with someone else's blood, clambered hurriedly into Port's truck, tossing a Springfield up ahead of him. Jurkovich had the truck rolling already, backing, turning, then again into forward. Behind them he could see another truck pulling up to follow them. Buffalo's truck was wrecked, one of his men dead, but he and Schaefer and Collins, the latter awkwardly swinging an arm that seemed to be broken, were yanked up into the captain's truck by sheer muscle. Collins, who couldn't help himself, screamed when a husky Marine hoisted him aboard by the wrong arm.

"Sorry, pal."

Collins, groaning, tried to nod an okay.

"Shut up, amigo," shouted Federales helpfully from where he was getting back into his own truck. "Doc's gonna fix you better than ever." Sure, a man hurt. He damn well shouldn't be yelling about it.

It was trickier rolling down the riverbank to the ice's edge than Port expected. Jurkovich had everything he wanted, more than enough, wrestling the wheel, pumping the brakes, hitting the gas.

"Steep as hell, Skipper." Slippery, too, with this fresh snow.

"Okay, okay, just don't stall. Keep it moving."

When they hit the ice the wheels slipped for an instant, losing traction, skidded sideways, and then caught, and as they sped out fifty or sixty yards onto the frozen river to halt and wait for the others, Billy was delighted at how smoothly they were riding. After the rutted chalk and gravel they'd been traveling for a thousand corrugated miles, this was a ballroom floor.

"It's lovely, Captain," the driver said. "Solid, too."

Cake, Billy thought, a piece of cake. We even have a little snow in case the planes come.

"Hold her here, Jurkovich, until the others are on the ice, too." They had a mile of river to cross and there were still Japs behind them that weren't dead. It was taking each of the trucks time to navigate the riverbank without stalling or tipping over.

When they were all finally on the ice, Port was still issuing orders.

"You and the heavy gun in that last truck, Top," Billy shouted. "Cover our ass! I want you back there and Federales between us in the middle truck."

"Aye aye, Skipper."

The three surviving American trucks started up again, heading north. North toward the distant shore and Siberia.

They were slowly away, still testing the ice, not wanting to skid, with the first sergeant once more staring through the snow out the back of his truck over the barrel of a machine gun, watching Mongolia fall astern. Federales with Dixie the mortarman and a half-dozen other Marines, Cantillon, the padre, and Leung followed Port in the second truck. The captain and Yusopov and now Buffalo were piled together up front in the lead truck, Billy and the prince on the running boards, cold as hell, but Jurkovich couldn't steer or shift gears with three grown men on his lap. The captain was beginning to concentrate on Siberia, on the Russians. And getting there without getting shot by the Soviets. That was Yusopov's job. And he'd better be convincing at it.

To their rear, on the south bank of the river there now appeared at the water's edge a large, open car with a big machine gun on its hood. It carried a couple or three uniformed Japanese, one Jap, bareheaded and with a bloody face, was standing, apparently giving orders to the driver at his side. Maybe arguing with him, you couldn't tell, and gesturing out across the ice to where the Americans drove steadily, easily, comfortably toward safety.

This was Jesse Irabu. Despite the blood running down his face and the bloody rag around his head, Port could see him easily, unmistakably, through the glasses. He wondered if Irabu, with those head wounds, could see Billy.

Joe Gang, glancing over his shoulder, watched the enemy; he hoped his commanding officer saw them.

"Top might turn our heavy gun on them fellows, Skipper. Pick off a couple we won't have to kill later on."

"Think he could hit them at that range while rolling, Joe?"

"He could sure try."

Billy was thinking. The enemy vehicle hadn't moved a menacing inch toward them. Did they need Jesse Irabu dead? They'd beaten him; let it lay.

"Skipper?" Joe Gang prompted him.

Before he could say more or Port answer, the Japanese scout car with its big gun, its two-man crew, and a dead man in the back had rolled out onto the ice. Jesse was coming after them.

No one needed prompting now. Federales and Port could hear the first sergeant's heavy machine gun starting up as Rafter took on the enemy vehicle at a quarter-mile range out on the Onon River ice.

"Give it to 'em, Top," Port shouted, no longer gentlemanly toward beaten foes, not with the Japanese coming after him with a damned .50.

Rafter's fire was hitting the enemy vehicle; you could track the tracers and see them hit. In the front passenger seat Colonel Irabu remained standing, holding on to the grip of the machine gun with one hand, wiping blood from his eyes with the other. And when his vision cleared, he leaned forward on his elbows, both hands on the machine gun.

The top's gun crew was still firing when the Japanese .50-caliber gun opened up, aiming at Rafter's truck, the one in closest range.

To no effect at first, the shots well left, ricocheting off the ice. Damned gunner must be blind, Rafter thought. No one shoots that bad.

Then Irabu jerked his gun back in the other direction, the pain causing his thigh to half give way, and he squeezed off a second stream of shots in the general direction of the first sergeant's truck and trailer, rolling smoothly north.

Something went up!

That damned gasoline trailer, towed behind. "Oh, hell!" Billy Port groaned, the gasoline trailer! Why hadn't they jettisoned the damned gas?

Rafter's truck and trailer blazed up and then burst into a stinking ball of oily flame, sloughed to a skidding halt and capsized, spilling out men to left and right, at least one of them on fire. That man fell to the ice and rolled, trying to kill the flames.

"Go back to them, Jurkovich. Do a one-eighty! I want those men!"

"Yessir." The driver had already turned the big truck, but cautiously, not wanting to go into a skid. He could see four men now, all of them standing or on their knees. The burning Marine was down. As for the truck, it was burning into nothingness on the blackened ice, sinking slowly to fall off to one side as the supporting ice thawed under it in the superheated gasoline fire.

And the Jap scout car was still coming on, and fast.

When Jurkovich hit the brakes and skidded to a halt, Buffalo and other Marines jumped out to hit the ice running, grabbing at and dragging the injured back toward Port's truck.

One burned man shouted up at the runner.

"The top's gone, Buffalo. He went up like matches and I jumped. Him and two others."

"Yeah, yeah. It's okay, we got you."

As soon as they were aboard, pitched in bodily over the tailgate, drawing groans of pain, Jurkovich had the truck back in low gear, but not before looking over at Captain Port. Without saying a word, he was asking about the top.

"Move it, Jurkovich. We can't do anything for him now."

"Nossir."

Jurkovich knew they were both talking about First Sergeant Rafter.

Behind him the enemy scout car was rolling faster, the big .50-caliber firing. Bits and pieces of Marine trucks flew into the air. Irabu was chewing them up. He was half dead himself of shock and loss of blood and concussion but he kept firing and the young lieutenant kept his vehicle moving. Irabu was intent on getting the others, getting all of them. It didn't take that much to squeeze a trigger and Port's trucks didn't have the speed to escape their pursuer nor the range to stand off at distance and fight it out with him.

They still had four hundred yards to go with the Japanese closing fast. Behind Port in the truck bed two Marines were down, dead or wounded he wasn't sure. To his left rear Federales's truck seemed to be taking even more of a pounding with the furled canvas burning and one fender hanging down and beating itself to pieces against the wheel.

And then Federales slowed, braking to a halt or stalled, Port didn't know. But that would be the end of him and his truck, with the Jap scout car still coming.

"Jurkovich!"

"Yessir."

"Federales and his people. If their truck's done for, can we make it back to them before the Jap does?"

The driver shook his head.

"I'll try, Captain, but I don't think we got a chance."

Port's eyes locked on Federales's truck where several men, Federales among them, were busily lifting and tugging at something or someone back there in the truck bed, getting their wounded up and out, Port supposed, but through the smoke of blazing canvas and the falling snow, couldn't be sure. Then, as he stared, he heard the distinctive cough of a mortar firing.

"*Chunk!*" And then, quickly, "*chunk!*" again.

And a third!

Perhaps two hundred yards away he saw the Japanese scout car coming. And then, *not* coming, but veering sharply left as the first mortar shell hit the ice and exploded in a red blast haloed with black smoke, sending up a spray of ice chunks and shrapnel. Then, as he continued to stare, the enemy car swerved right, once more toward him, when its front end suddenly lifted off the ice and vanished in a shower of flaming white, the burning phosphorus of the willy peter shell that had hit it square. The enemy car turned once in midair, twisted, slammed back to the surface of the frozen river, and exploded as the WP, burning at two thousand degrees, ignited fuel and ammo.

One Japanese soldier, his uniform afire, staggered a few steps before falling to the ice where he jerked spasmodically, and then lay still, flame licking at him and smoke rising into the snowy sky from what was left of his burning uniform. The others, well, you couldn't see them. They were gone, just ashes in the flame.

No one in Port's truck said a word, as, off to their left, Federales's truck resumed its limping way toward the Siberian shore.

A hundred yards farther along, there was a hard, unexpected bump as Port's truck bounced, then stopped abruptly.

"What the . . . ?" Had the Jap shots finally knocked out his truck? Jurkovich, a mad grin on his face, pounded the dashboard with a big, mittened fist and shouted at his commanding officer.

"The far shore, Captain. It's the riverbank! We're in freaking Siberia!"

60

*"This ain't the junior prom, amigos. You will be armed,
locked and loaded."*

BILLY Port tugged a Havana cigar from under his sheepskin coat, and
stuck it into his mouth without bothering about matches or lighting
up. He was sure it was Irabu back there dead, sure it was his .50-
caliber gun that killed First Sergeant Rafter.

Well, that's what they pay us for.

Federale's truck climbed the riverbank and pulled up alongside.
Port knew he owed Federales more than words.

The sergeant, looking jaunty, saluted and formally addressed his
company commander.

"Does the captain want me to go back out there on the ice and
finish them hombres off? If they ain't dead yet."

"No, amigo. We're out of China. Russian soil now. I don't want to
start another war here or get anyone else killed, now that we're home
free."

If Billy thought there was anything left of Rafter, sure, he would
have gone out there himself. But pawing over Japs for signs of life,
he'd give that a pass.

Federales didn't argue. It was the captain's call. And with all they'd
done, how far they'd come, how long he'd been in Dog Company, he
figured the skipper had his reasons for what he did. Or didn't do. And
something else was sinking in. Something that ever after, he would tell
Marines with whom he served: "Captain Port said he'd get us out and by
damn, he done it. Lost half of us doing it but he brung us out of China
and brung us out fighting."

It wasn't until much later that Federales, who'd scouted for both
Black Jack Pershing and Captain Port, realized it was the first time
either officer called him "amigo."

Just then they heard the plane. Their old companion, the Japanese
spotter, and Port instinctively went into a crouch and froze. Then,
realizing where they were, relaxed and watched as the enemy craft,
prudently remaining on its side of the border river, circled lazily

through snow showers and low cloud. Well, they'll be able to report back what happened to Colonel Irabu, Billy thought. Maybe someone could notify his folks, back in California if they lived there. The Marine Corps, sure as hell, wasn't going to do the job.

This line of speculation shattered on the reality of Federales's urgent words: "Horsemen coming, sir."

Port looked up from the frozen riverside through snow toward the forest of slender white birches at two wraithlike figures, fur-clad Red Army cavalrymen, carbines and cartridge belts crisscrossing their chests as they rode, trotting toward them on their big cavalry mounts. Yusopov, who'd come up to stand with Billy and his sergeant, stepped out in front and raised a friendly hand to call out in his native tongue to two men with red stars on their caps. Then, half turning to the Marines, "I told them, 'Long live Russia, Comrades!'"

Well, thought Billy Port pragmatically, it was a start. He still couldn't call his country "the Soviet Union," not without gagging on it. But at least the prince was "comrade-ing" the lads.

Siberia? Siberia was cold, spare, bleak, windswept, empty, Communist, edgy, maybe even hostile, and ten thousand miles from home. But, well, compared to being dead, or in a Japanese prison camp, Siberia was bloody gorgeous.

Port was here, he was alive, and in Natasha's country.

More than that, whatever country they were in, they were still Marines, and the first sergeant was making reports. A new first, named Federales. Why postpone it? The man earned the job.

"Six dead, eight wounded, plus burns. Only one Doc Philo thinks he's gonna lose. Two trucks destroyed, two damaged but running. Two light machine guns and one mortar operational. One heavy Browning lost. One Skoda 37mm field gun we don't know how it works. All present or accounted for, sir."

"Thank you, First Sergeant." Six dead. That was bad, but could have been worse. With Japanese troops before them and Irabu behind and the damned bridge barricaded, suppose the ice hadn't held; they would all have been taken.

During Billy Port's ride through Mongolia, Siberia had loomed before them as a sort of El Dorado, a glistening city of gold. For the younger Marines, it suggested the "Emerald City of Oz," where the Wizard dwelled, who could be relied on to supply their needs: a brain, a heart, or a ticket home to Kansas.

Or that's how it seemed. Now they would encounter reality.

As Port expected, and after exchanging compliments with the patrolling cavalrymen (they were scouting the riverbank for "Jap bastards"), it didn't take long for the Siberian Red Army to realize it had uninvited guests. Also as expected, the Russians were jumpy, suspicious, wary of armed foreigners, a glorious stew of Marxist paranoia and legendary Russian xenophobia. Anticipating this, Port and Yusopov had worked out a primitive opening gambit. With the prince translating and guiding his every move, Port led the shrunken convoy of two battered old trucks, crammed by now with twenty Marines, supernumeraries, and corpses, up from the riverbank to the nearest paved road where they simply sought out the first Russian military unit that came along, snapped off salutes, and announced themselves as an advance detachment of United States Marines arriving in the Soviet Union to join in the great Allied war against fascism.

And offered American cigarettes all 'round and asked directions to the nearest garrison town, of which by some miracle, Yusopov knew the name.

Japan, diplomatically and by Port's order, wasn't mentioned. The Americans were fighting the Japs but the Russians weren't, not yet at least. Let's not bog down here on the fine print, Billy decided. A nervous Soviet captain passed the Americans on to a major, the major to a colonel. With stunning speed, considering the infamous Red bureaucracy, before that first day was out, they'd actually been received by a one-star general. Up until and including that level of relationship, Yusopov had been introduced as a Russian officer seconded to the Americans.

Billy didn't go into details but grinned broadly as he puffed on a Havana, shook hands briskly, and slapped men on the back. And if the Russians were inefficient in some things, their small, local clinic worked. The wounded Marines, including Joe Gang minus his eye and one hand, were taken in with a cheerful enthusiasm by orderlies, nurses, doctors, even hospital officialdom.

"This place ain't bad, Skipper," Doc Philo commented in his official capacity as chief medical officer, "I seen crappier stateside."

When he wasn't visiting his wounded at the hospital and filing papers for burials, Port pestered any officer who understood English, submitting formal requests that the nearest American consul be notified, and promptly, that a detachment of American Marines had arrived in the Soviet Union to establish, here in Asia, a sort of Allied "Second Front."

The actual message Billy gave the Russians to send (he didn't really expect that they would) read: "Dateline, Siberia, January 24, 1942: The Marines have landed and the situation is well in hand. Captain William Hamilton Thomas Port, USMC 051313/0302."

The Russians smiled uneasily, nodded comprehension, and did nothing. At that point, everything bogged down in red tape, inertia, and the reluctance of officers to stick their necks out. Exacerbating delay, the Russian New Year's had recently been celebrated, with some men hungover and a few (including officers) still drunk.

By now Port's Marines, all the Marines, even blond-haired Buffalo with his all-American smile, the Cajun Thibodeaux calling everyone (including the uncomprehending Soviets) "ma cher," and the slightly sinister-looking, and newly minted Top Sergeant Federales, more resembled Chinese bandits than professional Western soldiers, in their fur hats and knee-length sheepskin coats, belted and cinched in by cartridge belts and bandoliers, and festooned all over with grenades, sheathed knives, bayonets, field glasses, and compasses. And, conveniently to hand, Springfield rifles, BARs, and Thompson guns slung or carried, with every man also toting a .45 automatic or Smith & Wesson .38 in his belt or shoulder holster or in gunfighter, quick-draw style, à la Wild Bill Hickok, holster tied-down snug with rawhide around the thigh.

Although, if you knew anything about Marines, you recognized their yellow canvas leggings, and the spare, jaunty way they carried themselves, and their weapons. No one had yet asked that they surrender their arms and the Marines did no volunteering.

The Russian troops, even their officers, crowded 'round, curious to see these strange but impressive Allied soldiers from across the broad Pacific.

Colonel General Arkady was anxious to see them for himself. He'd served as military attaché at the Soviet embassy in London in the early thirties and admired the Marine officers he'd met in his diplomatic rounds. Now, pending instructions from Moscow as to just what to do with these exotic interlopers, and acting in the spirit of Allied sportsmanship, he decided it might be politic to have a small party for the new arrivals, hosted by the Red Army. Arkady was the commanding general of the Army corps that defended the river borders with Japanese-occupied China. He had come all this way, over lousy roads in winter, from his HQ at Habarovsk, to see and welcome the Marines. A prudent man (after all, Moscow might disapprove), Arkady held the party not in a Red Army officers' club, but in the recreation room of the local "Young Pioneers League of the Komsomol," the Young Communist Party. But to have Arkady throw you a party at all, well, this was something, wasn't it? Port's men, stunned by the warmth of welcome, asked if they should go armed.

"Stack 'em by the door so they're handy, you people," murmured the top sergeant. "Never be embarrassed by your weapons. It's when you need 'em and ain't got 'em, that's when to hide your damned faces. And wear your sidearms at all times, You will be armed and ready, locked and loaded. This ain't the junior prom, amigos."

After all this time, with his Mexican accent, Federales enjoyed American slang.

The promised hospitality aside, Captain Port still had little feel for the Russians, what they meant and what they intended. About Prince Yusopov, Billy was tap dancing; so were the Soviets.

At first he'd proposed to the prince, "We might pass you off as a vaguely stateless person, under some non-Yusopov alias, that was assigned to this patrol because we needed someone who spoke a little Russian. Or throw them a bluff. Explain that you're a Soviet officer attached to the Marine Corps for liaison duty in case the USSR goes to war with Japan and we're all on the same side?"

"I don't think so," Yusopov said flatly.

"Okay then, give me a better idea. No pride of authorship, I just want to keep you out of trouble."

"Your ideas are fine, Billy. But they'd only postpone the day when I'd be exposed. By then the Reds would be furious for putting something over on them and they'll shoot me as a spy.

"I propose to offer myself up voluntarily, under my own name, confess past sins, sing a verse of 'The Internationale,' and swear allegiance to the Kremlin. Russia is, after all, my country, too, and I want to fight the damned Germans at the side of the gallant Red Army."

He paused. "What do you think, Billy?"

Port had to laugh.

"I think they're going to shoot you either way, Nicky. But if you're determined to turn yourself in, let's not do it to some panicky lieutenant who bumps you off immediately as an 'enemy of the people.' Get the most senior Red Army officer we can find and surrender to him. At least he'll have the muscle to keep you on ice until he gets orders from the Kremlin."

Yusopov agreed that made sense. "How about this General Arkady that's invited us to dinner? Some of these older Red Army officers are more 'Army' than 'Red.'"

"Okay. We go to his party, announce you're the last White Russian to see Anastasia, and have a vodka on it. You never know, they may kiss you on both cheeks and nominate you for commissar."

The Marines, all of them, were billeted down by the railroad station in a small hotel with minimal services but heated. On the day of General Arkady's reception, January 27, young Mr. Cantillon came up with a notion.

"Captain, I'm still monitoring radio with Sparks and we have reports General Timoshenko's Russian armies are driving deep into the Ukraine. Mightn't we announce that, toast the Soviets, and get their party off to a jolly start? Maybe they'll be impressed, think that we're in touch with Washington."

Billy said he'd think about it. He had another ploy. Dress uniforms.

Only Port's original Dog Company Marines from Shanghai barracks had their dress blues. Some had been destroyed in one or another of the abandoned trucks. "If you got 'em, wear 'em," he ordered. And a half dozen got into their blues for the first time since Shanghai. So did Captain Port. The surprise, Prince Yusopov's tsarist colonel's uniform. He didn't intend going gently, did he?

What with the Marines' dress blues, the prince splendidly outfitted, Father Kean in his roman collar and clerical black, Leung in a brocaded jacket, and in the presence of the gloriously bemedaled General Arkady, the festivities got under way in high style, despite the gloomy rec room's linoleum, cheap curtains, dog-eared magazines, Ping-Pong table, and the usual badly painted portrait of Stalin.

When the first round of drinks had been handed around by Red

Army enlisted men serving as waiters, Arkady, plump and genial, introduced his senior staff, and then it was Port's turn. He introduced everyone, including Mad Red Donnelly and Thibodeaux. The Cajun, resplendent in his blues, gave the general a vigorous "Ma cher General!" Nor did Billy overlook "our chaplain, Father Kean of the Society of Jesus and the British Museum." Yusopov, whose uniform and decorations had already inspired Russian glances and whispers, was left for last. And permitted to introduce himself.

"Comrade Colonel General, I present myself to you, sir, Colonel Prince Nicholas Ivanovich Yusopov, late of the White Army."

Arkady, smooth as you would wish, shook his hand briskly.

"Welcome to the Soviet Union, Comrade Colonel."

"Thank you, sir."

It was as simple as that.

There was plenty of good vodka and the Russians friendly, some even coming up to be introduced to Yusopov who by now was calling everyone "comrade" in the proper Soviet fashion and, in turn, by two or three of the Red Army officers, being addressed as "prince."

"Jesus," Port whispered to Federales, "I didn't think it was going to be this easy, Top."

"Evening's young, Skipper," said Federales. "And we don't know these hombres. General Pershing, he always said . . ."

Like poor Rafter, the new top soldier was good at restraining enthusiasm.

Of the two dozen Russians in the big hall with its scatter of tables, bar, and gramaphone, only a few hung back.

"The political commissars, I take it," Yusopov said. "Doesn't pay for them to be too chummy."

The Russians, too, were armed. Which was natural, their country fully engaged in a war of annihilation on their own ground against the Germans, and this close to Japanese-held territory. If the Red Army men were nervy, they had good reason. But with the Russians, it was only sidearms. No Thompson submachine guns or BARs checked at the door.

Then one of the commissars, the senior man by the arrogant look of him, came over. The introductions were made, Port being very specific in identifying Yusopov as having been seconded to the Marine

Corps for liaison purposes and subject to American military authority.

"Ah, yes," said the commissar, "except that this is Soviet territory. If and when we have a second front established by our gallant allies the Americans and the British, it will surely be ten thousand kilometers to the west of here. And you will be fighting the Germans. Here there are only Japanese. With whom the USSR is not at war."

Looking pleased with himself for having gotten off this neat summary of the situation, the political officer knocked back a vodka and waited for the Americans, or someone, to respond.

Port did, not with a rebuttal but with a toast, smoothly translated by the prince.

"To the gallant Red Army, to the Russian people, and to your great leader, Marshal Stalin. And to Marshal Timoshenko and his successful new offensive in the Ukraine, of which we have just learned from Washington."

"Amen to that," Father Kean muttered.

But the Russians seemed pleased. As well as impressed by Port's awareness of the Ukraine. Billy noted that Prince Yusopov had joined in the toast. Even to Stalin. "Good man, Prince," he told himself. "That's playing the damned game."

The Jesuit, who knew a little Russian from his adventures in Mongolia, and delighted to learn that Arkady had served in London, was enjoying himself fully, practicing his Russian and not sparing the vodka. Especially when the general mentioned his love for English literature.

"Dickens, the Brontë sisters, and Sir Arthur Conan Doyle were my favorites. In London I haunted Smith's bookstore. *The Hound of the Baskervilles,* what a thrill the first time one reads that. The moors, the gigantic hound, the sense of dread. Jolly good stuff, you know. Eventually I took up the modern writers. *Lost Horizon,* H. G. Wells, and the satires of Evelyn Waugh."

"You don't say, sir."

"But I do, Reverend."

"Do y'know, I baptized Waugh a Catholic?"

"No!"

"I assure you, I did. At Farm Street church."

"Tovarich!" the general declared, grabbing another glass from the passing waiter. "You are a splendid fellow, to actually know the clever Waugh. Just between us, Father, he's a terrible snob, isn't he?"

"Oh, dear me, sir. Terrible, forever cutting people."

"I was sure of it," Arkady responded, inordinately pleased.

Leung, being Chinese, behaved with a massive dignity. Let the foreign devils make fools of themselves.

Another commissar, more amiable than the first, was blathering on about the new system. Something they were calling the "Gulag."

"What's that, Yusopov? Another five-year economic plan?"

"Don't know. The word literally means a group of islands. A . . . what's the English?"

"Archipeligo."

"Yes, but in this usage of the word, the gentleman (meaning the political commissar) speaks of a series of camps. Where they send people like me, inconvenient fellows to be indoctrinated, taught the new ways, cuffed about a bit to catch our attention. That's where I'll probably be sent, to the Gulag. At least that's his guess."

Port thought that one over a bit. He was puzzled by these Russians. Cordial one moment, then a drink later, talking about sending people to "camps" where they might be "cuffed about." That had an ominous stink to it and he thought he'd better draw something of a line in the sand. If you could use such a figure of speech in snowy Siberia.

"See here, Major," said Captain Port, addressing the commissar, but careful to insure that Arkady, as senior man in the room, could hear him, "The Marine Corps is most grateful for your hospitality. And the excellent vodka. But it would be highly improper for me, as commanding officer of this detachment, to entertain any suggestion whatever about one of my officers, in this case, seconded, as Colonel Yusopov quite clearly is, being brought under Soviet government jurisdiction. Such things are surely not to be debated here and now under wartime conditions."

And then, permitting himself what one usually calls "a pregnant pause," he continued.

"Decisions such as these," Billy said with a dramatic turn of phrase, "are only to be made at the highest levels."

The commissar, slightly drunk, demanded, "And what levels are those, Captain?"

Port, seeing that he had Arkady's ear, maintained the arch tone:

"It's quite beyond my ability to comprehend such matters, Major. Perhaps even beyond your own, sir. Such things are negotiated on a global scale in inter-Allied councils . . ."

He let the word, with its overtones of bureaucracy, hang in the air.

"Councils?" the commissar echoed.

"Yes, Major. Roosevelt, Marshal Stalin himself, Winston Churchill. They meet monthly, at the Kremlin, in the White House, or over brandy and soda in London at Number Ten. Weighty matters are on the agenda and it takes great men to . . ."

"They say Churchill is drunk by noon each day," a Red Army colonel, regular army and not a commissar, said in an envious tone.

"I cannot confirm the report," Port said solemnly, "but I have heard it said."

"What a wonderful thing," another man responded, "to be drunk by noon and still to function. To meet in council, even . . ."

At midnight, they were still going strong, nearly everyone drunk, when General Arkady called up gypsy violins and a Cossack chorus that roared through a smashing "Red Army March," "Tipperary," and something Billy thought might be Tchaikovsky. Or Rimsky-Korsakov?

To which, Lieutenant Edmund Cantillon, United States Navy, splendid in his officer's uniform, responded, in tune if slightly drunk, with a rousing "Whiffenpoof Song," on which, after any number of roistering choruses, Marines, Cossacks, commissars, and even Father Kean joined in:

> "Gentlemen songsters/Off on a spree.
> Doomed from here/To eternity.
> Lord have mercy/On such as we,
> Baa, baa, baaaa."

At which, once the cheering ended, First Sergeant Federales, in that unmistakably if heavily accented top soldier's voice, called for order: "Gentlemen, and amigos, we will now sing 'The Marines' Hymn.'"

And they did.

61

"First Sergeant, please parade the command for the prince."

IN the morning the call came from a clearly apologetic Colonel General Arkady.

"Captain Port, Moscow has replied to my inquiry regarding Comrade Yusopov. Higher authority has taken over the case. I regret to say he must appear before a tribunal in Irkutsk. Competent counsel will be provided."

"Provided by whom, General?"

"The KGB, evidently."

Irkutsk, at the southern tip of Lake Baikal, was a provincial capital. It also had a regional KGB office.

The Marines were still in the small station hotel, a couple of Soviet sentries lounging outside, armed but not hostile, just keeping an eye on things. Billy sent Buffalo for the prince. In a parlor off the small lobby, the two men drank strong coffee as Port reported his conversation with Arkady.

"What will you do?" Billy asked.

"Make a case, defend myself as best I can, emphasize that I returned voluntarily, that I simply want to serve in some military capacity opposing the German invader, that sort of reasonable argument."

"Are they reasonable people?"

"No."

Yusopov was taking it all quite calmly. Port wondered if he would have been able to do so.

For the rest of that short, cold day Arkady permitted Billy to put and to argue his protest. Yes, yes, the general said frequently, but higher authority had . . .

"I know, I know. Had . . . 'taken over the case.' "

When they finally parted, Arkady rueful and shaking his hand vigorously, Billy dropped his own little announcement.

"I'd be most obliged, General, if you inform 'higher authority' that on behalf of the United States Marine Corps, Captain William Hamilton Thomas Port is 'taking over the case' as Colonel Yusopov's counsel, and will accompany him to Irkutsk. And that I formally request the presence of an American consular official to assist and advise me."

"You are a lawyer, sir?" the general asked, somewhat startled.

"No, sir, just a Marine officer doing his duty."

That night the Marines gave the prince a going-away party. The KGB would be arriving within a day. Perhaps two. In winter, on Siberian roads, who could say with certainty? Billy's case of Château Latour '24, none the worse for wear, was finally broken into and served, uncorked by Mad Red Donnelly, and pronounced first rate. Even among "us Cajuns of the Acadian bayou country of Louisiana."

"Thank you, Thibodeaux."

Sparks, who'd brusquely resisted a Red Army suggestion he give them his radio for safekeeping, prudently passed on the wine but provided Cantillon a news report that the naval officer read during dinner, or what their house Jesuit, with gallows humor, insisted on calling "The Last Supper."

"In Malaysia, forty-eight Hurricane fighters have been dispatched by the RAF to the defense of Singapore. The bad news, the twenty-second Indian Brigade is cut off near Layang-Layang south of Kluang."

"Ma cher Lieutenant," asked Thibodeaux, "could you Layang-Layang that again?"

On a serious note, Yusopov kept trying to dissuade Port from going with him to Irkutsk. "Please, Billy, you do not know these people."

Father Kean, who did know them, held his counsel, having earlier talked with Port at the Marine's request.

"Padre," Billy told the priest, "all my life I've gone into strange places and taken risks serving my country. Mostly trying to kill people. This once, I'll be going into a strange place and taking another variety of risk, to argue a good man's case and try to save a life. I think that's a thing worth doing."

The Jesuit, remembering their talk that cold day in a nomad's yurt, nodded solemnly. "As do I, sir. God bless you."

More surprising, the protests of young Cantillon. "Captain, your place is here, commanding the detachment. They're your responsibility. They're your Marines."

"He's right, Captain," Yusopov agreed, smiling. "They're your Marines and I'm just a White Russian along for the ride."

"No," said Port, "when you put on the uniform, when you fight as a Marine, when you join us, I will always be there for you. As an officer of Marines, I'm there."

In the end, as they broke for sleep, Billy knew exactly what he was going to do. "Let's breakfast together, Prince. We may not have time later to talk."

"Of course."

There was first a brief morning huddle with Leung, going over the state of finances. Port issued a few instructions regarding his brother Ned in Pinckney Street, Boston, and handed Leung an unsealed letter to Ned, before pocketing a substantial sum of cash from his cache, "the old exchequer."

"Never know when I'll need some of the folding, Leung."

"Very prudent, sir."

Yusopov came downstairs in the uniform of his Preotrazhensky Regiment, complete with decorations. Over coffee he told Billy, "I've decided not to be arrested here at the hotel. I don't want your men getting into a scrimmage with KGB thugs. Won't do them nor me any good. I'm going over to Arkady's office at Red Army barracks and announce, 'I hereby surrender myself as an officer of the late White Army to the officers of the victorious Soviet Red Army.' I will have surrendered officially to him. To the Army. As a prisoner of war and not a political prisoner. Let the Red Army bear the onus of turning me over to the KGB."

"Will that make any difference?"

"Probably not. But it'll make me feel better."

Trouble was, Arkady had left for Habarovsk and no junior officer wanted to take responsibility. Somewhat depressed by the anticlimax, Yusopov returned to the hotel.

Where the Marines were also making plans. Even Joe Gang, who'd checked himself out of the little Russian clinic, pale, a bit shaky, one eye bandaged, but standing. The Russkis, he said, had treated him okay. But he had his duty.

"I want to be here for the skipper. He believed me about Travis. He promoted me to sergeant. I don't take that lightly, boys."

"You ain't got no dress blues, Joe."

"You got dead guys my size. Maybe Rafter's would fit me. I'll borrow their blues, just pin up my sleeve neat. You'll see . . ."

Two cars drove up about three-thirty with the sun already down and the gray sky turning into dusk, again hinting of snow.

Two sentries flanked the front door of the little station hotel, wearing dress blues, rifles at present arms.

Then Billy came out, not only in dress blues but with his sword buckled on.

Ignoring the cold, not wanting to diminish the dramatic impact of his blues, Buffalo stood by holding the captain's long, forest-green overcoat. Federales, a revived Joe Gang, Thibodeaux, Donnelly, and the handful of other Marines who still owned or had been loaned dress blues, were in formation on what Federales, in the best first sergeant tradition, insisted on calling "the company street."

Billy thought in wonder of scenes out of *Don Quixote,* every bit as unreal, but did not say.

Two men in badly cut flannel suits and seedy overcoats of the sort winos wear who sleep in Boston doorways got out of the first crappy Moskva sedan. One of them had a sheaf of papers.

Yusopov now emerged for a second time, still in his uniform of a tsarist colonel. At which, with a nod from Captain Port, Federales called the detachment to attention.

Port and the prince, smoothly in step, inspected the men as the two Russians, standing by their sedan, went uneasily from one foot to the other. They weren't soldiers and ritual rattled them.

It was then that the prince, for the first time, even deigned to notice them.

"You have business with me, gentlemen? I am Colonel Prince Yusopov, at your service."

Since only Yusopov could speak both Russian and English, the prince was in the ironic position of translating his own indictment and explaining things both to Port and to the KGB agents.

When the niceties were accomplished, Port called Cantillon to him.

"I should be back inside the week if the roads hold, however it plays with the prince. You're in command until then. Use your head. And you know you can rely on Federales to guide you, count on the men. They're Marines. Keep trying to reach an American consul somewhere. Get Sparks calling en clair to Headquarters Marine Corps in the States. Maybe he'll get through. Someone's got to know where we are and what's happening. That's important to Yusopov and to me.

And thanks, Navy, you turned out fine. Might have made a pretty good Marine."

"Thank you, sir."

Then, in a parade ground voice all could hear, Port said, "Mr. Cantillon, as his commanding officer, I will accompany Prince Yusopov to Irkutsk to represent him in the tribunal. You will take command of the Marine detachment here in my absence. First Sergeant, please parade the command for the prince."

"Aye aye, sir."

All this had been worked out earlier, of course, especially the roles to be played by Cantillon and the top, but it went down well, impressing the KGB men despite themselves.

By now, snow was again falling.

"Buffalo!" The Dog Company runner had volunteered to accompany his company commander to the tribunal.

"Yessir."

"We'll be leaving now."

The big Marine, also in his dress blues, and still cradling the Thompson gun, opened the rear door of the sedan so that Yusopov and Port could get in. Buffalo then handed in their duffel bags and overcoats for warmth during the long ride, and got into the front passenger seat of the other car with two more KGB agents.

As the two sedans started up, headlamps piercing the heavily falling snow, engines laboring in the cold, First Sergeant Federales called the detachment to attention. And then: "Present, Arms!"

It was only a half-dozen able men by now, with a half-dozen old Springfield rifles, but as one, the half-dozen gloved hands slapped their weapons smartly, as, just barely, through the car windows, they could see Billy Port's crooked smile and his usual, cocky, snapped-off highball of a returned salute.

As the two Russian cars vanished into the gloom and the squalls of snow, Mr. Cantillon called out: "First Sergeant."

"Yessir."

"Dismiss the men, First Sergeant."

"Aye aye, sir," Federales replied.

It was the first direct order the naval officer had ever given a Marine.

62

Cantillon, with his own Navy Cross, wrote letters,
called on friends at Yale.

NONE of them would see Captain Port again. Not Mr. Cantillon or
Top Sergeant Federales or poor Joe Gang with his one arm or Doc
Philo or "ma cher" Thibodeaux would know exactly what happened.

Oh, there were stories, snatches of information, rumors, reports, a
few outright lies. But in the wartime Soviet Union the free press was
something of a fiction and the mills of what passed for justice ground
exceedingly slow.

Buffalo they knew about. The KGB shot him right away at Irkutsk.
He was only an enlisted man of no importance. But a young fellow
of his evident strength, well, you want to be careful. When at KGB
headquarters they'd manacled Port and the prince, Buffalo went ber-
serk, killing two warders with his hands. Word coming down from
Irkutsk claimed the boy had been injured in an auto accident and died
in the hospital. The Marines knew that his death was fact and no lie;
the Soviets having stupidly sent back the body. Complete with bullet
holes.

Of Yusopov and Captain Port, the Marines knew less. The prince,
one report had it, had been bundled into an unheated cattle car to
Moscow and the Lubyanka.

Port? Had some bureaucrat panicked and sent him off without
trial? Were there sinister motives? Or was it simply red tape and
wartime confusion and they didn't know what to do with the man?
Well, it was a large gulag, wasn't it? And who knew what went on
there, who lived, who died, who made an accommodation with fate
and endured? There were, after all, hard men who had survived previous camps. Perhaps other harder men would live through this,
would survive the gulag. Men surfaced after years. And unexpectedly.
Such marvels were rare but not unknown.

Washington was not about to unbalance the delicate and tricky
wartime alliance with totalitarian Moscow, not for the sake of one
decidedly junior and probably insubordinate Marine who'd gone freelancing on his own, God knows where in Asia, and in the doing had

surely exceeded his writ. Not when there were tens of thousands of other, more reputable Americans missing in action in various theaters of a global war.

It took months but in the end Cantillon and Federales and their tiny command were safely repatriated, following a ride on the Trans-Siberian Railroad across four thousand miles of Asia and the Middle East, released to officials in neutral Turkey.

Not that everyone forgot Billy. With his resources, connections, and native tenacity, Vintage Port was hardly your average helpless, grieving parent of a lost son, forlornly and impotently regarding a gold star displayed in the window. Billy's old man hated Roosevelt but political differences didn't dissuade him from pulling every string he had, or even imagined, in the capital. He flattered political enemies, insulted bureaucrats, offended high officials, made enemies, gave interviews, offered bribes, hired lawyers, wrote letters to editors, was threatened with lawsuits for slander, libel, and worse. The old man never quit.

But it was to no avail. The postwar world moved swiftly from euphoria to new antagonisms as the East-West Cold War kicked in.

Mr. Cantillon, as you might have imagined, tried his best to track down Captain Port, wrote letters to family connections, called on people at Yale he suspected of having influence, made strenuous efforts, even to the point of becoming something of a crank. But the war intruded. Cantillon ended up commanding a destroyer that was kamikazed off Okinawa, earning him his own Navy Cross (and a Purple Heart that was almost embarrassing, since his only wound was a broken rib suffered while being hauled out of the water).

Chesty Puller, busily slaughtering the Japanese on various South Pacific islands, weighed in, pestering the brass, making a damned nuisance of himself, but by then the pre-war Marine Corps of seventy-five thousand men had exploded into six divisions of nearly half a million. Who had time to track down one company grade officer who'd vanished, or run off, and was in any account most likely dead?

Father Kean, Society of Jesus, succeeded in an eventual return to London and actually did patch up that dusty old pile of bones at the British Museum. Then, on a sunny day in 1944 he was killed by a German buzz bomb in Mount Street, London W.1, on his way to cocktails with a Mitford girl at the Connaught Hotel. Federales fought all through the Pacific War, ending as a sergeant major, in the end outranking his role model Rafter. Joe Gang returned to Joseph, Oregon, as something of a hero. Rodeo riding was out, of course, not with one hand, one eye. But each year when they marked "Chief Joseph Days," Joe was trotted out to ride in an open car in the town parade, and to an enthusiastic ovation. Sparks opened a radio shop in his hometown and was one of the first local merchants to stock a Dumont television set. Doc Philo went to medical school in Austin and became a pediatrician. Thibodeaux also survived not only one war but a second in Korea, and returned to the bayous, retiring from the Corps as a gunnery sergeant, "Ma cher."

As for the 4th Regiment of Marines, lost in the final, awful battles of Bataan and Corregidor, exhausted, outgunned, trapped, hungry, fever-wracked, overrun and taken by the Japanese, their legend and a thousand stories live on. But as for proof of anything, forget it. What Colonel Sam Howard hadn't burned back there at Shanghai barracks in the late November of 1941, the remaining records, rosters, and files were lost or destroyed in the last hours of the regiment's existence. Or during the Bataan "Death March" that followed, starving, beaten men not being very punctilious about the paperwork.

War is hell on everybody, and especially on the archivists.

The unofficial monthly magazine of the Marine Corps, *Leatherneck,* years later published Colonel Dick Camp's account of what happened to the men who were left behind in China and didn't make it to the Philippines. Says Colonel Camp, 204 North China Marines were taken prisoner, and after forty-four months in Japanese prison camps, at war's end, 190 had survived and were liberated.

The colonel then adds, without elaboration: "Five Marines escaped and made their way back to friendly lands."

EPILOGUE

NATASHA Rostov had also gotten out. As U.S. Consul General Art Leavis grudgingly admitted during that final phone call from Captain Port, it was only the luck of the draw, and a few strategically placed cash bribes, that got the Russian girl aboard one of the last ships of any sort to depart Shanghai in those final frantic days before Pearl Harbor.

And, like the 4th Marines, she'd landed in the Philippines, though happily not in Manila that, by that time, December 8 and 9, was under heavy air attack by the Japanese. Natasha's ship, a rusty old bucket the unhappy Captain Henriques would have recognized, carried the refugee passengers (three hundred of them, Brits, Yanks, Dutch, and the occasional stateless White Russian) all camped out on deck for the entire voyage and living on slops. The ship docked and discharged its wretched cargo at Zamboanga, a Philippines harbor on Mindanao.

Zamboanga was an obscure place, a popular liberty port for the sailors of the American Asiatic Fleet in the twenties and thirties, best remembered for an old shipboard ditty. "The monkeys have no tails/in Zamboanga/The monkeys have no tails/They were bitten off by whales . . ."

Despite which, as one fleeing Briton remarked, it was "jolly good luck," getting to Zamboanga, since by the time the refugees from Shanghai had landed, Japanese ground forces were swarming all over Luzon, smashing MacArthur's half-trained Philippine Army units and intent on capturing, killing, or cornering Luzon's American defenders on the Bataan Peninsula and the fortress island in Manila Bay of Corregidor.

In Zamboanga, which had little, but what little they had could be bought, if you had the cash, Natasha arranged passage on an inter-island steamer that carried her south through the Banda Sea and into the Timor Sea and eventually to a safe berth at Darwin in the vast, empty tropical north of Australia, where, six months later, she gave birth to a healthy son whom she registered as William Port Rostov. By the end of 1942, by decidedly irregular means, which included the cultivation of men with dubious but influential connections, she and her boy were in Vancouver, in western Canada, and early in 1943 had succeeded in making their way to Pinckney Street, Boston, to the elegant town house where Billy was born and grew up. A house now converted to the headquarters of Port Distillery Brands Inc., where she presented a letter of introduction to Billy's kid brother Ned, now his father's right-hand man. And a good one.

The letter Madame Rostov hand-delivered gibed in all details with one Ned had received at the end of 1941 postmarked Shanghai, one of the last letters Billy mailed before going off on his ride. Those details very precisely included Billy's prediction that good Russian vodka was the "gin of the future" and that Natasha Rostov, with all her experience in the distillery trade and the hospitality business (a nightclub dancer; but didn't it sound better this way?) and her impeccable links to the very best White Russian circles, should enable Port Brands to steal a competitive march in cornering the vodka market immediately at war's end. And beating out Seagram, Smirnoff, and the rest of them, especially that son of a bitch Joe Kennedy.

Ned, no dope, didn't entirely buy Billy's pitch, but he saw the logic in it, and since this girl seemed a very nice young person, and since Ned loved his big brother, he fixed up Natasha and her child with a place to stay, put her on the payroll, and (deftly avoiding explicit explanations to his old man) introduced her to Boston society. Billy Port might be among the missing, but his last girlfriend would be suitably taken care of by the family. It was all very discreet, very decent, very WASP. And in the end, a glorious demonstration of the love of brother for brother.

By 1950 Port Brands was (despite the Cold War) riding the wave of vodka's popularity up the charts, and Natasha Rostov, the firm's director of marketing, now a very elegant twenty-eight, had been married for four years. The ceremony had been one of the Boston weddings of the season, solemnized, by family tradition (the groom was an Endicott, and you know what that means!), at the Old North Church, where long ago they'd raised Paul Revere's lamps, "one if by land, two if by sea." Her son William, a sturdy, happy four-year-old, was ringbearer, as Natasha wed John "Chub" Endicott, a very proper

Bostonian who'd been the captain of Harvard, owned a seat on the Exchange, and more to the point was a terribly decent fellow madly in love with this Russian beauty (and successful marketing expert).

They lived happily and very comfortably in a great house on a fashionable street off Commonwealth Avenue, and had a daughter and Natasha's second son.

Then, at Christmas of 1950, Natasha and Chub attended a Port family holiday party in the main second-floor dining room of the Ritz Carlton, with much caroling and eggnog and wassail of every manner and sort. Even the Old Gentleman was there, the great "Vintage" Port, a little sadder with the years, and less ferocious, though every bit as crotchety, intimidating, and benevolent at the same time (a Herr Drosselmeyer straight out of *The Nutcracker Suite*). Another war was on by now, with another generation of Marines fighting desperate battles, these against their old allies the Chinese at the Chosin Reservoir in the terrible mountains of North Korea. At some point, while Chub Endicott was huddled with other old Harvards bemoaning the fate of Crimson football, Ned Port broke away for a smoke and found himself alone with Natasha, enjoying a brief moment of solitude in the crowd.

She was still gorgeous, a "schoolgirl" no longer of course, but quite sophisticated and grown-up, the long hair no less golden but coiffed now, soignée, up in a French knot, the face lovely, the figure perhaps a few pounds fuller, more voluptuous. Ned had always liked Natasha, not only the look of her, her outgoing ways, but her courage and resource. He was aware, if anyone was, of her astonishing wartime trek halfway across the world. Ned, who knew her well by now, and was still under the spell of his heroic and only brother, understood why she'd attracted the notoriously choosy Billy. And he admired the job she'd done with Port vodka, her obviously successful marriage to Chub, and how well she was raising the children.

And knowing the story as few did was more than slightly in awe of her. Now, fueled by a third cocktail, Ned Port asked, quite impertinently: "Nataly. Tell me something."

"Yes, Ned?"

"Suppose Billy came marching home and walked through that door tonight?"

"Well, Ned, you know that is the stuff of dreams and fairy tales.

Stories that one tells children at bedtime. I know the Soviets. And I long ago came to terms with reality."

But Ned pressed. "I know, I know. But just suppose he came strolling across Boston Common in a Christmas snow and, drawn by the lights and the singing, came through the revolving door and into the lobby of the Ritz to ask whose party was this?"

Flirtatiously, she said, pleasantly champagned and with a half laugh: "You know your brother. He would shake off the snow and 'halloo!' everyone and call for a drink. And accustomed to giving orders, would surely add, 'And quite smartly, please!' "

"And then?"

She looked thoughtful. Then, her lovely green eyes crinkling at the corners, she smiled. And in that husky, still-accented voice, she answered, "Endicott is a very good man, Ned. I owe him much. And I love him. A wonderful husband and father. Not only to our children, but to my boy Will . . ."

"Yes, yes, but if Billy . . . ?" Ned said, impatient with piety and mischievously preferring truth.

She half turned toward one of the great windows framing Boston Common in the falling snow, so as to mask her face from Ned, who knew her too well. And so that he could not tell if she spoke truly or in jest, and giving Ned only her straight back, Natasha continued to look out at this Currier & Ives version of America and said, "But for Billy Port, if he returned, one might make a suitable arrangement."

- - - - - - - -

BILLY PORT'S RIDE
FROM SHANGHAI TO SIBERIA
(C. 1,500 MILES)

+++++++++
RAILROAD

N

U.S.S.R.
SIBERIA

OUTER MONGOLIA

G O B

INNER MONGOLIA

THE GREAT WALL

C H I N A

0   500
SCALE OF MILES

INDIA

BURMA